Abysmal

AN UNLUCKY 13 NOVEL

MARIE ANN

Cover design: Rebel Ink Co.
Editing: Tiff Reads Romance
Formatting: Marie Ann

Welcome to Black Diamond Resort and Spa…
An island dedicated to the world's elite and the place my father sent me to hide and rehabilitate myself after I made the biggest mistake of my life.
One that almost ended mine…
But Gavin, the bodyguard my father hired to protect me, sees more than those mistakes, than my defensive, bratty attitude.
He sees *me*. Takes care of me.
Gives me strength in times where all is hopeless with the utterance of a single word…
Boy.
With Gavin's need to claim me and my desire to be cared for, we form a bond that's all-consuming.
I can't hide how badly I want him, and what he gives me. *My Daddy*. He makes me feel alive for the first time… only for me to sink into an abysmal black hole when the truth smacks me in the face.
I may be his boy, but I'll never *be* his. The gold band still sitting heavily on his ring finger only proves that—even if he does hold me to his chest like it doesn't matter…

Playlist

ASCENSIONISM—SLEEP TOKEN
RAIN—SLEEP TOKEN
1800RAPTURE—LOSER
KILL THE SUN—CANE HILL
TAKE ME AWAY—THE PLOT IN YOU
DESCENDING—SLEEP TOKEN
DYWTYLM—SLEEP TOKEN
SMELLS LIKE TEEN SPIRIT—WITCHZ
LIPS OF AN ANGEL—HINDER
BATH SALTS—HIGHLY SUSPECT
BURN DOWN MY HOUSE—ARCHITECTS
HAPPY SONG—BRING ME THE HORIZON
TOO HEAVY—THE PLOT IN YOU
BLOODFEATHER—HIGHLY SUSPECT
LIKE THAT—SLEEP TOKEN
CHERRY WAVES—DEFTONES

DEADBOLT—THRICE
THE LETDOWN—BAD OMENS
SAVE ME—SHINEDOWN
HASTY—CONSCIENCE, SYNDROME
BROKEN—THE DEVIL WEARS PRADA
FEVER DREAM—GRAYSCALE
YOU'RENOTTHEGOODGUYANYMORE—THE VIRUS AND ANTIDOTE, TMTTMF
PINK LULLABY—HIGHLY SUSPECT
WRONG—FIVE AM, KELLIN QUINN
TOUCH, PEEL AND STAND—DAYS OF THE NEW
LONELY WORLD—ACRES
LONELY DAY—SYSTEM OF A DOWN
TELOMERES—SLEEP TOKEN
DISPOSABLE FIX—THE PLOT IN YOU
BEST OF YOU—FOO FIGHTERS
HIGH WATER—SLEEP TOKEN
YOU ASKED FOR IT—EMMURE
ALLEVIATE—IMMINENCE

To everyone who needed to escape a life they never wanted to live.
I hope you have found yourself and the life you deserve.

"It can't rain all the time."

—Brandon Lee, *The Crow*

Authors Note

Zevryn and Gavin's relationship developed into something I never anticipated, and because of that, I wrote a story unlike anything I've done before. It's very near and dear to my heart, and I truly hope you enjoy their love—as wholesome and emotional and possessive as it is.

Before you read, I do want to touch base on something real quick. This book is a work of fiction, which we all know, but I do want to stress this isn't a guide for any BDSM dynamics. If this is something that interests you, please do your research and always be cautious of your own comfort level, boundaries, and what is safest for you.

Every dynamic within the BDSM lifestyle is highly personal, extremely varied, and unique to the persons involved. And while Gavin and Zevryn's dynamic is within that realm, just remember that it is exactly what *they* need. What works for one couple's dynamic may not work for another—and that's okay. Each person and what they desire, crave, and need is different. It's a mutually beneficial relationship that is wholly valid and beautiful.

Abysmal does contain content and themes that may be triggering for some readers. Below, you will find a list of specific triggers if you wish to read them.

The following may contain spoilers. If you are comfortable going in completely blind, feel free to skip to the next page.

In this story, there is: substance abuse/addiction, mental health struggles, suicidal thoughts, physical violence, grief, death.

Welcome to Black Diamond Recovery Center

Black Diamond Recovery Center was founded in 2001 by father and son, Craig and Dexter Diamond. Wanting a place for those in the public eye to go to seek help with their addiction and mental illness, Black Diamond came to fruition.

We recognize that addiction and mental illness are complex diseases that affect every aspect of a person's life, and we provide comprehensive care that addresses all of our clients' needs. Unlike other recovery facilities, we don't just treat the addiction; we treat the whole person. Our approach is designed to provide support and healing for our clients' physical, emotional, and mental well-being, helping them achieve lasting recovery and a brighter future.

During your stay, you'll enjoy relaxing living quarters, gourmet meals, and luxurious amenities—all carefully curated with your healing and comfort in mind—while still receiving the utmost levels on anonymity.

Prologue

ZEVRYN

Faster and faster, I spin. The blue walls blur around me in wispy streaks as I twist my feet, holding my breath as my stomach lurches into my throat. I can feel my heart battering against my ribs so hard, it hurts.

I'm panting now. My chest is heaving as the room falls out of focus, my mind buzzing from the pressure in my skull.

Digging my toes into the carpet, I push myself even harder. My arms are held straight out so I spin like a top, my dark hair flying around me, fusing with sky blue walls.

Something twists inside of my stomach, making me gasp just as the floor tips, sending me flying.

I keep my eyes wide as I wobble around the room, the world as I know it nothing but a blurry mess as I stumble through it.

I whack my elbow, but I don't even care because this is the best feeling in the world.

I'm airborne, levitating with my mind alone.

I wish I could always float, stuck in a place where nothing exists.

But, like always, it fades so fast, and I'm left hunched over, hands on my knees as I nosedive my way back to reality.

It sucks. But I keep trying, hoping that next time, it'll linger for a little longer.

I remember how it used to be so fun when I first started doing it as a kid, but over the years, it got less exciting and more nauseating. And yet, I can't stop the childish notion that scrambling my brain will erase all my problems.

The carpet is a soft cushion against my back as I flop down to stare at the smooth ceiling, hands against my stomach so I can feel the way it moves as I breathe. The way my muscles contract and expand.

It never ceases to amaze me—what our bodies are capable of. What we can grow accustomed to. What we learn to crave...

A sharp knock on my door makes me wince, shoulders hitching to my pierced ears. Dad doesn't wait for me to answer before he's pushing it open and stepping into my space.

"What are you doing? There are people downstairs expecting you."

I roll my eyes as I stare up at the bright, white ceiling, blue blurring just at the edges of my vision.

"Don't roll your eyes at me, Zevryn. Get up." His sharp tone has me clambering to stand. I stumble as I find my feet, my mind still whirling.

"Jesus. What were you doing? You look terrible," he grumbles and starts readjusting my tie, sliding his hands briskly over my suit jacket until it's wrinkle-free and I'm presentable enough for his standards once more.

His dark eyes flit over me, gaze narrowing on my face. I feel my own cheeks heat uncomfortably at his scrutiny. I slide my sweaty palms over my thick curls, pressing them down.

"Lot of good that'll do you when it looks like you stuck your finger in a light socket." I still, my hand frozen in midair. His own hair is unkempt like he's been continuously running his own fingers through it, so who the hell is he to talk?

"If I were you, I'd watch your tone," he replies dryly as he takes a step back, hands fisted at his sides, a silver ring glinting on his finger. A miserable reminder.

I snap my jaw closed at his words, not having realized I said them out loud.

Shame eats away at me as I stand in front of my father, fidgeting. He's dressed impeccably in a suit, crisp white and inky black, the first button undone respectably. His tanned face is clean-shaven, the stubble of yesterday long gone, with his dark mop of hair slick with product in casual disarray.

Looking at him, even with the slight mess of his hair, no one would be able to tell his wife just killed herself and he's attending her sad excuse of a funeral reception.

The silence grows between us, not for the first time.

We've never been close. He's always worked too much, never home, and me... well. I always took care of myself, or I had nannies to do it. But Mom... she was still my mother.

But not anymore. Because she's fucking dead. And she decided her final act in this world would be to take me out with her.

I swallow the bile rushing up my throat. I sway, my hand darting out for balance. My father grips my fingers, steadying me. My eyes track the floor, unable to look up to see his usual stern disappointment.

Just... not now.

"Are you all right?"

I croak out a pathetic snort. "Sure, Dad. I'm dandy."

"Don't—" he snaps before cutting himself off abruptly. A sharp hiss sounds through the air as he sucks in a breath.

"What do you need?"

"I need to be alone," I respond without thinking. He releases his hold on me abruptly, as if I burned him. I take another step back, not stopping until the backs of my legs bump against the bed frame.

"You can have all the alone time you need—just not right now. We need to get through this, and then we can move on."

"Move on," I repeat, shaking my head. My unruly locks fall in front of my eyes, obscuring the pale carpet fibers.

"Zev—"

I hold my hand up, forcing my words through the impossible tightness in my chest. "No. I heard you loud and clear, Dad. *We'll go downstairs, cater to everyone else who apparently cared about Mom, while I force away the memories of her cold, vomit-covered body plastered against mine." The words almost make me choke, but I force it down.*

All of it.

"Or do you want to ignore the fact that she washed a bottle of Trazodone down with what was probably a few glasses of wine and then asked me to watch a movie with her so she could die right next to me? Or how about the fact that I woke up to her with blank eyes, staring straight into me, her body covered in vomit? Or *how you weren't fucking there when I tried calling you for help!" I'm screaming now, my body trembling from the force as it wracks me. My veins feel charged and white-hot as my blood chugs through me—a sick reminder.*

"Enough!" *he shouts so loud, it bounces off the walls. I drop onto the bed, head hanging between my shoulders as I force the sobs back deep inside my chest. His shiny shoes take a step toward me before stilling. I watch him shift a couple of times before retreating.*

"You have five minutes," is all he says before he disappears, leaving me alone, just like I wanted. But now that I have it, I regret it.

I never want to be alone again. The thought alone is terrifying, but the reality...

Paralyzing.

I'm not sure how long I'm stuck before Lara knocks on the door and makes her way inside. She's gentle as she coaxes me up and fixes my appearance once more, pulling me into the bathroom, where she wipes a cold cloth over my flushed face, rinsing the tears and snot away.

"There you go," she says gently, rubbing her hands up and down over my arms like someone would do if they're cold and trying to fight off a chill. I guess that's what she's doing—except I'm not cold, just disgusted and lonely.

"Thanks," I manage to croak, my throat raspy from screaming at my father.

"Do you need anything?" she asks, soft, blue eyes searching.

"Got any alcohol?" I just want to feel like I'm floating again.

She snorts, surprising me. I rear back with a small smile. "You're too young."

"I'm fourteen. And my mom's dead." Yeah, I pulled the dead mom card. Sue me.

Lara shakes her head in exasperation. "No." Then, she turns around. "Come on. Let's go before your father comes back up."

I ignore the photos lining the walls as we find our way to the stairs. I always used to think this house was so big growing up, but the longer we lived here, the more I realized it was a prison. A very nice one, but a confinement all the same. Created by greed for money and power and stature.

The low hum of chatter picks up as we near the landing. I can feel eyes on me from all around. My skin prickles with awareness. I shrug, readjusting my jacket, hating the thing more than ever.

"You'll be okay," Lara whispers in my ear before she makes herself scarce. I'm left fidgeting on the last step, the focal point of everyone's gaze.

"Aren't you all here to mourn my dead mother?" I snap loudly, startling myself with the brashness of my words. I want to swallow my tongue the moment they leave my mouth, but it's already done. There are a few loud gasps, but everyone eventually whirls around and goes back to their mindless gossip.

I slip through the crowds in search of the alcohol I smelled on my father's breath. Chances are he got his from his office, but I'm willing to bet there's some around here somewhere.

No one tries to talk to me, which I'm grateful for.

It's not until I'm in the sitting room, eyes scouring the tables, that I notice the coffin. Sleek, black. Big. So much bigger than my mother's body resting inside.

My feet stop moving. My lungs stop expanding. My heart stops beating as my eyes fall to Mom's pale complexion surrounded by cream-colored satin.

Her lips are painted a light pink, lashes dark with mascara, and skin pasty with foundation.

She looks like herself only... not.

Because she's fucking dead, *my conscience leers. It startles me enough to snap out of it. I rip my eyes away and book it out of the room, clutching my chest, nails digging into the cotton. The kitchen is less packed, the counters piled high with the food people brought—because casseroles are what we need right now.*

When my palm slides along the cold marble, I'm finally able to breathe properly again. Each breath still comes in short bursts, but I'm able to inhale a little deeper every time.

A hand grips my shoulder. "We're so sorry for your loss, Zevryn."

"Let us know if you need anything," another person says. Low, concurring murmurs continue in a stream of indistinct vibrations. I ignore every single one of them as my eyes zero in on the bottle of scotch inside the glass cupboard.

I swipe it and shoulder my way through the sliding glass doors, out into the bitter, winter air. Once the door latches, I exhale and trudge my way across the small yard until I reach the short, brick wall near the property line.

I stare out at the trees as the sun sets somewhere behind me, casting the sky in various shades of happiness. The booze is scorching and tingly as it slides down my throat—a sharp contrast. My eyes bulge as I splutter and retch, some of it spilling over my bottom lip, ironically staining my shirt.

After a few, long moments of wheezing, I'm back to chugging it, and this time, it's a little easier.

With every swallow, I float a little higher.

With every breath, I sink a little deeper.

With every thought, I walk the line between reality and a dream-like fantasy until I plunge somewhere into the abysmal depths of nowhere.

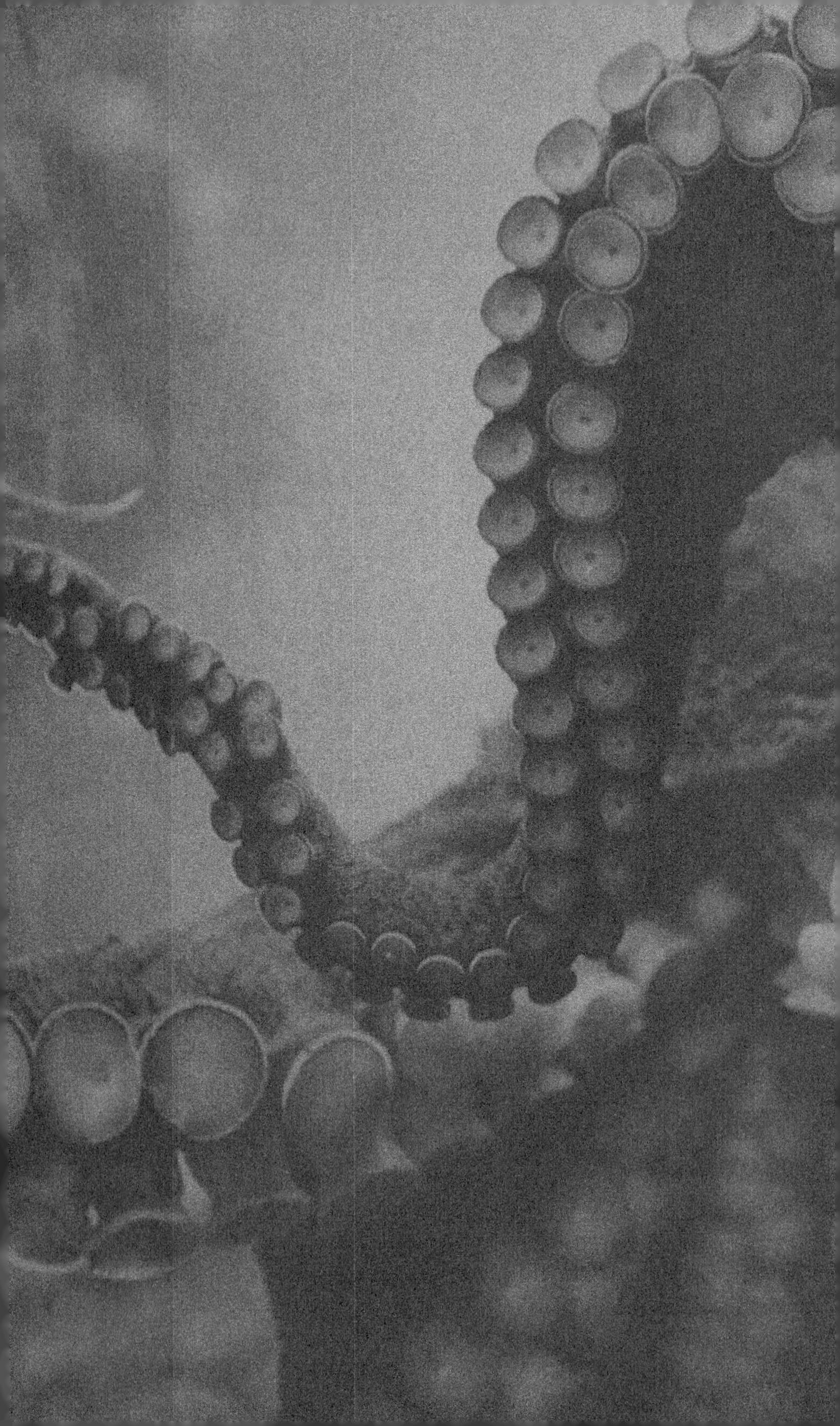

One

ZEVRYN

The ambiance of red and purple makes my head swim, and when I close my eyes, it seems the colors grow brighter, heavier. It weighs me down into the soft, buttery leather of the sofa. My fingers flex against the material, a physical reminder I'm here, in our own private area of the club, not thirty thousand feet in the air, floating with the clouds.

Glass clatters against glass, the sound muted in the pulsing waves of the music and bodies below. I drag my heavy lids open, the alcohol swarming my veins a hot and heavy pull. The body in front of me flickers in and out of focus—all I can see is the light refracting off the metallic material of her skimpy top.

"You good?" Dillon nudges his shoulder against mine. I drag my gaze away from the nearly naked woman plastered on top of my lap, meeting his bloodshot eyes. His blonde hair is swooped across his forehead, nearly covering one eye completely. Our eyes hold for longer than necessary, but I can't look away.

My tongue drags out across my lips as my gaze drops to Dillon's. His shoulder presses against mine again, insistent. It causes me to look up. His brow is quirked in question, a playful grin splayed on his lips I can't stop looking at.

"You're staring awfully hard, Z." His nose wrinkles as he leans forward to grab a shot off the glass table in front of us. The liquid inside is clear as Dillon upends it, his Adam's apple bobbing as the liquid makes its way down his tight throat.

I clear my own, shifting against the sofa. The woman on top of me giggles from the movement, and her fingers wrap around my wrists where I hold her by the hips. My attention's brought to her now, all sex and seduction. Her long, blonde hair hangs down her back and over her shoulder in flawless waves as she rotates her hips on top of me.

The friction feels good, flooding my groin with warmth as the material of my slacks chafes my bare length.

Long fingers brush mine over her hips. I drag my head to the left, finding Dillon helping me work her over my lap. He's not even looking at her. I'm the sole focus of his attention right now.

My hair falls in front of my eyes, obscuring my view, but I can't be bothered to care, not when Dillon brings a small, round glass to my lips. The scent of tequila wafts into my nostrils, making my eyes water in time with my mouth. I part my lips for Dillon, letting him tip the contents into my mouth.

I hold the hot liquid inside, relishing in the sting as I swish it around. *Fuck, it's so good.*

He hikes a brow once I finally swallow, as if he's asking, *more?*

Dillon and I have a mutual understanding. We're both aware of our... issues, how toxic and unhealthy they are. We just don't care.

Or, at least, I don't.

I know Dillion isn't as far gone as me. He's in control—just having fun. He cares what his father thinks.

I never have.

My father manipulates me, enables me, and I let him because I need it. The unbroken cycle of abuse that's only matured over the years. Because at least if he hates me, he's thinking about me. And I need someone to.

I nod my head, and Dillon holds his hand up. "Another round." His hand never stops brushing over mine, like he knows I still feel alone, even surrounded by the empty minds of strangers.

The woman on my lap is getting rampant in her movements, shaking me against the leather. It's so soft and soundless—probably for this exact reason. As Dillon's arm slides across my back, wrapping around my waist, my head lulls to the right. More people line the long, rectangular sofa, Carmen directly to my right.

She's lost in her own world with her own lap filled. The girl dancing on her has short, black hair and tattoos covering almost all of her exposed skin—which is a lot. I can barely make out her face, but Carmen seems to be more than enjoying herself, her own expression glazed and wanton.

When her eyes meet mine, having felt my stare, she grins. I think I return the gesture, too lost in the fog to really be sure, but then Dillon's nudging me, and I'm sitting up. The girl yelps and clutches my shoulders. The change in position makes me groan deep in my throat. Dillon's arm tightens around me now that he's fully pressed against my left side.

His breath fans across my neck, damp and hot. The air circulating around us feels buzzed and potent. The girl's fingers dig into my hair, long nails scratching against my scalp as she works herself on my lap, growing more frantic. The sensation feels sublime. I'm being touched everywhere and nowhere.

I wait for the desolation to surge forward.

Heat pools at the base of my spine. Voices concoct in a tumulus wave of intensity. Glass touches my lip once more, and I open without any thought. More tequila. Sharp, sweet, and smooth. The breath I huff out after I swallow feels hot as it bounces off the sweaty flesh inches from mine.

"You too far gone for more?" Dillon asks in my ear. I don't know how I manage to open my eyes. I don't even remember closing them. His face is pressed against mine, smooth and pale in the warm, wavering lights.

Do I look as broken as I feel?

Music vibrates into my body as the sound waves travel through the air. The floating intensifies, raising me higher. His left arm lifts from his side, and a small, white baggie comes into view. He's smirking at me when our eyes meet again for a split second before he disconnects from me to lean forward.

He's never willingly let me go so far before.

Without any regard of consequences—because for us,

there aren't any—he dumps some of the white powder right onto the glass table. The purple lights morph into blue as he cuts a few lines with a matte, black card, staining the sharp edge in white.

My mouth waters as I peer over the woman's shimmering shoulder. My hands shift from her hips to her ass, squeezing tightly for a minute before smacking the bare skin. "Off." I'm not nice about it—I don't need to be. It's her job to entertain me, and right now, something else is vying for my attention.

She gets off without a word and moves to find someone else to grind on. Won't be hard; we've got a full house tonight. My private section is full—all people I know, none I care about aside from Dillon and Carmen. Darien too, I guess. But that's just the life we all live. In the same circle, all with the same selfish, ill-intent.

Money.

It stains, changes, corrupts.

I used to care about it, worried I'd become just like him —my father—but somewhere along the way, the concern faded into nothing the higher I got. And now, I'm almost as bad as he is, using money to get what I want, be whoever I want, depending on my mood.

And I've gotta admit, it's fucking nice knowing you're untouchable. The high is almost better than this... but not quite.

Dillon drops to his knees on the expensive carpet and grabs a bill from his wallet. He rolls it up tight then looks back over his shoulder at me. He holds it out, and I follow suit. My knees thud against the soft fibers, slacks stretching taut over my bent joints.

We're touching again, from shoulder to knee. His touch

is intoxicating as I grab the hundred dollar bill—because we're that cliché—and bend over the table. The thin, white lines are a delicious taunt as the green paper grows near.

I swear I can feel my pulse slow in preparation for the kick my heart is about to take, like it needs a split second to prepare. Just as I press the tip to the end of the first line, I plug my other nostril and inhale sharply, swiping the bill up as I snort the first one.

I pinch my nose and throw my head back, eyes rolling back at the instant wave of euphoria before I'm dropping my head just as fast to suck up the second line in my other nostril. I hand the rolled bill to Dillon without thought and watch as he takes his lines just as easily, only with a lot more dramatics because he's not as used to it as I am.

It makes me smile, even though somewhere deep inside me—a place I don't like to think about—knows I should stop him. Before it's too late. Before he gets too deep.

Like me.

But the other, sicker, lonelier part of me wants more of this from Dillon, just so I don't have to be alone in my self-destruction.

When he's done, I swipe up the residue and rub it on my gums, making my tongue as numb as my face. My heart kicks, knocking against my sternum as my blood thrums inside my narrowed veins.

"Dance with me," Dillon murmurs in my ear as holds his hand out. I grasp it. Our skin is slick with sweat as our palms slide together on our way down the sleek stairs. As we near the bottom, sounds become louder, lights brighter. Bodies multiply by the second, all clustered together in unsynchronized waves.

Dillon pushes us through to the center of the floor, and despite the varying levels of inebriation, we make our way through without much difficulty. When we're where he wants us, he hauls me against his torso, fingers digging into my ass as he starts rotating his hips, guiding mine the way he wants.

We're the same height, so I'm panting against his face, but he doesn't seem to care. His pupils are huge, black depths. A perfect match to mine, I'm sure. Bass vibrates through me, making my blood dance, veins and tendons fluttering.

My clothes cling to my skin as perspiration multiplies. Bodies bump into me from all directions, every single one lost to either the music, sex, alcohol, or drugs flooding their systems.

Because in this moment, nothing matters more than flying sky-high, never wishing to come down.

TENTACLES REACH OUT, all eight of them gripping my throat and my face with their suckers. Fire rips through my chest as I'm sucked into the abyss.

I shoot up, my own hand against my throbbing neck. Fingertips trace my skin, over my thready pulse as heavy doses of oxygen fill my lungs.

Lips so blue, skin so cold. Stains in my memories.

My room is cold and empty as my eyes scour through the darkness, searching for something to hold onto, a beacon to a reality I don't want to be in. I heave out a breath and cross my legs under the thin, damp sheet sticking to me like a second skin. My fingers card through my tangled hair, and I hiss when I catch them on a knot.

Clarity creeps back in steadily. The fan circulating cool air, the low hum of some appliance, the lights of the city shining behind me, even this high in the sky.

But I'm still caught inside my dream—a very real nightmare.

I can't remember the good from back then—if there even was any. The moment I cracked my sleepy eyes open to find my mother, still as a mirrored pond covered in dried vomit—has defined my life for the last five years.

Everything circles back to that. Like that's all I am anymore.

The fucked up son with a dead mommy and cliché daddy issues.

I dig the heels of my palms into my aching eye sockets. My temples throb with the start of a heavy hangover, throat dry and stinging in desperation for water. I fall back onto the pillows, slapping my hand around my bedside table in search of my phone. Glass rattles, then something shatters. I don't even flinch.

When my fingers brush over the smooth screen, I bring it close to my face, one eye pinched shut as the bright screen sends needles into my brain.

The clock reads 5:27 AM. I would roll my eyes if I knew it wouldn't hurt so bad. My father's going to be calling me any minute, I bet.

Notifications fill the screen as I unlock it. I clear them all without looking before pulling up the message thread with Carmen and Dillon. The last text is one from Carmen saying she was home, but I don't even remember falling asleep, let alone leaving the club and coming back home. Before I get the chance to type anything, a bar pops up at the top of my phone through the Do Not Disturb I have turned on constantly.

Like fucking clockwork.

"Hello, Father," I rasp as soon as I answer.

"Where are you?" He doesn't waste any time getting down to business. Nothing new there.

"I'm at home. Sleeping. You woke me up." The lies flow easily, effortlessly. I can practically hear how hard he rolls his eyes.

"I wouldn't believe that, even if I saw it with my own eyes."

"Your faith in me is staggering."

"Cut the shit, Zevryn. Are you—"

"Woah," a voice bellows out next to me, jolting me in place. I shoot up in bed again, groaning as my head swims, a pounding pressure knocking against my skull. I sway back and forth, my phone loose in my grip as I breathe heavily through the blinding nausea.

"You've got to be kidding me," my father says just as the person next to me moans in pain.

"Zev?" I think the voice sounds familiar, but my brain is throbbing so intensely, it's hard to hear through the waves of pain.

I'm staring at the shadowed lump on the other side of the bed a couple feet away. I'm not surprised I didn't notice. The bed's fucking huge, and honestly, the last thing I remember is dancing against Dillon, lips molded together in desperation as the crowds piled in around us.

With another blacked out night, the possibilities are endless.

"Dillion," I breathe in some relief at something making sense. Though, I'm not sure if that's better or worse.

"Fuck." The sheets shift as he sits up. "What the hell?" My eyes have adjusted to the dark just enough I can make out his bare chest and blonde, pin-straight hair sticking up on all ends from dried sweat and... *oh.*

My eyes flick over Dillon's bare chest as a fractured memory from last night returns. Dillon and I plastered together against a wall, all teeth and tongue. It was so hot, but I was numb, foggy from the lingering effects of the coke and heavy presence of tequila.

Hands were everywhere. Mouths, too. I remember the hot sensation of cum slicking my fingers, more than just mine, onto Dillon's face, down his neck, in his hair.

My eyes roll back, my dick twitching at the distorted recollection.

"Zevryn!" My name being shouted rouses me from inside my own mind. I clear my throat to answer Zion.

"What do you want?"

"What do I want? Jesus. You're nineteen years old, and I *still* have to treat you like a child living in my home, telling you when to eat and sleep and go to fucking work," he snaps, letting the *fucking* slip accidentally, I'm sure. Because my father is nothing if not overly cautious of his words and his tone.

Lucky for me, I always seem to bring out the worst in him.

I can't help the dry, raspy laugh that huffs from between my lips. My eyes are still locked on Dillon, where he lays spread eagle below the sheet. I can see the outline of his flaccid dick.

"As if you've ever done any of that. That's what you hired people to do." The line is quiet as Zion mulls over my words, no doubt thinking of *exactly* the right thing to say.

"I supposed I could've let your mother do that, but just think about how much worse it could've all turned out if I did." His words are cold and cruel and, unfortunately, truthful.

The fucking bastard.

After a minute of tense silence, my father states, "This meeting is important. I expect you here at seven sharp. Make yourself presentable. And tell Dillon his father is expecting his presence as well," he adds with a sharp bite to his tone. "Do *not* be late, Zev." And then there's the click of the call ending.

I drop my phone beside me on the bed. Willing the call to be forgotten, I reach for one of the bottles not shattered on the floor. I dig my elbow into the bed as I upend it, taking a few large swallows of the liquor before sliding across the smooth mattress until I'm plastered against Dillon. He looks up at me with sleepy, hungover eyes, a small, tired grin twitching at the corner of his lips. "That bad, huh?" My jaw clenches, and he nods, his hair scratching against the fluffy pillow. "They want us there today, I'm assuming." He already knows, but I nod anyway.

"The usual," I reply, dipping my head down to mouth at his throat. He smells of sweat and alcohol. An escape.

"Don't you ever wish you just... couldn't," he breathes out

just as our mouths clash together. I'm sure our breath is foul, but neither of us cares because we've seen the worst of each other and stuck around. Carmen, too, but she's not here right now.

We are.

And I want to forget for a while.

"Yeah, but we have to." I wish I could say I don't know why we have to, but I do. Because as much as I've grown to loathe my father and his money, I've become equally dependent on it, on this lifestyle and all it brings.

Without it, I couldn't soar. I'd sink deep into the trenches where the water's black and creatures that have never seen a flash of sunlight live.

Dillon's hand reaches between us, gripping my hard length. I find his just as easily, sliding my palm over his silky skin with practiced ease. I've lost count how many times we've found relief within each other, but it works.

We know each other inside and out, no secrets, all our ugly truths not only bared but accepted. Desired, even. Just to know we're not alone in the bullshit.

My father's words still battering around my skull melt into the background as my veins hum with the simmering warmth of alcohol and arousal.

Dillon arches his back as I twist my wrist on a down stroke. I speed up, my own chest heaving as arousal takes charge over the traces of alcohol. Dillon's cock gets slick as precum dribbles from his slit, urging me to end this sooner than I should.

I want to take my time, to really draw this out just to piss my father off by being late for one of the most important meetings in Carver Breck Technologies' history.

Because fuck him.

My arm slows, causing Dillon to whine and arch his hips as he fucks into my loosening fist. "Zev," he pants desperately.

I dip down to swipe my tongue across his chest. His trembling fingers find mine, and he pinches my pierced nipple, drawing a hiss from me. I stop the motion of my hand altogether to roll on top of him and press our lengths together.

Dillon's hands grasp my ass, blunt nails biting into my skin as he pulls me impossibly closer. "Yeah," he groans, rocking his hips. My arms are already shaking from the strain of keeping my exhausted body upright, but the thrum in my balls is enough motivation.

I lean back to spit over our dicks before dropping down and frotting against him. The room is stifling; sweat clings to our skin. The sheet sticks to my back, the fabric flowing in waves with every rock of my body against Dillon's.

His whimpers and moans fill the air and my mind. His vocality keeps me here, while the mere prospect of what's next threatens to drag me under.

As much as I hate my father, he knows the power he holds over me. The kind I fight against every chance I get but eventually succumb to because of what I need.

Money.

It always comes down to the fucking money I grew up hating while learning to crave it. The power it holds, the possibilities it brings...

Dillon's nails dig into my back as he arches his own, eliciting a hiss from my lips at the combination of pain and pleasure. His dick is slick satin as it slides along mine. I drop down onto my forearms to give us both more friction. When my flared head bumps his belly button, I groan, arms shaking all the way through my shoulders.

Dillon's legs are spread impossibly wide. I can feel his sharp pelvic bone on every grind. It hurts, but when he wraps his legs around my lower back, heels digging into my ass cheeks, pinning me in place, I no longer care. I shove my face into his neck and breathe in the scent of sweat, sex, and alcohol.

We both reek of it, and I eat it up for what it is—desperation to escape.

Dillon shoves a hand between us to wrap his fingers around our lengths. I twitch under the touch, overstimulated to the point it almost hurts. He works us in tandem with our small movements.

I burn with a craving for so many things.

I push myself up, peeling my clammy skin from Dillon's. He huffs and grips my back, trying to pull me back down, but I hold my stance. I blow my curls out of my face, panting as I stare down at him.

The faintest traces of the sun starting to rise fills the never-ending skyline just outside the glass. It gives the buildings a warm glow, ironic for how cold and manipulative this entire fucking city is.

"Where are you?" Dillon asks out of nowhere, pulling me from the city outside. I glance down at him, and a bead of sweat drips onto the pillow beside his head. Neither one of us speaks for a minute before he's rolling from underneath me.

I let him go easily, sitting back on my haunches as he drags himself off the bed and digs around in my side table.

My mouth starts to water, already knowing what he's grabbing. What I've always tried to hide from him and Carmen.

When a flash of white skips through my peripheral, I hold my breath. *This isn't okay... but I don't care.*

Dillon finds his place underneath me again like he never left, except he did, because now he's holding a baggie loaded with coke, and he's currently dumping some out on top of his abdomen.

How does he know I need this?

Why?...

He has no idea what he's doing.

My hands tremble slightly atop my thighs where my fingertips are dug in deep, putting divots in my flesh. When he's done, he closes and tosses the baggie aside. My eyes drop to the small mound located in the space just between his lower ribs, inches above his belly button. Only enough for a bump.

Dillon's hands dig into my hair as I bend down and sniff it into my nose, chest thumping wildly. I wet my finger and swipe up the excess. Dillon's lips part without hesitation as I rub it across his gums. He smacks his lips, blue-green eyes as wide as my own. Hesitant. Maybe even a little scared.

I like it.

Just as our mouths clash, my phone vibrates incessantly from where I tossed it. The sound travels through the sheets, and Dillon stills. I grind my molars together and press my mouth even harder into his.

He shakes his head but flicks his tongue out. "We've gotta go, or we'll be late. It's why he's calling," he says breathlessly. My jaw pops.

"Fuck him."

"Zev, my dad..." he trails off. I resist the urge to roll my eyes. Dillon, as much as he *rebels,* it's always when Hugh doesn't know because Dillon still kisses his father's ass.

Shoving my anger with the whole fucking world to the back of my brain, I lean down to kiss him again. "Just give me ten more minutes of this," I plead with him. I do want to piss my father off by being late, but I want this with Dillon more.

My heart thrums wildly, stealing my breath as he nods. Our movements become rushed and frantic as we thrust and grind together. Dillon glides his now spit-slick palm between us and jacks us together in time with my thrusts.

The low hum of arousal floods my system again, and I feel like I'm soaring as I chase the sensation—mindless and free.

Dillon comes before I do, his back bowing, cock jerking against mine. His cum makes it so much better to move within the confines of his loose fist. He keeps jerking his hand, teeth bared as he works to get me off, too.

The sight of his displeasure, even just the flash of a tight jaw, makes my eyes roll back on a shout. The minute-high of coke mixed with the delirium of an orgasm is so contradictory yet ironically similar.

I feel sky-high, like I'm floating on nothing.

And I seek to have both simultaneously.

I collapse on top of Dillon, but he's already wriggling his way out from under me. I huff a breath and roll onto my back, letting him escape. He doesn't say a word as he hurries into the bathroom. Not a minute later, water hits the shower floor.

I turn my head to stare out through the glass, fingers tapping restlessly on my cum-covered stomach. The sun is breaking through the skyline now, heavily-red this morning.

It reminds me of that old proverb I heard only once as a kid but seemed to stick with me all these years.

"Red sky at night, sailor's delight. Red sky in morning, sailor's warning."

I used to think about it often, especially when I would wake from a nightmare before dawn and stare out my window, finding the first brushes of a red-painted sky.

Weather lore has been around for centuries from those desperate to predict the weather before we had people to do it for us. And while it's used in a literal sense, I'm sure there were people out there who took it as an omen.

I've never been a superstitious person, but I know for a fact, every time I've seen the sky glow red with the sun, something not so favorable has happened.

Of course, it's purely coincidence, but I can't help but wonder.

With a sigh, already feeling the effects of the coke dwindling, I drag my ass out of bed to join Dillon in the shower, the bottle of liquor between my lips again.

Maybe he'll give me another ten minutes if I beg with his dick in my mouth.

Two

ZEVRYN

"We're going to be fucking late," Dillon groans as he fixes his hair in the mirror, styling it a particular way.

"We'd have more time if you'd quit fucking with your hair," I remind him. His eyes find mine in the large mirror, narrowed into slits.

"No. We'd have more if you didn't swallow my dick the second you stepped in the shower." I shrug my shoulders. I've got no rebuttal. He's right. And I wanted to waste more time.

It's fifteen to seven now. The car is waiting for us downstairs, but there's still no way we'll make it on time—not with traffic. I smile to myself as I drag my fingers through my wet curls, displacing them. I tuck a few strands behind my pierced ear, showcasing the shaved side of my head.

My small acts of rebellion might seem petty, but as long as I receive a grimace or a tick of the jaw from Zion, it makes it worth it.

Dillon's grinning, though he's still trying to play pissed off. "You really hate him." It's not a question.

"Yep," I respond and leave him to find my phone. More notifications line the screen, the missed call from Zion and a couple of texts from Carmen sitting at the top—two of the three people whose notifications come through the do not disturb.

Ignoring the beacon of Zion's name, I pull open my thread with Carmen.

CARMEN:

Get your ass up and go to work! I don't care if you're hungover.

And tell Dill I said hi ;)

I smirk and roll my eyes. She doesn't give two shits if I go to work; she just wants to fuck with me. So, I tease right back.

ME:

Tell whoever was grinding in your lap I said good luck

And why don't you actually get a job

I lock my phone just as Dillon walks out of the bathroom, and damn, does he look good with his blonde hair slicked back, clad in one of my suits—Armani in the inkiest black, slim-fitted. No tie, but the white shirt underneath is crisp and subtle. It's tailored for me, but Dillon and I are similar to the same build—he's just more muscular since I've lost some weight recently.

I look down at my own dark gray Brioni hanging loose. No tie, three buttons undone. Zion's gonna hate it.

“Let’s go,” Dillon says after looking me over. I smirk.

“Go ahead. I’ll be down in a sec.” He stares at me hard for a moment before heading for the door. When I can no longer see him, I pop open the baggie and dump some on the back of my hand. I do a few quick bumps before shoving it in my pocket.

I grab a tissue off the stand and swipe it under my nose a few times before striding down the hall. Dillon’s at the elevator, foot tapping against the marble floor as he waits. My walk slows the closer I get, and I smile in satisfaction at his pursed lips.

We’re surrounded by sleek steel as we descend. My phone vibrates.

CARMEN:

Fuck you. Why would I do that when I can do this all day?

And then a picture pops up underneath her text. My grip on my phone tightens marginally as I take it in. Dillon must sense something because he leans over to look.

“Fuck,” he breathes, and I nod, my own lip sucked between my teeth.

Carmen’s on her back, long brown hair splayed against a pillow with a perfectly-round ass inches from her face, bare and tattooed. There’s a tiny peek of the woman’s pussy glistening from the sun shining through the glass.

I chuckle and shake my head as I blow out a breath.

ME:

You got me there. Have fun.

I pocket my phone and drop my head against the steel at my back. What I would give to be there right now instead of on my way to a fucking meeting for a company I don't give two shits about.

Zion only wants me there to prove he's in control. I don't contribute to anything of importance, just paperwork bullshit. But appearances, as my father likes to say, are of the utmost importance.

"Our faces are the faces of the company. I don't care if this is what you want or not. You will show up, and you will work if you want to keep spending my money and living the way you do."

And there we have it, folks. His blatant manipulation.

As a way to try and get back at him for it, I used to blow his money on the most ridiculous shit, trying to get some sort of reaction out of him, but he never said a fucking word.

After a while, it lost its appeal. Might seem far-fetched, but you'd be surprised at how boring wasting money can get.

The ride to CB Tech is long with the stuffy traffic. I have the window down, but it doesn't help much when all I can smell is burnt rubber and oil. I dig through the compartment in the center and pull out a cigarette.

When the smell of burning tobacco wafts over me, I smile, thinking about the tick in my father's jaw when he smells it.

"You really are self-destructive, you know that?" Dillon mumbles next to me. I arch a brow, blowing out a cloud.

"You already knew this," I reply hesitantly, curious as to where he's going with this. The coke is surging in my veins; my legs are bouncing and twitching. I sniffle the snot threatening to drop out of my nose.

"Yeah, but today of all days?" He finally drags his gaze from the window to me. "This isn't just important to your father, Zev. Or mine. I understand a shot to calm your nerves, but..."

"You act like they're not a couple of the richest fucking guys on the east coast. Hell, in the country." The words taste bitter on my numb tongue.

"This is about more than making money. It's about expanding, creating more jobs—"

"Oh, so now you're on their side?" I sound petulant, but I'm pissed off. It was always supposed to be me, him, and Carmen against it all.

I thought he was just starting to get *me after last night...*

"I'm not on their side. You know how I feel about it. But lately, I've been taking an interest in it because it's important work. I could really make a difference, Z." I look away from his pleading gaze to stare out at the packed lines of cars, mostly a sea of yellow and black.

His words draw me farther away. I don't want to drag Dillon down with me—it's the last thing I want—but I never wanted to plunge alone.

When we finally pull up to the building, it's half past seven. Fashionably late, or as Dillon likes to call it, *way too fucking late.*

He rushes inside without a backward glance while I finish my second cigarette. The air is stuffy, even out of the confines of the car, and it makes my undershirt cling to my skin. I pace the area in front of the doors, cigarette between my lips. One curl is hanging loose in front of my eye, brushing against my eyelashes as I pace on the concrete path.

A security guard comes up to me, probably to tell me to fuck off and not smoke on the property when he notices who I am. His stride stutters for a moment before he walks up to me, face set in stone.

"Mr. Carver, do you need assistance with something?" I can't help but smirk at the title. Everyone in this fucking building hates me, but they can't outwardly say it, and I just know it drives them all insane.

The billionaire's bratty son, being a menace yet again.

I drop the cigarette and crush it with my Louboutin. "Nope. All set." With a smirk, I brush past him and inside the air-conditioned building. People shuttle all around like little bees in a hive, slaving away for the queen—or in this case, Zion Carver and his partner, Hugh Breck.

The elevator ride up to the executive floor is long with the constant stops, letting people off and more clambering on. I keep my place in the corner, legs crossed in front of me, taking up the space of two people unnecessarily, but no one says a word.

Finally, the silver doors glide open, revealing Riley, my father's personal assistant, waiting for me with files clutched in his hand. His mouth is in a thin line, and it pinches tighter when our eyes meet. I stroll out with a smile, hands in my pockets leisurely, my fingers pressed against the baggie.

"You're late," he hisses as I stroll past, heading for the

conference room. Riley's hot on my heels, breath coming out in short pants as his equally short legs struggle to keep up.

"I'm perfectly on time."

"You reek of cigarettes, you're disheveled, and your fucking eyes are bloodshot." His sharp tone draws me to a stop. I whirl around to pin him with my glare, but he doesn't shrink under my scrutiny.

Riley may be small, but he's a tough fucker—it's why he's worked for my father for so long. And frankly, I have to give props to him for dealing with Zion for the last two years. No one else has been able to for so long. He's insufferable.

"What I do is none of your business."

"It is when you're here. And your father would not want you walking in there, forty minutes late, looking and smelling the way you do." The hall is empty, walls lined with glass on either side of us, blinds drawn so we're all alone.

I take a step forward, making Riley step back. "You work for Zion, not me. I don't feel like being hounded first thing in the morning." I smile, relishing in the way he glares. "Now, if you don't mind, I have a very important meeting to attend. And I think they need my two cents."

"Zev, don't you dare—" He snaps his mouth closed as I pull open the door a few feet away. Silence meets me as everyone's head swivels, dozens of eyes drilling into me.

"Sorry I'm late. Traffic was a bitch." I pull back the chair next to my father and plop down into it. It creaks as I settle down, and I stretch my legs under the long, amber-colored table.

When I chance a glance at my father, I immediately notice the bulge in his jaw near the top, where his molars are pressed tightly together. His eyes are narrowed, nostrils flared, but aside from that, he doesn't give much outward appearance to his irritation.

It's something though.

My lips twitch.

"Please, do go on," I wave my hand in the air before clasping my fingers together and placing them over my stomach. "Oh, coffee, yes, please," I say way too loudly when I notice the carafes spaced evenly along the center of the table, various breakfast foods piled on plates between. I reach across and slowly drag the pot across the smooth wood, biting back a smile at the long, high-pitched squeak it makes.

Everyone's gazes are hot on my face as I pour a cup, adding the fixings until it tastes more like sugary cream than coffee. When I finally settle back in my seat, everyone pulls their eyes away—except Zion. His are twitching.

Smirking in his line of sight, I roll around until I'm facing the projection screen lined with numbers and graphs I don't really understand.

"Sorry for that. May we continue?" Zion's arm stretches in my peripheral, gesturing toward the screen. The board members and some people I've never seen before all nod in quick succession. A woman in a sleek pantsuit clicks a remote, and the screen shifts. More endless fucking numbers.

My eyes lose focus as she drones on and on, other people adding in. Questions are asked. Zion remains silent. Dillon sits directly across from me in the seat right next to his father, utterly consumed by whatever's being said. Hugh Breck looks domineering sitting in the chair, broad shoulders lax, hands clasped in front of him. His blonde hair is cropped close to his square head, styled to perfection. The suit donning his body is a warm shade of navy blue, perfectly tailored to his body.

I purse my lips as I rove my gaze over him appreciatively. He's tall, well over six feet—just like my father. They're both indomitable men. Ruthless. Smart. *Vain.* And they're both assholes with a lot of secrets.

Dillon's piercing gaze catches my attention. I drag my eyes from his father's throat to him. He pins me with an icy stare, and I smirk, hiking a brow. His lips move, forming words silently.

"Knock it off," I think he says, then his lips flutter with a smirk. I shrug and reach across the table to drag a plate of pastries my way. I'm not hungry—far from it with liquor sitting heavy in my gut—but I know the sound of me eating will piss Zion off, and I'm all about that.

I shove a glazed donut into my mouth, shooting Dillon a wink before I pull my phone out and scroll through Instagram, my legs shaking restlessly, making my chair creak. I ignore the red dot near the top filled with notifications I never check.

The voices echoing throughout the room drone into a white noise as I get lost in the black hole of social media. When a foot taps into my leg, I jerk and almost drop my phone. Hugh is glaring at me. I turn my head, and would you look at that—so is my father.

"What?" I mouth, and he lifts a hand to point at my phone now in my lap. I look down, then back up, grinning. I waggle my brows at the innuendo, and he huffs a breath, rolling his eyes. He fixes his attention back on the front, ignoring me. *Rude.*

I sniffle loudly as snot drips down my nostrils. Taking another bite, I stare through the glass at the cityscape. Buildings just as tall—some even taller—surround us in blocks of steel. The sun reflects off the windows, bouncing off in sharp rays. It's noiseless, but I close my eyes and imagine the loud bustle of the city—car horns, incessant shouting, unidentifiable beeps and dings, motors in cars, the sound of tires eating asphalt.

A folder snapping closed pulls me out of my trance. Everyone pushes out of their chairs, the projection screen blank as someone rolls it up. The group I don't recognize huddles together with small murmurs as everyone who works here exits the room in a timely manner—everyone except Dillon, Hugh, Zion, and myself.

Oh, great.

I force myself to stand and shoot my hand out. An older guy with gray hair latches on and shakes over exuberantly. I fight a grimace and the urge to wipe my palm on my slacks when he finally releases me.

"George, this is my son, Zevryn." Zion clasps my shoulder hard enough to almost make me wince. I bite it back and give them a fake, beaming smile, hating his next words more than anything. "He's the heir to the throne, as they say, so we're making sure to get him involved early." *You fucking wish,* Dad.

"A good philosophy, Zion," someone else says. I'm already bored with these games. My skin's crawling.

I shove my hands in my pockets, feeling the smooth texture of plastic. I grasp the baggie tightly. "It was nice to meet you all. Please, excuse me." Turning on my heels, I push my way out of the room, beelining for the bathroom.

Glares follow me the entire way, drilling hot and heavy into my back. Luckily, the bathroom's empty as I enter one of the handicapped stalls near the back of the large, opulent room. I pull the baggie out of my pocket as I take a seat on the toilet. After dumping a small pile of powder onto the back of my hand, I snort it up one nostril and repeat it for the other one. Sucking air heavily into my nose, I pinch both nostrils, then rub vigorously.

The door creaks as someone enters, so I press the seal closed and shove it back into my pocket. It's already running low, so I'll have to give Darien a call.

I tear off some toilet paper and rub it under my nose to make sure there's no residue left, then I unlock the stall door with a loud click. Dillon is standing near the sink with his arms crossed over his chest, lips pursed in a frown.

I roll my eyes at his demeanor as I wash my hands, checking my reflection in the mirror. My dark curls are unruly and wild where they hang down, just below my ears. A rough shadow of stubble adorns my face, hiding the slight gauntness of my cheekbones, but there's nothing to mask the red veins stitching their way across the whites of my eyes. I blink a few times against the dryness and pull out my phone to text Riley.

ME:

Bring me some eye drops.

He responds almost instantly, and I can feel his annoyance through the phone—it's comical.

RILEY PRICE:

I don't work for you, remember?

And yet, I know by the time I get to my office, there will be a bottle waiting for me. Pocketing my phone, I finally meet Dillon's gaze. "What?"

"You're blurring the lines," is all he says, giving me pause. I grip the edge of the smooth, stone counter, sniffling. The side of my hand presses against Dillon's hip, the material of my suit smooth and silky against my dry hands. I rub my knuckles along his hip bone before straightening.

I stare into his blue-green irises, subtle red lines surrounding them. "What fucking lines?" I drag my lips across his cheek, following his jawline. My other hand finds his hair, and I delve in. A few strands of blonde come loose from the product holding it in place. He shudders when I pull back, his own mouth parted, cheek glistening with the faintest traces of my spit.

"You know this is how I am, Dill. You've always known." I look into his eyes as I tell him that. His throat bobs with a smile, eyes crinkling at the corners. "Don't try to change me. Not for them."

His fingers grasp my chin, his thumb finding the divot in the center. "I'm just worried about you. I thought last night was—" I dart forward and swipe my tongue over his lips, making him gasp and drop his hand as he wipes his sleeve over the wetness.

"Don't be. I'll tell you if I'm not." I ironically follow that line with a heavy inhale through my nose, sucking snot back into my head. I grip his nape and press a kiss to his forehead before exiting the suffocating room.

"LET'S GO." I shove out of my chair and brush my hair back from my face, sniffling, before pushing Dillon away from my desk and toward the door. He digs his heels in.

"Wait, we still have—"

I groan. "Don't even try to pull the ten minutes left card with me. We're the bosses; we can fucking leave when we want." I squeeze his hip, and he quits resisting.

"Fine, let me tell Dad I'm leaving."

I roll my eyes. "You're almost twenty-years-old. You don't need to tell Daddy you're leaving work."

He levels me a glare, a thick section of blonde hair blocking one of his eyes. "Zev."

I throw up my hands in a mocking, placating gesture. "Fine. Fine." I stare out at the executive floor in all shades of gray with navy blue accents. There are cubicles in the center of the large room, where keyboards clack and phones ring, followed by muted conversations.

Riley walks up to us, eyes pinned on me as Dillon's knuckles rasp on the door to Zion's office in a rapid succession of three. Zion and Hugh have been holed away in Zion's office all week—since the meeting on Monday.

"They're—"

"Come in," Zion's voice booms out, and I flip Riley off, making his small lips purse. Dillon pushes his way inside, and I follow behind, making sure to shut the door in Riley's face.

"Just wanted to see if you need anything before we head out," Dillon stands in front of them with his hands behind his perfectly straight back. I glare daggers into the back of his head. *What a little fucker.*

"Yes, actually," Hugh starts before Zion interrupts smoothly.

"We will be hosting a launch party for a new piece of tech being introduced and shifted into production. It'll be a week from today, so I expect both of you to be there and be on your best behavior." Zion's eyes are on me alone, narrowed into slits. "Nothing like that stunt you pulled at the meeting Monday."

"Stunt?" I mock gasp, pressing my palm to my chest. "What ever do you mean?" Dillon jabs his elbow into my ribs, and I grunt and hunch over, unable to bite back my smile. Zion bares his teeth, his hate of me so blatant, it makes me smile wider, while a weight settles in my chest simultaneously.

"Cut the shit, Zev," Hugh cuts in. He stands from the chair off-centered to Zion's large desk, broad shoulders cut straight across with another perfectly-tailored, blue suit. His square jaw is cut sharp as says, "You will not fuck this up."

I won't, huh...

If there is one thing I hate in this world, more than anything, it's being told what to do. *You'll do this; you won't do that.* And you know what I do in return? The exact opposite —because why would I *want* to do what's expected of me?

"I won't?" I ask, hiking a brow. Hugh's jaw tightens, but before he can say anything, Zion pushes himself out of his chair and rounds the desk, putting himself right in front of me, New York's skyscrapers the perfect backdrop. His white shirt is stretched tight over his torso, all buttons done up impeccably because Heaven forbid the mask ever slips.

"No, Zevryn, you will not." I part my lips to snap back at him, but he holds his hand up, cutting me off. "Because if you do, this very comfortable… exuberant lifestyle you have been living will disappear."

A lump swells in my throat as his dark eyes peer into mine. I know he notices my dilated pupils, the stark red veins. Bruises beneath my sunken sockets. I swallow against it, hating the way it chokes me.

My molars grind together, fingers curling into fists at my sides. "I can live without your fucking money," I snap at him petulantly. His face remains utterly blank, not even a twitch in his eye, when normally I can always drudge up some kind of reaction, no matter how small.

"Can you? Even when you're left without a job?"

"You'd fucking fire me?"

Dillon stiffens beside me, but he remains silent, knowing better than to get in the middle of me and my father. Because as much as we loathe our families, they hold all the fucking power.

Zion nods. "And I'd lock all access to your accounts—and that cozy little penthouse you're holed up in. Everything you own has my name on it, Zev. Remember that before you continue to push this." His shadow looms closer. "I'm tired of the games. It's time to grow up."

The threat of losing everything is the last thing on my mind right now. There's one detail shoving its way to the surface, something I've kept down for so long, but the threat of his words brings it forward until it's screaming at me.

"This is more important to you than losing your son." I don't say it as a question—because it's not.

His nostrils flare, and his jaw tightens, a bulge forming near his top molars through his five o'clock shadow. The silence in the room rings so fucking loud, it makes my temples throb. No denial. Not even a shake of his head.

Nothing.

And then...

"It's more important than your luxury." I nod my head, having heard enough. I reach out and clasp Dillon's hand, needing something to ground me here before I sink into the trenches I try so desperately to stay out of as much as I veer toward it.

Eyes locked on the buildings behind him, I utter my understanding. "No worries, Zion. I heard you loud and clear. I fuck up; you'll disown me." I spin on my heels and drag Dillon out of the room with me. It's not until we're in the elevator and it's descending that I feel like I can breathe—except when I do, it comes out in a wretched gasp. My lungs feel too small, incapable of holding air, so I gasp and clutch at my chest, tears stinging my eyes pitifully.

I've always known how he's felt, but to have it stated so plainly—and in front of Dillon so there's no possible way I can try and convince myself otherwise when he heard everything I did...

Dillon wraps his arms around me just as I sink to the cold, metal floor. My head slams against the steel over and over, the warped sound echoing around us. He rubs his palms over my arms, trying to soothe me, but all it does is piss me off.

Hugh may be a goddamn prick, but he loves Dillon.

My father has never loved me, but to hear him *finally* admit how little I mean, like it took no strain for him to do so…

He'd erase me from his life just as easily as he did Mom.

I let Dillon hold me as the numbers tick down to the first floor. When we reach the number five, I pull away and stand up, blinking my eyes clear of the tears threatening to fall. I clear my throat and crack my neck.

Three…

Two…

Ding.

The doors slide open, revealing the large, ostentatious lobby. Dillon and I make our way through the bustle of people and out onto the steaming concrete. The sun is blinding, and it's too hot for June, so I discard my jacket and undo the buttons on my shirt as we walk to the black car waiting for us near the curb.

My head throbs, and each step I take sends a sharp jolt into the back of my eyes.

Dillon climbs in first, and I follow. The second the door is slammed shut, I'm cracking the window and lighting a cigarette just so I can stink Zion's car up with the smell when his driver finally brings him home.

Normally, the thought would make me smile, but right now, I don't feel much of anything—or at least, I won't soon enough.

"Are you okay?" Dillon asks after a while of being locked in traffic. I've long since snorted a few lines, uncaring about Dillon watching my blatant self-immolation as my heart thrums with the shock to my system. My legs are bouncing, hands twitching, as I smoke another cigarette.

I can't even taste the nicotine.

"I've never been better, Dill," I drawl. Dillon's lips purse as he watches me pull out my phone. I scroll through my contacts until I stop at the right one and hit call. It rings for a minute before it's cut off.

"Hey, Zev. What's up?" Darien drawls.

"I've got some money to blow. Wanna come over?"

Three

ZEVRYN

With Carmen on one arm and Dillon on the other, I step through the front doors to CB Tech. It's surprisingly quiet as we make our way to the elevators, only muted instrumentals and soft, golden lights illuminating the way.

Carmen looks around, her dark hair swishing against her back and brushing my shoulder. Dillon's gaze is set forward, but I can see the excitement on his face, underneath the mask of indifference he's trying to portray.

We slow our steps as the group in front of us slows theirs, waiting for an elevator to open. It doesn't take more than a minute for the subtle ding to chime, and we all step on—elegantly, of course, because we all have an image to uphold.

Carmen's hold on my forearm is light, content. Dillon's is the exact opposite. He's latched onto me like he's afraid to let go. His eyes keep pinging around the steel box, foot tapping anxiously. His eyes are on me again.

It makes me smirk through the haze coating my eyes.

I nod my head at the other patrons and exit the lift when the doors glide open, revealing the usually empty space to be completely lavish. Lights adorn the ceiling, swooping down and twisting around with navy blue ribbons entwined intermittently.

There are tables spread out evenly amongst the open floor, all centered toward the stage at the opposite end, where I'm sure Zion and Hugh will show off their newest invention—or purchase. I don't know which one, but it doesn't really matter, does it?

"Damn, they really go all out, don't they?" Carmen asks above the muted trickle of music as we make our way to the center of the room. She releases my arm to do a dramatic 360. Servers walk around with trays of champagne and fancy-looking hors d'oeuvres. I reach out to a passing server and snatch a glass off their tray. It tips under the unexpected force, and I watch with glee as the glasses lain atop shift and clatter together. He manages to right the black tray at the last second, much to my disdain. The light directly above his head showcases the bead of sweat trickling down his temple.

His eyes find mine, wide and questioning. I lower my eyelids to half-mast and give him a sly grin. "Sorry about that." I upend the glass and swallow the bubbly alcohol with relish before slamming it back down.

He grits his teeth, but his bottom lip wobbles. "No problem, sir." Then, he disappears before I can push him further.

"Leave the poor kid alone, would ya, Zev?" Carmen nudges my side. It makes my penguin suit pinch. I shift uncomfortably, the alcohol I downed earlier long past the point of making me warm, but at least there's champagne.

"Come on, Dill. Show me around." Carmen grabs his arm holding mine, tugging him away. He releases me reluctantly, eyes flashing to mine.

"I'm *fine,*" I appease him. He doesn't argue. My eyes trail after them as they make their way through the thickening crowd.

I am anything but fine.

I find an empty table nearest to the wall and yank out a chair. Another tray pops up in my peripheral, so I hold my hand up to stop them. Black shoes falter and turn in my direction. I lift my gaze and hold up three fingers. Dark eyebrows form a perfect arc, but she doesn't argue as she transfers three glasses from her tray to the table. With a nod, she disappears back into the thickening group.

With a delicate glass stem between my fingertips, I down the first glass in two swallows, the expensive bubbly sliding down easily. I'm chasing it with the second when Zion finds me.

"That's your third, Zevryn," he murmurs from somewhere behind me, his voice sounding high up. I tilt my head to the side, and sure enough, there he is, standing at my back, hands clasped behind his, eyes scanning the room instead of looking at me.

He can't even fucking look at his own son.

"I didn't know you could count that high." I snap the petulant words before I can think better of it. Zion's eyes flash as they drop to me. His jaw ticks at the little quip, and I really can't help the way it makes me smile.

Whatever he sees on my face must really piss him off. With steady hands, he pulls out the chair next to me and gently takes a seat. His hands are relaxed against his thighs after he releases the tension in his slacks from the change in position. He leans forward, dark hair perfectly coiffed and smelling of what I'm sure is expensive product.

"You're drunk," he says gently, but his tone doesn't fool me. Zion's anger always leaks through his words and into his actions. He's cold and cruelly manipulative. "You've been drunk all week."

I can't help the way my face heats.

The shame he makes me feel...

"How the fuck would you know?" I finish off the second glass. I'm defensive—and he knows it. When I reach for the third—technically, my fourth—Zion's arm snaps out, covering mine just as my fingers brush the crystal base. His fingers are cold and heavy against mine, pinning my hand against the soft, white tablecloth.

His nose wrinkles in disgust as he leans in, careful to keep his words just for us. Because Heaven forbid someone found out we aren't the perfect family. Little does everyone know, we've never been a fucking family.

"The smell practically leaks from your pores, Zevryn. You're constantly in a state of inebriation, and I'm about done with your excuses."

I snort. "Excuses? Why do you even care? I'm showing up for work, just like you want, so what's it matter?"

He shakes his head like he can't understand why a toddler doesn't grasp the basic concepts of trigonometry. "The way we present ourselves to those around us is of the utmost importance." His breath is hot and minty as it fans over the back of my neck. "Everything we say—do—all comes into account in our business. A business you *will* take over someday, but I will not have an alcoholic sitting at the table, now or ever, so you need to get whatever your issues are out of your system now because, in a week's time, my patience will end along with my enabling."

He leans back, taking the flute with him. I let my hand fall away, eyes staring forward at nothing in particular. I ignore the way they sting and blur with liquid pooling over the surface. Zion rounds my chair, his black tux blocking my line of sight before someone calls his name and he's gone.

When I can no longer see him, I feel like I can breathe again. I suck in a breath and fucking choke on it. My hands fly to my neck as saliva tangles in my throat, constricting my airways. For a second, I panic at the loss of oxygen, my heavy beating heart chugging faster by the second, but then air travels through my snot-clogged nostrils. Just a whisper of it, but the sharpness is enough to send a signal to the neurons in my brain that I am, in fact, not suffocating.

Just drowning in my father's endless disappointment.

My chest heaves as I slump back in the chair, my buzz long gone, and in its place, a ticking time bomb.

It's heavy beneath my sternum, its effects traveling to my extremities, making my legs bounce against the marble floor in clacking taps.

The sense of time dragging pulls against my skin, making it prickle with pin needles. I'm alone, surrounded by a blur of people and the deafening hum of chatter.

"Do you ever check your phone anymore?" A voice drags me out, and I lift my head, finding Darien plopping down in a chair in front of me. He's dressed in black slacks and a dark blue shirt with the first three buttons undone, most of his dark chest on display.

"Zev," he barks, waving his hand in front of my face, and I blink.

"What's up?" I clasp his hand. "Didn't think you'd show up to this shit," I throw my hand up as I lean back, rolling my eyes up at the decorated ceiling. Even being this high up, I still feel too close to the earth, like gravity has increased tenfold, and I'm slowly being crushed.

"Eh, wasn't planning on it, but figured why not. Been a long time since I've been to one of these." He slouches back in the chair, a similar position to the one I'm in.

"You mean a dick-measuring contest? Speaking of, is your dad here?"

He chuckles, shaking his head with a smirk tugging at his full lips. "Of course, he's here. He'd never pass up the opportunity to show his face at one of their parties."

I roll my eyes, but a smirk stains my lips thinking about Zion running into Micah Richardson. He invited him, of course, with full intentions of Micah showing up, but the reality of it is always so different.

"That ought to be fun to see." Darien holds up a hand at a passing server, taking two flutes filled nearly to the top. He hands one to me.

"I don't plan on sticking around to see," he says before taking a sip. The echo of a mic being tapped rings throughout the room, drawing everyone's attention. Dillon and Carmen break through the settling crowd, warm smiles on their faces, Carmen's flushed with alcohol.

They look happy.

"D, good to see ya." Dillon nods his head as he pulls out the chair next to me. Carmen plops down on Darien's lap and wraps her arms around his shoulders. He embraces her as she settles on his lap, her freckled face glowing under the warm, ambient light.

"Dillon." Darien acknowledges Dill with a nod.

"Thank you all for coming tonight." Zion's voice booms through the mic, and I grit my teeth, avoiding facing the stage. Dillon's hand grips my upper thigh, sensing my tension. Then the heel on Carmen's shoe taps against my shin as she gives me a sad smile.

I look away, swallowing against the lump in my throat as my father's words batter around in my skull.

For the first time in my fucking life, despite how deeply I hate him and this business, I was making an attempt to show up. I think vying for a sliver of praise, but I should've known nothing would ever be good enough for him.

I couldn't do it sober. Hell, I can't do *anything* sober anymore. And I'm not really sure when it all changed. It's something that happened so slowly, I didn't notice until I was in too deep and stopping wasn't even a possibility anymore.

I had my first taste of alcohol at fourteen, and the liquor that burned its way down my throat seared a path straight to my brain. The way the world spun around me, tilting and whirling, my head as light as it had ever been, put my childish spinning attempts to shame. Had I known alcohol could have given me what I'd always been craving, I would've started chugging the shit a long time ago.

I was floating on cloud nine, veins warm and tingling. And then, I thought about Mom. How she was dead. *How* she died—right in front of me... and I didn't care. I laughed about it, so hard I couldn't breathe.

I've been chasing that high ever since.

Digging my fingers into my sweaty palms, I sink my teeth into the soft muscle of my tongue as I force my gaze to the stage. Zion's standing ramrod straight, and on most people, it would make them appear stiff—uncomfortable—but on Zion, he just looks domineering and perfectly in control.

I fucking hate him.

He drones on about how proud he is of what's been accomplished because of *everyone's contribution to this wonderful company they've built.* I can't stop the snort that bubbles up my throat. A few heads turn my way, gazes sharp as they drill into me with downturned mouths. Carmen giggles silently atop Darien's lap, and I watch as Dillon's lips twitch with amusement, his hand squeezing my thigh again.

Zion thanks everyone for showing up before exiting the stage, and then Hugh takes his place at the podium. I vaguely hear as he starts to explain the piece of tech and what to expect as my gaze tracks to my father. He takes a seat at the table directly in front of the platform. A woman I've never seen before gives him a bright smile and leans in, lips pursing as she whispers near his ear.

Zion smirks, and my teeth lock in a grit as I watch his lips move in response before they brush against her cheek, his hand subtly grazing her knee just beneath the table.

My vision blurs, something vile churning in my gut at the sight.

In the five years since Mom died, I have never once seen Zion entertain another woman. I know he's fucked around, there's no denying that, but at the very least, he's been *respectful* enough not to bring that shit around me.

Until now.

Another piece shifts into place, only solidifying the nasty thoughts articulating in my diseased brain.

I'm nothing but a mere piece of his DNA. Not worth the time, the effort.

Not worth his love.

My nostrils flare as I fight against the blinding sting in my eyes. I roll them up to keep the tears from spilling over. When I finally feel the pressure subside, I pull in a shaky breath and lower my head.

As I look around the room, I can't help but think that no one understands how hard it is to be in pain so silently.

So alone.

And so, so afraid.

Through a blurry gaze, Darien cocks his head, eyes on mine for a long moment before he gently lifts Carmen off his lap. She whispers something, and he shakes his head before pushing his chair back and meandering through the groups of tables, out into the short hall.

My brows furrow for a moment before I'm pushing out of my chair.

Dillon's grip on my thigh stops me. He leans in, eyes on the stage with his lips pressed against the metal in my ear. "Where are you going?"

"To the bathroom."

"They're about to present," he whispers like I actually give a shit. When he notices the expression on my face, he rolls his eyes. "Just hurry up. *Please,*" he adds with a pout, his thick, blonde hair covering one of his eyes. "I hate being alone at these things. People corner you," he whispers harshly, making me laugh.

Dillon always makes me feel a bit lighter, even when the swarm starts to suffocate.

"Yes, *Dad.* I'll be right back." I press a chaste kiss to his cheek before heading toward the bathroom. Hugh's voice reverberates along the walls, followed by a harmonized euphony of clapping as I yank open the door to the bathroom.

I blink against the harsh light stinging my retinas as the door swings shut behind me, effectively cutting off the worst of the noise. Water splashes in one of the sinks as someone finishes up washing their hands. I avoid their gaze in the mirror as I shuffle to a urinal, taking a piss as the dryer blows loudly.

As the door thuds closed, I rasp my knuckles on the stall at the far end of the bathroom. Darien pulls it open, dark fingers wrapped around the top of the white door. I step through, my heart thumping against my breastbone in anticipation.

"You look wrung out," Darien observes as I cross my arms over my chest. The material of my tux is tight, fitted to my body down to the millimeter, even with my recent weight loss. I can feel every shift of the expensive fabric against my chewed-up nerves.

I dig my teeth into the soft flesh of my cheek until I feel the flesh give way to the strong tang of copper.

"Wanna talk about it?" he asks as he plops down atop the toilet, making the porcelain lid rattle.

"Are you going to make me, or can we just get on with it?" I already know what this is.

He chuckles darkly, pink tongue darting out to wet his

bottom lip. "Nah, just trying to be a friend. You look like you need one."

"You are—but not that kind of friend." My words come out harsher than I meant, but he doesn't take it personally. Darien always appears perpetually unbothered—something I deeply admire about him but will never admit.

"Suit yourself. I'm just here for a good time." He digs into his pocket and pulls out a baggie. My lips curl in as I watch him spin around on the toilet and dump some of the white power on the back of the tank. His dreads dangle in front of his face, partially blocking my view of the thick, white lines he's forming.

I'm already digging a bill out of my wallet before he's finished. When he turns halfway, I hold the rolled hundred out to him. His shit—he goes first. He nods his thanks and dips down to suck up the first line. My foot shakes restlessly against the floor as I wait, leaning up against the wall.

My eyes close with bliss at the sound of Darien snorting, and I swallow the pool of saliva gathering on my tongue.

"Fuck!" he shouts a little too loudly as he stands. I grab the bill from him just as he stumbles into the wall, eyes rolling back into his head. His breathing is labored, almost a wheeze as he slumps against the side of the stall.

I blink once. Twice. My eye twitches at the corner, but then I look at the toilet and those lines call to me more than anything else around me. I lean down, bill pressed to my nose, my other nostril plugged. I suck in a breath, dragging the makeshift tube across the powder.

Time slows infinitesimally. My heart gallops. Euphoria licks across my brain.

The sound of gurgling cuts through the sharpness. I

blink. Sniff. Pinch my nose. One line, more than half of another stares back at me. I run my tongue over the fronts of my teeth as I spin around. Darien's slumped on the floor, jaw slack as he chokes on his own spit.

I blink.

Vomit?

His body wracks, shoulders shaking. It reverberates down his body until his hands, and even his feet, are shaking, too.

I blink.

My face is numb, my throat thick with the familiar drip.

The white of his eyes are all I can see through his fluttering lashes. "Darien?" I think I hear myself say, but my voice sounds so far away, like it's coming from someone else entirely.

The white walls close in around us, feeling darker and heavier by the minute.

I blink.

My hands tremble. The rolled-up bill hits the floor in time with my knees. My fingers find Darien's face, sticky with sweat and other fluids. I turn his head, watching the vomit spill from between his bluing lips.

"Darien?" I tap his face. When he doesn't flinch, I slap him a little harder. Nothing.

Everything feels sharp and sluggish as I choke on my heart, waiting for Darien to come out of it.

A creak, then footsteps. Knuckles rasp on the door. "Z? Are you in here?" It sounds like Dillon, but I can't be sure. It sounds like there are waves crashing in my ears like they do against the beach in a tsunami.

I'm drowning in the sound, in the feelings I'm forced to

bear as I stare at Darien's slack face. The gurgling has stopped. He's limp.

"Zev, come on. You can keep partying later."

I want to laugh. Cause that sounds nice, but I don't think that's going to happen. Because this *feels* bad. Impossibly wrong.

I'm confined to here and now.

The door rattles. I blink.

Help... I think we need help.

I part my lips, forcing a sound from my throat. I don't know what it is, how I manage it, but then Dillon's head is poking underneath the small gap between the door and the floor. He's still for a moment. "Oh, fuck!" he shouts.

My ears ring from the decibel. His feet slap against the marble floor, loud and jarring. And then, silence.

I remember the first time I ever heard silence this loud. It was moments after I woke up that morning and Mom's pale face was the first thing I saw. I didn't know what I was looking at for so long.

I kept trying to wake her up. Sometimes she slept so heavily, it took a while. Except that time, it wasn't. She just kept jostling with the force of my touch shaking her. Blue lips parted and soiled with vomit.

The smell stained my brain, my heart.

And now, I'm choking on the scent all over again.

My eyes flash open, and instead of seeing Darien, all I see is Mom. Her short, dark hair fanned across my lap as vomit pulses from her mouth in streams so thick, she's choking, asphyxiating in my arms while I sleep, none the wiser.

"*Help!*" I think I scream, my voice finding me just when I

need it most. "Please, someone help! She's dying!" A sob rips through my chest, and something shreds inside of me. Something visceral.

Something I know I can never get back.

All of a sudden, everything gets loud. The door rattles and then flies open. A large foot drops back to the floor. My eyes find Zion's, and for the first time in my life, I feel grateful seeing his face.

"Dad," I choke. "Help her—she's dying. Please, help. Help her!" My screams carry on as I'm shoved away from the body half-lying in my lap. My head hits the wall with a sharp thud, and I groan.

My face is wet and hot. Arms circle around me as the noises increase.

Yells. Screams. Shouts of panic. And in the center of it all is Zion. Calm, jaw set as he fixes what I broke.

He may not have been able to fix Mom before, but he can now.

Black creeps in slowly at first, but then, it's all I can see. All I feel is my heart battering and bruising my ribs. I think I claw at my chest, burning with the need to scream, to breathe.

To...

"Zev," someone rasps into my ear, "what did you do..."

Four

GAVIN

Sweat trickles down the back of my neck. The itch that follows makes me curl my toes into my shoes as I resist the urge to swipe it away.

It soaks into the collar of my simple, black tee with more soon to follow from the way the waves from the sun are hammering down.

My arms are locked tight behind my back, the fingers on my right hand curled around my left wrist. I scour the area with cold calculation, seeing nothing but green grass, trees, and semi-empty houses as most occupants are gone for their day jobs.

"You know you can come inside and cool off, right?" Ms. Warren calls from behind me. Jonah is right on her heels, leering behind her in the doorframe. I subtly grit my teeth, and the urge to roll my eyes is almost too strong to resist.

This woman has absolutely no concern for her own safety—like she didn't hire us to protect her from the man that's been stalking her for months. And one would think with the price tag involved, she'd want me to do my job properly, but no. She just keeps bugging me with the same question.

It's almost like she doesn't understand, worst-case scenario, I can't protect her from him if I'm in there and not out here watching like I should be.

"I'm all right out here, ma'am. Thank you." I nod my thanks and fix my gaze back toward the road. Jana's new house is located at the end of a cul-de-sac in an entirely different city, so it makes our jobs much easier.

For the last two weeks, all has been quiet, but we're still on alert because the cops haven't caught him yet.

"Is he always so stuffy?" I hear her whisper to Jonah, although she's not exactly doing a good job of that when I can hear her from across the porch. Jonah snickers, then the sound is cut off by the door latching shut.

Annoyed by my break in concentration, I walk around the perimeter of the house like I do every five minutes, ensuring all is well from all sides. I take a deep breath, grateful today's my last day in this stuffy town. Orson will be here tonight to take my place because, for the first time in years, I'm taking a vacation.

I was more forced into it, but after a long conversation with Milo a couple of months ago, I realized he was right—and it was something we *both* needed to do. Never mind the fact our anniversary is in two days, and I haven't the slightest clue what to get him.

Ten years with him and I'm still just as clueless as I was back then.

As I'm nearing the large, fenced-in backyard, my phone buzzes in my pocket. I dig it out, knowing it could only be one of six people—and with Jonah being inside, five. Swiping my arm across my forehead to keep sweat from stinging my eyes, I curl my upper half down to block the sun from the screen.

Deacon's name flashes, so I swipe immediately. "Yes?" I answer briskly, eyes back on the yard. I wander closer to the house, checking the windows are still locked, my phone pressed between my ear and shoulder so I can use my arms.

"Remember that we're friends after I tell you this," his gruff voice thunders over the line. I wince immediately, already knowing what he's going to say. I'm dreading it as much as anticipating it.

I blow out a long breath. "What happened?" I ask, knowing he wouldn't be calling me if it wasn't important.

"Zion Carver." I halt in place, the billionaire's name deafening in my ears. "His request was for only one of us—but it has a lot of stipulations. He needs someone who can be gone for a couple of months and is willing to leave the country."

"And I'm the first person you called," I reply, trudging through the grass to comb through the tree line.

"Yes. Your lack of stipulations veers you in this direction, but everyone's out on a job right now. You're our only option." Deacon sounds contrite. He knows how hard it was for me to even ask for some time off—and now, he has to ask me back.

I groan audibly and brush back a few sweaty strands of hair that have slipped from my hair tie.

Milo's going to be so pissed.

"When?" is all I ask, already knowing I'll take the job. Deacon's breath of relief is evident.

"Soon. He's agreed to pay more than your annual salary —for the business *and* you, personally." My eyes bulge, feet stopping inches from the porch. Jonah pulls the door open, lips parted to speak when I told up my hand.

"I can counter back with a higher price for you since it's last minute, and you will have to leave the country for two months. I'd bet he'd go for it—he sounded... desperate." I can hear Deacon's finger tapping against his desk in a methodical tune as he waits patiently for my answer.

"Desperate? Who's the client?" Jonah cocks his shoulder on the doorframe, listening in on the conversation. Even on a work call, I still keep my eyes peeled.

"His son. He wouldn't give me more details than that. Said he wanted to meet with you to discuss this in person due to personal matters."

"Yeah, I'll meet with him, just let me know when and where." I sound resigned, but somewhere, deep down, there's a part of me that's relieved I have an excuse to give Milo.

"Orson should be there within the hour. Head back here, and we'll talk. Thank you, Gavin." I hang up, but I don't pocket my phone. I pull up Milo's contact and stare at the picture I set for him.

His wet, golden hair is glowing in the sunlight, sunglasses perched on his nose, tattooed torso on display. His smile is so bright and wide. It reminds me of happier times.

Times that have long since dissipated.

"What was that about?" Jonah asks. I lock my phone and shove it back in my pocket. Standing, I face him, arms crossed over my chest.

"Just a job. Orson should be here soon."

"Yeah, all right." He nods and heads back inside, leaving me to wait for Orson's arrival so I can go home and tell my husband I lied to him.

ONCE I'M BACK in the city, I drive to Ayers Security's business office. Deacon meets me to give me a quick rundown before I'm jumping back in my car and heading toward Carver Breck Technologies for my meeting with Zion Carver.

I keep the radio on a low hum as I sit in traffic, thumb tapping the bottom of the wheel to the beat of "Fake It" by Seether. Milo's name pops up on the display, his photo in the background. My gut clenches as I hit the button on the steering wheel, answering his call.

"Hey, babe. Do you know when you'll be home? I was thinking about making your favorite for dinner but don't want it to get cold before you're home."

Fuck. "Uh, yeah." I silently clear my throat from the ball of guilt constricting my words. I glance at the clock on the dashboard. "Probably a couple of hours. Have a meeting real quick, then I'll be headed home."

I can hear his smile in his words. "Okay, drive safe. Love you." And then there's a click just as I'm pulling in front of Carver Breck's building. The skyscraper touches the sky from where I'm parked, all steel gray and glass.

Milo's carefree words bounce around in my head, tangling with guilt. In my mind's eye, I easily visualize his smile morphing into a frown. Lines of disappointment on his forehead. Bright blue eyes twinged with sadness. With anger. *Resentment.*

My watch buzzes with the appointment reminder Deacon added to my calendar. Steeling my expression, I climb out and easily make my way inside. After checking in with the front desk, the receptionist directs me to the executive floor.

As the steel doors glide open and I step onto the lift, I take one last glance through the lobby. At the high ceiling, ostentatious decor. The lavish yet sleek furniture.

This place screams money, which is no surprise to me knowing who Zion Carver is.

Billionaire business owner, started from the bottom, and now, he's one of the country's richest men.

I push the button for the floor I need—the highest one available—and move over so more people can get on.

It's a slow ascent with the constant ebb of movement, but finally, the doors open to the executive floor. A small, wiry man with yellow hair and freckled skin is the first thing I see. His arm darts out, hand in the air. I grasp it and shake. "I'm Riley Price, Mr. Carver's assistant. He's asked me to bring you to his office as soon as you've arrived. If you'd follow me."

He spins, and his short, skinny legs really book it across the sleek floor. The executive floor is more shades of gray with navy blue accents. Offices and conference rooms with glass walls line the perimeter, the cityscape an incredible background with cubicles focused more in the center of the room, each one filled with people clacking away on keyboards.

The energy isn't bad, just buzzing with focus. Like bees in a hive.

I glance around, eyes pinging across the ceiling and corners of the room, looking for cameras. It's become an instinct after years of working security, but I'm still aware of *when* I'm doing it.

Riley brings us to a large office with frosty glass walls. He knocks his knuckles against the door before cracking it open. Poking his head inside, he says, "Mr. Holt is here for you, Mr. Carver."

The door swings open, and Riley steps back to let me through. "Please, head in." Nodding my thanks, I step in, and he closes the door behind me with a soft click. Wheels dragging across the floor snap my gaze away from the stunning view just on the other side of the glass. Steel buildings backed by a densely blue sky. Sun rays shimmer on the glass, sending fractured beams bouncing. The roads below look small enough to pinch between my fingers, the cars lining them mere specs.

I've never felt so high nor so large in my life.

It's a thrilling sensation.

"Incredible view, isn't it?" Zion says behind me. I nod, a smile on my face as I turn to face him. He shakes my hand, his other clasping my elbow. I finally catch my first in-person glimpse of one of the most famous men in New York City.

He's dressed impeccably in a starched white button-down and black slacks that look to be made of silk. His hair is perfectly styled, stubble trimmed and lined up perfectly straight. He looks formidable and severe.

It makes me glad I decided a suit would be the best

option, even if I look slightly rumpled from the four-hour drive.

"Mr. Holt, thank you for meeting with me under these circumstances. I apologize greatly for any inconvenience this may have caused you." He holds his arm out, indicating the chair just on the other side of his large, sleek, wooden desk. I take a seat in the soft leather as Mr. Carver drops into his.

Now that he's seated directly in front of me, I notice the slight bruises under his eyes and the frown lines marring his mouth, along with deep-set wrinkles in his forehead.

I guess running an empire of this magnitude takes its toll.

"I suppose you have many questions related to the details of our contract."

I nod my agreeance. "Of course." I clasp my hands in front of me, patient. Mr. Carver digs his fingers into his eyes and rubs aggressively. Tension radiates in his neck and down his arms.

"I'm going to be blunt, if that's all right with you, Mr. Holt?" Zion blinks heavily, meeting my curious gaze.

"Please, call me Gavin, Mr. Carver. And of course. Candor is always the best bet, no matter how blunt."

"Then call me Zion. We're about to be on a first-name basis after this." His words make my ears perk. I raise my brows, lips pursed.

"My son is an alcoholic. Or, well—" He stops to take a deep, frustrated breath as he runs a hand through his hair, disheveling it. "I suppose an addict of more than just alcohol. He's been slowly declining for months, and even I must admit, I should've done more to stop him. Or to help him.

"But I didn't. I thought he was going through a phase—or was acting out of pure spite because of me. We don't have the best relationship, you see, so it wasn't a far-fetched notion in any capacity." He gives me a sad smile before continuing.

"But then, at a launch party we had just five days ago for our newest piece of tech, Zevryn did something—" He cuts himself off with a sharp inhale. I watch the muscle in his jaw twitch uncontrollably for twenty solid seconds before it finally relaxes along with some of the tension in his hands.

Zion places his palms flat on the desk, as if he needs something sturdy to settle the tremor controlling them.

"Someone died. An overdose. In my building, at my party. Because of *my son.*" I keep my expressions in check, not even allowing a single twitch of surprise to escape, but my mind is running rampant with scenarios.

The hows, the whys, the *because.*

Personally, I don't have any experience with addicts, so I have no idea what to expect—if it'll even *be* a different experience.

"What about the legality of it all?" I ask, needing to know the stance there before we move forward. One of Zion's brows raises expectantly, his expression flat and dry. I nod once, understanding dawning immediately.

"Money," is all I have to say. He nods, his features tightening into a grimace.

"Unfortunately, yes. Under any other circumstance, I would never use my money to ease someone out of their punishment, but he's my son." He says the words with so much remorse. "I couldn't just let him..." Zion clears his throat and then shakes his head. He pushes back from his desk and walks over to the window, staring out at the surrounding buildings.

"He's my son. And despite his role in what's happened, I do not believe it was a decision he made with malicious intent. Honestly, we don't even know exactly what happened. Darien is dead, and Zevryn refuses to speak—to anyone—about what happened that evening."

My mind is racing with the information overload. It seems Zion's just venting at this point, but I listen quietly. Every piece of information will help me do my job to the best of my ability—especially if my job involves someone so... unstable.

The thought sits bitter on my tongue.

I nod my head even though Zion's back is to me. "What do you need from me?" I don't bother trying to placate him by saying he made the right decision. I don't care, nor is it my right to have an opinion.

He turns to face me, leaning against the glass. "Part of the deal was that I get Zevryn some help."

"Rehab?" I guess.

Zion nods. "But that's not all of it. Micah, Darien's father. He's..." Zion blows out a breath, making the loose strands of hair across his forehead move, "a bit of a business rival. We've always been cordial—in the most professional way, if not cold—but it seems his son's passing has brought out the worst in him."

I feel the skin on my forehead tug as my brows furrow, pieces clicking. "I'm assuming this is where I come in."

"Yes. Micah has threatened Zev's life. I am not sure if it was simply in the heat of the moment, but one time is too many for my taste—especially coming from a man with his kind of power."

"But you have the same," I counter.

Zion pushes off the glass, coming to sit in the chair directly to my left. I turn so we're facing each other. The bags under his eyes seem more prominent, the blue-black color deepening by the second as the sun begins its descent from the sky.

"I do. Which is why I am using it to get him out of the country for a while. There's this island—off the grid to the general population. It's a resort and recovery center for those with enough money and stature to even know it exists. That's where I'm sending Zevryn for the next sixty days. He should be more than okay there, but I would like you to accompany him. Not only to ease some of my apprehension but to watch after him."

I lean back in my chair, gaze shifting to the outside. "Deacon did say it was an out-of-the-country job. Where is it located?"

"The South Pacific. French Polynesia." When I don't say anything, Zion continues. "Aside from your normal duties, I need you to make sure he's working the program, staying sober. Because I don't doubt for a second that my son could find a way to get high at a rehabilitation facility."

"That's not generally in my job description."

"Which is why I'm paying more than your annual," Zion counters. I let an amused smirk slip. He's got a point.

"I will email you all of the information on the island, along with a file on my son, Zevryn. I'll need you to start tomorrow." I inhale deeply through my nose, the back of my index finger pressed to my lips in thought. It's not going out of the country that bothers me. It's not even babysitting an addict—it's Milo.

I'm going to break a promise to him—one I decided was less important from the moment I got off the phone with Deacon. *That's* what unsettles me. How easily I can throw it away, only a sliver of remorse festering in the deepest recesses of my gut, far enough away I can easily block it out.

"Gavin, I'm desperate here. And I'm not normally a man to admit that kind of thing; my pride won't allow it."

As my eyes flit over Zion Carver's face, I see that—very easily. A prideful man showing a weakness. It's a sight to see.

"You said tomorrow?"

"Yes." He pushes up and rounds his desk. After clacking away at his computer for a moment, he straightens. My watch buzzes with a notification on my arm a few moments later. I glance down at the notification from my bank for a deposit. My eyes widen at the amount before I flick my gaze to Zion, an eyebrow arched.

Deacon must've pushed the payment through immediately. I can almost picture his fingers hovering over the keys, waiting. It nearly makes me crack a grin.

"I haven't signed anything, and you just gave me two-hundred grand."

"Call it an incentive. And once Zev is home, I'll send you another hundred. Does that seem fair?"

I suck in a breath between my pursed lips. Air whistles between my teeth. I nod. "Let me see the contract." Zion hands it over without preamble, and I spend the next twenty minutes in silence going over every word with care, looking for loopholes within the subtext.

Zion remains silent, sitting in his chair and staring out

the windows. His phone buzzes just as often as mine, and each time he checks it, the lines in his face grow tighter with tension. His fingers ball, knuckles whitening.

The verbiage is very straightforward, and I feel content with the decision as I take a fountain pen from Zion's desk and sign my name at the bottom. After handing it back to him, I say, "I'd like a copy of that for myself after Ayers signs, and then email a copy as well, please."

Zion nods, signing his name with a flourish. "Of course. I'll get this sent to them right now, and I will email you."

"As for the information—"

A few keys click, and then a whoosh sounds through the room. "Done." My watch buzzes with the email notification, a line of missed calls and unanswered texts from Milo sitting just beneath.

"Tomorrow, nine A.M.?" I ask. "And are we meeting here?"

"Yes, that works fine. We'll meet here so you can accompany me to Zevryn's penthouse. That's where he's at for the time being—his friends and my business partner are sitting with him currently."

Something niggles at the forefront of my mind. "Does he know about this?"

Zion blows out a breath, his cheeks puffing out. His hand drags through his hair once more, making some of the strands stick straight up. "No. And I don't plan on telling him until tomorrow when he has to pack and leave. He doesn't have a choice, and he'll know that."

Fuck, that's going to be messy.

"And I need you there because you will both go straight to the airstrip from his place. My private jet will take you to the international airport in Tahiti, and from there, you'll jump on a smaller aircraft to the island. Their airport isn't quite big enough for anything larger."

I nod in understanding. The buzzing of my phone grows incessant in my pocket, and I shift in place on the chair. Zion eyes it curiously for a moment.

"I think that's all for now. Look over everything I sent you, and if you have any questions, please don't hesitate to ask." He slides a card across the smooth wood of his desk. It's dark gray with silver holographic lettering. "This has my personal number on it. You'll need it." He holds out his hand, and I stand to clasp it.

"Thank you, Gavin."

"Of course, Zion. We'll talk tomorrow." After a tight squeeze, we release each other at the same time.

Without looking back, I walk briskly toward the elevator. Office hours must have ended at some point during our meeting because the floor is empty. Only the sound of my shoes clacking against the marble sounds in my ears. My mind is buzzing.

My watch lights up with Milo's face. I close my eyes for a moment before I pull my phone out and answer, eyes locked on the reflective silver of the elevator doors, the soft glow of the numbers slowly ticking down.

"Gavin! I've been trying to reach you for half an hour. Why the hell did I get that notification from our bank? What's going on?" He sounds shocked and confused. I touch my fingers to my temples and rub, digging in deep.

His face appears in my mind's eye. Dark blonde brows furrowed, his thick lips downturned, dimples popping out slightly.

My stomach flips.

"I was in a meeting; I told you that. So, I wasn't able to answer." My words come out sharper than I intend, but as hard as I try, my first reaction is to get defensive whenever tensions get high.

"I know, but that's a lot of money with no explanation, and I was worried something was wrong."

"Nothing's wrong. We'll talk when I get home."

"When will that be?"

"I'm headed there now."

Milo hangs up, leaving me listening to the loud blare of a triple ring followed by staticky silence. I don't bother lowering my phone from my ear until the doors slide open, revealing the quiet lobby.

My ears still ring as I jump in my car and pull into the city's stuffy traffic.

It seems no matter what decision I make, it inevitably brings me closer to my marriage's demise.

Five

GAVIN

The dinner Milo prepared sits untouched in front of us. It smells amazing, but my stomach twists at the mere thought of touching it.

His head is bowed, buried in his hands, blonde hair a curtain masking his anger-riddled pain. I reach across the table, wanting his skin on mine—if only to soothe my own discomfort—but before we touch, he jerks away and shoves back from the table. It scrapes a few inches across the floor, making me flinch.

I stare hopelessly at his back as he disappears down the hall. The bedroom door slams shut, and all I'm met with is silence. I drop my head back, staring up at the ceiling. The lights are dim because Milo tried to set the mood.

A mood I shattered because of my job.

It's always the same. Whether it's my job or his, one of us always has an excuse to be absent.

Our marriage has been strained for years. We both know it—it's why we tried to do this. Celebrate our ten-year wedding anniversary by *both* of us taking some time off for the first time in years with the singular intention to spend time together.

But I went and chose the job I love over my husband, and I know this is just another nail in the coffin.

I can't even explain *why* anymore.

In the beginning, being away from each other was torturous. We'd phone daily, text whenever I had a break, and he had a layover. We made it work for so long.

But eventually, all good things die. The calls became less frequent, texting nonexistent, until, eventually, we'd stop speaking while we were apart. We stopped *needing* to.

Now, we can go days without a word. Sometimes a week or more. The feeling of missing him is there, sometimes more prominent, but it's easier to push down beneath the focus of work.

I know Milo's the same. He's been a flight attendant since we met at just twenty-one years old. I was on a flight to the city, my first time in New York. I had just gotten the job with Ayers Security, and with my belongings already shipped to my new apartment, all that was left was *me.*

I still remember the first time I saw him. What first caught my eye were the faint shadows of tattoos under the sleeves of his white, button-down shirt. It piqued my curiosity, and I couldn't help but follow him with my eyes whenever he walked past, tending to other patrons.

He felt my eyes—I know he did—because every time he walked past me, he met my gaze with a cheeky one of his own, dimple etched in his cheek, golden hair short and cropped close to his head.

And the rest, as they say, is history.

Now, we're here, on opposite sides of the house, pretending the other doesn't exist because that reality is better than the one you love hurting you deliberately.

I pull down a glass and pour myself a stiff drink, swallowing it in one go. I don't allow myself any more because I need my head clear for tomorrow, but I craved *something* in my veins to deal with the inescapable fight with Milo.

I avoid the pictures of us lining the hall as I make my way to the bedroom, my wedding ring a leaden weight on my finger. I rasp my knuckles against the wood, ears strained as I wait for Milo's response. I hear his muffled voice coming from the other side.

Pushing it open, I find him sitting on the bed with his phone to his ear, laptop open on his thighs. He glances at me quickly before dropping his gaze. I walk into the closet to start changing clothes. I don't make it past undressing when I stop at the sound of his voice, hands midair, reaching for a white, cotton shirt.

"Twelve-hour flight, noon tomorrow. Got it. Thanks, Olivia." The snap of his laptop shutting lures me out of the closet. The curtains are shut, blocking out the lights of the city, with only the dull, white glow of the bedside lamp providing me with a view of his face.

It's set in stone, resolute in a way that makes my stomach sink uncomfortably.

I lean against the door to the closet, arms crossed over my bare chest. "Job tomorrow?" Milo's jaw tightens at my question. The shadows caressing his face make his gentle features appear even more soft.

It makes me regret my tone.

"Yep. Something last minute came up. Urgent," he adds.

"Then you understand." His head snaps up, and the glare he pins me with automatically makes me tense up, ready for a fight.

"Don't pull that fucking card with me, Gavin. This is not the same."

I push off the door, taking a step toward him. "How is it not?"

"Because." He stands so he's facing me, all the sorrow and regret on his beautiful face more than apparent. "I wouldn't have even answered the fucking phone if you didn't already fuck all of this up!" His chest is heaving, blue eyes glassy with unshed tears.

"I didn't have a choice, Milo." The lie slips effortlessly from between my lips, a whisper added to the mountain of dishonesty we've fabricated over the years. It's so large now, its shadow basks us in dreary gray.

When did lying become easier than the truth?

"Didn't have a choice," he mocks, then scoffs. His head hangs between his shoulders, hands clasped tight around his biceps. My eyes fall to his sleeves of tattoos, tracing them with my eyes for the millionth time, down to the golden ring on his finger that matches mine—the same color as his hair.

"Why are you lying to me?"

"I—" My mouth snaps shut at my immediate rebuttal. Milo's eyes peer directly into mine, seeing more than he should. More than I want him to. After a few seconds of silence, he nods. I hurry to fill it before he gets the wrong idea. "No one else was willing to do it, baby." I throw the endearment in. It's a cheap shot, but I'm desperate.

We can't leave it like this. Not before I'm going to be gone for two months with limited communication.

This is different. This fight feels… permanent.

"Yeah," he rasps, then clears his throat as he lifts his head, dragging his gaze from my feet to my face—a slow perusal. "And you were." Milo's Adam's apple bobs with a swallow before he collapses to the bed, head hanging again like it takes too much effort to keep upright.

The veracity of his words hits a place far too deep to explore, and the sight of his defeat kills all the tension inside me.

My arms wrap around him with ease, and when I coax him to lie back with me, he comes easily. He even curls his body perfectly against mine.

I've always wondered if we were two pieces of the same puzzle, etched with imperfect edges, but next to each other, no one would ever never notice a disconnect.

Now, though, I know better. He simply fits against me so perfectly because he *wants* to.

Neither of us speak a word as Milo drifts to sleep, spending one last night in each other's arms. Because after I get back, everything is going to be different between us.

My alarm blares at six, and I'm grateful for the early wake-up, even though I didn't sleep much. I spent long hours combing through the documents Zion sent me while Milo lay sleeping beside me. I went over every detail of this recovery center, the island itself, and the boy under my protection.

Even the photo Zion included in the file of his son, Zevryn, I could see the stark red veins in his eyes with pupils bigger than his irises. How wide and unseeing they are, glassy with inebriation.

The money better be worth the inevitable headache.

Rubbing the sleep from my eyes, I turn toward my husband. Milo's curled up on his side of the bed. There's a good two feet separating us, but it might as well be an ocean. I reach into the space, feeling cool cotton against my palm, my fingertips inches away from his tattooed bicep.

"I love you, Milo," I whisper into the darkness of our room, knowing he can't hear me but needing to say it, regardless.

With a silent sigh, I push out of bed and silently make my way into the wardrobe. I close the door behind me before flicking the light on, so I don't wake Milo. I pack quickly, the weather of the island this time of year at the forefront of my mind.

I don't need to dress in suits for this job, thankfully—not that that happens often, anyway—so jeans and t-shirts are essential and much easier to fit into one suitcase. After shoving in the last of my travel hygienic products, I grab my clothes for the day and slip into the bathroom for a quick shower.

Steam builds as I scrub every inch of my skin vigorously, taking out my frustrations on myself. My skin is red and raw by the time I step out, the cool air stinging.

Clearing the fog from the mirror, I stare at my reflection

as I scrub my teeth then go about drying my hair and trimming my beard.

After cleaning my mess, I drop the towel from my waist and yank on my underwear. When my foot slips against the cool, damp tile, a light chuckle permeates the room. I glance up through my brows, finding Milo leaning against the door, sleep etched into his face in the form of lines from his pillow.

"Thought you were mad at me," is the first thing that comes to mind, the words slipping from my lips without thought. I wince the moment his carefree face tightens at the reminder.

"I am," he says briskly, brushing past me to jump in the shower himself. I make quick work of getting dressed in slacks and a button-down. Dropping my towel into the hamper, I watch Milo through the opaque glass. The outline of his body—even obscured—makes my dick twitch in my pants.

It's been weeks—hell, I think months, at this point—since we've fucked. There's a passing chaste kiss or two, but nothing like it used to be.

We were insatiable, the passion between us never ebbing, always flowing... until it wasn't.

My skin itches with the desire to be touched, to just feel something tight and wet.

Need. Want.

With a twitch in my jaw, I pull my hair into a secure knot at the back of my head before exiting the steamy room to make some coffee, since it seems the both of us will need it.

Time ticks by slowly, neither of us speaking a word for over an hour. I let time drag to the very last moment before

I'm forced to leave. By the time my bag is by the door, I'm aching to leave, despite my heart lancing with guilt.

"I have to go," I say quietly, hand on the doorknob. Milo's standing in the entranceway, a few feet away. His blue eyes look so sad when they finally meet mine. It feels like a punch in the gut—and I hate myself a little more.

"I know."

"I..." I blow out a breath. "Fuck, baby. I don't know what to say."

"You've already said everything that needs to be said, Gavin," he accentuates my name, making me wince.

"You know that's not—"

"No, it's exactly how you meant it. Don't lie to me."

I take a step forward. "I don't want to fight. Not right before I leave for two months."

Milo's shoulders droop with defeat, the tension draining out of his body. "I don't either." I tug him into my arms, breathing out in relief when his own wrap around me. "Please be safe. Check in when you can."

I nod, my cheek scraping against his temple. Milo doesn't know where I'm going or why—NDAs and all that—but he does know I'll be out of the country, and cell service might be scarce. I'm honestly not sure how any of this is going to work, but I'll figure it out as I go. Like I always do.

"I will." I press a kiss to the top of his head. "But I have to go."

Milo drops his arms like I'm on fire, walking back until he bumps into the wall. With a grimace on my face and a heavy weight in my gut, I leave our apartment and my husband behind.

Zion's waiting for me near the front entrance to Carver

Breck Technologies when I pull up in my cab. He immediately pulls me into his black town car, and we head toward his son's place.

Car horns and vicious shouts drown us in a discordant melody as we drive through the city. "Zevryn got discharged from the hospital a couple of days ago," Zion says as he stares out the open window. "There wasn't enough Fentanyl in his system to do much damage, thankfully. But the other boy..." His throat bobs with a swallow, and with a sharp, pained grimace, he continues.

"It appears the cocaine they were snorting up their nostrils was laced. We're not sure whose it was exactly. Zev is refusing to speak to anyone still, and he's the only one that can give us insight. Of course, Micah is blaming Zevryn. Refuses to believe his son could be into substances, even though he clearly did them.

"I don't know what to believe myself, to be frank. I know Zev's been on a warpath, but like I said yesterday, I don't see him deliberately hurting someone." In this moment, Zion Carver looks decades older than his forty-three years.

"Many drugs nowadays are laced with something, unfortunately," I say, trying to ease his suffering, if only a bit. Only because it's the truth.

Zion sighs heavily. "Yes, you're probably right. Moving on." He changes the subject abruptly, making me blink a couple of times, eyes darting back to scan the other cars. "Did you get everything you needed from the information I sent you?"

I nod. "Yes, thank you. It was very thorough." I now know Zevryn Carver is nineteen-years-old, five-foot-eleven with hazel eyes—the brown and green kind, not blue and green.

Black curls adorn his head, and his face is all sharp, fierce angles. And as I glance at Zion, I can see the shocking resemblance. Only the boy has issues with alcohol and cocaine in a way I'm assuming Zion Carver never has.

It's why we'll be leaving today for Black Diamond Resort and Spa. An island dedicated to the world's elite. A place for rest and recovery where the elite don't have to worry about anyone finding them. Where they can bring their secrets and unmask their demons because everyone around them is hiding, too.

There are two sides to the island. One—a resort. A place to escape, to decompress. Reset. The other—a place where the unstable go. Whether it be addiction, mental health, and anything in between.

And that's where I'll be with Zevryn Carver for sixty days while he works the program and hides from a variant death threat.

We pull into the underground garage, where the driver parks in a reserved spot. "We'll be a while," Zion tells his driver, who nods. Once we're on the concrete, the air feels cooler, darker, and the elevator ride feels much of the same.

Eyes locked on the camera discreetly placed in the front left corner, I say, "You should call Ayers and get a security system put in place for your son's home. The security here seems to be more than enough, but you can never be too sure, and it would bring you peace of mind."

Zion nods. "That's a good idea. I will give them a call later today and get that set up. Thank you."

"Sure thing."

Zion clears his throat after a moment of silence. "Like I said yesterday, Zevryn does not know about this, so I do expect some blowback. I'm sorry you will have to witness it, but I wanted you here in case I need help dragging him to the car."

I balk at his words, slightly taken aback. "You want me to manhandle him into the car," I reiterate.

He nods once, sharp. Brisk. "Yes. If need be."

"Sir, I'm not sure if I'm comfortable with that."

"Well, you better get comfortable with it fast because Zevryn is a fighter, and he's going to push every single button the both of us have. He will hate this. He's always hated being told what to do. In fact, he does the exact *opposite* every single time just out of spite. Been that way for as long as I can remember, so you need to be prepared for that, Mr. Holt, which is why I deem it imperative you witness all that he is before you arrive on that secluded island."

Before I can think of a response, the lift dips as it stops. A second later, the doors glide open, and we step into a chaotic mess. Zion sighs heavily as we step into the penthouse, static crackling in the air.

My eyes scan the area, from the floor to the high-rise ceilings, in a quick assessment. There are clothes strewn about, empty food containers littering every available surface. Broken glass and potted plants shattered. Loud shouts echo, followed by softer, more placating ones.

My eyebrows hike, lips curled in as we step into the living area, the elevator—and seemingly the only exit—at my back. Normally, I would've requested a layout of Zevryn's apartment, but since this isn't where the job will take place, a quick analysis is more than enough.

And if he's going to hire Ayers to put a system in, then we'll have it on file if I ever want access to it.

"What is it now?" Zion turns toward a boy, who can't be much older than eighteen, his youth blatantly apparent. He's got shaggy, straight blonde hair, some of it covering his eyes as he stares blankly at Zion. His arms are hanging by his sides in defeat, the clothes he's wearing wrinkled and unkempt.

"Zion, I swear I didn't know."

"Didn't know what." It's not said as a question.

"There are a lot of hiding places. I thought Carmen and I got them all—" Zion holds his hand up, effectively cutting the boy off. "Leave it, Dillon."

Ah. One of Zevryn's friends. That name and another—Carmen—were in his file without photos. Now, I can put a face to a name.

Dillon's lips turn white as he rolls them between his teeth. His eyes are rimmed red and glassy. Like he's hungover—or he's been crying. Either seems plausible.

"Are you high right now?" Zion's turned toward his son now, voice dripping with ice. Zevryn is just an unfocused image in the background as my gaze flicks to Zion. His tone surprises me. The way he spoke to me about his son is drastically different from the way he's talking to Zevryn right now. Almost... bitter.

"The fuck does it matter?" Zevryn levels with his father. And for the first time, I take in the boy I'm going to be protecting for the next two months with every ounce of my undivided attention.

He doesn't seem to notice me stationed near the wall as my gaze rakes over him in a thorough inspection. He's twitchy, with eyes too wide to be normal. His skin gleams with sweat, baggy clothes clinging to him with wet stains.

He drags the back of his hand underneath his nose, sniffling loudly, leaving blood and snot smeared on his skin when he drops it to his side, making the black bands on his wrist fall back down.

He looks exactly like his picture, only more... wrecked. It's obvious he's been struggling with an addiction for some time. His body has lost some of its fullness. A decrease in not only weight but muscle mass, too. Even his face is more gaunt and bruised and hollow than it was in the picture.

A ghost of a man stands in the room, and I think I'm the only one who sees it.

"Please tell me that isn't a serious question."

"Why shouldn't it be?"

I stay in the furthest corner, watching the interaction in silence until I'm needed. A silent observer.

"You've got to be fucking kidding me," Zion hisses, making Zevryn laugh maniacally. He can't keep still—jerking around the open space, arms swinging haphazardly. His feet are bare, so every step is brought with heavy slaps against the marble—or whatever kind of stone it is. My eyes narrow, and my fingers twitch when he steps millimeters away from glass shards, but before I can react, he's whirling around again.

"What's wrong, *Dad*? Can't handle it? Yeah." He nods jerkily. "Just like you couldn't fucking handle Mom. What's it like? Having two of us like this? I would say two people you love—but we both know you don't love me, and you sure as fuck never loved Mom.

"I think if you did, maybe even a little, she wouldn't have killed herself, and she sure as fuck wouldn't have done it in front of me."

His words send a shiver from my nape down each vertebra where it settles at the base of my spine with chilling weight. His face, all sharp angles and shadows, is twisted in a wretched sneer, the drugs in his system calling the shots.

"You don't know what you're talking about, Zevryn."

"Don't I?" he screams, making his friend take a step back, shoulders hunching protectively near his ears. "Don't you think I fucking *know!*" Zion's back stiffens as the tendons in Zevryn's neck bulge from how hard he's screaming. "I've lived in the abyss of Zion Carver my entire fucking life. You're a poison to everyone around you. It's no wonder I need drugs to stay alive! You've made my life fucking miserable!"

My heart throbs for some inexplicable reason, and I'm unable to take my eyes off the boy filled with so much sorrow, I can feel it in my bones as it saturates the air we breathe.

"Zev," Dillon croaks, the word thick and warped with the tears clogging his throat. Zevryn lunges, and something sails through the air with a sharp whistle. It zooms past Zion's head, a good foot away, and smashes to the floor somewhere behind us. My body locks up on instinct as I near the disaster unfolding with slow, sure steps, gaze never straying from the distraught boy.

"Then, I suppose it's a good thing you're leaving for rehab today," Zion says coldly, unbothered by the bottle of booze meant for his head, shattered into shards behind him.

Zevryn's black eyes, wide and crazed, zero in on Zion with the kind of malice you don't see often in life.

Erratic, unhinged, and full of real, raw hatred.

I pull in a breath.

Zevryn's jaw grinds and ticks as he paces the floor, eyes darting from his feet to his father. Suddenly, he stops and whips around. Blood drips from his nose now, creating a rivulet down his lips and over his chin as points a finger in Zion's direction. "I'm not fucking going anywhere!" His hand has a tremor as it hangs in the air. Blood stains his perfectly white teeth. Perspiration licks his pale skin.

"You do not have a choice, Zevryn." Zion sounds bored. I flinch from his callousness, while my hands ball into fists, watching Zevryn's eyes pinch with pain.

With a shout, Zevryn kicks the coffee table across the room. It smacks into the glass with an echoing crash. The vibrations don't have time to settle before something else is launched across the room with a guttural cry. I can't see what it is as it whips through the air, but whatever it was, was most definitely breakable.

I stop with my hands tensed at my side, my eyes darting around, following the chaos ensuing as I work through when to step in at the exact right time.

The boy is just so lost, so broken, and his father is merely making it worse. Doesn't he fucking see that?

Why is he treating him differently than how he spoke to me about him?

Dillon takes a step closer to Zevryn. "Z, please. I think it might be good for you." His voice wobbles, and I can tell even without looking at him that he's got tears in his eyes.

"Oh, of course, you do, you *fucking rat!*" Zevryn crowds his friend against the wall until he is cowering, jaw vibrating from the force of his crying. Dark curls bounce as Zevryn weaves his head around chaotically.

"I know you were telling Zion shit. Ruining my goddamn

life!" His hand connects with the side of Dillon's head, making it thud against the wall. He stays stock still, chest heaving as he lets Zevryn abuse him—and he doesn't let up either. Both hands come up, and Zevryn shoves his friend again and again.

Every time Dillon lifts from the wall, Zevryn is shoving him back so hard, I can hear the way his bones crack every time. Dillon's sobbing uncontrollably now, and the sound of his pain echoes faintly into me.

My eyes drift from the drug fueled mess, finding Zion watching his son with pained interest. The way his eyes are crinkled at the corners, hands balled into fists, muscles rigid.

He cares, but he won't let Zevryn see it... *Why?*

I take a step forward to get between the two, but Zion holds his hand up, stopping me. The growl of protest that rumbles in my chest is almost too strong to force back.

"Zevryn, enough!" Zion shouts. Dillon slips down the wall to the floor, hands covering his face as Zevryn charges at his father with a bloody snarl.

This time, I do step in. The boy with sweaty, black, matted curls and equally black eyes launches right into my arms, a scream on his lips, fingers curled into claws, aiming for his father's face. I catch him mid-air and pin his back to my chest, arms wrapped around his bony torso.

He kicks wildly, bucking and screaming against my hold. I grunt when his head nails my shoulder, making it immediately radiate a throbbing heat. The stench of sweat and alcohol wafts into my nose, making it wrinkle.

How could they let someone they claim to love sink so deep?

"Get the fuck off me!" he screams, shattering my ear drums. Nails score my forearms, making me hiss as he digs in deep, fighting me tooth and nail for a swing at his father. His pain, even through this rage, rolls off his body in a current so thick, I feel it clinging to my own skin, unsettling me.

I squeeze him tighter, feeling every part of him against me as my own eyes pinch in despair.

"I fucking hate you! I wish you would've died instead of her. Maybe I wouldn't be so goddamn fucked up!" The swear words just roll right off his tongue, and if I wasn't so preoccupied, I might even be impressed by their fluidity if my first reaction wasn't to chastise him for his language.

"There is something severely wrong with you, Zevryn. Look at the way you're acting right now."

"Because of you! It's always because of you," he sobs. The fight seems to escape his body in an instant, leaving him heavy and limp in my arms. I'm panting, my breath making his hair flutter as I keep him pinned to my chest.

His head is heavy against my shoulder, face pressed into my neck as he sobs, his lithe, little body wracking from their force.

I don't know what to do, but my instinct is telling me to hold him, to comfort him any way I can, so that's what I do.

Lacing my fingers just beneath his ribs for more support, I hold Zevryn Carver with every ounce of strength I have, hoping some leeches into his pain-riddled body.

He needs it more than I do.

A few minutes later, when the boy has calmed some, my eyes find Zion's, and he nods. With regret, I release my hold gently, letting Zevryn sink to the floor. His limbs tangle around him in a heap as he folds in on himself.

The sight makes me want to reach out to him.

As I force myself to take a step back, the ding of the elevator breaks through the echoing cacophony of wretched cries. A young woman and an older gentleman enter, carrying bags of what I assume to be groceries.

"Dillon?" The woman asks, her long, brown hair twisted into a braid, hanging down her back. "Zev," she cries as she runs through the vast space, her shoes clicking loudly.

That would be Carmen.

My chest is still heaving from the exertion as I slip back against the wall. Carmen gathers Zevryn into her arms, and he sobs against her, his body still wracking from the staggering force. Dillon hovers above them both, hands outstretched, unsure after his friend abused him, I'm sure.

Snot and tears clog Zevryn's throat, making the noises coming out of him sound even more wretched and pained.

I'm dizzy, my body vibrating from experiencing something so chaotic. My strong feelings are even more unexpected.

Zion and the other gentleman move into the kitchen, while the two kids help Zevryn to his feet. My foot lifts from the ground to help before I stop myself.

He's limp in their arms, head shoved into Dillon's neck, giving me a peek at his half-shaved head. He stains the boy's clothes with blood as they shuffle down the hall and into what I assume is a bedroom.

When the door clicks shut behind them, I shake my head, clearing the building cobweb of thoughts before moving into the kitchen where I catch the tail end of a conversation not meant for me.

Zion's bent over the counter, head in his hands, and the

other man is leaning in close, face slightly wrinkled with tension.

He straightens at my entrance. "My apologies, Gavin. But I did tell you—"

You should be apologizing to your son, I want to bark, but I swallow the words like bile. "No worries, Mr. Carver," I say instead as I stand on the other side of the counter, eyes scanning the kitchen, the only room that seems even remotely put together.

Zion fixes his shirt, brushing his hand over the front to smooth out a crease. He nods his head toward the man standing next to him. "Gavin, this is my business partner and close friend, Hugh Breck. He's Dillon's father." Our hands connect on a brief, firm shake.

"Zev and Dillon have been friends since I moved into the city and became associated with Hugh. It seems they've both traveled the wrong path, though Zev is deeper in the darkness."

"Dillon still has his head about him," Hugh cuts in with a grunt.

"I think some separation will be good for everyone while Zevryn straightens out his life."

Why does every word that comes out of his mouth piss me off now?

Zion glances at his watch, making me glance at mine. We should've left for the airport a while ago, and Zion seems to realize that, too.

"I'll call and reschedule the flight for four. It's not an ideal time for arrival, but it must be done." He pulls out his phone and wanders to the other side of the kitchen as he speaks into it.

The flight to French Polynesia can range anywhere from twelve to sixteen hours, according to my Google search last night, which isn't ideal, but more than doable.

Leaning my hip against the counter, my eyes rake over the open expanse of the penthouse apartment, once more taking in the aftermath of Zevryn Carver's drug-riddled explosion in the form of shattered glass and split wood. Haunted cries and echoing despair.

The city standing beyond us in a sea of gray so large, I feel as if I'm suspended mid-air, looking across an impossible immensity.

Wealth surrounds me in abundance. It's evident in not only the quite literal New York City penthouse I'm standing in, but in the décor, the clothing, the personas of everyone around me.

They are the elite. Some of the country's richest men. Their stature knows no bounds. And that power is what brought me here.

Zion Carver hired me to look after his son. To protect him. A commitment I will honor, not only because I have to, but because I *want* to.

If only for a glimpse into the real Zevryn—a boy who's lost and alone in a world too big for him.

Six

ZEVRYN

My heart's hammering against my ribs. The sound reverberates against my eardrums, drowning out the words coming from Carmen and Dillon. They surround me in an attempt at comfort, but it only makes my stomach cramp harder.

Goosebumps mar my flesh, intense to the point it hurts whenever the smallest whisper of air caresses my skin. The bathroom floor does nothing to cool the inferno smothering me on the inside. Licking along my nerves, digging impossibly deep into my muscles and connective tissues.

My eyes sting as sweat drips into them. I can't blink, so I'm forced to feel the salty liquid absorb across the surface.

I deserve it. All of it.

"Zev."

I hear my name being called over and over, each time further away. Softer. Insignificant.

My brain pulsates with the effort of keeping myself upright, so I stop trying. When hard tile connects with my cheekbone, stealing the air from my lungs, I feel a little less heavy inside.

I vaguely remember how I got here. To this place inside my head. So deep, it's bottomless. I'm surrounded by waves of *nothing,* and I've never hated anything more. Being numb was always the goal, and I've always found myself somewhere between the two on the spectrum, but now I want to feel *good.*

High.

On top of the fucking world.

But all I see is Darien slumped against the bathroom stall as I turn my back on him to bend down and suck the powder up my nose without a second thought.

No matter how many times I replay it in my mind, it's always the same. My desires win out over everything—even my friend fucking *dying* right in front of me.

Everyone thinks it was my fault. That I'm the one who gave him the laced coke. I don't bother correcting them because what does it fucking matter anyway? Darien's dead. I'm alive. There's no moving past that.

Even my own father wants to get rid of me. Send me to some fucking place where he doesn't have to look at me, or even think about me. *Where people like me go to* get fixed.

Because there's something broken inside of me. But it can't be repaired. It's who I am at my core.

As my eyes flicker closed, my last high fading rapidly, leaving nothing but a bone-deep exhaustion in its wake, I hold regret for the first time, and it feels like an old friend welcoming me home.

When Carmen drops a duffle bag at my feet, I just know she found the rest. I refuse to meet her gaze, something akin to shame eating away at my innards.

The moment I woke up, sweaty and bloody and plastered to the bathroom floor, I knew what I'd become.

Dillon and Carmen were waiting for me when I came out after my long, exhausting shower. The moment I laid my eyes on Dillon and saw his own, bloodshot and glassy, I'd never hated myself more.

I haven't been able to look at either of them since.

I still feel buzzed, thank fuck for that, but the high I really need is long gone, always fading as quickly as it comes.

A dangerous, vicious, rapturous cycle.

"I'm glad to see you've gotten yourself sorted," Zion's voice submerges me in an ice bath. "You look like shit," he adds, making me snort dryly. My father, ever the empathizer.

"And I'm still not going anywhere. I'll stop on my own." An easy lie.

All of the fight has left my body, leaving me drained. Exhausted down to my very core. Only thoughts of *what's the point* circulating.

Zion scoffs, making me jerk from the unexpected noise coming from my very poised father. "This isn't up for debate, Zevryn. You will get in the fucking car, or I will make you.

Either way, you *will* go." His tone holds a specific bite I haven't heard from him in years, despite all my fuck ups.

It makes the lost, little boy inside me ache with abandon.

My arms hurt as I cross them over my chest, forgetting the people surrounding us, their eyes taking in the scene unfolding with hesitant scrutiny. "Fuck you, Zion. You can't —" Zion jerks his head in a nod, making my brows tug in confusion.

An, "I'm sorry," enters my ear in a faint whisper before two large, strong arms wrap around my waist from behind.

I jerk at the unexpected touch, but I'm held tight, not budging a centimeter. The hold feels familiar, strong and warm, but my mind is so fuzzy, I can't recall anything of significance. My feet kick out, arms flailing as I'm dragged toward the elevator.

"Get the fuck off me!" I scream, slapping my palms against the bulging forearms digging into my ribs. The elevator dings, and I'm pulled into it, my eyes locked on the people I *thought* loved me. Cared for me. Fucking *respected* me.

Carmen and Dillon stand side by side, arms intertwined and wrapped around each other. Their eyes are shining with tears as they trickle down their pathetic fucking faces.

"Fuck you!" I scream at them, hating the way my voice cracks from the pain I can't hide. My own tears spill, but they're out of anger. Betrayal.

Don't they fucking know this will kill me?

I can't *be* sober.

Zion picks my bag up from the floor and steps in next to me and whoever the fuck has an iron-tight hold on me. Whoever it is, is much bigger than me.

As the doors shut, cutting off the pathetic expressions of my friends, I don't stop fighting. Even as my stomach drops when we start the descent into a proverbial hell.

"I don't want to do this," the voice whispers again, so faintly I don't think I heard him right.

Either way, I still scream out my rage. "Liar!" I kick, bellow in frustration, claw, and mark my detainer with every floor we pass. I get a few low grunts in return when I hit something vital, but the goddamn brick house never falters.

"You fucking son of a bitch," I seethe, unsure if I'm talking to my father or the other dude.

Neither one bites. "We'll talk on the way to the airport," Zion says instead, making me stiffen, my fingers scraping against one of the arms against my torso. Skin gathers under my short nails with a hiss.

"I'm not getting on that fucking jet," I force out between clenched teeth, glaring at my father.

The elevator levels out, and my stomach swoops into my feet, making me clutch the hairy arm around me.

Zion sighs, head dropping as he rubs his temples. "I don't have time for your insolence, Zevryn. You've already delayed everything significantly. We'll talk. *In the car.*" He steps off the second there's enough space between the heavy doors. When he turns, his dark eyes drill into me, making me shift on my feet that still barely rest on the floor. It feels like all the barriers I've built against Zion no longer exist with a tired blink of my eyes.

I'm bare. Raw.

Vulnerable.

"Carry him out. I don't want him making a run for it," Zion says tiredly like I'm not even here. The body behind me inflates with a deep breath before my feet are lifted off the floor once again, making me yelp as I flop against a hard chest.

I'm forced to close my eyes when we step out into the blinding sun. It's sweltering as the sun's rays hammer down, making my stomach flip. Heat oozes from the concrete, directly into me, forcing me to bury my face into the brute man's neck for some sort of solace from the throbbing in my temples and right behind my eyes.

Through the sounds of the city, a car door opens, and then the sun dims as leather glides across my backside. I keep my eyes pinched closed, light still shining through the opened door. It's not until I hear it slam closed that I pry them open, breathing heavily through my parted lips as a wave of nausea circulates at the lurch of the car.

My vision's blurry, so I focus my gaze on the black, luxurious fabric between my shoes.

"At this rate, you should get there close to the facility's opening hours. I don't think you'll have any issues checking in." Zion's dull voice pulls me out of my pathetic wave of misery.

"Excuse me?" I yell, finally lifting my head, blinking rapidly to focus my stinging eyes. The man beside me, sitting nearest to the door we entered through, stiffens, and I have the joy of watching some of the muscles in his perfectly fitted shirt ripple.

Damn, he really is as big as he felt. Not huge but strong enough to manhandle me easily, his obvious muscle hidden behind a layer of soft cushioning. Visible, yet... almost squishy. Like a real-life teddy bear.

The thought makes me scowl.

Zion lets out a heavy breath at my comment. "What do you want, Zevryn?"

My eyes flick down, then back up. His side profile is strong, brown hair pulled into a bun with a trimmed beard lining his jaw and upper lip. Scruffy in a way that I just know if he were to rub it across my skin, it'd burn its own path.

"Who the fuck is he?" I snarl. His eyes snap to mine the second the words leave my lips, making my mouth snap closed. His dark eyes narrow as they peer into mine. A wrinkle forms on his forehead before his broad chest lifts with a breath, and then it disappears.

"I'm Gavin."

I huff out a breath of irritation and have the joy of watching his top lip twitch.

"Gavin..." I drawl, circling my hand.

Gavin's eyes flicker to my father. Zion shakes his head, making the man's jaw tighten before fixing his gaze out the window. Zion ignores me as his thumbs fly over his phone screen.

I glare at them both for an immeasurable amount of time.

Finally, Zion puts his phone down just as signs for JFK pass overhead. "Gavin is the man I hired to protect you while you spend the next sixty days in a treatment facility."

His words make my stomach turn. Sixty days.

The withdrawals...

The thought makes my skin crawl.

"That's the sweet way of saying rehab, *Dad.* No need to fucking sugar coat it now." My words are as venomous as I'm feeling as panic licks my veins.

"Yes, *rehab.* This isn't like most places. You'll be flying to an island, a place only meant for people..." Zion seems to struggle with what to say for a moment, and it brings me a flicker of satisfaction, seeming him not so put together.

"People with your type of... dispositions in a similar lifestyle."

"What the fuck does that even mean?" My skin flushes with heat. I can feel beads of perspiration pooling on the surface of my skin, even with the cool air blasting from the vents around us.

"Look, Zevryn," he snaps, seemingly having lost all his patience—which he never really had to begin with. "This is an island for people like you: rich and addicted to things they shouldn't be. We don't have to worry about the paparazzi or other people finding you. They are thorough with who they allow in, and it is all very discreet."

I sit back against the leather, making it creak. "People finding me?" I ask because that's the part that stuck the most out of all that jumbled nonsense. My brain's not firing on all cylinders, and I know when I sober up completely, I'm going to hate life more than I already do.

Zion's jaw ticks in its usual way as he looks me over with something akin to disgust on his face. Just as I drop my gaze, unable to stand the sight—and the feeling of inadequacy any longer—his eyes flick toward the man seated next to me.

His body takes up too much space, the heat radiating from him nearly suffocating.

My gaze drops to the gun on his hip, locked in a simple, black holster. And even through the buzzed fog in my mind, I'm able to click pieces together. Zion's words reverberate in my mind.

"Is he a fucking bodyguard, Zion?" My blunt use of his

first name makes his head snap up. "Why?" Fuck, my head hurts. "Wait—for me?"

"Because you killed someone," Zion replies, blunt as ever, only his words pack a fucking punch, and they hit straight to my gut. I wheeze out a breath, hating the way water pools on my eyes at the fucking *casual* mention of Darien's death. Gavin's head jerks toward my father, nostrils flared.

"I didn't fucking kill him," I growl, low and angry. Zion's jaw ticks faster.

"Regardless of the hows or whys, he's dead all the same, and his father is pissed." Zion looks me directly in the eye as he says, "He wants revenge, Zevryn, and even through all of your stupidity, I do not wish to see you hurt."

I scoff indignantly. "We both know that's not true."

Ignoring me, he continues, "Gavin will accompany you. He will be by your side, protecting you and making sure you complete the program. When you return, I want to see the man I know is buried inside there somewhere back, living and breathing in front of me. Not whoever this shell is that you've become."

His words bring a tense stillness to the car. One I fucking drown in as flashes of dead memories flicker through my consciousness as cars blur through the window.

DEAD EYES HAUNT ME.

Wide, unseeing. Glassy.

It's all I see as I stare up at the textured, white ceiling of the hospital room.

I'm alone with my thoughts for the first time since I woke up. Reality doesn't seem... real. It can't be. Not again.

But no. It's true.

Someone else died in front of me. Only this time... it was different. Worse. Because it was my fault. I may not have put the shit into Darien's body, but I was culpable all the same.

I'm the one that turned a blind eye to his stumbling, the white lines on porcelain calling to me, tempting in a way that was impossible to ignore. The shiver of doubt that slithered down my spine was no match for my lust for cocaine.

A lover of death, of peace of mind.

Of sanity and life.

And yet... I know I won't stop. Even knowing what I've done. The repercussions of my disgusting behavior.

It doesn't change a fucking thing.

THE INTERIOR of the jet is as opulent as one would expect from a billionaire—or more specifically, my father. I've never had the *luxury* of being on it since, you know, my father fucking hates me and all, but I'm not surprised by its grandeur.

I scoff as I drop my ass in one of the oversized, leather chairs that's as silky soft as I'd imagined. I hate the way I sink into it with a sigh, exhaustion weighing heavily in my bones despite the anxiety flickering in waves.

My father's voice still echoes in my head, despite how hard I tried not to listen. He told me more about this rehab facility I'm going to on some island called Black Diamond. How I'm supposed to really *work on myself*—his words not mine.

I tuned him out after that, not wanting to hear any more.

The fact is, I'm on the fucking jet, whether I want to be or not. The bodyguard he hired to babysit me—because let's be real, that's all he's here for—slowly pulled me up the steps, my back latched to his front. The contact kept my complaints to a minimum, as I was more focused on the way I was being held than anything else.

Heat flames my face as I watch Gavin through the small window as he speaks with Zion, my duffle and his suitcase placed on the ground next to him. With his back to me, and my father otherwise occupied, I rake my gaze over my bodyguard's back. The crisp white button-down adorning him is a tight fit but not constricting. His shoulders are broad with a thick neck and even thicker arms.

I drop my eyes, and my mouth instantly waters. His black slacks curve over his ass like they were perfectly tailored for it. So round, I know nothing but rock-hard muscle lies beneath his skin.

When Gavin turns around, I avert my gaze, thinking I'd been caught, but not even two seconds pass before I'm peering through the glass again. The phone in his hand makes me realize I don't have mine. I pat my pockets, even though I know they're empty. And that bag Gavin's carrying won't have it either; I'd bet everything I own on it.

"That fucking asshole," I growl, hands balling tightly atop my thighs. I grind my teeth as I watch my father dip back into the black town car before it pulls away, leaving Gavin where he stands. He dips and grasps our bags before hauling them up the staircase.

Gavin ducks slightly as he steps inside. He situates our bags before taking a seat on the opposite end from me, dark eyes flickering around before settling on the small window to his right.

His hands are laid flat atop his thick thighs, the material of his pants stretched taut. His black boots look out of place amongst the rest of his clothes, but it kind of works on him.

The longer I stare, the more my eyes narrow on him as I glare across the cabin.

He may be hot, but he's just a means for my father to control me, and I have to remember that.

"Where's my phone?" I ask Gavin as he pulls his back out of his pocket. His eyes finally meet mine again, and I hate the way their dark depths make me shift against the leather.

"You're not allowed a phone." His eyes crinkle at the corners like he's slightly confused, but his expression straightens out as I blink.

I groan out loud. "You've got to be fucking kidding me."

"Mouth!" he barks, startling me. I blink at him with wide eyes.

His own eyes are just as wide as mine as we stare at each other across the intimate cabin. His lips part, and a small grunt escapes them before his jaw snaps closed, the muscles in his neck corded. With a swallow, he jerks his gaze away, down to the cellphone in his lap.

"So, you get a phone, and I don't?" I snap. I have the joy of watching his fingers curl tightly around the phone that looks so small in his hand.

"Yes." He answers without looking at me. My mouth pops open to argue when the rattle of bottles echoes from the back room. It has my ears perking up, and despite my exhaustion, I sit up in my seat just as the steward steps out from behind the curtain. I blink a couple of times, eyes wide as the man makes his way toward me, dressed in a crisp, white shirt with a dark blue tie and slacks to match.

His golden hair shines as it catches on the rays of sun beaming in through the open windows, and as he draws near, I think I notice black ink staining the skin beneath his shirt.

"Good evening, Mr. Carver. I'm so sorry for the wait. Would you like something to drink?"

"You know..." My eyes flick to the shining name tag pinned to his left pec. "Milo, I would love a glass filled with whatever tequila you have on hand." I rest my head against the seat, giving him a wide smile as the tips of my fingers brush over the top of his thigh.

A low growl rumbles out just as Milo stiffens. A shadow looms behind him, dragging my gaze from his to... "Fuck," I grumble, slumping.

I glare at Gavin over Milo's shoulder with a pout. His front is pressed close to the steward's back, making my eyebrows furrow.

"He is not allowed any alcoholic beverages, Mr. Holt, per Mr. Carver's request. If you have any questions, do call him, and he'll be sure to straighten out any confusion."

I roll my eyes through my headache.

"Yes, sir." Milo steps back—right into Gavin. He fumbles, face flushing red as an arm bands around him automatically. An arm I have become well acquainted with in the last couple of hours. Dismay festers in my gut at the sight.

"He'll have a water. I'd like a coffee," Gavin's voice has taken on a lilt of a different tone. My eyes squint until I can barely see the two of them in front of me.

"Actually—" I'm cut off by the glare Gavin drills into me.

The steward's face tightens with a grimace as he steps away. Gavin's arm drops heavily, and he straightens as the guy slips past and disappears back behind the curtain.

"I know you think you can tell me what to do—"

Gavin faces me head-on, large body looming, taking up too much space. I press back into my seat.

"You know you're not allowed any alcohol, Zevryn, so why are you pushing?" Before I can respond, he adds, "Do you even want any?" He's sitting in the seat in front of me now, hands clasped in front of his knees where he's hunched over. A few strands of his brown hair have escaped from the knot it's tied in, framing his face as he peers at me.

His thumb flicks over a ring on his left hand, a continuous twisting motion. Once my eyes lock on the golden ring, I can't stop staring.

My head hurts just as badly as my body aches.

Why is this my fucking life now?

"Do you?" he asks again.

"Do I what?" I blink in confusion, trying to clear the fog from my mind.

"Do you want alcohol?"

"Yes," I answer automatically because that's the truth, and with where I'm sitting, on a fucking jet getting ready to head for rehab, there's no point in lying. Especially not when he's already seen what I am.

"Why?"

I drag my gaze from the window to my bodyguard. He's still messing with his ring, and I don't know why, but it pisses me off. "Why did you take this job when you're married? You're gonna be gone for a long time—enough to put a strain on any marriage."

Gavin rears back. "Excuse you?" Something clatters from behind the curtain, making Gavin stiffen as he rotates toward the noise.

I jerk my head toward where the steward, Milo, disappeared to. "He your husband then?"

"You don't need to worry about things that don't concern you. Get some sleep." After pushing to his feet, he gives me one last look before moving back to his original seat.

I force my eyes away from him before he catches me staring. It hurts too much to look outside anymore, so I let my lids fall closed and welcome in the dragging lull of sleep.

"FUCK," I groan, my hands flying up to cradle my head. I swallow against the burn in my throat, almost gagging at the rotten taste lingering on my tongue.

As I peel an eyelid open, I notice it's dark inside the cabin—and I'm alone. I search out Gavin automatically, but I don't find him in the chair he's claimed as his own, only his laptop pushed to the side with a plain, white mug next to it.

I push to my feet, swaying when they touch the ground, and vertigo hits me like a gut punch. I grit my teeth and bite back a moan of pain as hushed, angry voices filter through the cabin.

My limbs lock as I hold my breath, fighting against the strain to breathe. It's quiet for a moment, but then I hear them again. They're coming from behind the curtain, so I shuffle across the soft, padded floor, refusing to acknowledge that we're thousands of feet in the air because that thought alone makes me want to shove my head in a door and slam it shut repeatedly.

Despite my efforts, nausea still swirls as I walk, clutching each seat I pass for support until I reach the partition separating the crew compartment from the cabin. There's a soft, yellow light glowing beneath the edge of the curtain with black shadows of separation.

I peel back the curtain nearest the edge, finding the steward and my bodyguard inches from each other, faces turned in, harsh whispers exchanged.

"You're leaving the country with Zion Carver's son?" the blonde asks. I wrack my brain trying to remember his name, but I come up blank. All I remember is how hot he is.

"You know I can't tell you anything, Milo. Why are you so upset?"

Ohhh, Milo. Right. I mentally nod to myself, but even that fucking hurts.

"You know why. Nothing has changed. But this is my job. And *yours.* Now's not the time."

"When is it ever?" The muscles in Gavin's back bunch and roll with the movement of his arm as he shifts to clutch the counter at Milo's back, his large frame towering over the smaller man. And he's not even that small. In fact, Milo's bigger than I am, but Gavin's mass could make anyone shrink in size. Milo sucks in a breath at the movement, forcing his chest against my bodyguard's.

Gavin growls low, dragging his face against Milo's to whisper in his ear. I can't hear what he says, but whatever it is has Milo slumping, releasing all of the tension in his body as his hands clutch at Gavin's shoulders. Another gold ring glints in the yellow light.

"Shit, Gavin. You—" Gavin captures his lips in a kiss that steals my breath, a noise ripped from the back of my throat.

Gavin pulls away from Milo with a heavy breath, his body tense from head to toe. Milo's panting, eyes closed with his golden hair brushing his neck.

"Eavesdropping is very rude," Gavin's voice is sharp and tense as it rings out loudly in the mostly silent cab. I'd freeze if my head wasn't spinning so badly. I clutch the wall for support, but my grip is weak, and I slip.

"Shit." Arms wrap around me, and then I'm weightless, pinned against Gavin's body as he carries me to the small sofa. The moment my body is dropped onto the leather, I release a pained moan, curling in on myself.

"Go back to sleep," he tells me after long moments of silence.

"Don't fucking tell me what to do," I snap, the words coming out weak and raspy as I pathetically stand my ground. A heavy sigh meets my ears, and then my feet are lifted. Gavin places my legs in his lap and wraps his fingers around my clothed ankle, thumb pressing into the divot just behind. When he meets my gaze, his eyes crinkle at the corners.

"Now get some sleep."

I swallow the lump pressing against my throat as I bury

my face into the crook of my elbow. The burn of tears clogs my nostrils, making breathing harder as it wheezes in and out. But Gavin's touch makes finding sleep easier—gentler—despite the agony rippling through my body.

As I sink into unconsciousness, I relish in the innocent touch of another human.

Seven

ZEVRYN

"I think that is probably for the best," Gavin replies, his voice heavy. I'm grabbed under my armpits as I'm planted on some sort of seat. I sway without any support, my brain flipping in my skull. A grunt hits my ears, and then a hard, warm body is sliding against mine.

I fight against the pained urge to keep my eyes closed, barely peeking through the hazy film covering them to see Gavin covering my body with his much larger one. His thick arm wraps around my back, fingers biting into my ribs as he holds me against him.

"Whass—" I slur heavily, my tongue a lead weight in my mouth. If my heart could, I'm sure it'd hammer away in my chest from the anxiety licking through my veins—but even my fear is no match for the booze coursing through me.

"Shh," Gavin barks, making me wince as the rough tone hammers against my skull. His fingers tighten against my ribs, making me wheeze.

"Hurts," I pant as we lurch over a bump. *Are we moving?* My stomach churns.

Oh, gods, we're moving. I'm too focused on breathing through the drowning waves of nausea swelling and cresting with every passing second to completely make out Gavin's response.

"I'd imagine so after you stole a… and downed half… sleep with…" His voice flutters in and out in drugging waves. I swallow against the knot in my throat, the thickness choking me.

The continuous motion stills, making me jerk. The arm around me loosens, allowing me to slide off and fall to the soft ground with a pained groan. My stomach cramps, and I let out a strangled noise as vomit spews from my lips. My eyes roll into the back of my head as my body convulses.

Heat flashes and burns, followed by bitter cold, making me shiver.

Hands clasp my shoulders, my arms, rubbing up and down with more flaring heat.

Muffled voices sound around me, unintelligible and muted through the roaring in my ears. My hands dig into the soft earth, and the uniquely fresh scent wafts into my nose. A smell I don't recognize.

Tears prick my eyes as fear becomes one with the dizzying agony.

I just wanted to forget, but I'm so far gone. Everything fucking hurts.

How did I even get here?

When my stomach finally quits contracting, I'm left panting and drooling on the grass, vomit staining my lips.

My eyes are bleary, temples throbbing to the beat of my

heart as large legs shift into view inches from my face, the searing heat never leaving my shoulders. The shadow drops, and then Gavin wraps his arms around me and hauls me to his chest.

A form of protest spills from my lips, embarrassment for being so feeble surprisingly finding its way to the surface through all the bullshit my body is putting me through.

"Quiet, Zevryn." His large hand presses gently against the side of my face, pushing me against his broad chest. With a weak cry, I burrow into the soft, unyielding muscle with a sigh. The putrid smell of vomit wafts into my nose, and the water pooling on my eyes spills over as I suck in weak lungfuls of Gavin's soothing scent.

Other voices filter in as the jolting rhythm of his walking halts. I can't hear what they say, but I feel the vibration in Gavin's chest as he replies, a low, calming sensation amidst the molten lava boiling in my veins. I tense up as a bead of perspiration trickles down my temple. Another between my shoulder blades.

Noises I don't recognize tear from my throat as I lash out, hating the sensation eating me from the inside. My hand connects with flesh. Vertigo hits, and blackness oozes in.

I let it swarm me with welcome relief.

THE BED BENEATH offers no comfort as I twist and writhe within the thin sheets. Even the cool fan circulating above is useless.

I scramble to sit up, but when I hit a vertical position, my head protests with loud screams, and I'm forced back with a pained jolt.

"Are you awake?" Gavin's voice sounds from just beside me, shocking as it shatters the silence. I startle as I peer through the darkness, one eye pinched closed as it's being used as a focal point for a particularly nasty migraine.

He's sitting near the foot of the bed, hands clasped in his lap. His shadow looms.

"No," I croak, rolling to my side, but it's not until my gaze focuses again that I realize I rolled in the same direction he's facing. I slam my eyes closed. It feels safer that way—the world much smaller, though my torment is amplified with no direction.

I don't know where I am. I think I vaguely remember the horrendous ride here followed by faint, chattering voices, but then...nothing. And I'm worried it was all a nightmare.

It's all dark, all the time, as my body wars with itself, time nothing but a slow crawl meant to antagonize.

I know what this is. I've *seen* it up close and personal. How desolate and life-altering it is—what a body allows someone to bear before it becomes too much and the person expels whatever's inside—literally and metaphorically.

Though, the agony of withdrawal was never enough for my mother to stop. But me...

My veins rub together like two pieces of sandpaper, pulsing and shredding wide open. I feel my eyes stretching as they roll into the back of my head, a hoarse scream ripping from my throat. My body contorts—not because it has to but because staying still is just as excruciating as moving.

Air whistles between my lips in haggard breaths. My fingers dig into the soft fabric below out of spite.

It doesn't make me feel better, but it's *something.*

I always thought I wanted to feel over the empty despair of nothingness, of being lonely. Alcohol made me numb, but the coke...

It made me feel on top of the fucking world. Sky high and fucking soaring through the stratosphere.

Now...

I've never hated the concept of feeling more in my life. Not even the affliction of my mother's death or watching Darien die right beside me can compare.

"You need to drink some water." The abruptness of Gavin's voice makes me flinch, then cry haggardly. Footsteps thud across the floor, and a shadow looms closer. Peeling back one eyelid, I take in the way the brightness of his shirt appears almost reflective this close-up.

It makes my brain pulsate.

"Does your husband bleach all your shirts for you?" I rasp with a sneer as I try to swipe the bottle of water from Gavin's hand. The condensation combined with my weakened grip has it slipping from my tingling fingers. Gavin's curl into his palms as he glances down at the floor. He silently picks it up, popping the cap as he straightens.

The cold rim is placed against my lips, and I have no choice but to part them and allow the slow trickle into my mouth and down my throat. I moan at the relief, even if it hurts just as much.

After a few swallows, my stomach cramps again, making me jerk inward. The bottle sloshes over and spills over my face, but I don't have the energy to protest the tissue dragging gently over my skin, absorbing the spill.

Shame heats my face, but it's probably just the fever.

The damp collar of my shirt is ice against my feverish skin, and I shiver. The blanket is pulled upward and tucked around my neck. My hair is brushed away from my face.

Staring at the geometrical galaxy behind my eyes, I wallow in all I'm feeling because, for the first time in my life, I truly accept that I deserve this.

"Go back to sleep. You need rest."

"Give me some fucking booze, and I will!" I shout in a hoarse whisper, swallowing against the abrasion in my throat.

"I understand you are in pain, but you need to watch how you speak to me, boy." His voice sends a shiver down my spine.

"Please," I beg, shuddering in my own shame. I try to lift an arm, but it flops back against the bed helplessly. "Please, help me." Tears clog my throat.

"I am," I hear faintly as a finger drags across my forehead. "Do you realize where we are, Zevryn?" he says, softer this time, though his voice still holds an authoritative bite. A tone that never ceases to me make me defiant, to go against everything it stands for, but right now... I welcome the security of it.

That at least *someone* knows the truth and can help me.

I peek out from behind the blanket now covering my face. My surroundings come into view in blurry segments. It looks like I'm in a bland, modernized hospital room. The bed I'm in is similar to a hospital bed—only slightly bigger and nowhere near as bulky.

The room itself is cold and clinical, but the carpeted floor, padded furniture, and framed art on the wall make their attempt at giving comfort apparent.

I just want to get drunk, get high, and fuck my life away. Not lie in this torture chamber.

Is that too much to ask?

"Apparently," Gavin replies dryly, arms crossed back over his chest. The position makes his pecs bulge, which is just ridiculous. Never mind the fact I said that out loud.

The lines between reality and unconsciousness have long past vanished.

"Please just get me out of here. Whatever he's paying you, I can double—triple it! Fuck," I wail. Tears stream down my face. My hands shake against my face as I scrub and scratch violently. Digging until my fingers feel wet.

Anything other than this.

Hands, arms, and a body much stronger than mine envelops me. My own are ripped away from my face and pinned near my waist. I scream and lurch, fighting against the confinement.

I need... I need...

Please.

"Shh, Zevryn. It's going to be fine. Just hold on." My body shifts with Gavin's movement.

"Hello, this is Gavin Holt, Zevryn Carver's bodyguard. Yes, Zevryn seems to be in a rough patch, and I'd like someone to come in and check on him, please. Okay. Thank you."

The bed dips, and heat swarms me. It's suffocating, but the tight constriction grounds me, even as I plunge into darkness.

Eight

GAVIN

Zevryn's back is against my chest. The fever consuming his body radiates into me, making me itch. His dark curls are matted to his head due to the sweat dripping from his pores, making the room smell of stale musk and vodka.

Watching his nails dig and scrape across his skin with mindless desperation made something inside my chest lurch. Something raw and primal. Haunting and alluring.

I've never experienced the kind of physical agony he seems to be in, but I can *feel* it by simply watching him. The way his body is eating at itself, pining for what it craves.

It's eye-opening—witnessing addiction from this side. So close and personal, raw and malignant.

I must admit, observing the withdrawal Zevryn has been enduring sheds a whole new light on addiction and on addicts themselves.

It makes you wonder *why*. Why would they put

themselves through this? Why would they risk everything for the high?

What is so horrendous, they can't stand to go through life sober?

I sink my teeth into my bottom lip as I stare down at Zevryn. The sharp slope of his nose, the way it flares at his nostrils. His lips twisted in agony, even in sleep.

Deeper than that, I think back to the first moment I saw him. The wild, pain-riddled abandon in his gaze. The way every harsh strike of his father's words would hit like a whip against bare skin.

It's not as black and white as I once assumed.

We all have our reasons for what we do, and I'm sure Zevryn has his. I just hope his stay here—away from his father, from the life he lived—only shows him how good sobriety can be.

That even when it's hard, it's better than hurting himself.

With every ragged breath, tortured scream, and contorted limb, I see his pain. His desperation for it all to end. The way his craving has ravished everything left, leaving nothing but a shell in its place.

Zevryn Carver is irrevocably broken, and I want nothing more than to hold him against me as I piece him back together.

I don't know where this fierce protectiveness has come from. I could say it's just me doing my job, but I know it's more than that.

Zevryn... is more. He needs someone to help him, to care for him. And I can be that person.

No one needs me anymore, but he does.

A soft knock sounds before the door cracks open. It's

dark in the room, but my eyes have long since adjusted. I keep them strained on the door as a tall, lanky man in scrubs steps through.

"Hello. I'm Justin Miles, an RN. I'm just coming in to check on Zevryn." I nod from my position on the bed, trying to keep as still as possible so I don't wake Zevryn from his sleep. He'd been tossing and turning, stuck in the place between awareness and unconsciousness for endless hours —apart from his little outburst—but now he seems to be resting peacefully, and I don't want to disturb that.

The nurse crosses the room quickly and pulls a stethoscope from around his neck and places it against Zevryn's chest. While he listens to Zevryn's heart, I take in the man in front of me. His hair is dark, scrubs a charcoal gray. He appears even taller up close with long fingers.

When our eyes meet, he gives me a small smile before his gaze flickers back to Zevryn, hands nimble as he checks Zevryn's vitals. I sit quietly, letting him do his thing while holding the frail boy in my arms.

When Justin has finished, he wraps the stethoscope back around his neck and tosses his other things back into the bag he brought with him.

"How is he?" I ask quietly. My fingers have carded through Zevryn's sweaty hair, brushing it away from his face.

"He's exhausted. His body is completely drained, and these next few days are going to be the hardest, but despite the pain he's in, he seems to be in good health otherwise. Maybe mildly dehydrated. So, we'll push fluids and ensure he gets lots of rest."

I nod my acceptance. It is my job to protect him, so I'll make sure he gets everything he needs.

"His withdrawal is a lot more intense than we anticipated. Was anyone aware of how often he was abusing drugs?" His tone is soft and gentle, a mere whisper in the darkened room. I shake my head.

With a sigh, I tell the nurse what I know. "He stole a bottle of tequila while I was sleeping on the flight here. He drank half of it before I woke and discarded it. So, I feel his drunkenness has partially masked the severity of his withdrawal from harsher substances, but I could be wrong on that.

"I also witnessed extreme, erratic behaviors the day we left, but that's all I am aware of." His sweat clings to my warm palm.

"That's fine. I'll just make a note of this in his file."

"Thank you."

"Of course. Let me know when he wakes so we can try to get some food in him." I nod at Justin as he exits the room, leaving us alone again.

Relief settles in my chest knowing he'll be all right—physically, at least, because the way his body was contorting had my own stomach twisting.

I'd never seen anything so demonic; it's no wonder he's lashing out.

Zevryn groans and rolls to his side, curling against my left leg, all naked skin hot with fever. He rests his face against my upper thigh, hands tucked against his bare chest. Curls fall across his nose, so I gently pick them up and tuck them behind his ear with my free hand, the shaved hair on the side prickly against my fingertips.

I reach behind me and adjust the pillows as best I can before slumping back, ignoring the persistent ache radiating in my lower back. My eyelids grow heavy, but I scan the room one last time. The door is locked—only mine, Zevryn's, and the staff's bracelets can open it.

It's not ideal for that many people to have access to this room, but until Zevryn is out of the medical wing, this is the best they can do. The staff have all been vetted—otherwise, they wouldn't work here—so I'm confident I don't have anything to worry about. But still, the holster on my hip makes slipping into sleep a bit easier.

THE DAYS PASS IN A BLUR, so I can only imagine how they've been for Zevryn.

Every day has consisted of the same: him in pain, acting out, and sleeping. And I've held him through it all. The cries, the dry heaving, the relentless bitching and moaning.

I've never disliked and admired a person so intensely in my life.

The moments when he was sleeping—or close to it—were some of the softest experiences of my life.

Zevryn was clearly vulnerable, whimpering and crying, huddled against me for comfort, and I gave him every ounce of strength I have, knowing he needed it more than me.

It was easy for me to find sleep in those moments too—peace of mind, a tranquil experience. But when he was awake... it was an entirely different story.

He threw insults left and right. Made comments about Milo, about me. He cursed his father and best friends to hell.

I don't think I'd ever been so verbally abused in my life. The boy sure does have a colorful language, and I felt myself tensing up more often than not with the urge to chastise him. I even slipped up a few times, earning me even more insults, but for the most part, I had to let it all slide off my back, hoping it was the detox talking and not a rotten personality.

I accept that I've never known Zevryn sober, so I have to assume all of this erratic, nasty behavior is coming from the part of him that craves what it can no longer have.

"You're always hovering," Zevryn grumbles, pulling me from my musings. He's sitting on the bed, clad in loose-fitted clothes with his legs crossed, a tray of food resting on his lap. Fruit and toast. Light enough for his stomach to handle but gives enough sustenance, which he needs after making it through the worst of it. According to the discussion we had with the staff earlier this morning, Zevryn should be able to move into his own room later today.

They offered to give us a private VIP villa near the water, due to the unique nature of Zevryn's attendance. I swiftly took them up on the offer with a generous thanks. While it would be easy to monitor from a room in the main building, having a private space with limited access gives me the isolation I prefer when working.

And it has nothing to do with the desire to still keep Zevryn to myself.

"It's my job to hover," I reply easily.

A grunt meets my ears. "Not literally."

I resist succumbing to the twitch in my lips. "*Quite* literally." My watch buzzes, making me drop my eyes to the small display as it illuminates.

"Whatever," he mumbles through a mouthful of food. My eyes narrow.

If there's one thing I've learned about Zevryn during this time alone with him, it's that the boy has absolutely no manners. He talks with his mouth open *and* full. He doesn't say please or thank you to the staff that brings his food in—per my request since I can't leave Zevryn's side. I'm not even sure the words are in his vocabulary.

The boy is every bit of a spoiled rich kid, and I still can't figure out if it's purely an act or not.

The two very drastic sides to him I've seen don't give me much insight as to who he *really* is.

"Finish your breakfast. You know the counselor asked to meet with you today since you're feeling better."

"No," is all he says, keeping his head down so his thick curls block my view of his face.

I stride toward the bed with purposeful steps. Pressing a finger beneath his chin, I lift his dimpled chin so I can see his face.

"No?" I ask with a brow raised in question.

Zevryn's eyes never stray from mine as he rips out of my grip. "I'm not fucking meeting with anyone."

"You will do as you're told, boy," I bark, grabbing his face once more. His angry eyes make me soften my tone as I rub my thumb over the dimple in his chin. "This is what you're here for."

"I didn't fucking come of my own free will."

His mouth!

I sigh. "Well, of course not. I don't think many would willingly suffer through a detox like that." Zevryn winces, eyes scrunching shut as his lips turn down. My gaze flickers to the soft creases near his pouty mouth.

"Didn't have a choice in that either," he mutters, trying to pull away from my touch again. I frown at the top of his head as I drop my arm to my side.

"You must realize this is the best thing for you."

He laughs dryly, chin to his chest as he picks the crust off his dry, wheat toast. "The best thing?" He finally lifts his head, giving me his bloodshot, hazel eyes again. Brown with a ring of green on the outside. Endless depth.

"You think *this* is the best thing?"

I lift a brow, not sure where he's going with this. "It must be."

"You have no fucking idea," he scoffs and shoves the tray off his lap. It clatters to the floor, and the food spills across the carpet. I stare down at the mess inches from my feet. *This boy tests every shred of patience I have.*

"Are you going to pick this up?"

"Nope. I'm going to sleep." Turning his back to me, Zevryn yanks the blanket over his head and goes completely still. I stare at his unmoving body for long minutes, my molars grinding silently, before I bend over to pick up his mess for the last time.

Setting it all back on the tray, I slam it down on the stand, making him jolt, the fabric flowing upward.

"Knew you'd clean it up," he snarks, making my eye twitch uncontrollably.

Swallowing my disdain, I walk the perimeter of the room with nothing else to do. But I need space because this boy is suffocating me.

Luckily, we're near the center of the main building, so

there are no windows in this room, making my job a lot easier but also a lot more boring.

Sit. Watch. Wait. Repeat.

For the next fifty-three days.

"Quit walking. I hate the sound of your footsteps." Zevryn's words draw me to a stop. That little...

I pick up the pace and slap my feet down harder with every step. Not even thirty seconds later, he shoots up, the white blanket falling around his waist. His lips are twisted in a sneer, eyes narrowed and pointed at me. The frizzy disarray of his hair brings a snort to my lips.

"Fucking *stop,*" he snarls before confusion morphs in place of his annoyance. "What the hell are you laughing at?"

Ignoring his question, I reply, "I'm doing my job. If you want me to stop, I suggest you do what you're supposed to do."

"What the fuck does that mean?" he shouts. I want to sigh in exasperation. The boy really needs a lesson or two... or fifty.

"I told you. It's time for your first therapy session. You've been holed up in here for seven days—and only because they respected the fact you've been in pain. It's time to start working on your recovery."

He snorts. "Yeah. I don't think so." Back under the blanket, he goes.

Such a little brat.

I stomp over and rip the whole thing off his body. Zevryn gasps and reaches for it. "Hey!"

"Get up," I tell him after tossing the blanket into the chair across the room.

"Excuse me?" The way his face twists up makes me want

to bellow in frustration. No one has ever gotten so deep beneath my skin before, but it's like every little thing Zevryn does pricks tiny little holes into me, leaving me a little less whole every time.

"You heard me, Zevryn. Get. Up."

"I'm not fucking listening to you, and if you—" I drop down and lift him into my arms with ease. He bucks, forcing me to tighten my grip. Despite his fight, he's easy to carry, bringing me absolutely no strain.

"Put me down, you prick!"

I stop in my tracks. Keeping ahold of him with one arm, I use the other to grab his face, squeezing his cheeks as I force him to look at me. His hazel eyes are hard with defiance.

"Do not call me a prick again," I tell him, my voice low. "I let the name-calling slide when you were in pain, but I am done with your constant disrespect, Zevryn." He winces, but his eyes never leave mine.

"I've done nothing but take care of you the last week. Every time you threw up, sobbed, screamed, and moaned, I was there to hold you, clean you up, keep you hydrated." I don't say it with intended malice but to remind him. "And all you've done is treat me like shit.

"This isn't an ideal situation for either of us." Taking a deep breath, I try for some honesty. Something I don't think he gets very often from people. Because despite how badly he pisses me off with his acting out, I don't think he *wants* to be so unruly.

"You think I want to be away from my husband for two months, stuck on a secret island with a little rich boy who couldn't care less about anything?" The mention of Milo after barely thinking about him for a week is startling. It brings me pause. I can't even remember the last time I thought about him or our last conversation on the jet. Or even the pained glance we shot each other as I stepped onto a much smaller aircraft on the mainland that brought us to Black Diamond.

My chest rises with a deep breath at my unexpected realization. I don't know why it feels different than any other time I'm on a job. I go days without talking to or even thinking of my husband with no second thoughts, but the awareness here, on an island that seems impossibly far away, seems... strange. Almost surreal.

Zevryn's trembling brings me back to the moment. My arms strain slightly from the added movement, and the friction of his clothes against my healing forearms smarts, but I don't even contemplate putting him down. Or moving my hand.

His bottom lip quivers as he stares past me at the wall, full lips pouty and curved downward, the pressure of my grip making them puffier. The dark shadow of stubble dusting his face makes him look much older than his nineteen years.

Fuck, he's only nineteen, and he's this lonely.

It wrecks me.

It's silent for a few moments while we both gather our thoughts, mine turning more melancholy by the second.

"From what it sounded like, *your husband* probably doesn't care much about you being gone," he says through puckered lips.

"Excuse you?" Heat rises inside me. My grip tightens. *Just when I think...*

Zevryn winces but doesn't pull away. This time, he looks

me right in my eyes—no shame. No contrition. "How long have you been lying to your husband, Gavin?"

His words hit like a punch in the gut. My hold on him loosens, and he drops to the floor unsteadily. There are red blemishes on his cheeks from where I held him, and I'm forced to dart my eyes away in shame at the immediate twitch in my cock.

As I stare at my boot-clad feet, I know deep in my wounded gut just *how* long.

Years of lies, broken promises, and altered truths.

But for a *stranger* to see that so clearly... *Maybe I've been failing this whole time. Trying to keep pieces of us together that no longer fit—if they ever did.*

"Do you ever wonder if he's lying to you as much as you lie to him?" My head snaps up, finding Zevryn seated in the chair I normally sit in. He's hunched over with his elbows digging into his knees. The sweatpants covering his legs hang off his hollowed form, his shirt much the same.

"You need to quit talking," I growl. It makes his eyes narrow as he stares up at me with sharp defiance through his thick dark brows.

"Why? Seems like we both have some issues to sort through, and what better place to do it than fucking *rehab?!*" He shoots to his feet, throwing his arms in the air. His curls bounce as he jolts around, a sour grimace marring his face.

"I'm not the patient here."

He stares at me head-on. "Well, maybe you should be."

I CAN'T STOP THINKING about the crimson blemishes I left on his face.

The way they stained his pale, porcelain skin. Or how they brought some much-needed color to his washed-out face.

"Fuck," I grumble, dropping my head against the door at my back. Maybe the boy was right.

Zevryn's just on the other side—finally speaking to the therapist.

After he blew up on me, it got silent. Intensely so—but only on the outside. Inside, my anger is festering. But I don't think it's vexation for him.

Leave it to the little brat to drudge up *my* shit when we're here for *his* treatment. I want to hate him for it, but I can't help but feel relieved at the truths swarming the surface.

My phone buzzes in my pocket, so I pull it out. A quick glance at the screen tells me who's calling. The same man who's called every day since we arrived, and each one has pissed me off a little more.

"Mr. Carver," I drawl after bringing the phone to my ear. My eyes scan the hall I'm standing in. Cool, lightly-colored linoleum floors, bright white walls. Closed doors lining the short hall. The scent of the sea wafting in.

"How is he doing?"

"They've told me he is through the worst of it." Short and to the point. Maybe now he'll quit calling so much.

"Aside from physically..." he trails off. I let out a slow, even breath.

"He's very reactive. Explosive and quick to anger. But I think it will be that way for a while." *I fucking hope not, but according to the staff, it's part of rehabilitation.*

"Yes, well, that is to be expected. Is he doing what he needs to be doing?"

"He's in therapy right now." A shout from the other side of the door has me jolting, heart slamming into my throat. "I have to go." I hang up and shove my phone in my pocket before whirling around and knocking briskly on the door. After two seconds of not getting an answer, I shove the door open. It slams into the wall as I step over the threshold.

The counselor's wide eyes are on me, her mouth slightly agape, and wire-framed glasses perched on her nose. "Did you need something?" My eyes shift from her to Zevryn, where he sits in a chair opposite her, legs pressed against his chest, arms wrapped around his shins. He doesn't even lift his head from where it sits atop his knees.

"Gavin," he says dryly like he didn't just shout moments ago.

"*Hmm,*" I grunt, taking a step further into the room, letting the door close behind me.

Zevryn shakes his head. "Dr. Weaver, this is the big, bad bodyguard my daddy hired to protect me for no reason." He sounds so sarcastic, it makes my fingers twitch.

"Not for no reason," I grit, molars clenched. The doctor makes a small humming sound, a warm smile on her face. My eyes narrow at the sound.

"Does the reason really matter as long as you get your money?"

"It isn't just about the money," I growl. *Or at all.*

"Just," he scoffs.

That's fucking *it.*

"Zevryn!" I bark, so loud it makes him jolt, head jerking back off his knees so he can stare at me with wide eyes. "Quit pushing me, boy," I tell him once I finally have his attention.

"If I may interrupt," the doctor cuts in with her sweet voice, severing my connection with Zevryn.

"Yes?" I turn with a flash of annoyance, and even though I've already scoped out the room, I do it again out of habit. The light from outside is blinding as it shines through the windows lining the room. The view of the sea is extravagant, making me crave to feel the water against my skin.

My eyes catch on the diplomas and certificates on an opposite wall, Dr. Weaver's name in bold near the top of each one.

"It seems you two have formed a connection of sorts that I'm worried can impact Zevryn's recovery." She's blunt but gentle with it, which I can appreciate.

Still staring out the window, I ask, "How do you mean?" *Did I do something to fuck this up for him?*

I notice that Zevryn stays quiet.

"I think with the amount of time you two will be spending together, it might be important to work you into some dual therapy sessions." I jerk back, not having expected that.

"Excuse me?" I ask at the same time Zevryn blurts, "I don't fucking think so."

"For once, I have to agree with the boy," I grunt, crossing my arms over my chest as I turn away from the iridescent waves.

It reminds me of Milo and how much he loves to be in the water.

We always talked about vacationing to somewhere with water this clear and blue—and now I'm finally here. Without him.

I discreetly dig my fingers into the flesh just beneath my pectoral. I think that should hurt more than it does.

"Tell me this." I hear her chair creak. "You've been here for a week so far, correct?"

Zevryn grunts.

"Right. And how many of those days have you spent together?"

This time, I answer. "All of them." *What kind of question is that?*

She nods. "How many hours?"

How fucking specific do we need to get? "I'm his bodyguard," I say like it explains everything—because it does. Does she not understand that?

"I know."

"Then, why are you asking?!" Zevryn snaps. She doesn't seem fazed by his abrupt outburst, though I suppose she's probably used to it working here.

"So, you will be spending every moment of Zevryn's stay here with him?" Her question is directed at me, her kind eyes seeing more than they should. I shift on my feet.

"Yes, ma'am. It's my job."

"Well, then I think this is included in your job description."

"I don't fucking want him here," Zevryn snarls. He shoots to his feet and strides right past me to stare out the window at the crystal waters.

"Zevryn," I growl in warning, but I go ignored.

"Why is that?" the doctor questions.

He doesn't answer for a few minutes. Each one that drags on makes me feel like an intruder. I start across the room, but the counselor holds her hand up, stopping me before fixing her attention back to Zevryn.

"Do you know why you feel that way?" she prompts gently.

"I don't even want to be here."

"I know, but you are, and I think, together, we'll be able to help you through his despondency."

"What if I don't want to get through it?" He turns around, and the drowning sadness in his eyes steals the breath from my lungs. "What if I'm content where I've been?" I can't take my eyes off of Zevryn. I'm reminded of the affliction of his detox, what he went through, the pain I felt as my own.

I feel it again as if it never left. All of my irritation is gone in a blink as I stare at the lost boy in front of me. Hopeless, helpless, and needy for something he doesn't know he needs.

"Why are you?" she counters.

"Can he leave?" Zevryn mentioning me draws me back into the conversation instead of listening in from the outside. Dr. Weaver turns and lifts a perfect brow. I stride across the room quickly.

As I reach the door, I glance back at Zevryn, finding his sorrowful gaze already on me. "I'll be waiting just outside."

"I wouldn't expect any less." His quip makes me roll my eyes—but not before I give him my back.

And the brat is fucking back.

Nine

ZEVRYN

"Why are you?" Her question feels *so* fucking heavy. Heavier than anything I've felt before.

I hate her for asking it—but I hate myself even more for saying what I did. I don't need anyone picking apart my brain, seeing the shattered person I am at my core. It's bad enough I have to feel it every waking moment. I certainly don't want to piece apart *why* I am the way I am.

I know enough. Self-discovery is above me.

"Can he leave?" I can't look at him. His presence in this room fucking suffocates me. The way he lurks. Hovers. Fucking controls.

The annoying sound of his purposely heavy footsteps draws my eyes to his muscular back, clothed in a dark, plain T-shirt.

I hate it when my eyes search out his when he turns. "I'll be waiting just outside."

I already don't want him to go.

"I wouldn't expect any less." I almost miss the roll of his eyes as he leaves silently. For some reason I don't want to analyze, it makes me smile.

"You've already nurtured a connection with him," Dr. Weaver observes. I want to deny it. I even open my mouth to do that exact thing, but I pause. What's the point? It's not like it matters when I break it all down to the nitty and gritty bits of my center.

Because there... Nothing worth a fuck is to be found.

"Apparently," I snarl, hating the truth as it is. It's not like I fucking planned on the asshole taking care of me while I was delirious. Or that it would affect me the way it did to wake up with my face pressed against his jean-clad thigh, the scent of his fucking manhood wafting into my nose.

Or every time I woke up, shaking uncontrollably, sweating through the fever devouring my organs, I would reach for him and find solace in his stability.

I *needed*, and he *gave.*

How fucked up is that, anyway?

"How does that make you feel?"

I sigh. "You know, doc, I'm already tired of the questions."

"That's fine," she replies easily. "We can talk about something else. Tell me about your life."

"What do you want to know?"

"Anything you want to tell me."

I slouch in the chair, keeping my eyes on the water beyond this small room. This entire place smells like the sea and the jungle surrounding us.

Their vibrant colors call to me. I've never seen anything so vivid, so... real before. I crave to go out and just fucking *live* in it—just to make sure it's even real.

"There's nothing to talk about really," I reply after a while, fiddling with the black band on my wrist. I glide my thumb over the smooth, oval-shaped sensor in the center. "My daddy's rich. I'm a spoiled brat, who has a very cliché coke addiction. That about sums it up."

"That's not all you are," she states easily, making my jerk my head toward her. She's giving me a small, open smile. I don't want to trust it.

"You don't know me."

"True." She shrugs, then pushes her glasses back up her nose. She sets the pad of paper on the armrest of her chair. "But I'd like to, Zevryn. If you'd let me."

"Zev," I correct her.

"You prefer Zev?"

"Yes. My father named me Zevryn," I say without thought.

"And you don't like that?"

"I don't like my father." I wince. "But I don't want to talk about him."

"There's a lot you don't want to talk about."

"Is that a problem?" I grit, hating the insecurity already weighing on my shoulders.

"Of course not. This is for you, Zev. To help you." Her gaze becomes too much. I stand and walk away. "Why don't you take a few minutes to gather your thoughts?" she says to my back.

I nod, tucking a loose curl behind my ear. It tangles with one of my piercings, so I unwind it easily before fingering the strand, needing something to do with my hands.

My stomach twists with a cramp, and I suck in a breath as I curl in on myself, planting my free hand against the glass to steady myself. I let my eyes fall closed as I take a deep breath.

I thought the cravings from before were intense—back when I was living my fucking life before my father inserted himself and my friends betrayed me.

But now, my muscles cramp with desire. My veins pulsate with longing. My organs twist themselves inside out for another hit.

I'm full of a never ending need I can't satiate. And it's so fucking lonely—a loneliness that started all of this.

It seems I've reached an impasse.

"I keep seeing dead people," I say out of nowhere. The rustling of papers stops.

"Hallucinations?"

I can't stop my dry cackle. "Nah." I shake my head. "My mom. Darien. Memories of them dying."

"Why?"

Isn't that the million dollar fucking question.

I sniffle against the trickle of snot running down my nose. It makes me clench my hands into fists. "They both died in front of me. Mom... I don't know. I knew she had a problem with her pills, but I guess I didn't know how bad it was until I woke up and her dead body was just..." I stretch my arms out as I turn around to face the therapist. "Right there. And I think she did that on purpose. Like... she wanted me to see her that way.

"Maybe as a reminder of how badly I fucked up her life. Or maybe she was just miserable. I don't know. Zion and I never talked about it, or her—for good reason. Mom has always been a sore spot between us, and it's always been easier to just... *not.*" I clear my throat from the lump clogging it and scratch my head. "But Darien…that *was* my fault." I can't meet Dr. Weaver's gaze, knowing what I'll find if I do.

"I didn't give him the coke. It was the exact opposite actually—not that anyone would believe it. I was always blatant about my drug use. Darien kept his shit hidden because of his father." The breath I suck in doesn't make me feel any better.

"They all think I killed him. That I knew it was laced or I just wasn't careful enough. I don't fucking know." I yank on my hair with both hands, gritting my teeth against the sting in my scalp as it radiates into my chest. "But it doesn't really matter, does it? Cause he's still fucking dead. And I'm here. But it should've been me. Darien was *good.* I never have been."

The doctor's quiet for a minute. "Why don't you think you're good, Zev?"

I scoff, but it comes out wet and choking. "Look at me," I cry, slamming my palms against my chest. I can feel the bone against my palm, the thump of my heart just beneath. The room blurs in glossy waves.

A knock sounds at the door again, jarring me. Gavin pops his head inside. A few hairs have come loose from his bun, and they frame his face as it hangs just inside the doorframe. "Zevryn?"

I huff out a breath, planting my hands on my hips. "I'm fucking *fine,* Gavin!" My words are watery and high-pitched. Gavin's dark brows bunch in the center of his forehead as his eyes skim my body before darting to the doc, then around the room.

I know I *should* feel grateful for his protection, but I fucking don't. Micah Richardson might have threatened my life in passing, but who cares? My father certainly doesn't, despite his feeble *attempt* at pretending by hiring a bodyguard to come all the way to Black Diamond *Resort and Spa.*

The name makes me snort. Such a nice way of *not* saying there's a fucking rehab for the world's richest located just on the other side of the island—the dark, ominous trenches money allows us to sink into.

But me being here doesn't even make sense—it's the one thing that I keep circling back to now that my mind is free from the haze of pain.

Zion told me he'd disown me if I fucked up—and I did more than that. I made the biggest mistake of my life when I chose my lust of cocaine over my dying friend. And yet... here I am.

I can't help but wonder what his endgame is.

With one last look at me, Gavin slips back out, leaving me feeling exhausted. I find my chair again and curl up in it. The clock on the wall shows the session is just about over anyway.

I've said too much and yet, not nearly enough.

Dr. Weaver doesn't say anything either, which I'm grateful for. Between Gavin's hovering, the way my brain and my body are warring with one another, and my own personal desire to not fucking be here, I can't take another second of this shit.

"You can spend the last few minutes decompressing. Take your time; there's no rush. I want to thank you for opening up for me today. I truly want to help you, Zev. To see you be the best version of yourself."

"Yeah, sure," I huff, shaking my head against my knees.

"You don't think so?"

"Nah. It's what you're paid to do."

"You seem to have thoughts about certain people's jobs," she counters quickly. My brows pinch as I ruminate on her words.

"What do you mean?" I ask after a minute. Dr. Weaver clasps her dainty hands in her lap, glasses perched on her nose.

"Earlier, you mentioned Gavin getting paid to protect you, and just now, you mentioned my pay."

"Yeah?" I cross my arms over my chest, unease twirling in my gut.

"Does money bother you?"

I think about her question for a minute as I stare out the window. I feel her eyes on me, but they don't make my skin crawl—not like most people's.

"Not specifically," I answer after a while. I'm pretty sure our time together is already up, but the doc doesn't seem to be in a hurry to kick me out, which is kind of nice.

"So, it's safe to assume money's not the issue, but *who* receives the money for what they do. Is that more accurate?"

I hate her prodding. I don't want to think about this shit!

"I don't fucking know, doc," I snap with a click of my teeth. "I don't exactly feel comfortable with people being paid to pretend they fucking care about me." My chest is heaving, and my eyes sting with a wave of fresh tears. I grit my teeth and hold them back, blinking furiously up at the ceiling.

Why does everything feel so much more?

Oh, right. I'm fucking sober.

This is great. Real nice.

When Dr. Weaver doesn't say anything for a while, I risk a peek through my lashes. She's observing me quietly, a small, sad smile on her pretty lips.

"What?" I snap harshly, making myself wince. She doesn't deserve my attitude after she's been so kind, but I can't help it.

It's just easier this way.

"People generally don't do things they don't want to do, Zev. Even when money is involved. I can't speak for others but for me... Yes, this is my job. I went to school and got a doctorate so I could help people.

"While I do get paid, I don't have to pretend to care, nor do I use money as an incentive to. I care about every single one of my patients dearly. Yes, it is strictly a professional feeling in the sense I want to see you be the best version of yourself. Watching people grow and find themselves with my help is the best gift in my life."

I can't help but to peer at her curiously, not having expected that. She meets my gaze head on and doesn't look away.

"Thank you for telling me that."

She smiles warmly, and I feel a little... *more.* "I will always strive to be honest with you. You deserve it—and I do as well. What do you say?" She stands from her chair and walks over to me, holding her hand out. I take it in mine and shake her hand, some of my unease filtering out.

"That sounds nice." I croak the words, my throat feeling tight, and I clear it a couple times, hating the way my cheeks flame with embarrassment.

"Good. I'll see you in a few days."

I actually find myself smiling as I walk to the door, but as

I step through and catch my first whiff of salt water along with the heavy, manly scent of my bodyguard, it drops in an instant.

Gavin half-huffs, half-snorts. "How was therapy?"

I roll my eyes, but I'm unable to stop the way my left arm presses against his as we walk side by side through the hall.

"Confidential," I snap, baring my teeth at him before dropping my gaze back to the floor. Gavin's boot-clad feet are bigger than mine, and the canvas of my sneakers are worn and stained. He's wearing jeans and a t-shirt, whereas I'm in athletic shorts and a loose cut-off.

He's so large and manly, and as I look down at myself, really seeing who I've become for the first time. I notice the loss of muscles in my legs. How chicken-y they look under the flowing fabric. The way my bones protrude more than they should.

Just a shell of flesh and bone. Hollow and ghastly.

We turn another corner, and the scent of the sea grows stronger. I perk up at the thought of floating in the aqua water.

"Where are we going?" I ask. Gavin seems to know exactly where we are, which is confusing because I'm pretty sure he's been holed up in my room with me since we arrived.

"Since you've been healing the last week, it's time for our tour. They're going to show us around and then take us to your private villa afterward."

"Private villa?" I repeat, eyes widening as I step outside for the first time in a week. I inhale deeply, my eyelids fluttering closed. Salt water and Earth fills my lungs with every deep breath.

"Yes. Our situation is unique amongst the rest, so you are able to have a private space. But that doesn't mean you have all your privileges. You have to earn those."

"Privileges?" I ask, but before Gavin can respond, a voice interrupts.

"Zevryn, hello! I'm Lawrence. It's nice to see you again—and feeling much better, too. That's wonderful. If you would just follow me, we'll get started." He turns his back and jumps on a fucking golf cart before he finishes yapping.

I blink at his back before glancing up at Gavin. His eyes are scouring the outdoors, twitching a little as they move. I nudge him with my elbow, making him grunt softly.

"What is it, boy?"

Deep breath.

"Do we have to do this? That dude looks like a prick."

"You seem to like that word. And yes, *we* do. So, get your little ass up there." A palm connects with my ass in a short, sharp swat, making me gasp. I stumble forward before whirling around. Gavin's hair is messy from the wind, and his hairy cheeks are tinged in pink.

"Did you just... *spank me?*" I balk as I press my hand to my smarting ass. He got good contact, even through clothes.

"Yes. Because you're a brat who needs his attitude adjusted. Now, get on the cart before it happens again." I swallow and jump on the back, gripping the small, metal bar next to me for dear life.

As Gavin settles in beside me, his wide body taking up every last inch of available space, I can't fight the way my eyes rake over him. He's stiff, fingers curled into his palms as the cart roves down the path, jerking occasionally when the stupid driver takes a curve too fast.

His voice delves on like a radio on for background noise. I don't pay it any mind as I take in the nature around me.

I've never been out of the country before. Hell, I've never even left New York, believe it or not. So, this is all kind of a shock to my system—that our world can be this beautiful and not stink of burnt rubber and garbage.

It's beautiful.

The jungle we're driving alongside is dense with thick foliage, palm trees lining the opposite side of the path. I peer into the depth, noticing vibrant signs of life.

As we slope downward, water draws nearer, along with the presence of villas.

"This one right over here will be yours for your stay. Your bags have already been set inside. Gavin here has already taken care of the rest, so I will let you two off here. Please let us know if you need anything else."

I hop off at the same time Gavin does, and then the dude is driving away, a whistle trailing after him. *What a douche.*

A hand lays on the nape of my neck, and I press into it as Gavin leads us to the front door. The water is a very short walk away with the thick foliage of the jungle to the left. It feels secluded and private in a way that brings me so much fucking relief, every step I take has my shoulders dropping more and more.

Gavin waves his own black band in front of the door and unlocks it. He steps in front of me, cutting me off. "Hey," I snap, but he holds his hand up.

"Let me look around."

I huff but wait by the door as he scopes out the villa, his hand pressed against the holster at his hip. The view through the glass windows is sublime: the turquoise ocean, multiple vibrant shades of green vegetation, the long, textured trunks of palm trees.

They're actually kind of surreal to see in person. Almost like only ever seeing them through photos made them somehow… illusory in my mind.

I didn't want to come here—and a part of me still doesn't want to be here solely because I don't want to pick myself apart—but since the blinding convulsions of withdrawal have minimized, at least physically, I can see with a clearer head, and all that's in my line of sight is fucking *peace.*

Not having my father's suffocating presence down my throat has been a relief I never thought I'd experience. He's always just *been* there. And never in a way that I've needed.

Gavin steps back into view, and I straighten from my slouched position. The hair in his bun sits perfectly against the nape of his sweaty neck, a few loose strands twisted as they stick against him.

"All good, Mr. Big Bad Bodyguard?" I push off the wall to sit on the sofa placed in the center of the large room. It faces the sliding glass doors leading to the high-rise steps, which then dissolve into a path that leads down to the beach.

"Watch it," he growls, rounding the couch as he comes into view.

"Or what?" I lift a brow, sliding my arms along the back. The cream-colored material is textured but soft against my bare arms.

"Zevryn," Gavin sighs, digging his fingertips into his temples. His head hangs marginally between his shoulders, making the muscles stretch. "You push every one of my goddamn buttons."

"Not the first time I've heard that. I'm gonna go unpack. See what the fuck they even gave me."

"Your mouth!" Gavin's sharp shout has me whirling around, eyebrows sky high. His jaw is pulsing as he grinds his teeth together, dark eyes wide yet scrunched with irritation.

"Why the fuck do you keep saying that to me?" I ask, taking a step toward him. His watch buzzes with a notification, making me glance down at it, but it darkens before I can make out what it said.

"You were hired to protect me." He's inches away now, his heat sucking the air from the small room. "Not fucking tell me what to do. You should remember that."

Before I can step back, a hand is around my throat, and my back is pressed to the glass. It should've been jarring, but I've never felt a gentler touch in my life.

His grip isn't tight, merely a hold of dominance. I squirm, my breath coming out in quick pants, each one hitting Gavin's throat as he looms over me.

"That's where you're wrong, boy. I'm here to do it all. And not because I've *been paid* to." He throws my words back in my face, making me flinch. He presses even closer, every inch of his covered skin against mine. "So, the next time I tell you to watch *your fucking mouth,* I suggest you do that." He enunciates his words with a gentle squeeze.

I'm paralyzed. Stunned utterly fucking stupid as my legs buckle. Gavin's left arm snakes around my back, catching me before I fall, but that just means every inch of me is pinned against him.

I can feel the ridge of his package behind his jeans. He's not hard, but fuck.

With his hand still around my throat, he traps a curl beneath his thumb and tugs, drawing my gaze to his. Dark, molten irises see through me, to every gnarly, worthless shred of my existence.

"Can you be a good boy for me?" he asks softly, his rumbling tone sending vibrations directly from his chest to mine. His fingers flex against my ribs, and I suck in a breath as the hard ridge of his wedding ring slides against bone.

His words bring tears to my eyes, and I can't stop their escape as I blink through them, hating as each one falls, staining a path on my burning skin.

I can barely feel his thumb pressed on the underside of my jaw, tilting my head back until the tears cascade down my temples instead, soaking into my hair.

When I gulp, his hand on me bobs with the movement, but he keeps it in place. Warmth licks my veins.

With my left hand, I wrap my long fingers around his hand keeping me up, intentionally brushing his ring as I do.

With one last aching swallow, I say the words I've told myself more times than I can count, but now, for some reason, I feel a shame that hurts more than the truth itself.

"I've never been good."

Ten

GAVIN

I blink up at the ceiling from where I lie on the sofa, my mind churning and keeping me from sleep. I twist my ring around my finger as my mind drifts to Zevryn and his self-deprecating words.

The boy thinks so low of himself, and I itch with the desire to shake it out of him. I know he's not always well-behaved, or kind, or even fucking respectful, but he's *good.* I can feel it down in the very marrow of my bones, and hearing him speak so lowly of himself with tears in his eyes, pleading up at me to make it all go away…

But then, my fucking phone rang, and one look at Milo's name shattered the moment into a thousand fragments. Zevryn withdrew fast and hasn't spared me a single look since.

I shouldn't hate it as much as I do, but I like it when he looks at me, whether it be the brat in him or the vulnerable boy hiding inside. I crave the way he seems to need me, whether he wants to admit it or not.

I didn't even answer the call—I couldn't after the way Zevryn looked at me. A mere flash of loneliness before he disappeared.

With a heavy sigh, I scrunch my eyes closed with my hands clasped behind my head. I've barely slept in the last week, and even though I only have a sofa to sleep on until we leave, it's a hell of a lot better than the chair I've been stuck in.

The villa is locked up tight, curtains pulled over the large glass windows, dousing the space in shadowy darkness with the ever-prominent scent of the salty sea. I relish in the refreshing smell with every breath I take, using it as an attempt to ease some of the heaviness in my chest.

Zevryn tosses and turns on the bed a few feet away, the soft rustling of the sheet hitting my ears. I lift my head off the pillow, peering over at him. My eyes have long adjusted, so I can make out his form easily.

He's curled into a ball near the center of the queen-sized mattress, dark curls fanned across the bed sheet, a few sticking to his forehead. The air circulating from the fans above doesn't do much to quell the humidity in the air. It's why I'm only in a pair of loose shorts.

Zevryn cries out, and I'm out of bed and at his side before I realize. He's trembling, his puffy lips quivering as he presses his face harder into the soft mattress. I slide onto the bed, lifting the sheet to get closer.

As gently as I can, I wrap my arms around his torso and pull him against my chest, similar to the way I held him when he was going through detox. Zevryn curls his leg around mine, his head resting just under my ribs.

Leaning back against the headboard, I let my eyelids

droop as I card my fingers through his hair, gently tugging at the strands when the coils knot.

Zevryn relaxes against me at the soft scrape of my nails on his scalp and the brush of my roughened palms against his bare back. His spine is knobby, creating a ripple in my arm with every pass, a movement I repeat until my hand starts to tingle as it goes numb.

Warmth buzzes in my veins with the boy in my embrace, finally sleeping peacefully. Without moving my head, I lower my gaze to the top of his. His nose is buried so deep into the soft muscle of my stomach, I can barely see it. The thick bar in his right nipple glints in the shadows, and I swallow against the dryness in my throat as I curl my arm higher up his ribs to graze it with my nail.

I can't even feel it as I add pressure, causing it to slide through his pointed nipple. My breath catches as Zevryn's leg twitches before stilling, curling tighter. His leg hairs scrape against mine, and I can't fight the goosebumps that scatter across my bare flesh, the sensation so foreign.

Milo has always shaved. His legs, arms, chest—all of it—so it's been over a decade since I've felt another man's natural body.

It's as surreal as it is addictive.

I slowly pull my leg up before pushing it back down, dragging my flesh across Zevryn's. I shiver as he groans, both of our holds tightening.

He starts to squirm against me, the small rocking making my dick twitch from the friction. I drag my finger off his nipple to press my hand to his back in hopes it helps calm him, but as my hand moves, so does he.

Still lost somewhere in sleep, Zevryn scooches up, his

flared nose dragging across the thick trail of hair on my abdomen until his cheek is pressed against my chest.

The loss of weight on my abdomen makes it easier to breathe, and I don't bother hiding my amused smile as Zevryn snuggles in, his legs now between mine as he curls into me.

It's not the first time he's done this. When he was detoxing, the second night when it was really starting to get bad, I had him pinned against me to keep him from hurting himself—and me, if I'm being honest. He fought so hard for so long that when he finally gave up, he slumped in my hold and drifted off into a fitful sleep.

That was the *first* time he crawled on top of me and held on like a boy cuddling a stuffed animal. The surprised groan that came out of me made me more than glad the boy was delirious *and* unconscious.

Now, though, I relish in his hold. In being the one that brings him comfort when his nightmares strike.

Zevryn talks in his sleep, and while I don't know the specifics of his dreams, I do know the boy feels too much, and it consumes every part of him. So, if I can be a sliver of solace for him amidst his own mind's damnation, then I will without hesitation.

My eyes finally slide closed as the boy and I drift off wrapped in each other. It's been years since I've been held quite this tight or this intimately, and I can't deny the soothing peace that settles in my gut.

Zevryn's stubble scrapes against me as he moves his head, making my eyes roll back. Color bursts behind my closed lids as a white-hot wet suction closes around my nipple. I cry out, my hands fisting as Zevryn draws me into his mouth with a slow, drawn-out suck.

My eyes snap open, dropping to the boy latched to my nipple, full lips curved in a perfect O. His eyes are still closed, black lashes brushing his high-cut cheekbones, and I can't hold back my grunt when he sucks gently again, sending shockwaves straight to my groin.

My fingers entwine with his hair until my knuckles bump his scalp. I don't pull him off but instead use my hold to hold him in place, ensuring he doesn't move an inch.

"Are you awake, boy?" I ask, my voice so raspy, I can barely understand myself.

I don't receive a response, just more soft suckling followed by a contented sigh.

I force myself to breathe slowly and precisely through my nose, each inhale bringing more clarity, while every exhale sinks me deeper into it.

"Zevryn," I grunt as I tug on his hair, drawing his lips away from my swollen, puckered bud. The flash of damp air makes me hiss, and Zevryn cries out at the loss in an endless stream of whimpers.

"Tell me what's wrong." I keep my voice sharp but soft, not wanting to startle him, but fuck, my dick is aching in time with the pulses in my nipple, and my brain is starting to feel hazy.

"Please," he mewls, lips parted as he sinks onto my nipple again.

"Fuck," I gasp, head thudding against the headboard as fire douses my veins. Zevryn whimpers again, shaking as he wraps an arm over my ribs, the other curled by his face as he suckles on me.

"You want to suck on me? Is that what you need?" I ask, giving up. It feels too good to question. He nods, the movement so small, I probably wouldn't have noticed if I didn't have my fingers curled so tightly in his hair.

"Okay, boy," I sigh, petting his head as he swallows in small draws of his mouth. The tip of his tongue massages the underside of the bud, making my vision white-out.

While my dick is the hardest it's ever been, the comforting weight of being desired pulses at my core, bringing me a sense of peace I'm not sure I've felt before.

"I'll take care of you," I tell him with finality. "I'll give you what you need." I press his face harder against me, making him moan. The vibration makes me twitch, and I dig my fingers into the sheet as a flimsy anchor.

Zevryn rocks his hips in a slow grind, like it's unintentional, his dick firm against my upper thigh. The sheet ripples and flows with his unhurried movement, and even through the tight material of his underwear, his length slips through the crease of my leg and hip.

I keep my eyes opened a crack, too blissed out to keep them fully open, but desperate enough to watch the boy's every move.

There's not a single crease or wrinkle of tension on his youthful face. In fact, I've never seen it so smooth, so flawless.

He's truly an art form. Crafted from the most devilish hands to bring me temptation. And it's been nothing but a rapid descent into the abyss of betrayal as he gives me what I've always wanted.

To be needed. Desired. Craved and depended on.

The lonely boy with sadness staining his eyes has a chokehold on me—one I don't care to fight.

Zevryn

I FEEL HIGHER than I ever have—my mind in a place I didn't know existed.

The colors in my mind feel brighter, the smell of Gavin's unique scent stronger, the nerve endings in my body fervent.

I swallow the saliva pooling on the back of my tongue. Gavin's taste slides down my throat where it shoots straight to my cock.

Salty sweat and musk.

A whimper escapes my throat as his nails scrape gently against my scalp, followed by a gentle tug. His soft flesh is all around me—on me, in me.

I ascend higher. I'm so gone, my body doesn't feel like my own, a mere relic holding me to the planet, when in reality, I'm lost somewhere deeply above in a place that shouldn't exist.

The lingering nightmare of long tentacles wrapped around my throat is long gone as I anchor myself to Gavin's supple flesh, pulling him into my mouth with gentle sucks until my tongue goes numb and I no longer feel myself.

"I KNOW YOU'RE AWAKE, BOY." Gavin's voice cuts through the silence like a hot knife through butter.

I try to hold back my wince, and he chuckles. "Don't act shy with me now." He yanks on my hair, stretching my neck taut until I'm looking into his deep, brown eyes. He stares down at me from his raised position against the headboard, looking ever the domineering man he is.

"I'm not shy," I say, pulling against his grip. His eyes narrow slightly, his fingers tightening.

"I know."

"Good. Glad that's settled." I try to pull away from him, but he doesn't release his hold. "Let me go."

"No. We're going to talk about last night," he says calmly—gently—like it wasn't the most Earth-shattering moment of my life.

I don't want to talk about it. I don't even want to think about it and the way it made me feel—the sensation of being so high still lingering in my brain. In my muscles.

In my fucking veins.

"Talk about what?" I try for confusion. Gavin's not impressed if the deadpan look on his face is anything to go by.

"Don't be fucking smart with me, boy."

"So, you can swear, and I can't? That seems fucked up."

My head is yanked back so hard, I yelp as the tendons in

my neck are stretched past their capabilities. My hair brushes against my back, my watering eyes forced to the ceiling.

"I will not tell you again. I don't like those words coming out of your mouth." His flash of honesty surprises me.

"Why?" I croak. He releases me instantly, and I drop back down, my chest heaving. Gavin's dark brows are furrowed, the tail ends partially blocked by his long, shoulder-length hair.

"Because I said." His words come out slowly, like even he's confused by them. I know I sure the fuck am.

I shake my head with a sigh, wracking my brain as to why *his* demands feel soft and gentle, versus my father's that sink into my gut with cold spite.

Feeling too confused to work through it, I pad across the hardwood floor, swiping my bag from the corner of the room before I hide myself in the bathroom. With the sliding brown door against my back, I take in its opulence. There's a huge walk-in shower to my left, the tile a shiny, aqua blue to match the sea, with more than enough room for two people.

I zero in on the space, my thoughts veering in a different direction. Gavin's looming at my back, his thick, hairy arms bracketed around me as the waterfall showerhead spills water down atop the both of us.

Our skin slides together, creating an effortless glide for his hand as it traces the gaunt planes of my torso, trailing down to my aching cock, straining between my thighs.

A knock sounds at the door directly against my back, jolting me back to reality.

With a huff of irritation, I slam my head back against it,

ignoring Gavin, even as my face burns with my wayward thoughts.

A thick wall separates the shower from the rectangular space just in front of me. It houses two white vanities with large mirrors, and just to the right is another smaller, brown door with opaque glass, where I assume the toilet is for optimum privacy.

I slide down the door, dropping my head into my hands. My tangled curls fall around me, obscuring my view.

Before I can even take a breath, another soft knock vibrates the door. Rolling my eyes into the back of my head, I sigh. *I won't be able to get out of this.* "What, Gavin?"

"Open the door and talk to me."

"Why?" I stare at the plain, white wall.

"Because I asked you to," he growls. The low tenor sends a vibration through my stomach.

"You didn't ask. You demanded," I snark.

I flop backward as the door slides against my back. Gavin steps beside me, turning once he's in front of me so we face each other. I try to stare through him at the wall I *was* looking at, but his broad, strong body is impossible to resist —especially without a shirt.

He's only wearing a pair of loose-fitting shorts that hang low on his thick hips. There's a dark smattering of hair from his chest to his cum gutters—because let's be fucking real, the man's *got 'em*—made more prominent by the roundness in his abdomen.

I sharply remember burying my nose in that exact spot just below his belly button, suffocating myself in his softness.

I swallow and choke on my fucking spit. I splutter, my eyes bulging as dry fire licks my throat. Gavin gets to his knees, hand against my back patting and rubbing gently as I wheeze through my constricted airways.

When my vision clears, I notice his thick brows pinched together, creating a deep wrinkle in the center that's only partially covered by his loose hair. My mouth hangs open. Gavin is inches away, his scent all I smell, his touch all I feel.

My eyes drop to his nipple, red with small, purple blotches and slightly swollen from a night of continuous abuse.

My face ignites.

I needed that. Needed *him*. I didn't think—I couldn't. All I *could do* was feel. And Gavin was right there. Soft and gentle as he pulled me against him like I fucking *mattered*.

Gavin slows the calming movement of his hand before slowly pulling back. The absence of his touch leaves me feeling cold. I don't fight the shiver that washes over me, choosing to feel every small prickle as it imbeds in my skin, sharp and painful and fucking lonely.

"Tell me why, Zevryn."

The use of my full name has me snapping my head up until it smacks against the door with a loud thump. Staring into Gavin's eyes with every bit of my shattered soul, I rasp, "Because I fucking needed you." *And I don't know why I needed you that way*. "But it won't happen again." I have the sick, pitiful joy of watching his eyes crinkle at the corners and his small, curved frown before I'm scrambling to my feet and running from the room, heart in my throat.

I'm able to get the sliding glass doors open easily with a

quick wave of my black band, and then the path leading to the sea is beneath my feet.

Each slap has my heart pumping faster, my breath coming out in heavy pants as I lose myself to the rush of oxygen in my lungs and the sting against the soles of my feet.

The gentle breeze whips my hair around, small flashes of black amongst the vibrant green as I pick up speed, my vision narrowing at the soft, crystal water growing closer by the second.

A second set of footsteps coming from somewhere behind me infiltrate my mind, making me speed up to keep the distance between us.

I need space. To breathe. To fucking think about the new mess I'm becoming when who I am—or who I was, I'm not really sure yet—is still so close to the surface.

"Zevryn!" Gavin calls out, the singular word a knife to my back.

With a huff, I land on soft, stinging sand that gentles the impact of my leap. A smile breaks out on my face as I near the shore, my clothes peeling off my sweaty body faster than ever before.

I delve into the warm water in nothing but my briefs and lost thoughts, salty air filling my lungs.

I feel so fucking alive, and despite the way my neck prickles from Gavin's heavy gaze, I've never felt safer, either. Free to be myself. Away from the pressure of it all.

My bodyguard is still very much at the forefront of my mind—how can he not be—but it's easy to push him back as I dunk under the crystalline water.

Despite the stinging from the salt, I keep my eyes open

wide as I bury my toes in the sand, anchoring myself in place as I hold my breath, waiting for the moment when black creeps in at the edges of my vision, threatening to take me under.

The promise of it makes my heart skip a beat.

Eleven

GAVIN

The twitch in my eye is impossible to ignore as Zevryn runs away from me—literally. His little ass is already halfway to the beach by the time I manage to kick my own ass into gear.

For someone that was so sick only days ago, he sure can run fast.

I'm panting through the burn in my lungs as I finally catch up to him near the end of the path, unlit tiki torches lining the way. Sand flies in all directions as he beelines for the shore, his clothes floating into the air as he rips them off.

I wipe sweat from my brow, slowing my pace as he dives into the ocean, tiny, black briefs all he's left on. His ass sticks in the air for a split second before going under, and I'm held utterly rapt, blinking helplessly at the crystal water.

Shaking my head, I continue my walk through the sand, just at a much slower pace as I scour the beach front, picking up Zevryn's discarded clothes as I do. There isn't a lot of activity this early in the morning, which gives me a breath of relief as I plop down, shaking Zevryn's clothes out before settling them in my lap to keep sand off them.

The only other people I see are two men a distance away. I peer at them out of curiosity since no one else is out just after dawn.

They're huddled together near the shoreline, but far enough away, the tide barely grazes their feet. A guy with shaggy, blonde hair holds an acoustic guitar in his hands while pressed impossibly close to the other. The soft ripples of the cords travel out, the melody carried in the breeze.

The other man, smaller and lither than the blonde, visibly appears tuned into the other, his head turned to the side, long, black hair flowing in the breeze as they gaze at each other. The blonde cracks a wide smile, and it's so genuine, I drag my longing gaze away instantly, feeling like I'm intruding on an intimate moment.

After one last glance around me, I focus on the water and where I last saw Zevryn dive under. He still hasn't broken the surface, and it's been… I glance down at my watch, brows furrowing at the time. Nearly a minute and a half have passed with no Zevryn in sight.

I scan the water, but I can't see him from where I sit. I jump to my feet, his clothes clutched tightly in my right hand as I jog to the water, uncaring as it seeps into my boots.

My heart thuds in my throat, making every breath feel labored and intense as I search for him. My mind's in disarray. He's been under too long. He's still recovering; he can't hold his breath for that long.

I drop his clothes to the sand along with my phone as I start to wade into the water, boots and all. It laps over the tops, up to my shins. It's warm, like bathwater, and it causes goosebumps to lick along the back of my neck and down my arms as I trudge deeper in, the crest lurching higher as I push through the resistance.

With a spluttering breath, black curls send water flying as Zevryn launches out of the water, a lively, bright smile on his pale, gaunt face. The sight of him looking so alive after feeling so near death... something tight and uncomfortable squeezes the muscle in my chest, stealing my breath for an impossibly long moment.

The boy notices me almost instantly, and his smile drops immediately, making me wince even while having his eyes on me makes my lungs refill with air.

"Gavin," he murmurs, palms splayed flat across the surface of the water, long fingers dipping down before flicking back up.

"You're such a brat," I mutter, shaking my head. Zevryn cocks his head to the side, that smile flickering at the corners of his mouth even as his face blooms with a gentle flush of crimson.

"I know," is all he says, making me bellow out a hearty laugh. *If only he really knew...*

"I should beat your ass for it, too," I grumble, halting my steps as the water licks across my waist.

"Is that what you're into?" Zevryn asks breathily, crouched a few feet away, keeping a sure distance. I take a step, ensuring to keep my hands above the surface so I don't ruin my watch.

"Is that what *you're* into?" I ask, referencing last night's... whatever that was. *Odd... but good.* His sharp Adam's apple bobs with a swallow before he turns away, giving me his bare back. I notice a few freckles spread out across his shoulder blades, beads of water running down and dripping from the ends of his hair.

I let it stay quiet for a while, enjoying the silence between us, even if it is subjective. The water laps around us in gentle waves, skimming Zevryn's face while it brushes my waist.

"I don't really know who I am when I'm not high," Zevryn says after a while. I release a breath through my nose, thoughts churning. I don't want to say the wrong thing because this feels important. Vital in a way I *know* I don't want to fuck it up.

Zevryn may be a brat, but he's such a needy, gentle boy at his core. I'm certain of it.

"How long have you been getting high?" I ask after a moment of deliberation.

"I had my first real drunk... experience at my mom's viewing. It wasn't more than a month after that I was smoking weed and popping pills. Mainly hers until they were gone. Her dying really fucked me up." He snorts.

I bite my tongue so I don't reprimand him. That's not what he needs right now. "How old were you when your mom..." I trail off, not wanting to trigger him.

His back stiffens, causing a wave of water to lap outwards, but he surprises me by answering my question. "Fourteen."

"Fuck, Zevryn. That's so young." My molars snap together in shock—and in fucking anger because his father *allowed that.* He should've intervened back then. Not wait five goddamn years—

"Yeah. It was always hard. With Mom poppin' pills and Zion always gone. But when he was home, they fought.

Constantly. After years of it, it just became who we all were —until Mom died and everything changed. Zion became colder—if you can even believe that. And I... was a lot more broken."

His words lance straight to my heart. My eyelids fall shut at his admission. The despondency laced in his tone. So young to have lived such a tragic life.

"I needed to forget what she did... *how* she did it. In front of me. So, I drank. Smoked pot. Numbed it all with her pills —and then more. But it didn't take me long to realize it wasn't because of *her* that I was doing all of that... it was everything else. Real life. *Reality.* And how daunting it all was—" Zevryn cuts himself off with a shaky inhale. His body trembles, sending small vibrations through the water, and I feel each one like a nail in the coffin of my resolve.

Long fingers wrap around my wrist, startling me. My eyes drop to meet Zevryn's gaze. He peers up at me through wet, clumpy lashes. My heart slams against my sternum, stealing my air.

His eyes reflect the water, creating a pool of crystal blue, amber-brown, and moss green.

Beautiful.

"Gavin..." Zevryn gasps, full lips parted, and the heaviness suffocating both of us just falls away. His eyes dart from my face to my chest, and my nipples harden, remembering his lips wrapped around me, sucking me gently—reverently.

I flex my fingers on my left hand as they dip into the ocean from the weight of his grip. My other arm wraps around his waist. Digging my fingertips into the curve just beneath his ribs, I press him against me until every slick inch of his torso aligns with mine. His deep sigh is immediate as he lays his head against my chest, mass of unruly black curls like a halo around him.

Zevryn's bare feet shift on top of my boots, giving him a couple of extra inches. The top of his head settles just beneath my chin as he wraps his arms around me, settling his long fingers over my spine in a hypnotizing pattern.

"I don't want you to feel sorry for me. Or think I'm weak," Zevryn says quietly, his swollen lips brushing over my skin. Goosebumps follow their trail, making my eyes roll back.

"What I've seen you go through this last week only proves how strong you are, Zevryn. And as for feeling sorry for you—that's not it. I'm *angry* for you." My fists clench of their own volition as I think about Zion Carver and the way he treats his son—like he's malleable garbage.

Zevryn pulls back to peer up at me. "Angry?" He looks confused, and it breaks my heart that he doesn't even see it.

Or maybe he does, but it's always been a part of him, so he's grown numb to it all.

I'm not sure which is worse.

"Yeah, boy." I drag my thumb along his stubbled cheek. The dark shadow of hair coupled with his rosy blush adds a slight nuance of color. "So fucking angry."

When he parts his lips, probably to ask me why, I press my thumb to the center of them, keeping them closed. His skin is slick and wet, and I can't fight the way my eyes zero in on his plush mouth, still vividly remembering the way he sucked me so gently, like there wasn't a single thought in his beautiful head.

I haven't been able to stop thinking about it. How... right it felt. To just be.

Zevryn doesn't move an inch as I pin him in place. He just stares up at me with reckless loyalty, like anything I say will be the right thing and he'll obey blindly. But it's a good thing I know the boy better than that.

Clearing my throat, I release my hold on him, unable to bite back my grunt as he slides, so fucking slowly, down my torso until his toes dig into the soft sand. I incline my head toward the endless water surrounding us in indescribable beauty.

"Swim—I know you want to. We don't have to be anywhere for a while so just... live, Zevryn." With a hurried, chaste kiss to the top of his head, I turn around, giving him my back as I push through the density, heading to shore.

Each step feels heavier than the last—in my legs and in my chest.

When I'm finally sliding across the sand, each granule sticking in places it really shouldn't, I'm breathless and lost.

Zevryn bobs in and out of the water, his smile vibrant, even from here. It only makes everything worse.

The sun, high and bright in the sky, doesn't shed any light on the turbulent thoughts vacating the most pained recesses of my mind. My eyes drop to the gold band I'm twisting around my finger. The sight alone makes me recoil in confusion.

Milo...

He's always been *right* for me. Beautiful, smart, independent, and loyal to a fault. He was everything I needed—but I'm not sure when that changed.

This time away, even though it's only been a week, has shifted my perception. This island feels like a whole new world, the people in it even more so.

The way Zevryn has been with me is only because he's healing. Lost in a whole new world he's trying to navigate as someone he hasn't been for far too long—and I'm his crutch.

I see now how... ill-advised that was. To attach myself to him so soon into his recovery, but at the same time, what else was I supposed to do? He *needed* someone, and I was the only person there. I *felt* every scream, gasping breath, and pained groan like it was a part of me, too.

He only needs me because we're here together, and he doesn't have anyone else. That truth sits awkwardly, but I know that's how it is and no more than that—it *can't be.*

But the way I need him? That I can't explain. From the moment I saw Zevryn Carver wreaking havoc in a drug-induced state, I've wanted to protect him—especially after seeing the way his father treated him. And the burdens he carries.

Even if the people in our lives pretend they care, we know the truth.

He's alone—just as I am. But loneliness never bars any good intentions.

Still pinching my ring between two fingers, I twist and pull until it almost falls off before sliding it back down until my skin chafes and goes red from the friction.

The beach is still quiet, a few people wandering about but keeping their distance. Even the air feels lonely, with only the scent of salt and unreachable certainty lingering.

My eyes catch on Zevryn—or maybe they never really left.

I can't deny my need to shelter him with every best interest at heart.

Watching over someone, ensuring their safety, has never

been an issue for me—or something I ever had to question. I've been doing this job a long time and it's always the same—a very distinct line separating business from my personal life.

But now, the both are impossibly intermingled, and it's paralyzing. Each stinging verity burns my skin in the shape of my mistakes.

The lines aren't even blurred. They're fucking obliterated.

Zevryn.

Milo.

The way one needs me and the other never has.

But I made a promise to Milo many years ago that I would love him and remain loyal till *death do us part.* And I can't help but wonder… does the death of our love mean anything? Or if that's even what has happened between us. Because I do love him. Deeply. In a way that has changed me into a much better man. But is it the same love I went into our marriage feeling?

I groan loudly, dropping my head into my hands. My temples throb in beat with my heavy heart, each rapacious thought battering my skull with ill intent.

The sand piled beneath me is hot, working with the sun to dry the water from my shorts. My boots, on the other hand, are probably just ruined as water continues to lap against them.

I drag my head across my kneecaps, glancing to the left at the sound of footsteps, followed by hushed voices. Our eyes meet for a moment, each of us flicking a quick, fake smile before they pass. I follow their trail for a moment, eyes scouring their frames instinctually before they're far enough away, the thought of any threat is long gone.

I pick Zevryn's clothes up off the ground and shake them out. The loose tank is two sizes too big, the shorts near the same. He doesn't even have shoes on because he just ran out of the villa in a fit—which reminds me I'm going to have to reprimand him for his carelessness.

The fabric flips around in the sudden gust of wind, bringing with it Zevryn's scent—straight up my nose and into my brain. My eyes close as I bring the fabric closer until it's pressed to my face. I inhale deeply, almost choking as a few sand granules shoot up my nostrils, but the burning doesn't surpass *Zevryn.*

He smells like the ocean. Salty, fresh, and endless.

I dart my eyes to the boy so I can see him as I smell him, but when I locate Zevryn, I find him already staring back at me, many feet closer than he was before. I drop his shirt into my sopping lap, and a carefree laugh spills from his mouth, carrying in the waves and the breeze, bringing a part of him back to me.

I swallow, fighting the warmth burning my skin. I have never been more thankful for my thick beard than in this moment.

Zevryn shakes his head, bright teeth glinting as he tilts his head back, letting the long ends of his hair dip back into the water, throat perfectly arched. I greedily drag my gaze all over him.

My watch buzzes, drawing my eyes to it. The name illuminating the screen makes everything around me dull into an endless sphere of reverie.

With a pained closing of my eyes, I feel across the sand

for my phone. It's hot to the touch, making me hiss as I drag my finger across to answer before pressing it to my ear.

It's been too long, and yet not nearly long enough.

The heat seeps into my head with an ironic burn, each millisecond that passes filled with poised silence until Milo shatters it, bringing every plaguing thought to the forefront of my mind like a tsunami. I swallow hard, fighting two warring emotions with every ounce of strength I have.

"Gavin." Milo releases a breath.

"We need to talk," I mumble, already losing my resolve.

Twelve

ZEVRYN

Three weeks later

My eyes keep straying to Gavin, no matter how hard I try to keep them focused on the window behind Dr. Weaver, who is, of course, not saying anything to break the tension, knowing full well we could use some of her doctorly wisdom right about now.

These last three weeks have been... exhausting. After the morning at the beach, where I finally shared a small part of myself with Gavin and I felt *something* between us pressing in places I didn't even know existed... he shut down. Completely.

And I don't think anything has ever hurt this bad before. The rejection from the one person *paid* to watch over me. Like even money isn't enough to keep him interested.

Guess that proves it wasn't about the money for him. How fucking ironic this *is how I find out.*

He's followed me everywhere I've had to go. Therapy,

fucking *group therapy*, which is the bane of my existence. I've taken up yoga and music therapy, two things I actually look forward to every week. They clear my mind in very different ways. Something I apparently need to do more often than not.

I never realized the way my thoughts churn, each mood heavily influencing my emotions in any given moment. In yoga, the physical strain on my body—from the way my muscles scream, the sweat leeches from my pores, and the burning ache in my lungs—clears the cobwebs, zeros my focus.

Music therapy... that just makes it all disappear for a while. After three weeks, I can still barely hold a guitar properly—or any instrument, really—but the vibration of the music cascading into my body in cosmic waves settles the disquiet at my center, if only for a little while.

I've grown to need it. To crave them. Because the moment they're gone, it all comes back in a suffocating swell, dragging me under, where all is dark and inescapable.

"Zev?" Dr. Weaver's voice cuts through, making me jolt. Gavin's gaze sinks into me, making me shift in place on the chair.

He hasn't touched me since we were in the water. In fact, he's kept such a wide berth, a fucking wooly mammoth could fit between us—and I don't only mean physically.

I thought we shared something. Had... some sort of connection. But with the way he's been acting, I see now it was only ever in my head. And that's a scary fuckin' thought.

"What are you thinking so hard about?" the doctor questions softly. I think through *what* truth to give her. I can't say a lot with Gavin in the room because this is supposed to be mine and his bi-weekly *therapy session.*

It's a load of shit, is what it is. And that's what I tell the doc.

"Why do you think that? You don't think this is important or valuable to you?"

"Why would it be when Gavin's been nothing but the *most professional* bodyguard to ever be hired." The words come out with a bite I don't intend to let slip, but oh well. Who the hell cares at this point? Certainly not him—or me.

"What is that supposed to mean?" Gavin grunts, still staring at the fucking wall like it's actually interesting when everyone in this fucking room knows it's just a wall.

I can't help the way I add *boy* into his question because I know three weeks ago, he would've said it.

I miss it. And him. But it doesn't matter because it was just a lie—like everything else in my life.

But this... what I have here at Black Diamond Recovery, it's real. Or as real as anything I've ever known, even if it doesn't feel complete.

"It means everything is different now. You are. I am. And it's perfectly fine." I sound petulant and pissed off.

"That's not true, Zevryn—"

"Don't fucking lie to me!" I scream. Gavin rears back, eyes going wide at my unexpected outburst. My chest is heaving. It's hard to breathe.

I blink rapidly through the sting scouring every inch of my eyes. There's a deep prickling in my optic nerve, making me dig the heels of my palms into my sockets to alleviate the throb.

"Zev—" Dr. Weaver starts but stops when Gavin holds up his hand, cutting her off, his eyes never straying from mine.

His hair is pulled tight, knotted in his usual bun at his nape, a few wayward strands framing his face. One sticks to his beard, moving with every word he says.

"I am not lying to you. There are things that are simply not your business," he grinds out through gritted teeth. I scoff, huffing out a breath. It makes the curls in front of my face fly up before settling back down.

I tuck them behind my ears, feeling self-conscious. "None of my business."

"No. We're here for your recovery—not mine. My life is not your business."

"Your life?" I ask. "So, it's personal." *I knew it, but fuck, does it hurt hearing it.*

"Zevryn." Gavin groans, dragging his hand down his face and over his beard. He pinches it at the end as he nears his chin, eyes wrinkled at the corners. "That's not what I meant."

"But that's what you said. It's fine. I get it." I swallow through the disappointment. Every word that comes out of his mouth just proves that it was all a lie. The way he held me to his chest, the words he whispered to get me through the drowning agony I was burning alive in. His fingers playing with my hair as I suckled on his nipple, higher than I'd ever been, but in a much better, *safer* way.

And he doesn't even fucking *know* that that happened to me. I was too scared to say anything in fear that he'd take it away or ensure it never happened again. Or even worse, tell Dr. Weaver and she'd just fucking tell us both how unhealthy our relationship was—not that we even have one of those because my two-faced bodyguard is married.

"Gavin." Dr. Weaver diverts her attention to him, startling us both. He lifts a brow, shifting in his chair to face her. "Have you ever divulged anything personal to Zev?" His fingers curl into the fabric, but otherwise, his face remains blank.

"He knows some things," he replies easily, and I snort, making him scowl.

"Like?"

Gavin shifts again, appearing uncomfortable. I scoot up in my chair, resting my chin on my knees as I take in their exchange, grateful as fuck the questions aren't being directed toward me for once.

Yeah, Gavin. What do *I know about you? Other than you're selfish and kind of perfect and utterly aggravating.*

"Uh..." He glances down at his watch, probably checking the time. I snicker, smiling even wider at his glare. "He knows I'm married."

Dr. Weaver's perfectly plucked eyebrows arch on that one, making me curl my lips in. "You're married."

"Yes," he snaps, twisting that goddamn ring. "You'd think as a therapist, you'd notice the ring on my finger."

"Oh, I noticed the ring, Gavin. But thank you for bringing it up. You don't think your relationship interferes with your bond with Zev? Or even the other way around?" Dr. Weaver doesn't take his bait.

"No." Gavin doesn't elaborate.

"No, Dr. Weaver. It doesn't matter because there is *nothing* between me and Gavin. He's my bodyguard, and that's all. *There is no bond.*" I can feel Gavin's eyes drilling into the side of my head, but I stay focused on the counselor until the tell-tale sound of Gavin's watch buzzing signals the end of the session.

He silents it quickly, not moving from his spot.

"Well, thanks, doc. See ya in a few days." I push out of the chair and hightail it for the door.

She sighs. "See you soon, Zev. Gavin."

He's hot on my trail. I can feel his looming presence like molten lava. I shove through the door and keep near the wall, my head down as I work through the maze of halls. I've been here a month and still get fucking lost, and honestly, if it weren't for Gavin always veering me in the right direction, I'd never find my way.

"Zev, slow down." My steps falter at the sound of him saying my nickname—something he's *never* done. I'm either Zevryn or boy, and lately, it's only been Zevryn, much to my disappointment. Which pisses me off because I know I *can't* want that.

"Can't. Got activity," I tell him as I push outside, heading toward the trail. This afternoon is the wilderness hike, and I'm actually looking forward to it. I've traveled the trails but not far because I couldn't get lost in the vibrance of nature with Gavin's stiff ass up mine.

When thick, hot fingers sear a scar into my skin with their grip, I falter to a stop. We're a few feet off from the small group gathered near the entrance to the jungle, a few people leaned in and talking to themselves quietly. I vaguely hear the name Josiah and the hushed mention of weed, which has my mouth salivating before I'm yanked away and shoved against a tree.

"Are you trying to piss me off?" Gavin growls in my ear, his large frame curled so perfectly around me, I know if someone were to look over here, they probably wouldn't be able to see anything other than my shoes.

The thought has my breath coming out faster, heavier. He's so big and soft and... *Fuck. Is my face flushed?*

"Why would I do that, Gavin?" I cock my head to the side, biting back a hiss as the wood scrapes against my scalp, curls tugging as they're caught on sharp edges.

At least when you're pissed at me, I know *you feel something,* I want to say more than anything, the words resting just on the edge of my lips, but by some miracle I can't fathom, I'm able to hold them back.

He lowers his head, eyes narrowing into slits. A strand of his hair sticks to my stubbled cheek as he leans in closer, arms bracketing me in. "You're pushing me, boy, and I only have so much patience when it comes to you."

Boy...

Oh, gods. I'm gonna cave. I'm so weak for him.

I inhale his scent and immediately regret it. "Really? I thought you had an endless amount with the way you've been acting toward me. Ignoring me with that stick up your fucking ass." I try to push him away, but the second my fingers connect with the soft fabric of his T-shirt and I graze his supple yet rock-hard skin just beneath, I lose all resolve. Each modicum drains out of my body in an instant.

"All right, folks. Let's get started!" Sterling, the events coordinator shouts. Gavin doesn't budge. I try to look over his bulging bicep at the moving group, but he presses even closer, blocking everyone but him out completely.

"Fucking asshole," I growl, tired of it all. The cold shoulder after what we shared and now this alpha, macho bullshit.

"Excuse you?" he snaps, eyes bugging wide, top lip curled.

"I don't need this shit, Gavin!" Unfisting his shirt takes effort. I honestly don't know how I manage it, but when I'm free from the suffocating tangle, I shove my hands against his chest, over and over until his looming shadow drifts further away until there's enough of a gap, I can slip through.

I run toward the mouth of the trail, nearly tripping over the foliage scattered just around the bend. I can barely make out the tail ends of conversation, the group already far ahead in their hike, uncaring I was left behind. But the freedom they allow here is one of the things I like most about Black Diamond.

As long as I keep up with mandatory activities, the rest of my time here is pretty much mine. The trust given to be able to heal in our own way really sets the path for a long recovery.

Knowing that *someone*—whether you know them well or not—trusts you, makes you *want* to try.

Righting myself with a huff, I book it along. Tucking my hair behind my ears to keep it out of my eyes, my fingers graze the soft hairs growing in on the side of my head. I tug against the short strands, undecided if I hate that it's growing out or not.

I always shaved the side of my head to piss off my father, but being away from him with a clear head and absolutely no contact sheds light on how... different I am when he's not around to eclipse me.

A sense of peace settles over me as I delve deeper into the jungle, the buzzing of bugs and animals flitting around.

Sunlight beams down between the breaks in the foliage, almost blinding with the intensity.

Footsteps thud along the path behind me, only ensuring my tranquility despite our previous interaction.

I've wanted to hate Gavin for the cold shoulder he's given me, but I also understand. It's something Dr. Weaver and I have discussed heavily the last two weeks when keeping it all to myself clearly wasn't working when I felt as low as the ocean floor.

I like talking to her, getting everything off my chest. Already the oppressing weight of Mom's death feels surmountable. Like every day that passes, it feels a little less. Even more so, she's given me homework that... I don't exactly like *doing,* but I *do* like that it makes me think.

She has me write down everything that comes to mind between our sessions that directly correlates to my mood or a certain thought that doesn't sit well with me, no matter how random or seemingly insignificant.

I've written so much, I think I have carpal tunnel. But the words written within the pages of the black and white composition notebook she gave me... those words are my truth. The good, the bad, the ugly—and there's a lot of that.

It's who I really am, flaws and all. But accepting that is an entirely different story. Especially when Gavin takes up a lot of space within those pages.

Dr. Weaver's never asked me to share what I've written, but I have more often than not. The one thing I'm actually scared to talk to her about isn't my addiction to coke or alcohol. It's not my hate for my father—or even my mother.

It's the high that suckling on Gavin gave me.

I... can't have her tell me it's not good for me. It'll ruin what it was, even if it was only a blip in time. It's a blip I think about every time I close my eyes. Every time I look into Gavin's. When we get close enough to touch. When his eyes dip down to my mouth mid-conversation.

I need *something* to hold onto. A good memory I've formed here that helps dull the ache of every past mistake I've manufactured. And Gavin houses every single one of them.

The bed, the beach... his light, carefree banter.

It's like we were friends... only so much fucking more.

But it wasn't a truth—merely a diversion from it.

Birds chirp over the cascading rush of water. I crane my neck upward. Colorful wings flap elegantly in vivid colors I never knew was possible, and my mouth drops open in awe. The thick, almost choking scent of flowers sticks to my tongue, flooding my mouth with its perfume.

Talons rake across my scalp, drawing a scream from my throat as my hair is pulled, yanking a few strands loose, but before my scream has time to form into anything other than a rough croak, fingers scrape across my throat, clasping tightly against my pulse point.

"Is this what you wanted from me, boy?" Teeth sink into my earlobe. I jolt, pressing my Adam's apple deeper into my throat, choking me further.

Gooseflesh stings my skin as it breaks out far and wide, traveling to every inch Gavin touches and beyond.

"You want *feelings* from me? Well how about *pissed off.*" An arm bounds around my waist, using that as leverage to push me off the trail and into the trees. I stumble over the upturned dirt, but Gavin's arm tightens automatically, catching every misstep.

My heart's in my throat, my stomach, my fucking balls as they all throb and pulse in tandem with every heavy step he takes, dragging me through the jungle until we're fully covered by Earth's creation.

I barely have enough time to lift my arms to catch myself before my front is slammed into a tree. The trunk isn't thick, but it's enough to grip as my entire front is shoved against it.

"You don't need this, is that it?" Hot breath whispers into my ear, wet lips grazing my flesh with every curve of his mouth.

I drop my head against the bark, shivering despite the way I'm burning up.

"You think I fucking need this? You think I need everything complicated and muddled?" His teeth scrape over my shoulder in warning. It only makes me hotter.

"This isn't fucking easy for me, boy. It's all messy and confusing, and I was *trying* to do right by you *and* my fucking husband, but you can't let me, can you? You're so needy, you don't care how badly it fucks me up as long as you get what you need, right?" He sinks his teeth in, and I cry out, throwing my head back. His hand slams down over my mouth, muffling the sound as it tears from my throat.

My chest heaves, pain and desire coursing through my bloodstream, dulling every sense except for touch and taste—those are magnified tenfold.

Gavin is all that exists in my world, and I'm flying high on everything he gives me with no regard for the consequences.

"Tell me, boy." Fingertips dig into the hollows of my cheeks, causing my teeth to sink into the soft, inner flesh of my mouth.

"W-what?" I pant the question, which comes out muffled through his hand.

"Tell me you don't care how bad this is. That you want it anyway because I'm so fucking tired of resisting you."

My eyes roll into the back of my head hearing his words. There is no way this is real. "Gavin," I whine, pressing back against him. His cock nudges against my ass, hard and hot through the fabric of our clothes.

I'm burning up, sweat trickling down my temples and splashing onto my shoulders. Gavin's tongue swipes against a drop, making me shudder, my head rolling to the side to give him full access to my throat.

He drops his hand to circle it around my nape, shoving me harder into the tree. The rough scrape against my cheek sends me higher, my thoughts jumbling until nothing makes sense.

"Yes. Please. I-I need..." Gavin presses closer, every inch of him barricading me.

"Tell me what you need."

"You. Just you."

His groan rumbles through his chest. My eyelids droop, body going slack, the tree and the pressure of Gavin's body the only thing keeping me upright.

The rush of water cuts through our labored breathing, bringing a steadiness to the mounting intensity.

"I've been trying to keep you safe. Do what's best for you —and for me." A deep breath. "But you keep pushing..." He mouths at my neck with harsh swipes of his tongue, nails scraping across my over-sensitized skin.

Every second that passes sends me higher, the pain of

the last three weeks nearly nonexistent as Gavin erases every moment spent apart.

This is real.

Gavin steps away from me, leaving me cold and alone. I whimper at the loss of him, tears pricking my eyes at having him ripped from me again, the tree I'm holding onto my only comfort.

Not again... I can't do this again.

A sharp crack rings out, and then my ass is engulfed in flames. My eyes fly open as I lurch forward, pulling away from the heat—but it spreads rapidly, seeping deep into my muscle. "Fuck!"

Another swat comes down, a hair gentler this time, but it still stings like a motherfucker. I try to pull away, but Gavin's hand on my nape keeps me pinned exactly where he wants me—which is against a tree that'll leave its mark the same as he does.

"Watch your mouth!" he barks, hitting my ass two more times. I clench my ass in a pathetic attempt to divert his palm, but the flexing of the muscles only makes the throbbing heat worse.

Fuck, it hurts.

I whimper, squeezing my eyes shut as tears pool over the surface, clumping my eyelashes.

I don't realize how badly I needed Gavin's touch until he's pressing against my left side, lowering his head until his forehead rests against the top of my head. His broad chest is heaving, each panting breath fanning across my face, making me boil.

He drops his hand to my ass, rubbing over my shorts. The friction of my clothes dragging over my tender flesh makes me hiss, but Gavin's touch is a livewire straight to my cock. I didn't even realize I was throbbing until he touched me so gently, rubbing the soreness in.

I arch back into his touch, needing more. He brings his hand down again, but it's softer with almost no weight behind it. I wriggle, forcing his hand to brush across both cheeks. His warm chuckle travels into my ear. Goosebumps skitter over my scalp, raising my hair and sending chills across my body.

"Please," I plead, pushing back again. "Hit me. Hurt me..."

"Does my boy need his ass beat? Would that help you feel better? Clear out all the bad thoughts fogging your brain?" He kneads my ass, digging deep into the tissue.

"You... you know..." I trip over my words, unable to form a sentence with the way my leaden tongue sits heavily in my mouth, my psyche already drifting away.

"Yeah, baby. I fucking know." With a hard, lingering kiss to the top of my curls, Gavin holds the side of my neck in place as his other hand rains down over my ass.

He starts off softer than he started, each swat warm and tingling as he gradually builds up to hot and heavy. My vision glazes over, growing fuzzy at the edges, my body no longer my own.

My eyes roll into the back of my head, my only tether Gavin's hands. One keeps me immobilized, while the other sends me to a place I've only ever been once before.

Where nothing exists but Gavin and this rapturous elation.

Thirteen

GAVIN

Each whimpering grunt that spills from between his scraped lips settles deep in my gut, unfurling warmth and sedation.

"You sound so beautiful," I purr in his ear as I drag his shorts and briefs down over the swell of his ass. The elastic waistband settles just under the crease of his smooth, round cheeks bloomed crimson in the shape of my fingers. My palm connects with his bare flesh, and the crack that rings out has my head dropping back between my shoulders, a groan vibrating my lungs.

Zevryn has long since stopped crying out. His cries transformed into wonderful pants and whimpers—sounds I never knew I needed to feel whole.

His eyes are glazed when they're not rolled into the back of his head.

Still keeping hold of his throat, I shuffle in the dirt, scraping my body against his over-sensitized skin as I lean over him, lips to the back of his sweaty neck. His flush extends all over his body, coloring his pale skin pink.

My slaps have slowed into a deep, rough massage, kneading the blistering heat into his muscles. Every time I press too deep, he twitches, tensing up.

I chuckle deeply, scraping my beard over his shoulders. "Feeling better?"

He doesn't answer for a long moment. "*Mmm.*"

My eyes droop, loving the sound of my boy feeling good. I delve into his hair, gripping the strands to pull his head back. His Adam's apple bulges from the strain, creating a beautiful array of ridges in his slender neck. I trace each one slowly with my index finger.

When I reach his chin, I dig my blunt nail in to create a puffy, red line from the dimple in his chin to the furrowed crease between his dark brows.

His pale eyelids peel open at the halt of my touch, revealing pupils so blown, they eat up over half of his hazel irises. They have a glassy sheen, one I've seen in them before, but this time, it's different. Clearer in a way it never was.

It looks *right.*

I lean in close. "How are you feeling, boy." It's not a question. This time, I need a real answer so I know I didn't fuck him up—fuck all of this up before it ever really started.

As I wait, not very patiently, I continue my massage, each pass of my hand nearing the crease of his ass. "Zevryn." I mouth his name into the flesh of his shoulder, sweat smearing across my mouth.

He nods, eyes falling closed like keeping them open takes too much effort. "Yeah," he breathes.

"Too much?" I ask as I slip a finger between his cheeks. Damp warmth meets my fingers, and something akin to guilt hammers away in my throat, but the oppressing feeling isn't enough to stop me. Zevryn's breath catches in his throat. A strangled noise escapes in its place.

"What about this, boy? This too much for you to handle?" I dig in deep, unable to contain my growl at the soft, damp hairs surrounding his tight furl. I scrape a nail over his entrance, relishing in the way his back bows, pushing the tip of my finger just inside.

"Oh, gods!" he shouts at the same time I lose all sense of reason. Something in me snaps.

"The gods have nothing on me, boy. You won't even remember your fucking name when I'm through with you." I yank my hand from between his cheeks to reach around and shove my fingers into his mouth, fighting against the clash of teeth as he tries to bite down. "Don't be a brat, baby," I growl as I sink them into the back of his throat until he retches. The second the constriction releases, I push deeper, remaining in through his choking gags.

"Just tap my arm if it becomes too much," I whisper the words into his ear before pressing a kiss to the delicate skin.

Zevryn needs to know that even like this, he *always* holds all control.

Once the tendons in his temples bulge and pulse from the lack of oxygen, I drag my fingers from his mouth, smearing his thick spit over his lips and down his dimpled chin before I take my arm away and thrust my fingers between his cheeks, soaking his skin as I press against his furl.

I wrap my own fingers around the trunk of the tree,

needing stability for myself as I circle my boy's tight, little hole. It flutters against the pad of my finger, teasing and taunting, just begging for my attention. And who am I to deny my boy?

The first ring of muscle I breach traps the air in my lungs. It builds in pressure and intensity as Zevryn's silky heat envelops my finger. He ripples around me, groaning and sinking heavier against the tree. When my knuckles bump against his crease, I pull out, a smile twitching on my lips as I slam back in, this time with two.

Zevryn shouts, the sound echoing through the jungle in a reverberant melody. His muscle stretches, accommodating the extra thickness, but I know he feels the sharp ache deep inside.

I want to stain my essence on and in every inch of him.

I dig my fingers around inside him, preening when I rub against his gland. Zevryn shoots to his toes, lurching up the tree. I hear the way the rough wood scrapes over his skin, the sharpness only heightening the fervor devouring him.

I chuckle, feeling wild and untamed as I bruise my boy's prostate with reckless abandon. The boy grabs onto my hand for support as his legs buckle beneath him. His nails dig into my flesh, shredding the first layer of skin. I hiss, baring my teeth.

Zevryn whimpers as he brushes over the gold band against my knuckle. Him touching that single reminder that this isn't what it should be has my eyes widening and my heart thundering just below my throat, low enough I can breathe, but it still feels like it's choking me.

He doesn't falter as he pulls against my hand. I release

the tension in my muscles and let him pull me wherever he wants.

Maybe this will be over before it even started—and it's my own fault. But the lines between my loyalties have long since crashed and burned since the moment I got my hands on my lonely boy and he wanted this as much as me... even after I pushed him away.

But what choice did I have?

I've never had one where Zevryn is concerned.

With dark lashes staining his damp cheekbones, Zevryn sucks my finger—oh, *fuck... that* finger—into his mouth. He hollows his cheeks as he increases suction, dragging his plump lips down over each thick knuckle until he reaches the ring that sits like a caveat between us.

He drags his eyelids open, dilated, hazel eyes shining with mindless devotion. He twirls his tongue around the band, tonguing the edge and making it slide up on my finger.

A rumbling growl vibrates my chest, sending white-hot heat straight to my cock. I curl my fingers inside him, spreading them to stretch him out. My boy cries out, causing my finger to slip from between his spit-soaked lips. He pants heavily in the small space between us, black curls unruly. A perfect fusion to the untapped wilderness we're losing ourselves in—because that's exactly what we're doing.

Falling so fucking deep into an impossible trench I never want to crawl my way out of.

"Mine..." That single word is said like a question, a soft lilt to his raspy voice. My heart slams against my breastbone, stealing my breath—or what little I had left. His eyes hold questions I can't answer.

"I'm yours, my boy. And you're fucking mine." Zevryn's wide eyes light up. His lips part as he turns his head. I shove my finger back into his mouth, already knowing what he was searching for. The resounding hum vibrating my digit shoots straight to my cock.

"Remember, tap if it's too much, and I'll stop." I wait until he nods his head, showing me he understands, before I allow my brain to shut off. Between his ass sucking at my fingers and his body, sweaty and slick against mine, I'm nearing the edge of my control, the thread whittled desperately thin.

I curve around Zevryn, sinking my teeth into the exposed skin of his shoulder, not letting go as I fuck him with my fingers, pushing in a third as he sucks in a breath through his flared nostrils. I know it has to sting without proper lubrication, but he seems to welcome the ache. His skin is soft and pliant, the muscle beneath tense as my teeth dig deeper until copper explodes on my tongue.

I growl, thrusting my hips, grinding my cock against his bare waist. The material of my jeans is thick, the zipper digging painfully into my throbbing flesh, but the bite of pain just sends me higher.

Ripping my finger from his hot, wet mouth, I reach between us to shove my jeans down, fighting with the button before groaning in relief when the humid, tropical air caresses my throbbing flesh. The dull thud of my holster hitting the ground is merely background noise.

Zevryn's fingers dig into my wrist as he brings my hand back to his mouth, this time sucking three fingers to the back of his throat. He gags before pulling back for a breath, then immediately dives back in.

Sensation licks all around us, our mutual sounds flooding with those of nature.

My cock drags over his hip as I angle my hips towards his ass. I hunch down, dragging my length across his taint. My head nudges against his balls. They're hot and drawn up tight, more than ready to release his load for me.

Blood coats my lips as I drag my mouth over his traps until my nose is buried in his hair, my front to his back, my hand still shoved between us. Hooking my fingers in his hole and pressing the edge of my thumb to his swollen rim, I pull against the tissue, making Zevryn cry out.

I grin wickedly, pressing a nipping kiss to his neck before digging my chin into the top of his head, forcing his face harder against the bark. He whimpers, muscles loosening the harder my fingers drill into his channel, and my cock drags back and forth over his taint.

Green and black fill my vision as heat burns through me with fervor. My thrusts get shorter and harder. My hand cramps and aches, making me growl as I home in on his prostate, nailing it with accuracy.

My soaked hand falls from his mouth as Zevryn wails, the sound like music to my ears. I wrap my wet fingers around his throat, squeezing the sides until he stops breathing and I know his head swims from dysphoria.

When the whites of his eyes are all I see, I press harder against his swollen, abused gland, still fucking ruthlessly between his legs, my dick chafed from the friction. "Come on my fingers, boy," I growl.

Zevryn's ass milks my fingers like a cock as he comes, spraying the jungle floor with his seed. His textured, silk walls squeeze my fingers so tight, I can't move them. The smell of his sex—all man, salt, and musk—wafts into my nose, blackening everything around me.

I lose it all as I fuck the tight space between my boy's thighs, the crease of his ass slick from spit and sweat that pools off Zevryn's back in rivulets. "Fuck, you're gonna make me come."

I throw my head back, letting a deep, echoing roar rip from my throat as my release barrels through me. The base of my spine pulses in drugging waves as my balls unload, my dick jerking uncontrollably as my orgasm keeps throbbing, never-ending and blinding.

The sound of rushing water and animals rustling through the jungle comes back in small, dousing waves. More potent is Zevryn's skin stuck to mine, the way his hammering heart radiates throughout his entire body.

I slowly peel my eyes open, and the first thing I see is a small smattering of freckles trailing the ridges of his spine. I trace them with my tongue, lapping the salt from his skin as I force my weight off his body.

He may be filling out now that he's sober, actually *eating* and working out, but I'm still a great deal larger, and I don't want to *really* hurt him.

My eyes catch on the two crescents oozing blood in the shape of my teeth on his shoulder and the sharp, puffy scratches marring his skin.

Okay, maybe a little.

Zevryn's trembling pulls me out of my reverie. I unpeel myself from his flushed skin with much regret. It takes my shaking hands way too long to do the button on my jeans and readjust the holster on my hip before I dip down to gently drag Zevryn's shorts back over his hips, painfully forcing myself to ignore the mess dripping from his thighs. He hisses as the fabric drags over his inflamed ass, the skin swollen and radiating heat.

Once his shorts are in place and settled, I wrap my hands around his biceps and pull him away from the tree. My eyes catch on the pool of his cum decorating the scattered leaves and palm fronds—a milky, elegant contrast.

Swallowing the emotion tightening my throat, I grasp his chin so I can see his eyes. They're closed, lashes clumpy and wet, streaked with tears, skin blemished from the rough bark. I inhale deeply at the sight of my boy irrevocably wrecked.

"You came so beautifully for me, boy. Thank you." I kiss his forehead, feeling a peace I didn't know existed in this world. Zevryn's lower lip trembles, and his legs give out. I easily haul him into my arms. He drops his head to my chest, burying his face.

"Ar-are you still m-mad at me?" he chokes the words out through silent sobs, and my heart splits right in half. I tighten my hold as I turn us around, taking the non-existent path back to the trail we were *supposed* to walk.

"No, baby, of course not. I was never mad at you. Just myself." My jaw locks as true, blinding guilt creeps in—and not because of my ring, now sticky with my boy's saliva. He settles even deeper at my confession, nuzzling me.

"Did I hurt you?" I ask as I step onto the trail, heading back toward the entrance. Fear niggles in my brain, but it's hard to think past the numbing fog wrapped around me and dug deep within.

"*Mmm,*" he hums, no longer moving, still as can be with my every jolting footstep.

"Baby." I nudge his head with my chin, worrying my bottom lip. His eyes crack open, bright and clear, but still trapped in that haze I saw earlier.

I wonder if it's the same as mine.

"Did I hurt you?"

"*Mm,* yeah. Perfect."

I round the bend, eyes scanning the greenery fervently, but we're still alone. "You liked it?"

"So high," he whispers so quietly, I'm not sure I heard him correctly. I think I know what he means if the way *I'm feeling* is anything to go by, but the phrase he used has me erring on the side of caution.

With him, I have to be certain of *everything.* There's no room for doubt when Zevryn's mind is already in such a fragile state.

"I'll take care of you, boy," I promise him easily, never more sure of a commitment in my life.

The walk to the villa is long since I stay along the bordering jungle, trying to steer clear from prying eyes. Zevryn's in a vulnerable place right now, and I know he wouldn't want others seeing him this way.

Splitting my focus between the boy in my arms and the world around us is harder than I thought it would be. I want every part of me tending to him, but first, I have to get him home.

Safety concerns on this island haven't been an issue since we arrived. Of course, I'm still cautious because it's my job to be and I have a very important—the most important—boy to protect, but it's easier to let go a bit while we're here.

Secluded and surrounded by nature and other people focusing on themselves.

Watching Zevryn work through things all on his own these last few weeks has altered my state of mind.

I've kept myself away because I knew it was the right thing to do. He's vulnerable as he recovers and works through his traumas and addictions, and I was merely a crutch. Unintentionally, but intent doesn't matter when the result is the same.

I hurt him. I saw it every day with his lingering glances and down-turned lips. With every snarky, bratty word passed from his lips. Every fitful night's rest as he called out for no one in particular, but I knew it was for me.

I should've fucking controlled myself. And there's no excuse for it other than he makes me weak. Vulnerable and susceptible to his unintentional pleas.

Zevryn's eyelashes flutter against his cheeks, the simple, gentle movement vying for my attention. *And now that I've had him, I know I won't let him go. Consequences be damned.*

The door to our villa unlocks easily with a wave of my wrist, the black band on my wrist and Zevryn's the only way to enter. Holding my boy steadily in my arms, I lift my foot to kick the door closed before flipping the lock again.

The open layout of the villa makes scoping for possible threats easy, Zevryn pinned to my chest as I do. The curtains are still drawn, blocking out most of the setting sun and keeping the space cool and dark.

I carry Zevryn into the large bathroom area, setting him gently on the countertop. He sways, eyes closed, skin still beautifully flushed. I hold onto his waist with one hand as I drag his tank over his head and drop it to the floor at my feet.

The rustle of clothes has Zev's eyes fluttering open. They're unfocused but locked on me as I lift him off the porcelain to pull his shorts down, followed by his tight, little briefs. He sucks in a breath when his raw, bare ass meets the cool countertop.

"*Nngh,*" he groans.

"Shh, boy. Just let me take care of you. Here." I wrap his arms around my neck. "Hold onto me." I cup my hands just under the crease of his ass and lift him against me. His cum-stained thighs wrap around me easily, smearing my release all over my jeans, but I couldn't care less with him in my arms.

I try to sit Zevryn on the edge of the oval bathtub, which is large enough to fit the two of us, but the second my grip loosens, he whines and tightens his arms. I sigh warmly, simply tightening my hold as I bend over to flip on the tap.

Water rushes out, filling the basin steadily. I adjust the temperature and add some lavender bath oil before turning around to sit, letting Zevryn cling to me as the tub fills. The soothing scent of lavender fuses with the ever-present scent of the sea, but both of those potent smells have nothing on the sex oozing from my boy's pores.

When the water reaches halfway up the porcelain, I ease Zevryn's hands from around my neck. He digs his fingers into my wrists, clutching desperately. I kiss the top of his head. "I'm not going anywhere. Let me clean you up."

With a soft whimper, he lets me set him in the warm water. He falls back, splaying himself as wide as he can as the water laps against his nipple ring. The sight of it alone has my spent dick twitching against my zipper, but now is not the time. Not when my boy needs to be taken care of.

I settle on my knees beside the bathtub as I reach for a cup to pour water over Zevryn's uncovered torso.

Goosebumps rush out, pimpling his skin. A contented smile pulls at my lips as I bathe my boy, washing our cum and sweat from his body.

When the water cascades over his shoulder, he hisses, lurching. My hands still, heart thumping heavily against my ribs as I slowly sit him up to trace the wound. It isn't terribly deep, but the ridges are stark, and I'm worried it will scar.

"S'okay," he murmurs into my ear, wet lips brushing my skin. Water drips into my beard as I hold Zevryn's face against mine.

"You're perfect." The depth behind those words clogs my throat, and I blink a few times to clear the potency.

The boy is lost in my arms as I wash every inch of him. I work the suds deep into his curls, massaging his scalp to ensure I get every bit of dirt and grime, and do much of the same as I drag the cloth over his body, inch by inch.

By the time I reach his groin, he's hard, his long, slender cock bobbing in the water. I grip the base and drag the cloth over his hardness, paying extra attention to the ridges of his bulbous head. Zevryn shudders, moaning and wriggling in the water, sending small waves lapping against the side of the tub.

"Hold still, boy," I admonish him gently but release him to move onto his balls. They're heavy as I lift them and scrub his taint before dragging the cloth across his hole.

Zevryn lurches, his rim twitching repeatedly against my finger as I gently rub, cleaning as gently as I can. But it doesn't matter how tender I am; Zevryn is just so responsive, he's nearly inconsolable by the time he's finally all clean.

His pretty, little cock is red and swollen, a thick vein running down the shaft pulsing with his impending release.

I lick my lips, tongue scraping against my mustache. I suck my bottom lip into my mouth, sinking my teeth into the flesh.

I can't let my boy suffer like this.

"It's okay, baby. I've got you," I murmur as I wrap my fingers around my boy's cock and stroke upward. "You can let go for me." I don't make it past three upstrokes before the muscles in his thighs go rigid, and his length pulses so beautifully in my hand.

I'm rapt as I watch his cum spurt from the slit in his cockhead, creamy and thick as it shoots into the water.

When he's finally done twitching with aftershocks, my hand slowly working him through it, I grab him under his armpits and haul him to his feet. He has a dopey smile on his face as I wrap a fluffy, white towel around his shoulders and help him step out of the tub. Water drips all over the floor as I grab another and work on drying the excess water from his hair.

I've never seen someone look so at peace as I have right now. Zevryn looks blissed the fuck out, and I know exactly how he feels.

It's an indescribable feeling, but him saying he felt high… it makes sense. And I now know with certainty, *this* kind of high is the best thing for him.

And I can always give him what he needs.

At least while we're at Black Diamond.

He holds his arms out for me as I drag the towel down each arm, legs spread as I work between them, finishing off by drying his cock and in between his cheeks. I drop to my knees behind him after I toss the towel in the hamper. My eyes scour over the swollen handprints marring his pale flesh, spreading outward in the shape of my fingers. I trace a crimson mark near the base of his spine, swallowing a groan when he leans into the touch.

I spread his cheeks and lean in to inspect his hole. My thumb brushes his rim, and Zevryn half hisses, half moans. It's puffy and red, surrounded by a few dark hairs that I want to twirl around my tongue.

The thought makes me pull back with regret, but my boy needs rest. I push to my feet and cradle him in my arms as I take him to bed. It's unmade because Zevryn isn't the type to make it. Ever. Simply arguing, *"What's the point when I'm just going to sleep in it again tonight?"*

He wouldn't listen to my rebuttal, but that's not surprising, either.

With feigned annoyance, I drop him on the soft mattress and pull the unkept blanket over him as soon as I pull the towel off. Zevryn shivers as he dives deeper under the blanket, pulling it up to his chin.

I smile warmly down at him, dragging my thumb back and forth over his stubbled cheek, every pass swiping across his full, bottom lip. He looks at me like I'm the center of his world, and I want nothing more than for that to be true.

As I pull back, Zevryn whimpers, reaching out. "What, baby?" My eyes prick.

"Please don't leave me." The words are almost inaudible, but they lance my heart all the same.

I drop my clothes to the floor in a rush before climbing in next to him. Spreading my legs, I pull him between them, sighing as he rests his full weight against me, his skin still radiating warmth from the bath.

"I'm not going anywhere, boy." My fingers find his curls,

and I brush through the wet, silky strands until the tips feel numb and Zev is all but purring. He turns his head, searching, and I breathe out heavily in relief as he mouths my nipple.

"Go ahead, boy." I rumble deep in my chest, groaning silently when Zev latches on, suckling me in gentle pulls. He melts against me as the last piece of awareness shatters, disappearing to a place we're long gone from.

I hold him to my chest as I lean against the headboard, eyes closed in rapturous bliss as my boy finds his peace within me, and me in him.

Fourteen

ZEVRYN

My ass may be on fire, but I have never felt more centered in my life.

Air rushes in and out of my lungs heavily but evenly as my feet slam down on the treadmill. Sweat licks along my skin, slipping into every crevice. It stings where it seeps into the teeth-shaped cuts on my shoulder, but I don't mind. It's a reminder of how Gavin couldn't control himself.

My blood runs hotter than my ass as our eyes meet in the mirror just to my right. He's across the room, thick fingers curled around a dumbbell as he curls it toward his bicep. Drool nearly drips from my mouth at the sight of his veins bulging.

When he catches me staring, he shoots me a wink, and I fucking trip over my own goddamn heart. My feet tangle, and I slip on the rotating belt, narrowly missing the handrail as I manage to right myself at the last second.

Gavin's slamming his finger down on the emergency stop

button before I can even take a breath. The belt stops beneath me, and I jolt, panting.

"Are you okay?" He dips down to meet my eyes, which are drilling holes into my own shoes, face burning with embarrassment. I make an ass of myself far too often around Gavin, something I've never thought would bother me before.

But I guess that's another reality I have to learn to accept. How much *more* everything is when you're not numb to feeling.

I thought when I was high—or drunk—I *did* feel. That's what I liked about it. How different it all was.

Everything around me was less important, while what was happening *inside* me was the center of all my focus. Liquor made me numb while the coke sent me flying. Not always at the same time, but there toward the end, it was.

I swallow the lump in my throat, my mouth dry and aching for the all-too-familiar drip.

Fingers grasp my chin, yanking my head up. I flinch when Gavin's steely gaze burns into me. "Where's your head, boy?"

I try to shake my head. I don't want to talk about this. About the way I'm feeling—or *not* feeling—but just like I knew, Gavin doesn't budge.

"It's not up for debate. You need to talk to me."

"I'm embarrassed. And feeling that way makes me want to get high." I choke on the words; admitting them hurts worse than the act of humiliation itself.

Gavin's eyes crinkle, the crow's feet at the corners deepening. "Baby..." He drags his thumb back and forth over my stubbled jawline. The rhythmic brushing of his calloused skin eases the pressure building rapidly. "You have nothing to be embarrassed about. You tripped; it happens. And I kind of like knowing it was because you were staring so hard at me." He flips me a wink and a small grin, his mustache twitching with his top lip.

He leans in until his lips are pressed to my pierced ear. "And if it makes you feel better, I fell flat on my ass a few weeks ago when I was chasing you out of the villa. Think I even bruised my tailbone, but definitely my ego."

The picture he's painted obliterates every pathetic doubt in my mind. I giggle, imagining Gavin's face after the fact, the utter bewilderment I'm sure was present.

With his bottom lip trapped between his teeth, he watches me so intently. The path his eyes take over every inch of my face sends me a little higher.

I bask in the attention Gavin gives me, each moment engraving itself into my core.

He takes care of me like no one ever has, and I already know I'm falling for it—for him. Too fast and too hard. When I *know* it's impossible.

He's married. To a really fucking hot guy that seems genuinely nice. There's no way Gavin would ever give that up for someone like me.

Someone lost and broken and not worth the trouble it'd take to fix, even if I'm trying my hardest to get there on my own.

The kiss to my sweaty forehead yanks me out of my reverie. The pull from deep inside my mind back to reality is dizzying, and I clutch Gavin's forearm as my mind spins precariously.

"Are you feeling any better?" he asks quietly. The sound

of the doors being opened steals both of our attention. A guy walks in and heads to a treadmill on the opposite end of me. Gavin's eyes narrow, raking up and down over the dude before he huffs.

"Disappointed or something?" I ask with a bit more snark than I meant. Gavin arches a brow, seemingly unbothered.

"You want to try that again, this time with a little less attitude?" He pinches my ass, making me yelp at the flare-up.

"Did you like what you see, sir?" I bat my eyelashes and clasp my hands in front of myself. Gavin snorts and rolls his eyes before pushing off the treadmill.

"Only have eyes for you, boy. Just have to keep everyone else away from you."

"Oh, right. The *death threat*." I mock my father's words. That life seems so far away from here, and I really wish I didn't have to go back in a few weeks.

"Don't take it lightly, Zevryn. There may not be a threat here, but your safety is still my number one priority. I will never take you for granted."

I'm left staring at his back as he makes his way back to the weights. *No one has ever said anything like that to me before.*

Carmen and Dillon care about me—love me even. I know they do. We've been through some shit together, and that's not something I'll ever forget. And looking back, I know they were just trying to help when they involved Zion.

It's all a blur when I try to think about it, but I *know* I wasn't in a good spot. I felt it, so I can't even imagine how it looked from the outside. And I may be grateful for their intervention, but that doesn't mean I'm still not pissed off—if only because I'm allowed to be.

That's what Dr. Weaver told me anyway—that my feelings, logical or not—are always valid.

I do miss them, though, and I wish I could talk to them. But I'm not there yet.

I purse my lips as I start the treadmill again, on a lower speed this time as I ease back into it. I wonder if I should talk to Dr. Weaver about making amends—something we've started discussing not only during my sessions but in group, too.

The thought of speaking to my father, though… I'm not ready for that.

I work up a steady rhythm once more, my eyes almost rolling back with every shift of my shorts against my bare ass. I was so sore when I woke up, I couldn't stand the feel of something so compressing, so no briefs it was. And with the way Gavin's eyes are locked on my crotch, I'd say he likes it, too.

As I lick sweat from my upper lip, Gavin pulls his phone out of his pocket. With one glance at the screen, he goes stiff, and my heart sinks to my feet. He presses it to his ear and dips his head, his lips moving slowly as he speaks into the phone.

I stop the treadmill, walking with the belt as it slowly churns to a stop, and I'm left panting, worry gnawing my gut right open.

Gavin flexes his fingers before fisting them, his grip on his phone tightening. I step off and grab a towel to wipe my face, wrapping it around the back of my neck as I make my way toward my bodyguard.

When he catches sight of me moving toward him, he holds up his hand, stopping me in my tracks. Rejection instantly slams into my chest where it sits, growing in weight with each passing second.

By the time the phone call ends, I can hardly breathe, and the edges of my vision swarm with pools of tears I can no longer hold back. I blink, letting them slip down each cheek in paths of shame and dismissal.

The tension in Gavin's face hasn't eased, increasing my trepidation, even as my feet carry me toward him, his domineering strength an anchor to the threat of my abysmal trenches.

"What's wrong?" I rasp. I'm standing a mere foot away, his boots the focal point of my attention.

"Nothing, boy."

"I told you not to lie to me." I don't know where the strength comes from. Maybe it's because of the way his lie slipped so easily from his tongue, but it doesn't sit right, bringing up a cluster of unresolved emotions. My hands ball into fists at my sides.

I'm pissed off.

"Zevryn—"

"No, Gavin. You can lie to your husband all you fucking want to. About me, about what you *really* want, but don't lie to me. About any of it." With grit in my teeth and steel in my gut, I spin on my heels, giving the only man I feel anything for my back because he just doesn't get it.

I need honesty. The hard, unrelenting truth every time.

It may fucking hurt, whatever it is, but that's the point. I need to *feel* those things, experience them and work through them on my own while I still have access to help before I'm alone again.

I can't drown once I'm out of this place.

Because at the first threat of the water spilling over, I'll succumb. Out of fear, of panic. On pure instinct. And I don't *want* that anymore.

I want to be better. For Gavin. But for myself too because I think I deserve that.

"Don't walk away from me!" Gavin calls out from somewhere behind me, but I'm already pushing into the bathroom with more tears in my eyes and hate in my heart. Or at least, I wish it was hate, but it's just good old-fashioned disappointment.

In myself and my… I slam my palm against the wall, dipping my head. My nails scrape over the paint until they dig into my palms. I don't even know *who* Gavin is to me.

He's… everything, but he *can't* be. So where the fuck does that leave me?

Alone. Like I always have been—and the thought is still just as terrifying.

The door to the bathroom slams open, startling me. My head jerks toward the noise, even though I already know who I'll find. Gavin's nostrils are flared, his hair hanging loose around his shoulders.

I want to pull it. Yank until it rips from his roots just to see him grit his teeth.

"I'd like to be alone, Gavin." I hiss his name, hating how good it feels slipping from my tongue.

"There's no way in hell that's happening right now, boy." The door snaps shut with a dull echo. The once-empty space fills with the smell of him, and I can't take it a second longer.

I push up to him, shoving my finger into his chest, digging the tip into the soft, top layer of flesh. "Move. Now."

He doesn't budge a fucking inch.

"Gavin..."

"No, Zevryn. You need to talk to me. Right now. It's not up for a debate." He crosses his arms over his chest, easily pushing my hand away. Another wave of dismissal washes over.

"I'm not fucking talking to you about anything when you sit there and continue to fucking *lie* to me!" The last few words come out croaked from the strain my volume puts on my vocal cords.

"What am I lying to you about?" He sounds calm, wholly put together, and I hate the way his stability grounds the chaos.

"When you got off the phone. I asked you what was wrong—because something *clearly* was—but you *lied,*" I hiss the word like the venom it is.

Sobriety has shed so much light, and now I know how blind I was.

But no more.

"There are some things you just don't need to concern yourself with. Not right now, anyway. I want you to focus on your recovery, not your father's bullshit."

"That was my father?" I ask, voice small and meek. I haven't talked to him since I boarded the jet, and as far as I knew, he hasn't even called. But then again, I don't ask, and Gavin doesn't tell.

I think he knows how... rocky things are between me and Zion.

"Yes." He doesn't elaborate.

"What did he want?" My fingers twitch at my sides.

Gavin breathes out heavily between his lips before taking a step forward. His movement causes me to step back, and that's the dance we waltz until my back slams into a stall door, and suddenly, I'm falling inside of it.

It thuds shut with a resounding echo, the slide of the lock a cinderblock to my brain.

"Would you just let me take care of you? Let *me* worry and take some of your burdens until you're able to carry them without drowning."

His words are distant, trapped in a place I can't reach as it all comes screaming back. As my eyes stare at the porcelain toilet, all I see are white lines cut on the back, thick and screaming my name. Beckoning me for a taste.

I take a step without realizing, almost slipping as my ankle buckles.

Darien's gurgling behind me, a distant noise I willfully ignore.

The first burning rush up my nose, a hit straight to my brain like liquid fire that sends me soaring.

"Zev!"

I gasp, choking on nothing as I'm knocked back to wherever I am. I whirl around, panic sealing my throat until I can't breathe. I claw at my skin, my face, anywhere I can reach. "Baby, stop." Hands trap mine, making me cry out, fire ripping from my throat.

"Yeah, this is Gavin. I need your help. Zev's—"

I scream. So loud, my eardrums pop, and my brain inflates from the force within my body.

Fifteen

ZEVRYN

"How are you feeling, Zev? You look more clear minded." I nod, wringing my hands together in my lap. Sweat still clings to me like a second skin, and with every breath, I can smell myself, but Dr. Weaver doesn't seem to care.

"I'm okay." It's the most honest thing I've told her so far. Because I surprisingly am.

"We don't have to do this right now." Her voice is soft, giving me the courage I need to push through this.

"I know, but I want to. That isn't the first..." I trail off, trying to find the right words through the pounding in my skull.

"Panic attack," the doctor offers, and I give her a grim smile, not meeting her eyes. I focus on the ocean in the distance, the clear waves lapping in the breeze I ache to smell.

"I guess it was, huh." I huff a pathetic laugh before shaking my head and crossing my arms over my chest. I glance at the door, breathing a bit easier knowing Gavin's just on the other side. My eyes prick thinking about the way he tried to take care of me.

He was as panicked as I was, but even still, he called Dr. Weaver to help when he didn't know what to do.

He's always taking care of me.

When will it become too much of a burden?

"Do you know what triggered it?" Her hands are free of her notepad and pen. Her well-manicured fingers rest gently in her lap, her face open and expressive as she waits patiently for whatever I give her—and I think it's time I finally open up.

I've given her a lot of pieces over the last month, but I've kept some things to myself. Unsure or probably just terrified of speaking certain truths, but after the fog of my panic cleared, I realized *why* Gavin's lie stung so badly.

It's because I've done nothing but lie to myself for as long as I can remember.

"I have a lot of triggers. But this time, it was the bathroom stall. Gavin..." I swallow, flicking my eyes up to her before dropping them and rushing the words out before I lose my resolve. "Gavin pushed me into the stall. At first, all I could think about was him, but then the sound of the lock sliding shut felt like a hammer to my brain and... then, I just couldn't stop it.

"I was drowning inside my own mind. Like..." I puff out a breath between my lips. "It wasn't even pictures or a memory. I was *there,* all over again, experiencing it for the first time, only the high was different. I wasn't numb.

"I was so fucking self-aware, and yet I made all the same decisions. I snorted the coke and watched my friend die." My nose twitches as it burns. The sensation travels up the bridge of my nose to my eyes. With a blink, the tears fall.

I don't bother wiping them away.

"I'm scared once I leave this place, I'll make all the same decisions..."

"And end up right back where you were," Dr. Weaver effortlessly finishes my thought. I let out a shaky breath, bottom lip quivering.

"Yeah." *She understands...*

My heart squeezes in my chest.

"Zev, I just want you to know, the level of self-awareness you have right now is the best thing for you."

I pick at a loose thread at the end of my shorts. "What do you mean?"

"You know of the decisions you've made. How they brought you here, physically and mentally. That's an amazing realization to accomplish, and I am so proud of you for getting there on your own."

Her words knock the wind out of me. I don't know what to say for a long time, but I'm comfortable in the silence, each tick of the clock adding another clean line of separation to my thoughts.

"I'm scared of it happening again. But next time, I'll be alone in it."

"That's a reasonable fear to have. And sometimes, we don't realize something is a trigger until it's too late."

I nod, agreeing. "Yeah. Not knowing fucking sucks."

"It does, Zev. We can talk about different methods to help you. There are different forms of therapy, medication—"

The thought of medication makes me uneasy. "I don't think I want to be medicated," I tell her honestly.

"I understand, and I respect your decision. I'm not here to medicate you if that's not something you want, but just know that medication can be very beneficial." Dr. Weaver smiles warmly at me.

"Thanks. Can I think about it?"

"Of course. For as long as you need."

Knowing the decision lies wholly with me eases some of my discomfort just thinking about taking pills.

It's a crazy notion, knowing that your brain chemistry is so off, artificial chemicals are the only thing that can balance you out. It's actually terrifying.

"Mom was on pills. I think that's why I'm probably nervous to even think about taking any."

Dr. Weaver smiles warmly. "That makes sense. We've talked some about your mom over the last couple of weeks. And you mentioned you've been writing in your journal about her. Has anything new surfaced?"

I shake my head before she's finished. "No, just been thinking about the same things. How she died. Why. How we don't really have any answers and never will. I think that's what gets to me, over all the rest."

"What's that?"

"That I don't know why. I mean, she took an entire bottle of trazodone. She clearly wanted to die. Which I, unfortunately, understand more than I'd like to admit. The need to *escape*. To be done. I don't want to accept what she did, let alone relate to it, but I can't help but feel that way. And... I don't know... it makes it easier to think about. Like it doesn't sting as much because after all these years; my head's finally clear enough to understand."

Dr. Weaver blinks at me for a moment, then her face

curves into a wholesome, bright smile. "That, Zev, is what we call a breakthrough."

I scoff and shake my head, dropping my eyes. But her words warm a coldness inside me. Fills part of the hollow. Silence settles around us as I churn through my thoughts. I don't feel different, but I do. Maybe a little.

It's... nice. Feeling a sliver of peace. Just a taste of what I could have. But peace makes me think of Gavin and what *we* share. What he did...

"Gavin lied to me," I blurt. "And I think it bothers me because that's all everyone has ever done. All *I've* ever done. I've lied about my addiction. My mom lied about hers. Zion... every word that comes out of his mouth is a fucking lie, and my best friends lied to my face to get me here."

The chair creaks as I uncross my legs, feet slapping the floor as I stretch my legs out. My shorts chafe against my bare ass, sending a wave of heat radiating outward.

"That's a lot to unpack, but it's all within the same focus: lying."

"Yep." I pop the P.

"Did you ask Gavin why he lied to you?"

"I think he said there were some things he didn't want to concern me with because of my recovery. It was about Zion. But I don't think that's fair. Is it?" I look up at the counselor for guidance.

"Why don't you tell me what you think?"

I roll my eyes. Typical therapist's response. "I thought you were supposed to have the answers to my questions."

"I'm not a mind reader. Besides, I like to make my patients use their brains."

"Mine hurts right now," I mumble.

"We can stop if you'd like. You have your usual session scheduled for tomorrow and group as well." She pushes her glasses back up her nose.

"Nah, it's fine. Might as well get through this now while I can still think." She nods, urging me to go on. "I don't think it's fair because I deserve the truth, especially where I'm concerned. I know..." *Why does this hurt so much to say?*

"I know I'm fragile right now. Especially when it comes to Zion—and no, I don't want to talk about him yet. But I just thought..." My words come out choked. "I just thought Gavin would be the one person who *wouldn't* lie to me."

"Why?" One word. One question. The impact, shattering.

"Because he takes care of me. Protects me in a way no one ever has. Like I matter to him." My eyes fall closed, Gavin flooding my mind before reality snaps back. "But lying *isn't* protecting."

"Have you ever considered that it might be Gavin's way of protecting?"

My brows pinch in the center. Goosebumps burn down my arms. "What do you mean?"

"Well, we all have different definitions of the word. What's yours? How does Gavin protect you through your eyes?"

We're jumping into uncharted territory here. Gavin's been mentioned in many sessions but never this deeply.

I let my head fall back against the chair. My hair brushes over my forehead until it settles against my ears. My hands rub up and down over my thighs, each shift of the fabric bringing my smarting ass back to the forefront of my mind.

Even when he was spanking me, he was still taking care of me.

"He—" I clear my throat, fighting past the heat I know is blooming on my pale face. "He holds me to his chest and wraps his limbs around me. Basically pins me against him. His body is so big and hairy and soft, yet it's also so hard and intimidating. Comforting and gentle.

"I think he knows I have bad dreams. I don't usually remember them, but the lingering traces of exhaustion tell me I had them. It started when I was detoxing. Or, I guess, on the jet here?" I dig my hand into my hair, yanking on the strands. "I don't even fucking know because I think I remember his arms around me in my own apartment. Telling me he was sorry and whatever else.

"What the fuck does that even mean?" I'm questioning everything now. When this started, when it all began to change.

"He's fucking married. And Milo, who was the steward on my father's private jet—did I tell you that?" I dig the heel of my hand into my chest, rubbing at the ache. "Anyway, his husband, Milo, is hot as fuck. Blonde, tatted. Fucking *nice.* I saw them kiss, and it looked good. Familiar, you know?" I lift my eyes. Dr. Weaver's looking back at me gently, no judgment on her face.

It's relieving.

"But then, Gavin fucking held me when I got sick. And after we got here, he was by my side through every tortuous moment of my withdrawal. I thought I was dying, and it was the most terrifying experience of my life. I can only imagine how Darien felt in his final moments..."

"Do you want to talk more about Darien and what happened?" the doc asks after a long blip of silence.

"Nah. Just trying to get my head straight, doc." *And deciding how much I should tell you.*

"You can tell me anything that you're comfortable with. This is a safe space."

"Yeah, yeah. I know" I flip her a smile. "Gavin protects me by giving me what I need. Which is to feel taken care of because I've never had that before. He seems to want to do it?" I phrase it like a question. "I don't know where Gavin's head is at, but it's how I feel. And it works, you know? But something happened... It's actually happened a lot, and I've wanted to talk to you about it because I don't know exactly what it means, but I haven't because I've been scared you'll tell me it's not good for me. But what I want you to know, doc, is I *want* it. I don't... I think... Fuck!"

The door swings open, and I'm smiling before it even bounces against the wall. I turn, giving Gavin my eyes. "I'm okay. Just... working through some shit." His mouth tightens, fingers strangling the doorknob in their grip.

"Sorry—mouth. I know." His top lip twitches, dark eyes warming before they scan the room. With one last, longing glance at me, he pulls the door shut silently.

The room is awkwardly tense now. Or maybe it's just all in my head.

"As I was saying, I don't need it the way I need to get high, but that's kind of the problem? When Gavin does these... things..." My hands wring together, sweat slicking my palms. "I sort of feel high after or even during. It's like my brain shuts off, and I'm kind of just floating. It feels really good, like I don't have to worry about anything because Gavin will take care of it all."

My heart slams against my sternum. My foot bounces

restlessly against the floor, the motion vibrating up each leg. I stare at my shoes, watching them fly up and down over the carpet until my vision unfocuses.

I shove out of the chair to pace the room. My shorts rub against my ass, making my breath hitch.

It sounds so much worse when I say it out loud. Am I addicted to Gavin? Did I just replace one high with another? Is this the worst thing for my recovery?

What the fuck do I do?

Fighting against the urge to keep it all inside, I spill every tormented thought to the doctor sitting patiently behind me.

"Zev." I turn around after she calls my name. My stomach churns with apprehension. "I think you know what addiction feels like. You've experienced it; you still are. And you already know my professional advice on your relationship with Gavin.

"I don't believe you should be focusing on anyone but yourself right now. Something so new has a chance of souring, and it is a risk to your recovery." Her words make me blanch, all the blood draining from my face in an instant as my stomach drops to the floor.

"But," she adds quickly, "I understand that what you have with Gavin is a bit different. It is unorthodox *and* something that was technically started before you were admitted. And the circumstances behind your interaction aren't going to change for a while, so I do think it is in your best interest to work through this in a way that will be the best and healthiest for you."

Her words are a breath of relief. I slump against the wall, needing something solid for support. This is all just so confusing.

I don't know what I'm feeling, what it even means. I start pacing again.

"Okay, Zev. This is a bit unconventional, even for me, but I feel like saying this is what will help you the best, and that's what I want."

Dr. Weaver's voice brings my pacing to a halt. I whirl around to face her. The bow of her glasses is pinched between two fingers where they rest in her lap.

"Uh..." Unease festers in my gut all over again.

"Don't worry. It's nothing bad. Like I said, just unconventional." She laughs lightly, loosening the knot in my stomach. "So, you've been writing in your journal, right?"

"Yeah, I really like doing that."

"Good. Good. Okay, so this isn't exactly homework but a suggestion?" She phrases it like a question, so I nod. "Do some research. And I know you don't have access to your phone or the internet—by your choice—so this means you will have to talk to Gavin about this and what you will be doing."

"What, exactly, will I be researching?" *And talking to Gavin about...*

"What you feel when you and Gavin have intimate moments. I think willfully searching for the answers you have questions to will help. Especially with Gavin since he is intimately involved."

"Ew, doc, please stop saying intimate." I fake shudder, and she laughs.

"All right, sorry." She holds up her hands, still chuckling. "When you find answers that make sense, if you're comfortable, maybe discuss them with Gavin. Encourage him to do the same. I think that will also bring more honesty between you two.

"I'm not going to berate you or even criticize you, Zev. I can see your embarrassment, and while that feeling—and every other feeling you hold—is valid, I want you to know I would never judge you.

"I am here to help you not only with your recovery, but I want to help you find yourself—whatever version of you that is. Be proud of who you are because the Zev I've gotten to know this last month is a very bright, young man with a long, healthy future ahead.

"You've already come so far, and I can feel your desire to live. It's wonderful to see, and I am so proud of you. I know you talked about a lot today, and tomorrow, we can dive a bit deeper into it all, but right now, I think it's best if you go and do that. I think once you have the answers you're looking for, it will help to clear your mind to focus specifically on all the other things."

I wrinkle my nose at the onslaught of tears burning their way through me. They fall from my closed eyes before I can stop them. Each drop onto my shirt solidifies so much. Who I was, who I am *now.* What I want and what I *know.*

"Thanks, doc," I try to laugh it off, but my voice comes out choked. "I'll see you tomorrow."

"Yes. And don't forget group. Maybe you should try participating tomorrow?"

I huff a laugh as I grip the doorknob, turning, but not pulling it open. "Nice try."

She shrugs her shoulders, laughter written in every delicate crease in her face. "I had to try."

The scent of saltwater hits me as soon as the rush of air

from the door opening wafts into my nose. A grunt hits my ears, and I halt in surprise. Gavin, my very large, very bossy, bodyguard scrambles up from the floor, his cheeks ruddy under the thickness of his beard.

"Were you sitting on the floor?" I ask, eyes traveling down the length of the hall. Gavin shoves his hands in his pockets, something I've never seen him do before. I arch a brow, the other still furrowed in confusion.

Tucking a stray curl behind my ear, I jerk my head toward the front entrance. "Walk with me, Gavin?" I ask, ignoring the slight flush saying his name brings to my cheeks. He swipes a stray tear away from my face, crow's feet present as he sucks his thumb into his mouth, swallowing my tear.

I have to turn away before I jump him in Black Diamond's main facility.

He grunts and falls into step beside me. "Where else would I be?" He murmurs the words, almost soundlessly, and I can't help the way they drill straight into my raw, fragile heart.

"You're not just here because of the job, right?" I hate to ask, but it's better to know. "And the truth, please." *Deep breath.*

It's time for some honesty—or a lot of it.

All part of the steps or whatever the fuck. I think so, anyway. I haven't exactly been paying a lot of attention in group.

I tell Gavin the same thing I told Dr. Weaver about honesty and why I need it. Gavin listens quietly, but attentively, his fingers brushing my forearm occasionally or his feet hitching as he takes a step.

"I'm just trying to protect you while you recover," he tells me as we travel along the path toward the villa. The breeze is warm and damp against my skin, the sweat once dried coming back full force as the sun's heat hammers into me.

I lean into his side, looping my right arm through his left. Gavin stiffens before relaxing a second later and tugging me closer. "I know, but that's not the kind of protection I need."

"It feels right."

"What does?" I ask as we round another bend, this one drawing us closer to the dense jungle to my left. Tiki torches are spaced along the path, unlit. The howl of monkeys and the flapping of birds' wings fill my eardrums. Our feet crunch over a few fallen palm fronds, their splayed, green design creating an asymmetrical pattern as they overlap.

My fingers find the band wrapped around Gavin's ring finger. I press a blunt nail under the edge, pulling and pushing against it. He curls his fingers, halting my movement. My breath hitches, but then he relaxes, letting me have free rein again.

"Protecting you the way I have. Not necessarily keeping things from you but not telling you *right now*."

"Why?" My eyes are downcast, darting between the ground and Gavin's heavy, black boots. He stops, pulling me with him. Fingers clasp my chin, tugging my head up.

Gavin's dark eyes search mine. I don't know what he's looking for, but I let him see me for what I am.

I don't have anything to hide. Not from him.

Not anymore.

"Because you're my boy, and I don't want to see you burdened with the weight of things out of your control. Not when I have the power and the ability to ease some of it—at least for a little while."

My eyes search his endless depths, looking for any sign of dishonesty, but all I see is *truth.*

"Your boy?" I whisper the words, my throat tight. Gavin digs his thumb into the dimple of my chin, his other fingers splayed along my jaw.

"Yeah. Is that okay? If you let me take care of you for a little while?" I twist his ring down his finger.

"How long's a little while?"

He hesitates. "I think you know..." He says the words with a soft edge as he tucks a loose strand behind his ear. It hurts to hear, even if I did already know there was never anything *but* a time limit to what we have.

My eyes rove over every inch of my bodyguard. From his beautiful, shoulder-length, wavy, brown hair, over his thick beard of the same color. His beautifully sculpted face that matches the rest of his hard body padded with a soft, outer layer I love to bury my face in.

"For four more weeks, I'm all yours." His chest deflates as he exhales, stepping closer. His thick arms curl around my waist as I'm pressed against him. He kisses the top of my head, and my eyes flutter closed as his warm breath floats over my scalp, sending gooseflesh scattering outward.

"And after?" I ask, face buried in his chest. I immediately regret blurting the words. At Gavin's inhale, I blurt, "Don't answer."

"Zevryn..."

"No." I nuzzle deeper into his soft flesh. "Don't. This is good. I like this." I push up on my tiptoes, and Gavin chuckles halfheartedly, the sound vibrating into me. He clasps me just under the crease of my cheeks and hauls me against him.

I wrap my legs around his waist and bury my face in his neck, nuzzling the grown-out hair he hasn't trimmed. "We need to talk, boy," he says as he takes us toward the villa. All I smell is salt, Earth, and Gavin.

I sigh, already feeling warm and tingly. "Yeah, there's a lot we need to talk about."

Sixteen

GAVIN

I've never had so many thoughts churning in my mind at once. Each one is a battering ram, heavy and jarring.

Zevryn and his panic attack. The way I was utterly fucking useless as he was lost inside his own torturous mind. I knew he'd seen things, experienced even worse, but hearing it all while he was so lost...

It fucking killed me that I couldn't help him. But I was smart enough to accept that it wasn't about me and remember who *could* help him.

Dr. Weaver remained calm as she eased Zevryn through his panic attack. Each heavy breath he took centered him a bit more until some of the fog lifted, and left in its place was glassy terror.

I remained by his side through it all, holding him in my lap as he tried so desperately to hurt himself, unaware he was even doing it.

It was torturous, sitting on the other side of Dr. Weaver's

door, listening to Zevryn. I couldn't hear most of their conversation, but the snippets I did manage to catch told me enough. And while I felt slightly guilty for trying to eavesdrop, it wasn't enough to stop me.

About his mom and his new revelation with her death. Hearing the few, distorted sentences of his newfound understanding made my heart leap from my chest with pride. The way he's working *so* hard through all of his trauma... *Fuck.* He's amazing. Even the way he handled his panic attack with such strength is admirable.

But hearing him explain our connection liquified something inside of me. Something once deep and unforgiving now raw and exposed.

According to the good ol' doc, I'm not good for Zevryn. Or, at least, our relationship isn't. Hearing that brought forth a bout of anger I didn't expect, but I have no right to be pissed off or even defensive. Not when I know how wrong this is.

But is it wrong when it's never felt more right?

I've found something within myself in Zevryn. A fragment I've snuffed out for years as I put work above all else.

The irony isn't lost on me that a job I took, resulting in betraying my husband, is what brought me to my truth.

I need to be needed. Desired. Cherished and depended on. Zevryn gives all of that to me and *so* much more. When he lets go, he gives me his pain, his burdens and tragedies, and while we're together, he lets me bear the brunt so he can be free. Weightless and untouchable—exactly how he's meant to be.

But the boy is still healing the lost, broken parts of

himself, and I'm terrified my involvement will only end badly for him.

I can endure the pain of our inevitable end, but what if he can't? What if he's still too fragile and vulnerable?

And then there's Milo... Our last conversation was brief and... conclusive. We didn't discuss anything of importance, but it wasn't a good conversation either. I'd started, ready to spill everything, but something held me back—respect for him and our marriage, ironically.

It felt like we've both found our truths in this unexpected but willful separation, and the thought is agonizing but also enlightening. I'm just not sure Milo *accepts* that.

He's always been my best friend. The first person I've always run to, the only one I've wanted to share everything with—including my life. But maybe we've outgrown the love we once had, leaving us with a gentle, honest, pain-riddled devotion.

And I've cheated on him. Not only physically but emotionally. My mind is attached to Zevryn as equally as my body craves him.

Thinking about what I'm doing to Milo doesn't bother me like it should. I *know* this would hurt him, greatly and deeply, and that is the last thing I would ever want, but Zevryn and what he needs comes above all else.

Even my marriage, however broken and fragile it might be.

Zevryn tugging on the ring on my finger draws me back from my reverie. "What is it, boy?" I ask. Each footstep is effortless, Zevryn's weight against me like a second skin.

The boy doesn't answer. Instead, he wriggles his hips, slipping his hard cock up my abdomen. I shake my head, admonishing him with a *tsk* even as I tighten my hold, sliding my hands up to his ass.

I squeeze the tender flesh, drawing a hiss from my boy's lips. "You needy, baby?" I ask as I climb the steps, each one jostling Zevryn in my arms. He grunts and presses closer, nodding against my neck.

"Not right now," I say with authority as I lock the door, double-checking it before taking him to the couch. He's reluctant to let me go, but I'm much stronger than he is. With a huff, he plops down on the sofa, arms crossed petulantly over his chest. He even juts out his bottom lip.

I take a step back, one brow lifted as I stare down at him. "You think that'll work on me?" I ask, raking my gaze over his perfectly curated body that's only just begun to fill out again after he was so sick.

I hope I'm around long enough to see him wholly happy and healthy.

The thought has me bringing my hand to my chest to rub against my sternum. When Zevryn's eyes catch the movement of my hand, I drop it to my side.

"Yes?" he says hopefully, making me shake my head with a chuckle.

"We need to talk, boy."

"But—"

"Nope." I turn away from him to do a quick scan of the villa before pulling open the mini fridge and grabbing a small snack for Zevryn along with a bottle of water. "Let me take care of you. Let me know best," I plead, even as I demand.

His eyes soften, peering into the exposed depths of my soul, every inch of my internal pain flayed and bare for him.

"Okay," he rasps, taking the food and water from my hands with ease.

I release the breath I'd been holding and ease down next to him. I don't even realize how stiff I am until Zevryn presses against me. He lays his head on my shoulder as he pulls back the plastic wrap on his cheese and crackers.

I press a kiss to the top of his head, lingering to breathe in deeply. His hair smells like musky sweat with faint traces of lavender. My eyes close of their own volition, basking in everything he is.

Zevryn's soft chewing broken up with intermittent gulps of water fills my mind with peace. I splay my left hand over his left thigh, rubbing back and forth in gentle swipes of my hand.

When the crinkle of plastic sounds, I lift my head from his. "All done, baby?" I hold out my hand, and he places the empty container in my palm.

"How are you feeling?"

"Better, actually. Thank you," he says so softly, my heart aches.

"Baby..." I drop the trash onto the table so I can pull him into my lap. Zevryn curls effortlessly into me, arms and legs finding their respective places. He nuzzles my cheek before burrowing his nose into my throat. "Don't thank me for taking care of you. It's what I want to do."

"Would you still do it without the money?" It's a hesitant question but one I can tell he wants the answer to. And I'll give him every truth he wants—as long as it won't hurt him.

I refuse to do that to him.

"You know I'm here because it's my job." He stiffens and tries to pull away, but I growl and pin him in place. "Don't fucking move," I growl, "and let me finish." I yank Zevryn's head back by his hair. When he tries to nod, I release him.

"Thank you. As I was saying, I am here because of my job. But that's not what this is. Yes, I have my responsibilities. But protecting you has become so much more than a duty, boy. I don't know what you did, if you've got irresistible allure coursing through your bloodstream, but you fucking hooked me."

I take a deep breath, feeling unsteady at the truths laid bare.

Everything's on the table, and there's no turning back.

"I don't believe in love at first sight. Never have, still don't. I do, however, believe in lust at first sight, which I had for Milo." Saying his name with my boy in my arms is jarring, but when his lips, wet and sticky, glide over my throat in a spray of soft, gentle kisses, I have to swallow the urge to veer this conversation in a very different direction.

But I can't, so I resist by the skin of my teeth—but my boy sure as hell doesn't make it easy.

"Milo's been my best friend for a decade. A perfect partner to go through life with. But we've been... lost for years, I think. Trapped in a place we're unsure of how to escape. We've tiptoed around it, but we haven't been okay for a while.

"And this job was another excuse to be apart. But to take it, I broke a promise, and it wasn't difficult." The words, no matter how truthful, bring the realization I really am a piece of shit.

"It sounds awful, but trust me, it's even worse. I was grateful to just be away, so I didn't have to face the reality of what my marriage has become. But then... I fucking saw you.

How lost and in pain you were. And how *no one* but me noticed."

I swallow against the buildup clogging my throat. Zevryn trembles in my arms. I reach across the sofa and grab the blanket I've been sleeping with. I wrap it around Zevryn, tucking it in around him.

He settles instantly, snuggling against me. I smile warmly, eyes locked on the curtains blocking the glass wall, locking us in our own little world. "I have feelings for you, Zevryn. Deep feelings. But they're as complicated as this entire situation.

"I don't know what to do about them other than to just *feel.* To be with you while I can, but I refuse to hinder your recovery in any way. You are my first priority, and if that means we cannot *be...* then we won't."

I don't realize how tight my grip has gotten until Zevryn's hushed grunt fills my ears. I immediately loosen my hold, but he scrambles to capture my arms. "Don't. I like it."

"I don't want to hurt you."

He snorts, his flared nose wrinkling. "Yes, you do." He wiggles his ass on my lap to prove his point. I roll my eyes.

"Don't be a fucking brat, boy." I nip the end of his nose. He yelps, and the sound warms me.

"Don't be a *fucking* brat, boy," he mocks me, dark curls flopping in front of his face as he bobs his head. My hand slides to his throat effortlessly. I squeeze the sides, effectively cutting off blood flow.

Zevryn's hazel eyes widen before they glaze over, and his eyelids droop. Every ounce of strength drains from his body in an instant and zaps into mine like a livewire straight to my brainstem.

I grit my teeth and gently release my hold, relishing in the harsh inhale he sucks in, eyes rolling back at the rush. *Fuck, he's so perfect for me.*

"Now is not the time," I remind him against my better fucking judgment at the moment, but someone has to keep us on track, and it sure as hell will not be him. "And watch your goddamn mouth before I shove something in there to shut you up."

He leans back and parts his lips. The sight alone sends my dick from half-hard to pulsing and leaking. I tweak his jaw, making him flinch.

"That is the literal definition of a brat. Don't test me right now, boy." I lower my voice and sharpen my tone to get my point across. He shivers but obeys, just like I knew he would.

We're quiet for a while as I let my boy gather his thoughts. I push the water bottle to his lips every so often until it runs dry.

"I talked to Dr. Weaver about us, about how I... feel with you." His words are quiet and unsure.

I clear my throat, adjusting my hold against his back. "I know."

"You know..." He tilts his head, cocking a brow. "You were eavesdropping."

"Yes." *I promised no more lies.* "But I didn't catch most of your conversation. Just a few bits here and there and most near the end. I've never done that before, just so you know. But today, after..." My throat cinches, "after what happened, I was worried and—"

"It's fine. I'm not mad." Zevryn placating me feels *wrong.*

"No, it's not. I invaded your privacy."

"Yeah, but I like it. Means you care. Right?" he adds after a moment of hesitation.

"Yeah, boy. I care. Too much."

"I don't think there's such a thing as too much."

"With the thoughts running rampant in my head about you... Trust me. There's *too much.*" He giggles, the sound muffled and vibrating into my shoulder.

"Anyway, she said I should do some research to better understand it all. So, I'll have to use your phone."

"Okay, baby," I agree easily, making Zevryn's eyes widen.

"Just okay?"

"Yeah?" I ask, questioning his confusion. "You've already earned the privilege of phone access according to the counselors."

"But Zion..."

"I don't give two fucks about Zion and his goddamn rules." I spew the words with as much venom I can muster—which is *a lot.* My boy's eyes shoot open wide, his mouth dropping open.

"What happened with Zion?"

I force myself to take a deep breath. "Nothing."

"Gavin—"

"No. This is not up for debate. Nothing happened; that I promise you." He eyes me warily before conceding.

"Fine. But I'm not gonna drop it entirely."

I roll my eyes. "I wouldn't expect you to."

"I need to tell you about my... panic attack." He says the word with bite. I grasp his face, forcing his head back until he meets my eyes.

"There's nothing to be ashamed of, Zevryn."

"Yeah. I know." He shakes his head. "Anyway. The

bathroom stall brought back what happened with Darien, and I kinda just got lost in my head."

Darien... the boy who died.

"Because it happened in the bathroom..." I fit the pieces together. Each one that clicks into place makes me want to slam my head into a fucking brick wall. *Gavin, you stupid son of a bitch.*

"No, don't." Zev grabs at my arm. "It's not your fault—at all. You couldn't have known. I didn't even know, okay? It's just... a trigger. And I have to be careful; that's all."

He's so fucking strong. Stronger than anyone I've ever known.

I hold his face, bringing it close to mine until our noses brush, and I feel the soft whisper of his exhales against my lips. "I'm so sorry."

His smile is weak but genuine. "I know. I am, too."

Tension lifts from the room and off our shoulders, each verity revealed lessening our burdens, together and separately.

Zevryn idly plays with my nipple through my shirt, teasing it to a peak so he can pinch it and roll it around between his fingers, the touch almost mindless.

After playing for a while, Zevryn wriggles in my lap, sending his ass grinding right over my cock. I grunt and try to hold him still, but he does it again.

"I have to pee," he whispers, and I chuckle.

"Okay, boy. Let's go." Readjusting him across my lap, I carry him bridal style into the bathroom, not setting him down until his feet are in front of the toilet. I take the blanket from his outstretched hand and toss it over my shoulder.

His eyes rake over me. "Are you going to watch me?" He shifts on his feet. *As a matter of fact...*

I round the toilet and lean against the wall, spreading my legs. "I am."

"Um..." Zev fidgets, face beautifully flushed.

"Do you want help?" I push off the wall.

"Help?" he rasps, staring at me with impossibly wide eyes. I step into his space, leaning down to whisper into his ear.

"Yeah, baby. You want me to pull your shorts down and free your little cock from your briefs? I'll hold you in my hand, let you release into the toilet effortlessly. Then, once you're all done, I'll shake you and put you right back inside your pants. Maybe even give you a few strokes for being so good for me."

I'm panting heavily against Zevryn's face, the scene playing out like a movie in my head. *Fuck, I want that.*

He shudders. "Y-yeah," he finally breathes out, and my heart slams into my throat.

I pull back. "You want that, boy?"

"Please," he whispers. My smile breaks my face. I turn his face up and crash my lips to his. He grunts in surprise but immediately opens up for me. His tongue is soft and pliant against mine as I wrap around him, sucking it into my mouth and sinking my teeth into the muscle.

We groan in unison as our flavors mix into a heady concoction I wish I could swallow forever.

It takes strength I didn't even know I had to pull away from him. Pressing my sweaty forehead to his, his curls blocking my view of his eyes, I say, "Thank you, boy. I am so proud of you."

Discarding the blanket on the floor, I press against his back and reach around his waist to pull his shorts down. Each step I take is exactly as I described, so he won't have any surprises.

The longer my hands are on him, the more he seems to relax. By the time his dick is in my hand, it's a semi. I chuckle against his neck. "You gotta relax for me, boy."

He whines and stomps his foot. "I'm trying, but you're *touching me.*"

"I know, but if you can't do it, I'll do it for you."

"Can you?" He rubs his ass against me. "Please just make it go away; I have to pee." He sounds frantic, and from all the water he drank, I'm sure his bladder is full. Pressing one hand to his abdomen, I dip down and grab his balls, tugging and massaging.

When I squeeze my fist, crushing them in my palm, Zevryn cries out, bucking away from me. "Oh, gods, that hurts," he cries, and I nod.

"I know, baby, but look." I grasp his cock again, and it's perfectly flaccid. "You're ready to go." I kiss his neck. "Let go for me, boy. Give Daddy what he needs." *Fuck, I just said that.*

Zevryn gasps, turning his head into my neck, face wet with tears as he releases his bladder. "Oh, fuck. Oh—" He groans into my neck.

For the first time since I've met him, a curse word flowing off his tongue does nothing but make me hotter. Urine streams from the head of his dick, directly into the toilet bowl. My gaze never strays as he relieves himself, wholly and completely.

He's mine.

"That's it, boy. You're doing so well." He groans as a few

last drops trickle out. I shake them away before patting him softly. I make a fist around him and stroke a few times, just to feel his soft, silken flesh before I easily tuck him away, giving him another small pat.

"That was beautiful, baby. Thank you," I rasp, kissing every inch of him within reach.

"Daddy," Zevryn cries, whirling around and jumping into my arms. I grunt as I catch him, taking two steps back from the force. His mouth is all over me, wet and hot and needy. "Please. Oh, gods, *please.*"

My blood burns in my veins, each saturated, salacious moan ripping from my boy's throat only sending me deeper into an inescapable place.

"What are you begging for?" I lick a stripe up his neck, making him buck. The need for conversation is long gone as I lead my boy to the bed and throw him down. With a breathless squeal, he flops against the bed, long, dark curls splaying wide across the white duvet. His face is perfectly flushed, adding a deeper layer of color I wish he could always wear.

"You," he whines, reaching for me. I shake my head and take a step back. I whip my shirt off and drop it to the floor at my feet, baring my torso. Zevryn's eyes drop as he greedily takes me in. The little brat swipes his tongue across his bottom lip.

So alluring and impossible to resist.

Forgoing my jeans, I crawl between his spread legs, dropping my mouth to the inside of his ankle. I nip at the bone before sucking the tender skin into my mouth. Zevryn jerks, so I clasp his calf to keep him still.

I do the same to the other side, covering his ankles in

stark bite marks, soothing each one with a delicate swipe of my tongue.

I dip down to his toes and snake my tongue between them, lathering them in my saliva before sucking each one into my mouth with harsh pulls.

"Oh, gods." My boy groans as I suck his toes, making me chuckle as I pop the big one out, leaving it glistening. "That—that's..."

"You like that, baby?" I drag my tongue up his calf, turning his leg so I can reach the sensitive underside. Gooseflesh breaks out over Zevryn's skin, each hair prickling against my tongue. My eyes roll back from feeling my boy's inescapable pleasure.

There is nothing like knowing you're giving someone something they've never felt before.

Ultimate rapture.

"So much."

"You ever been cherished like this before?" I bite at his meaty thigh, loving the give of his relaxed muscles.

"Never." It's a whisper that floats into the air, the singular word motivating me to make sure he feels every ounce of my devotion. To him, his body, and his fucking soul.

All mine for the taking.

I litter his legs in dark, purple bruises, each one swollen and hot to the touch by the time I'm nearly satisfied.

Zevryn's shaking, his legs twitching against the bed, the movement far from his control when I finally pull back, hovering above him on steady arms. He's red and sweaty, his skin coated in a thin sheen of gloss.

I hook my fingers into the waistband of his briefs and rip them down his legs, my chest heaving with anticipation. They get tangled around his knees, making me growl.

"Da—" I yank, ripping the fabric, leaving it to dangle from my boy's thighs in frayed scraps. But now he's bare and free to spread himself as wide as I want, which is all I care about.

"Fuck, that's hot." I look up through my lashes. Zevryn's propped on a shaky elbow, staring down at me inches away from his straining erection. His eyes dart to the shredded fabric clinging to his skin before flitting back to my face.

He sucks his plush, bottom lip into his mouth, barely managing to block a moan. I wrap my hand around the base of his erection and hold him straight in the air. His head is an angry shade of red, his slit shiny with the first traces of precum prepping to ooze from him.

With a growl, I drop my head and sink my teeth into the spongy flesh. Zevryn screams and tries to buck away from my mouth, but the threat of my teeth has him stilling in an instant.

"Hurts," he pants, and I smile, still latched on. I keep my hold as gentle as I can, so there's more of a threat of pain than any actual damage being done, but he still feels the sting all the same.

After counting to thirty in my head, relishing in each shudder emanating from my boy, I release him. He sags against the bed, chest heaving. "Why'd you do that?" he whines, tears in his eyes.

"I've told you numerous times to watch your mouth, but I've never exactly followed through on the threat. But you need to know I'm serious about that, hence your punishment."

"Punishment? Why can't I cuss? I'm fu—I'm nearly twenty years old." He corrects himself hastily. The reminder of his youthful age is like a punch in the gut I have to swallow down like bile.

"Because it pisses me off hearing vile words coming from such a pretty mouth." I thumb his lips, pressing them into his teeth.

"That's not fair." He pouts.

"There are a lot of things that aren't fair, baby. But you'll listen to me, regardless, won't you?" I grab his throat and dig in, relishing in the graphic displays in his eyes before he succumbs to the feeling of being wholly owned.

"Yes, Daddy," he rasps through my grip.

"Goddamnit." I slam my mouth to his, hissing as our teeth clank, the jarring sensation only spurring us on. I choke my boy, stealing his oxygen selfishly. Each thud of his chugging heartbeat ramps mine up in speed until I'm dizzy.

Zevryn lurches into me, locking his legs around my waist and his arms around my shoulders. He digs deep into my muscle, blunt nails ripping their way through my skin. I hiss, nipping at his lip until the faintest traces of copper seep into my tongue.

Our cocks align, and I drop down, grinding into him. He mewls beautifully, trying to wriggle beneath me, but my hips keep him pinned to the mattress.

With a growl, I rip my mouth away and slide down his body until I'm face-to-face with his crotch. His balls sit tight against his body, so close to release. I nip at the wrinkled skin before sucking a ball into my mouth. I roll it around with my tongue before popping it out and moving to the next one.

Zevryn's legs shake against the sides of my head.

I grin, feeling high as I drag my mouth up, teeth scraping the sensitive, inner flesh of his thigh. I bury my nose into the thick patch of hair at his groin and inhale as deeply as I can, groaning deep in my chest.

Fingers sink into my hair, tugging at the long strands. "Gavin, don't," Zevryn pleads. Still breathing him in, I peer up. Nervousness and embarrassment stain his face, adding to his ethereal beauty.

With a grin he can't see, I nuzzle into him, his cock sliding alongside my face, smearing precum all over me. Zev flinches, and his fingers tighten, making me grit my teeth against the sting.

"Are you embarrassed about me smelling you, boy?"

"I... I haven't showered or anything..." His Adam's apple bobs with a swallow. I chuckle and press a kiss to the head of his dick before sliding up until I'm straddling his shoulders, keeping him pinned in place. My dick bobs in his face, and he catches it with his tongue, flicking it along the sensitive underside.

I hiss, biting my bottom lip. "Brat."

He responds by licking harder and faster. I buck my hips against the sensation. It's painful to pull away from my boy's precious mouth, but what I want right now isn't that.

"I love the way you smell for me, baby." I sink my teeth into his trapezius, near the other bite mark I gave him. "My dirty little boy. I want you filthy for me, covered in your cum while mine leaks from your little hole for days..." I lick his pierced nipple as I delve my thumb into his shallow belly button.

"What do you think about that? I think your little belly

button would look so cute filled with your cum, baby. We should do that." I press deeper into the divot until he squirms, then I pull away.

"Da—Gavin..." Zev trips over his words.

"Daddy or Gavin—which is it, boy?"

"I don't know what to call you," he wails, throwing his head back and slamming his fists into the mattress.

"Who am I to you? I can't give you the answer, but I will tell you, you're my fucking boy, and nothing will change that."

"I wanna call you Daddy but it's..."

"What did I tell you about being embarrassed?" I brush my thumb over his stubbled cheek, catching a tear and sucking it into my mouth. "It's just us. We can be who we are." The words seem to drain the tension from his body. He smiles up at me with a dopey look, eyes half-lidded.

"Okay," he agrees easily, making me give him a smile in return.

"See? That wasn't so hard. Do what feels good. There is no right or wrong," I tell him.

Gripping the backs of both his thighs, I push his legs to his chest, exposing him. The muscles of his ass flex as he clenches. His hole is tight and hot beneath the pad of my thumb.

"I wanna fuck you, baby, but I don't have any lube. And I may like hurting you, but not like that." I massage his rim as I talk, relishing in the way it twitches against me.

"I... uh. There's lube in the drawer." I arch a brow. "Dillon and Carmen," he says like that explains everything. The confusion doesn't leave my face. He sighs. "They packed my bag, and they packed my bottle of lube, too. They know

I'm a pretty sexual person…" He trails off, plucking at the sheets. "And Dill knows I don't like jacking it dry, so I'm assuming that's why it's in there."

"Your friends know these things about you?" I ask. My words come out stiffer than I intended, but thinking about that blonde boy touching *my* boy…

"Yes. We're best friends, and we're close, Gavin. No secrets—aside from my addiction." His words are resolute, and his eyes are clear.

I force myself to breathe in deeply. Jealousy flares like never before, nearly blinding me. I search Zevryn's eyes, but I don't have to dig for the truth that's so plainly on display.

"I understand." I kiss his belly button before reaching for the drawer. "Thank you for telling me."

"Are you mad?"

"Oh, I'm fucking irate, baby." I swipe the bottle and douse my fingers, not even bothering to warn Zevryn before I push two inside him. He grunts, eyes scrunching shut. "But not for any logical reason." *I crave to know you like that.* "All that matters is you're mine now, aren't you?"

"Yes," he moans. His ass is hot around me as I work my fingers to the hilt, then spread them. My vision tunnels, filled and drowning with Zevryn.

My fingers squelch as I slide them out to add a third. The stretch against his rim has his breath stuttering. "Tell me if it's too much." I glance up for confirmation, noting the small, shaky nod of his head. I breach him with three thick fingers. My grip on him tightens as I watch him stretch, the skin thinning so miraculously.

"You look fucking perfect." My left hand holds his right leg to his chest, his left wrapped around my waist. I drop my head to his shin and kiss him, relishing in the way his hair tickles my lip.

I catch sight of the bruises I put on his skin, and my vision whites out. I fuck into my boy desperately, needing it to be my cock.

"I'm ready," he tells me. "Please fuck me, Daddy."

"Oh, someone's using his *manners,*" I tease him with a growl, twisting my hand to press against his prostate. He lights up exactly like I wanted. "I've been saving playing with your special little spot in hopes you'd be a good boy." I swallow his tongue before ripping away, panting. "And you were. So good for me."

I drench my length with lube and press against his hole. Breaching the first ring of muscle is life-altering, but as I push past and sink into my boy's inner heat, everything I have ever known shatters into a euphoric elation.

Seventeen

ZEVRYN

"Wanna be good for you," I sob, but my voice sounds far away, like it belongs to someone else and I'm merely hearing the echo.

"You're perfect for me, my boy." Gavin's mouth latches onto mine, and I cry into him, letting him swallow my sobs as he takes me and fucking obliterates me.

My skin feels so hot and tight, too small to keep every muscle, bone, vein, and organ trapped inside. My nails dig into whatever I can reach, needing something to ground me before I disappear.

"Breathe for me, baby. Feel me." Gavin slowly rocks his hips, not taking me hard like he did with his fingers in the jungle.

No, the primal animal with rough, angry foreplay has receded, and in its place is my Daddy... gentle and soft and giving.

I need both parts of him, and Gavin seems to know

exactly what I need—always. Like he's entwined with my mind.

Gavin drops down on top of me, trapping me against the bed with the immensity of *him.* His arms shake slightly next to my head from the strain of not crushing me, and I hate it. I claw at his biceps, needing it all.

His hair dangles in my face as he rocks in gentle sways, his cock dragging along every groove in my internal muscles. I've never felt so full in every inch of my body. Inside and out.

"Please," I cry, digging into his skin, pulling him closer.

"I don't want to crush you," he breathes softly against me.

"Need all of you. Need it." I'm mumbling, mewling. I don't know how he understands me when I barely understand myself, but he seems to know exactly what I'm talking about. He drops on top of me, and the full density of his weight sends my eyes rolling back as the air escapes from my lungs.

I don't even care if it never comes back as long as I have this.

Gavin's body pins me to the bed, keeping me here while my mind soars in a place only he can bring me to. The white ceiling is brighter, his hair softer, the scent of his skin headier. Drugging.

Gavin digs his fingers into my hair, pressing the tips to my scalp as he grasps my curly strands in his fist. His legs flex against me as he pulls out until nothing but his bulbous cockhead rests just inside me, keeping me stretched.

The stillness has me peeling my eyes back open, unsure of when I ever closed them. Gavin's deep, dark irises are all I see as he stares into me, every inch of my tortured soul barred to him in hopes he'll see the *real* me.

The person he's helped me become.

Better. Stronger. *Healthy*—mostly, anyway. I am a work in progress after all.

His lips curve upward into a smile so warm and gentle, tears leak from the corners of my eyes and spill down my temples. Gavin catches one with his lips, then drops to the other side to kiss another.

"You're so beautiful when you cry, baby." He plunges back into me so fucking slowly, I feel like I'm losing my mind. My back arches against the mattress, forcing our chests to smash together. Gavin pins my hips to the bed with an iron-tight grip. As his fingers dig into my flesh, I moan, knowing there will be bruises in the shape of his fingers blemishing my skin for days.

I want to be marked by his touch forever. I'd carry each one on my skin and on my soul like a scar. He'd never fade from me.

He uses his grip on my hair as support for every slow plunge he takes back into my body. Every time he drags his cock out, I cry out, already missing him before he enters me again, completing me once more.

The cycle is endless and vicious and all-consuming. I lose everything but this. My skin is a live wire, set to detonate at the briefest touch. Gavin seems to know this because he slows even more, drawing out the throb in my core.

Our abdomens are slick as we glide together, my cock trapped between us, the scratch of the hair on Gavin's stomach only adding to the blissful friction.

I scream when he stops altogether. I can feel his cock

flexing inside me, his control nearly gone. I squeeze my muscles as tightly as I can, throwing my head back with a groan at how much bigger he feels because of it.

Gavin's arms buckle, and he drops on top of me. His mouth slides across my neck before he sinks his teeth into my shoulder, making me lurch with a scream.

"Such a brat." He smooths the sting with his tongue, lapping at my salty skin.

"Please," I cry, shaking my head back and forth. My face is wet with fresh tears and itchy from dried ones. My balls ache from how long I've been teetering on the edge, waiting for Gavin to finally let me fall. Whenever he feels me right at the precipice, he grabs my balls and squeezes, sending my cum back down with even more agony than before.

It's gone on for so long, I don't know which way is up or down, if I'm dead or alive. All I know is, I *need.* More than I ever have, and I can't take it.

"Please, Daddy!" I scream, letting my sobs break free in full force. My body wracks with them, and it feels so *good* to let it all out, each one that escapes making me feel lighter, the weight of pleasure bordering on pain lifting into...

Ecstasy.

Only this version is *so* much fucking better.

Gavin's growl thunders into me, but it's more a vibration than a sound. I tingle from it. My mouth falls slack, and Gavin slips his tongue inside, licking every inch of my mouth.

He devours my body and my soul in tandem, and *I've never felt so cherished.*

"Fuck, that's it, boy. You're there, aren't you? In that place?" he asks hesitantly. I can't see him; it's all a galaxy of blinding colors behind my lids, but I think I nod because then he grunts and his hand is around my throat, stealing my breath, too.

"Give Daddy your cum, boy. I wanna taste it again." His words take me there, just like he knew they would. Screams bounce off the walls and back into me in waves so strong, I convulse and writhe, clenching helplessly around my Daddy's cock as he fills me up.

His cum is hot inside me, filling parts of me I didn't know were so empty before. But now that I do, I know I'll always feel a little hollow without him there.

Air fills my head as my throat opens back up, making my head swim. The sensation of Gavin pulling back makes me panic. I lurch up, digging my heels into his ass cheeks, keeping him pinned. My thighs ache from how long they've been spread and stretched, but I *need* him.

"Stay," I whisper, keeping my eyes closed as shame lights my face. A warm, scorching chuckle vibrates my chest, forcing me to open my eyes.

Gavin's grin is bright, almost blinding, his eyes half-lidded just like mine. Like he can't possibly open them any wider without it causing physical pain.

"You want me to keep my cock inside you, boy?"

I nod, flushing deeper at his dirty words. I mean, fuck, I've never been a prude before. Far from it, actually, but there's something about Gavin that gives me back an innocence I barely remember losing.

He's changing everything.

"You're going to have to say it." He's teasing me—I know he is—but the embarrassment of asking him for something so... *dirty* eats me alive.

I swallow against the lump of desire choking me and force myself to say the words. "*Fuck...* Please keep your cock in me, Daddy. I... I like it." I wrinkle my nose like the brat I am. Gavin wraps his arm around my waist and rolls us effortlessly so I'm lying on his chest, legs spread wide around his hips.

My own protest the stretch, but when he thrusts, sending his semi back into me an inch, his cum squelching inside me, I lose all train of thought.

Gavin *tsks* with a chuckle as he guides my head toward his nipple. "I'll let that one slide since I technically told you to say it."

I flick my tongue against his peaked flesh, twirling my tongue around the small tuft of hair surrounding it. "Why don't you like me cussing?" I ask tiredly, my words slurring. I'm still in that place, and it takes so much out of me to focus this hard when all I want is to float, to drown in *Gavin.*

"Just feels wrong hearing it come out of your mouth. I'll be honest, sometimes it's hot, but my boy doesn't need to be using language like that."

"Hot?" I hum, sucking his nipple into my mouth. Gavin twitches as I hollow my cheeks. He swats my bare ass with full contact, making me lurch up his body and his cock. I groan, the sound muffled through my busy mouth.

"That's not an excuse to be a brat. It may be hot to me *sometimes,*" he enunciates, "but I'll still beat your ass over it." He squeezes my smarting flesh to prove his point.

I hum as I drift into the air, floating with the atoms that create the space around me, endless and abundant, as my Daddy keeps me safe below, his arms never lifting from my sweaty flesh.

"YOU'RE FINISHING your food before we go anywhere." I hike a brow but shovel in another bite anyway. There's no point in arguing—not that I would.

These last few days have been... surreal almost. I've been in my head a lot—I know that—and I know it upsets Gavin from the way his eyes pinch when he catches me deep in thought. But he's letting me process in my own way, which I appreciate more than he knows.

But today... today's a good day with only brighter ones ahead. *For now.*

I'm feeling good. Clear of the impending doom that seems to be leering around every fucking corner. So, no more corners. I'm keeping my vision straight ahead until I slam into the inevitable brick wall—i.e., the jet that will take me back to New York. Back to my huge penthouse apartment, where I will be all fucking alone again.

"Hey." Gavin's fingers grip my wrist and tug.

"I'm okay." I cough and shake my head, dispersing the nasty thoughts that just won't fucking *leave.*

"Do you wanna talk about it, boy?" My eyes flutter closed hearing that word spill from between his lips so effortlessly.

I just want to be your boy forever. The words sit on the tip of my tongue, but I don't say them.

I can't be that selfish. Not anymore. And definitely not with him.

But as I open my lips to tell him no, I realize I can't *say* no. and I can't say yes, either. I won't lie to him, but I can't talk about it right now.

"Fu..." I suck in a breath, shooting Gavin a beaming smile that is so fucking fake—and he knows it. He arches a brow, lips pursed, as if saying, *you wanna try that again.* "Fudge." He rolls his eyes.

"What I *mean* to say," I try again, "is that I do want to talk about it, but I can't right now, and I don't know when I'll be able to." The words leave me in a rush. Gavin nods and rubs his hand down over his beard in thought.

"I understand. Thank you for being honest with me."

I nod, chest deflating with relief. I look down at my food and push it away, my appetite long gone, even after the intense workout I had this morning. "Full?" Gavin asks.

"Yeah." I hold my stomach. "Think it's nerves."

"Nerves?"

"I'm gonna talk in group today." Gavin's eyes light up, making me blush and squirm. It's been a few days since my panic attack. I've had group and another session with Dr. Weaver. I didn't say anything in group, like usual, but I did pay attention. I listened to every person's admission with reverence.

How they can just open up like that in front of strangers is fucking crazy—and brave. But I think now I see it.

Knowing someone feels or has felt the *same* exact way as me is fucking validating. And it almost helps that they're strangers. Well, not exactly *strangers*, since most of them have been there longer or around the same time as me, but there's a new face occasionally, which honestly makes it a bit easier to open up. Knowing I'll never see said people again after I leave.

It gives me a sense of freedom.

"I'm so proud of you, boy."

I dip my head down until my chin bumps my chest. My hair falls in front of my face, hopefully blocking out the pink blushing my cheeks. Gavin's hand dips between my gnarled strands I hate to brush. His fingers trace my warm cheek before he grabs my chin the way he always does and lifts my head.

"Don't hide from me." He searches my eyes.

"I don't want to…" I don't miss the tightening in his eyes before he smooths out his features, replacing every trace of uncertainty with something kinda like love.

He pulls me from my chair and wraps his arms around me, pressing a kiss to the top of my head. I probably smell like sweat from all the moving around we've done today. We worked out, walked along the beach. I did some yoga, while Gavin shamelessly stared at my ass the whole time, and now we're eating before I have group. There wasn't time to shower, and now I feel the layers of sweat and grime like they've formed a second skin.

I wriggle, making Gavin tighten his arms. His chest rumbles with a growl. "Quit trying to pull away from me. I want to hold you."

"I'm all gross. And I stink." I sound whiny because I am. And self-conscious. Gavin dips his head and drags his mouth across my neck, his beard rough and burning against my skin.

"I thought we established I love the way you smell, dirty boy. The raunchier the better, if you ask me." He nips and tugs my skin between his teeth, making me yelp. My eyes widen, searching around the restaurant, but surprisingly, only a few people glance our way before going back to their meals.

Gavin shamelessly palms my ass for anyone to see, and I try—*I swear I really do*—to resist pushing back into his hold, but I can't. I hump against his leg like the dirty boy he says I am in the middle of a restaurant, and I'm fucking *sober.*

Oh, how things have changed.

Gavin presses a kiss to my lips before spinning around, eyeing up the person walking toward us. How he even heard them coming, I have no idea, but Gavin's always super alert to our surroundings, like all the time.

I know it's because of his job. He told me he's been a bodyguard for ten years, which is crazy to think about in terms of our age difference, but I try not to dwell on it because if I do, I'm sure he will, and I don't want him to question this... thing between us even more than he probably is.

"Can I help you?" Gavin says, tone perfectly respectable if someone doesn't know him like I do. I can't hold back my snort at his nearly disguised irritation at being interrupted, I'm sure.

"Sorry to, um, interrupt," the guy stammers, shifting on his feet as he drops his gaze to the floor, "but I'm supposed to ask you to..." He glances back over his shoulder, to someone in a suit with their arms crossed over their chest, looking displeased.

Awe, the poor guy is embarrassed. That's so cute.

The thought makes me still. *Is that how Gavin thinks of me?*

"Sorry... we'll be going." We probably shouldn't have been all handsy in the restaurant anyway. I tug on Gavin's arm. He doesn't budge, still glaring at the poor guy. "Gavin, come on." He holds his ground, pissing me off. The guy looks like he's about to keel over from embarrassment. I keep tugging, but the fucking brute won't move.

"Daddy!" I screech, stomping my foot down on the ground with a loud *thwap.* Gavin's head snaps toward me, eyes wide, lips parted for a split second before his entire expression morphs right before my eyes.

Oh, shit.

That's the man who beat my ass then fucked said ass with his fingers until I came against a tree, screaming into the canopy of leaves above us.

Wild. Desperate.

Formidable.

Waves of a predator fill the small space between us, making my brain go fuzzy. It all happens so fast. Gavin dips down and throws me over his shoulder, his pace fast even for my added weight as he takes us right out of the restaurant.

I don't want to *fight* him, but I do want to fight back… just a little.

I squirm against his hold, bucking my legs wildly once we get away from prying eyes. Gavin strides down the hall easily, his hold never loosening, no matter how hard I fight.

Oh, gods, he's so strong. He could really fuck me up if he wanted to—and knowing he has the power to but is still so gentle with me is such a turn-on.

"Put me the *fuck* down!" I yell, hammering my fist against his back. My voice bounces off the walls of the nearly empty hall. A group of people all swing their heads toward us as Gavin strides by without a fucking word. I bury my face into his back to hide from their prying eyes.

It's one thing to fuck my bodyguard and walk around holding hands. I don't care about any of that. But it's entirely different to be hauled around like a fucking ragdoll.

"Daddy," I whine in his ear, trying a different tactic.

Silence. Just the steady rhythm of his footsteps.

"Where are you taking me?" He rounds a corner. I try to figure out where we are, but everything is upside down and that coupled with the blood rushing to my head, it's all distorted.

With a huff loud enough for him to hear, I slump, letting my head thump against his lower back with every step. I drop my hands to his ass and dig beneath the waistband. I mean, if it's gonna be in my face like this, I might as well touch it.

I groan out loud when the muscle flexes and swells in my hands. I dig in deep, relishing in the scratch of hair against my palms. Each step is like a chisel to my control—and I never had any to begin with.

A door clicks, and then we're bathed in darkness. Gavin digs into my waist and drags me down his body. The moment my feet hit the floor, he's slamming me back against a shelf. Boxes slide around; some fall to the floor with dull thuds.

I gasp at the jolt, but it doesn't have time to escape my lips before Gavin's capturing them, stealing everything I have. My legs buckle, but he catches me. *He'd never let me fall.*

The thought makes my eyes prick with tears, even as Gavin turns my blood into molten lava in my veins.

I grasp at his jeans, digging my fingers into the waistband. I flick open the button and yank the zipper down, hissing in relief as his cock is freed from his boxers. He chuckles into my mouth, making me shiver—a shiver that turns into a full-body tremble when my dick is freed.

Gavin wraps his large hand around my girth and uses his grip to tug me forward until our cocks align. He's silky and hot as he slides against me. The friction is rough, making us both hiss, but the slightest flash of pain only makes it better.

Gavin doesn't waste any time fucking his fist. I thrust with every movement. The grip isn't tight, but it's more than enough. Haze licks across my brain like a black veil. My head falls back, thudding against a shelf. Dust wafts into the air and into my nose, making it burn.

"Everyone heard you call me Daddy," Gavin growls into the damp air circulating around us. He tightens his fingers, making me grunt and thrust harder. My dick chafes and burns, so I know his does too, but *fuck,* it's good.

Gavin and I haven't done our research yet. I've been putting it off because I'm kind of scared about what I'll find out, but this... *thing* between us grows stronger every day. It's not just the Daddy thing, but the way I *need* him. Like... how sucking on his nipples gives me peace and him taking care of me, cuddling me. Hell, even carrying me does the same.

And that's not even mentioning the way he helped me pee...

My teeth sink into my tongue to hold back my scream as my release shoots through me at the memory. But even that's not enough to stifle my cries and whimpers that flow with every pulse.

"Fuck, baby, you're filling my hand." I clutch Gavin's broad shoulders, needing something to ground me. He dips down and sucks my bottom lip into his mouth as he finishes himself off.

Feeling the way his movement loses its rhythm and becomes erratic before he stills with a long, drawn-out groan only makes the blissful haze ten times better.

Warmth coats my pelvis in sticky spurts, smearing into my pubic hair and dripping down the crease of my thighs. The sensation makes me wriggle, and I sigh when Gavin's cum drips onto my balls.

We're still kissing, slowly, lazily, both trying to catch our breath but unwilling to part. Gavin releases me and slides his hand between us, smearing our cum all over my groin and abdomen.

I sigh contentedly, rolling my head between my shoulders. Fingers press into my mouth, warm and sticky. I wrap my tongue around each digit, willfully sucking off our combined releases. And just because I can, I pay extra attention to the ring on his third finger.

We're salty, a tiny bit sweet, and all man.

"Well, now I'm even more dirty."

Gavin chuckles, and the sound shoots straight to my heart, making it skip. "My dirty little boy." He nuzzles my neck and sucks part of my flesh into his mouth with vigor. Each harsh pull draws more blood to the surface, and the area throbs with its own heartbeat before Gavin pulls away.

I can barely make out the shape of his head in the darkness, but I don't need to see him to know how he's looking at me.

His hands find my shorts, and he pulls them up for me, careful not to smear cum on the outside. He pats my softened length. "Now that that's out of the way." Before I can protest, I'm being spun around and shoved face-first into the shelves. My nails scrape across plastic as I search for purchase.

Gavin's hand slams down over my clothed ass before I can even take a breath, his other slapping over my mouth with a sting. He curves over my back, putting his mouth to my ear.

"This is for throwing your little tantrum." He swats me four more times, each thudding hit making me grunt.

"You were so hot screaming my name and stomping your foot," Gavin growls, nipping my shoulder. He humps against my ass, showing me how hard he is again. "Like a spoiled little brat vying for every ounce of your Daddy's attention." He slams his hand down again, this time on my bare ass.

I squeal and arch back into the flash of heat, my back bowing. "You're mine," I try to say, but it comes out distorted through Gavin's palm. He pulls away.

"What was that, boy?"

"You're mine." I try for a possessive growl like Gavin's, but it comes out raspier and much needier. Gavin chuckles and nuzzles between my shoulder blades.

"Don't laugh at me," I pout.

Gavin laughs harder. "I'm not laughing at you, baby. You're just so cute, all possessive over your Daddy." *It sounds so right...*

"Would you rather I didn't care?" I snap. Gavin slaps my ass in retaliation.

"Don't even."

"Sorry," I mumble. Gavin pulls away, putting my shorts back in place.

"Don't be. It's cute."

"Cute," I huff as I turn around.

"I am yours, boy. You know that." He wraps his arms around my shoulders when I drop my head to his chest, searching for his nipple even through the cotton. When I find it, I bite down gently.

His ring feels heavy against my back, the weight impossibly tangible, like the longer he holds me, the deeper the scar will become.

Eighteen

ZEVRYN

Everyone's eyes dart to me when I hold my hand up in the air. I can't fight the rush of blood, so I hold my head up high, swallowing the rush of bile.

"Zev," Kevin, the group therapy leader, says with genuine surprise. "You'd like to share?"

I drop my hand with a nod, feeling the weight of my choice like a cinder block to the chest. He smiles encouragingly at me. I keep my eyes locked on the floor, but I can feel everyone's gaze burning into my face from all angles.

I close my eyes and take a breath, remembering what Dr. Weaver said the other day.

"Remember, this is for you. Not them. There are no stipulations, and it's all on your terms."

"Name's Zev, which you all know," I start, making a few people chuckle, which is nice. Encouraging, even. "I, uh..." I drag my hand through my hair, forcing myself to sit up. "I'm a coke addict. Alcohol too, I guess. Doing both together was even better." More people murmur and huff out breaths of relation.

I finally lift my gaze, flitting it around the room. Each face is raw and honest, not a single one of judgment.

It's because they know. They've been there, and they fucking get it.

"Really loved the shit. Still do, but you know. Anyway, I feel good now. I don't want it like I did or even feel like I *should,* even if I don't *want to.*" A few nods follow the circle.

"But I'm scared as fuck to leave in a couple of weeks." My eyes find Gavin across the room without thought, but he doesn't say anything about the word slipping. He gives me a warm smile, wholly supporting me.

"I'm supposed to be making amends. I've thought about it. Talked to my fuckin' therapist about it, too." Gavin's eyebrow arcs, making me blush. "But I don't know. The thought of talking to anyone from... well, my other life, my *real* life... scares the shit out of me."

I drag my palms down my shorts, the silky, athletic material doing nothing to help clear the sweat. "While I'm here, it feels easier. To stay sober, to *want* to. But knowing once I leave, I can make a single phone call and have a baggie in my hand in minutes makes me a little fucking nervous. Because what if I can't resist the temptation? What if I don't have anyone to help me?

"I mean, I've got my two best friends. We grew up together in the same fucking world with basically the same, neglectful parents. They know, and yet they *don't,* and I don't think they ever could. So it's not like I can depend on them if

I need them?" I phrase it like a question as I glance around the room. A few eyes are on me, some are nailed to the floor. All different people from all different parts of the world, and yet we're all here at Black Diamond Recovery, trying to better ourselves.

Or at least, some of us are. Who knows.

It's quiet as my words settle around the room. I can feel Gavin's eyes on me, heavy and searching, but I *can't.* With shame, I keep my head down, twisting my fingers together.

"What if they don't forgive me? What if I can't ever forgive myself? I think the worst part of it all is I don't regret *everything.* Only the shit I did that hurt my friends. I don't regret trying to escape my father or the life I was forced into. The money, the fame, and all the weight it carries. This may be an excuse, but my father fucked me up, and I have no desire to fix things with him. Is that wrong or, like, bad for my recovery? 'Cause even though my mom's death was... I don't know. Not the start of all this, but you guys know what I mean. It was everything else that kept me there."

I wonder while speaking aloud, knowing I won't get answers to impossible questions, but it helps to voice my fears.

All of them.

"What if once I'm back in my fucking penthouse, the loneliness creeps back in like white static burning my brain, and the only option I have to shut it off is the coke? Or fuck, even booze. *What if I can't resist?*" My words are a mere whisper now as my voice cracks, then breaks from the sob I didn't even feel. Tears stream and drip onto the floor. I drop my head in my arms, resting them on my thighs as I sob uncontrollably, letting everyone in the circle of chairs see me at my most vulnerable.

"The *what if's* will kill you and all your progress if you let it," someone reminds me, their voice soft but stern. I nod against my hands, hearing the words deeper than ever.

"I did phone calls," another voice says. "I knew I wouldn't be able to face them once I got home, so I called. Hearing their voice was enough, and I didn't have to worry about schooling my face. And if it was too much, I could mute the call—or just hang up."

"But is that the same?" I ask with a flash of hope. I didn't even think about a phone call.

"Yeah. To me, it was. We're on a fucking island in the middle of nowhere, dude. A phone call suffices just fine. Especially when they know we're trying to work through our own shit. And if they don't understand or respect that, then maybe they shouldn't be in your life. This is the time to figure out what's best for *you,* even if you are trying to make amends with those you hurt."

Their words wash through me like a gentle, salty breeze. I breathe a little easier, feel a little lighter. I lift my head, searching the faces for the one who spoke, but I can't tell with everyone looking at me. My brows tug in the center as I search, but no one pipes up to it.

Huh. A mysterious liberator with all the right words. Who is he, Jesus fucking Christ?

The thought makes me snort. Like Jesus would be *here,* amongst the damned, of all places.

Gavin steps away from the wall, stealing every fiber of my attention like he always does. His face is tight with an emotion I can't read, but his eyes are still so gentle.

"Thank you for sharing, Zev," Kevin says, tweaking his teal-framed glasses with a smile. I nod and slump back in my seat, but I think there's a smile on my lips because Gavin can't stop staring at me. And I have to admit, I do feel a bit lighter than before.

Less burdened with my thoughts or whatever the hell.

Nineteen

GAVIN

"It's all set up, as of this morning."

Steam billows out behind Zev as he steps out of the shower with a towel wrapped loosely around his waist and another to his hair as he dries the dripping strands.

The sight of him has my steps faltering. My phone almost slips from my hand as I rake my eyes over my boy, dripping and flushed from the warm water.

He eyes me curiously as he walks to the small, walk-in closet housing all of his clothes. He pulls on a pair of sweats, sans underwear, throwing me a smirk over his shoulder. His ass clenches as he steps into them, making me grit my teeth.

"Gavin? Did I lose you?" Deacon's voice floods my ear, making me flinch. I shake my head and blink a few times, forcing myself to turn away from Zev, glancing at my watch as it buzzes with an email notification that has me stilling.

"Gavin?" Zev questions behind me. I hold up my hand to my boy before stepping outside. The sun is hot as it glares down. Sweat instantly beads on my skin, making me roll my shoulders.

"I'm here—sorry. Got distracted."

"Apparently, which isn't good since you're on a job." Deacon keeps his tone light, but I can hear the underlying questions.

"I'm aware," I spit the words out as my eyes scan the surrounding area. The island is full of lush vegetation—a never-ending sea of vibrant greens and blues.

"Are you okay?"

"Fine. Just tell me what's going on."

Deacon huffs. "Like I said, it's installed. Got finished up this morning. We've been working with Zion to get it done."

Deacon's mention of Zion makes my hackles rise. "Did you run into any issues?"

"No, it went smoothly. It helps that Zion's got more money than the fucking prince of England, I'm sure." I bite back a growl. *All that fucking money and he couldn't manage to help his son until it was almost too late.*

"Good. Is the feed live on the site?" Zevryn's eyes burn into the side of my face. I sneak a glance at him through the reflective glass. He's sitting on the sofa, staring down at the empty dishes from the meal we shared earlier.

The sight of his downturned lips makes my skin crawl with the urge to wrap him in my arms and make it all go away.

He shouldn't ever look like that.

"Yes..." Deacon trails off. "You know they all are—for *security* purposes," he enunciates. I scoff. "Why are you asking, Gavin?"

"No reason."

"Don't lie to me. You've been really invested in all of this. More so than what is necessary. Zion told me the system was your idea—which is good for business, don't get me wrong—but do you wanna explain?"

Zevryn's eyes meet mine, making my breath catch. I spin around and drop my elbows to the wooden rail. "First of all, he should've gotten the ball rolling on it after I *told* him to before I even left. Why he didn't makes no goddamn sense to me when he quite literally hired me to protect his son from a death threat. Wouldn't installing security measures at his penthouse be a part of that?

"Second, I care about Zev's safety. And we'll be leaving in just two weeks, so I need to know he'll be safe when I'm no longer with him to ensure it."

My breath comes out faster, each exhale making the line crackle. It's quiet for long, drawn-out moments.

"What's going on, Gavin?" Deacon finally says something, but goddamnit, that's not what I was hoping he'd say.

"Nothing, Deac. I'm just doing my job."

"It sounds like you're doing a hell of a lot more than that." His tone is accusatory, making my hackles rise.

"What the fuck is that supposed to mean?" My grip tightens on my phone, making it crack and groan from the pressure.

"*That* is what I mean. You don't swear—at least in any professional situation. And while we are close friends, this is a business call." His words are like a douse of ice water. "You also have not been checking in with Zion Carver like you're supposed to. He's had to call me for updates about his son."

"He acts as if he gives a fuck about anything other than

his investment," I snap, the words coming out before I can think twice, and the moment I say them, they're followed by regret. It's not my place to speak on Zion and Zevryn's relationship, but fuck, after this shit my boy has told me about his father and the way he treats him coupled with what I have personally witnessed... I do not fucking like the guy.

In fact, I kind of want to break his face for mistreating my boy and putting him through a hell he never deserved.

"Goddamnit, Gavin. That's not your place! What the fuck is going on?!" Deacon shouts into the phone, letting curse words of his own slip through. My anger deflates in an instant, the need to be defensive draining out of me. What's the point in keeping up pretenses that don't fucking matter?

"I care about the boy," I admit to Deacon, taking a deep breath of relief at the joy it brings.

Honesty.

"As in, you care about his safety and want to make sure he makes it home safe," Deacon says, deadpan.

I scratch the back of my neck, my hair brushing my knuckles. "Not exactly."

"Oh, you stupid, *stupid* son of a bitch. Please tell me this isn't what I think it is."

"Deac—"

"No! This is not good, Gavin. At all. I'm not even going to mention that you're married because if anyone is blatantly aware of that, it's you. What I am going to bring up is the contract you signed when you were hired. And I know, it was about a decade ago, but I'm sure you remember the fine print that pretty much goes without saying."

I hear a few clacks of a keyboard before his voice drowns on.

"Section 18:1. *Employees of Ayers Security are encouraged to develop and maintain professional relationships in the workplace. Sexual or romantic relationships with clients directly violates the fundamental principles of professional and ethical behavior. Therefore, those types of relationships are prohibited. If one infringes—*"

"Enough!" I shout into the line. "I fucking get it, Deacon."

"Do you? Do you really understand what this means, Gavin? For fucks sake, I *never* thought you'd be the one I'd have to worry about."

"Fuck," I mutter to myself, tugging at my hair. "I know. And you know me. You know I'd never jeopardize my job."

"Yeah, I do, which is why this doesn't make sense."

"I love him."

Deacon splutters into the line, making my lips twitch, despite my resolve. I lean my head back between my shoulders, squinting my eyes as I stare up at the bright, blue sky. I never thought to say the words I've been feeling out loud. I wish I could've said them to my boy, but I don't think that's something I'll be able to do for quite a while.

There are far too many loose ends we both have to work through before we go muddling what we are with the tangles of our pasts—and presents.

"Love? What the hell?" he mutters. "What about Milo?" Deacon asks the question I've been dreading myself.

What about Milo... my husband, my partner, my best friend for the last ten years.

What about him?

"I love him. I always will, but it's not working. It hasn't been for a long time, and we both know that."

"Does he know?"

I shake my head, even though he can't see me. "No. Well, maybe—but not about Zevryn. I wasn't going to have a conversation like that over the phone. He deserves far more respect than that."

"So, what? You're going to drop the kid off at his place, go divorce your husband, and then run to your little boyfriend's apartment?"

Well...

"Hey," I grate. "Watch the tone, Deac. It's not that simple, and you know it."

"Shit. Sorry. I'm just... This is confusing, Gavin. This *isn't you.*"

"That's it, isn't it? *This isn't me.* But what if it is? What if this is who I have always been? It just took Zevryn to shed light on it."

"You can't be that naive."

"Who says it's naive?"

"He's nineteen-years-old. You're thirty-three."

"And?" Is this how it will always be for me and Zevryn? Everyone spewing their opinion like it has any relevance, like they could ever understand what we have.

I know it's wrong, in more ways than one. He's vulnerable; I'm breaking vows.

All I've done is chew over every possible way this can't and will not work, and I'm done with it. Zevryn doesn't deserve my persistent, negative thoughts when he's the only one to make me feel alive.

He deserves respect and for me to trust that he knows what he wants. Dr. Weaver said Zev is more than capable of making his own decisions. And while she advised against a relationship, she knows she can't stop Zev, and she *trusts* his decision-making.

That's how far my boy has come. How hard he's fucking worked, and I refuse to belittle his perseverance just because of a few entanglements.

"You've never once thought that you were taking advantage of him?" Deacon's voice sounds too much like my own. It draws me up short for a minute. My eyes cut to Zevryn. The glass reflects the oceanfront behind me, but as I take a step closer, my boy comes into view.

He's curled up on the sofa, his chin resting against his knees, damp curls plastered to his slender neck. He must have shaved with my razor because his skin looks soft and smooth. My fingers twitch with the urge to drag my palm over every inch of him.

But it's the vacant look in his eyes that solidifies every lingering question festering because of Deacon's questions and judgments.

With my eyes locked on my boy, I speak slowly and deliberately into the line. "Of course, I've thought about that. Way too much, actually. But Zevryn deserves more than my doubt. He deserves respect and love. He's strong—stronger than anyone I've met—and he's a fighter. You can't even imagine half the shit he's been through, Deac. Enough to cripple anyone and keep them down.

"But not him. He's fighting. Getting stronger. He wants to live, and he wants to be fucking happy. All I want to do is protect him. Keep him safe. He wants the same from me, and I really can't tell him no. I don't want to."

Static rips through the other end, and I'm met with pregnant silence. "I care about him—deeply. I love all he is, and I'll do whatever it takes to protect him. So, if you need to fire me, you can. I'll respect your decision because I respect you and the fact you have a business to run. But don't expect me to leave my boy, regardless of your decision. He's mine, and he's not going anywhere."

I hang up the phone, then make my way inside, shivering when the cool air from the fan drifts across my heated skin. Zevryn glances up at me as I slide the door shut and engage the lock.

My phone feels heavy in my palm, so the moment I'm close enough, I toss it on the coffee table. My gun is put away in the drawer—per Zev's request when we're in the villa and most places anymore. I protested at first but ultimately obliged because I know he isn't in harm's way here.

It took me far too long to realize Zion hired me to *literally* babysit and spy on Zevryn, only using my job description as an excuse to get what he wanted.

I hate that I was hired to be used, but I can't bring myself to regret a single moment of it.

Zevryn is my life now.

"Hey, baby," I murmur as I sit down beside Zevryn. He's still in the same position—a close mirror to his posture when he's in therapy. It makes the hair on my arms rise.

"What's wrong?" I brush a few locks of hair away from his eyes, then grip his chin, my thumb finding the dimple there. I tilt his head back until the strain of keeping his eyes downcast becomes too much.

His hazel irises appear glassy. I swallow, squinting. "Tell me what's wrong." I don't pose it as a question, so he knows he doesn't have a choice on answering me. "Honesty, remember?"

His Adam's apple rolls with a swallow. He darts his gaze away, making me stiffen further. "You looked upset on the phone. Worried, maybe?" His eyes dart to mine before dropping again. "Did something happen?"

My chest deflates. I grab onto Zevryn, clutching him and digging my fingers into any space of skin I can reach as I haul him into my lap. He gasps as he flies through the air. I wrap my arms around him the moment he settles in my lap. Pressing a kiss to the top of his head, I murmur, "Baby, nothing happened. I was on the phone with my boss, and he said some shit that pissed me off."

"What'd he say?" he asks timidly. I nuzzle into his hair, breathing in the scent of lavender.

"Just questioned my intentions with you."

He gasps and tries to pull away, but I keep him pinned to my chest. "What does that mean?" he rasps and buries his face in my chest, making me hum. I lean forward, balancing his weight easily as I pull my shirt off and toss it on the back of the couch. I delve my fingers into my boy's hair and grasp the strands near his roots, using my grip to guide his head to where he wants to be.

The second he latches onto my nipple, he sighs heavily and contentedly, practically melting into me. I hum, playing with his hair as warmth seeps into me. My boy curls into my lap, legs bent near my chest as he nestles his ass perfectly between my thighs.

I pat his left ass cheek in a steady rhythm, timed almost perfectly with the drugging pulls of his mouth on me. I drop my head to my shoulder opposite of Zevryn's so I can watch him while he settles.

All traces of unease have left him, and in its place is a tranquil peace I feel deep in my marrow.

"It means I care about you, baby," I whisper softly.

"Feeling better, boy?" I ask after an unmeasurable amount of time has passed. Zevryn's still suckling me, but his pulls have slowed from his near-frantic desire. He nods against me, so I tweak his pierced nipple through his shirt. He jerks in my arms, then groans loudly. The vibration shoots straight through my nipple and to my cock.

Zevryn needing to suckle me isn't always sexual in nature. Sometimes, he just needs something to suck on to calm down, to center himself. Other times, he does it just to get me riled up.

My boy got what he needed to ease his worries, so now he's teasing me like the brat he is.

I swat his ass playfully, making him grin around my nipple. He peers up at me through his long, dark lashes, eyes sparkling with a new light. He pops off, swirling his tongue around his swollen lips. My nipple is puffy and swollen with its own heartbeat. Each thump sends a fresh wave to my groin.

"Thank you..." he trails off, looking sheepish. *That reminds me...* I palm his cheek, rubbing my thumb over his smooth skin.

"We never did that research you brought up," I remind him.

He shrugs. "Yeah, I know. We... got distracted the other day, and then I just didn't know how to bring it up again."

"Baby, you can talk to me about anything."

"I know." He nods, smiling up at me. *Fuck, I wanna crush him to me so hard, he just slips right inside and burrows into my thoracic cavity.*

"But I was kind of embarrassed to bring it up again. And Dr. Weaver said to take my time when I told her I actually didn't get the chance to do it."

I arch a brow. "Did she ask why?" Zev nods but doesn't elaborate. I pinch his ass.

"I told her we had sex instead," he blurts, face flaming bright red. I click my tongue before running it along my teeth. Zev fidgets, so I hold his arms down, stilling the movement.

"What did she say?"

"Nothing really." He fingers the coiled hairs on my chest. "Just for me to be careful and remember how important my recovery is."

I can't bite back my growl. My arms tighten around my boy on instinct. "Your recovery is always on my mind. I would never—" Zevryn silences me with a kiss to my Adam's apple. He keeps his mouth to my neck, lips brushing over the hair there as he speaks.

"I know, baby. All it was, was a reminder *for me.* So I don't forget that life exists outside of you, even if I forget that when we're together."

Words I crave to say sit heavily on my tongue, the three syllables weighing me down, but I can't do that to Zevryn. Not now and especially not out of selfishness.

I hold in a breath, count to ten, then exhale. "That makes sense."

"Yeah. But it's nice knowing you get defensive over me." His nails scratch along my skin, igniting a trail of goosebumps. I tighten my arms around him.

"Of course I do. Have you thought about what you want to look up?" He nods but doesn't answer verbally. "Do you want to do that now?"

He sits up, and I instantly miss the heat of his mouth on me. "Yeah." I narrow my eyes, making him roll his own, which earns him a swat. "Please," he mocks.

"Brat." I nip the end of his nose and move him to the cushion.

"It would be nice to know things." I nod my agreement as I grab my laptop.

"You don't know?" Zevryn questions, and I shake my head.

"No, baby. I've never felt this way about anyone before. These… thoughts and urges are new to me."

Zev squirms. "Oh." I huff.

Handing my laptop to Zev, I tell him, "Password is capital A, lowercase W, capital RT, zero, two, lowercase MN, exclamation point."

He stares up at me, jaw slack, eyes squinted. "What?"

"Oh, just—" I snatch it back to type it in, then hand it back to him. He smirks as he drops it onto his lap. His fingers hover above the keys.

"What is it?"

"Seems surreal to have access to the internet again," he tells me.

Oh, my poor boy. I sit down next to him and haul him

against me. “Feels like a lot, huh.” He nods, dropping his head to my shoulder.

“A little scary but in a good way? I don’t know if that makes sense.”

“It does, baby.”

“It’s like the seclusion of the island is fading the less time I have here.” He sounds despondent, and it makes my heart clench painfully. I rub my hand up and down his arm.

“I know exactly what you mean.” *All too well.*

I’m terrified he won’t want me anymore once we leave. He can need me, but if he doesn’t *want* me...

I shove down the stinging thought. “I’m here if you need me, boy.”

The smile that lights up his face eradicates every shred of painful doubt. His eyes are brighter, skin colored the prettiest pink. “Always?”

Oh, damn it all to hell.

“Yeah, my boy. Always.”

If only always was forever.

Twenty

GAVIN

It's late into the night when Zevryn starts squirming. He's lying on his stomach across the foot of the bed, cute little ass bouncing inside his sweatpants. I peer over my phone at him, watching with amusement.

He lost his shirt after I fed him a late-night snack, having made quite the mess with water because he was far too engrossed in the screen to listen to a word I said.

I wasn't bothered in the slightest. Feeding my boy and even cleaning him up after felt like another piece clicking into place. It did for him too, I think.

"What are you reading over there?" I ask, only slightly teasing, but when my boy's eyes dart to me before slamming the laptop closed, my curiosity piques.

I set my phone on the stand next to me and push off the headboard, crawling down the bed. Zevryn scrambles to sit up, but I throw my leg over his waist, keeping him still. I sit on his ass and rock my hips against him just to hear that soft mewl as he buries his face in the comforter.

"Ohhh. Must've been naughty," I lean forward and suck his earlobe into my mouth. I flick my tongue over his piercing.

"Da—" He cuts himself off by shoving his face into the crook of his elbow. I snatch his hair up and yank his head back.

Pressing my cheek to his, I growl, "Say it." *I've been doing enough research of my own to be burning up from the inside out.*

"Daddy." It's a breath of relief—for the both of us.

"That's right, boy. Don't ever fucking hesitate." I snag his skin between my teeth and pull until he yelps. After kissing it better, I sit up and dig the heels of my palms into his shoulder blades, keeping every inch of him pressed into the mattress. He tries to move his hips, but I drop more weight down.

"Tell me what you were reading."

"Please..."

"Please..." I taunt him. "Please what? Make you?" I follow the curvature of his spine. "Please don't make you?"

"Both," he whines, trying to arch his back. I chuckle.

I dig my nails in. "Tell me."

"It was a forum where, uh, people tell their real-life stories and experiences." The words fall out of his mouth in a jumbled rush.

"*Hmmm.*" I kiss his neck, flicking my tongue out to lap up some salt. "And?"

"And?" He whimpers.

"Did it turn you on? Reading about other boys being fucked by their Daddy?" I sink my teeth into his neck just so I can feel his pulse flutter against my tongue.

"Gods!" he screams. I slide down his ass and stretch out,

pressing my clothed cock between his cheeks. I grind down against him, eyes rolling back at the painful friction.

"Yeah, we've already established the gods situation, baby. Tell me what you learned."

He turns his head to the side so he can look at me. "Do I have to?"

"Yes. I want to make sure we're on the same page."

He takes an unsteady breath before trying to hide his face again. I snatch up his hair. "No. I want you to look at me when you talk to me."

"Fuck." I wrap my hand around his throat and squeeze. "Sorry, Daddy," he rasps, sounding contrite. I kiss him.

"Better."

"In, uh, BDSM... There's a Daddy Dom, little boy dynamic. I don't... I don't know if that's exactly what we are?" He worries his bottom lip, so I lean down to kiss it.

"I'm so proud of you, baby. Keep going." My praise urges him on, filling me with pleasure.

"Anyway, I learned every dynamic is different and unique to the couple. It doesn't have to be one thing or the other. You don't even have to label it as long as we're on the same page and we're both consenting adults." He stares up at me with wide, questioning eyes.

I've never felt so full of love before.

"And... what I feel is called subspace. It's different for everyone, and it happening or me enjoying it doesn't mean there is something wrong with me..." I delve my fingers into his hair and clench, drawing him back until we're eye to eye.

"You're absolutely right about all of that, boy." His eyes flutter closed. A small smile pulls at his lips.

"What do you think is the most important thing you

learned?" I dig my fingers into his shoulders, massaging the tension away. He groans, melting into the bed, but I can feel him thinking about my question.

I give him time, not pressuring for his answer. After a minute or two, he wriggles beneath me. With one last grind against his sweet little ass, I help him sit up. He crosses his legs and places his hands in his lap.

So fucking cute.

I tweak his nose, making him grin. He looks up, right into my eyes as he says, "I don't need to be ashamed."

"Fuck, baby." I slam our mouths together, needing to feel every inch of him. "I can't tell you how proud of you I am," I say against his mouth. I breathe in his every exhale until I feel faint.

My boy clutches my shoulders as he drops back on the bed, pulling me as close as I can get. I drop on top of him, pressing our hips together until our bones grind painfully. I rip myself away from my boy's mouth, panting as I stare down at him.

The soft light from the lamp coupled with my hair hanging in front of my face casts dim, distorted shadows on his face. I lean to the side, and a yellow beam casts across his face, skimming directly over his left eye.

I lean in, transfixed at the ring of green surrounding the warm brown in the center. His lashes are long and black, curving upward, almost brushing the edge of his bushy brows every time he stares up at me, eyes wide and feigning innocence—like now.

His nostrils have a permanent flare, and that fucking dimple in his chin calls to me, a perfect divot for my thumb to rest. I grab him now, placing my thumb exactly where it belongs. I turn his head from side to side, taking in every possible inch of him while I still can.

Dark stubble lines his sharp, angular jawline, making my mouth water. I dip down, testing the roughness with my tongue. My boy lurches off the bed, pushing his head into the mattress. I hum contentedly as I continue my way down his throat, nipping at his Adam's apple before tracing the lines defining his pectorals.

I tease his pierced nipple, tugging the silver bar between my teeth until his pink bud is stretched to its capacity. Zevryn's whimpering, fisting the sheets, and trembling uncontrollably. I ease up and suck the irritated bud into my mouth, lapping at it to ease the throb.

"I'm gonna worship your body, boy. Lick, suck, and fuck every inch of you." I follow the line of hair down his abdomen until it melts into the hair on his groin. I bury my nose in the dark curls and fill my lungs with his scent.

My boy squirms against me, pressing on my shoulders. I have to force my eyes from the back of my head to stare up at Zevryn. His face is bright red with embarrassment. The sight sends liquid heat through my extremities, making my toes curl.

I keep my nose engulfed as I skim my way down until his hard cock slips between us, radiating heat. He's hard with skin as soft as silk as I pull him into my mouth slowly. I focus on sucking his cockhead, my lips pressed just beneath the flared glans.

Salty-sweet drops of precum linger on my tongue, urging me on and increasing my need tenfold. I drag my mouth down his length, tongue curved to fit around him. My boy's hips flex as he tries to fuck into my mouth, but I drop an arm across his hips, stilling him so I can work him the way I want.

When his head bumps against the back of my throat, I inhale deeply through my nose and swallow, opening my throat to allow him entry. My vision darkens at the corners the longer I go without oxygen, but the drugging pull of having my boy's hard cock lodged in my throat is all I care about.

Zevryn's hands clutch the sides of my head. My hair tangles around his fingers, tugging against my scalp with every bob of my head. The burst of oxygen is like a hit. I'm dizzy and disoriented. My only focus is devouring the slim, long cock attached to a boy who smells of a lavender sea.

He's my Achilles heel.

"Gonna c-come," Zevryn cries out. I pop off to catch my breath and let him come back down. I massage his balls, which are heavy and drawn up tight. I trace the line down the center, reaching back to his taint to press against the pad of flesh with my thumb. Zevryn's legs twitch, and his head rolls to the side with a groan. My jaw aches as I smirk down at him, reveling in the way he seems so undone already when I've only just gotten started.

I massage that same spot with two fingers this time as I suck one of his balls into my mouth, then switch to the other until he's dripping. I push his legs back and out, spreading him wide.

His pale skin glistens with saliva. I follow a trail of it as it travels down his taint and into his crease. I drag my index finger through it and press it to his pucker, swirling it around through the damp hairs there.

My eyes roll back into my head when my boy's hole

winks at me, a heady invitation. "You want me in here, baby?" I press just the tip of my finger inside, drawing a sharp breath from my boy. He nods frantically, dark curls splayed across the white sheets.

"How bad?" I tease him with the tip. It's barely an invasion, more frustrating than anything.

"Please," he whines, shaking his head. "I need to come. Need you inside me."

As I inhale, I let my eyelids close for a moment. When I catch my boy's eyes, my heart gallops in my chest, overcome with it all.

I sink in up to the first knuckle, knowing he feels the sting. "Tell me how badly you need me. I want to hear it."

Zevryn's pale skin has flushed a rosy pink, glistening with beads of perspiration. I want to lick every drop from him.

"I need you more than I need to breathe. I wanna drown in you." Tears leak from the corners of his eyes.

It's like he stole the words right from the abysmal depths of my soul.

"Anything for you, my boy." I press a gentle kiss to his shiny lips. "Just relax and let Daddy do all the thinking, okay?" I wait until he nods, dragging his lips over mine. I can't resist swiping my tongue out to steal a deeper taste before I'm sucking his cock back down my throat.

Zevryn must not have been expecting it because he screams, his upper-half lifting from the bed. I work him over until I feel him twitching—which happens much too quickly, to my dismay. He whines when I slide off.

I pat his dick, eyes blazing as it bobs in the air, his head flushed and glistening with my saliva. I shuck my clothes easily and finish peeling Zevryn's off, where they hang around his ankle.

Once we're both bare to the humid air, I swipe the lube off the stand and drench my cock before sliding to the center of the mattress. I tug on Zevryn's arm, dragging him across until his sweaty skin is plastered to mine.

His eyes are lidded, lashes fanning his cheeks as he pants against my chest, arm slung across my torso.

It always feels heavenly when he holds me. Like his sinewy arms are the only thing keeping the pieces together, but that's exactly how it *should* be.

I reach down and lift his leg, dragging it over until he's straddling me. As my cock slides between his cheeks, Zevryn peels his sweaty face from my skin to push up, adding more friction. He arches his back like a little kitten as he slams his ass down. My hands find his slutty, little waist, and I dig my thumbs into the V of his hips.

Zevryn grinds against my slick cock without having to be told. His own bobs in front of him, slapping my chest. I fist the base so he fucks into my hand with every flex of his hips, giving him dual sensation.

"That's it, boy. Get yourself nice and wet for Daddy's cock."

The sounds ripping from his throat burn through me. When my cockhead catches on his rim, we both suck in a breath. Zevryn stills like he got burnt, chest heaving, fingers flexing against my chest. He licks his lips as he stares into my eyes before dropping his upper half to mine and arching his back to better the angle.

My dick slides inside him as he slowly pushes back. He's so fucking tight, I groan, letting my head relax against the pillows for a few moments of rapturous bliss before I pop the cap on the lube and squirt a generous amount on my fingers.

With a grunt, I push up on an elbow and reach around my boy's waist. "What's wrong?" he asks on a whimper as my movement pushes me deeper.

"Not wet enough, baby." I force the words out through gritted teeth. Fingers clamp down on my wrist.

"Like the sting."

I suck in a breath through my nose. Zevryn's front is centimeters from mine, skin so hot, I can feel each heat wave as it reaches outward, licking across my flesh like his wicked tongue.

"I'm not gonna hurt you. Not like that." I kiss his collarbone as I lift him from my lap. I hiss when my cock slaps against my stomach, smearing lube into the hairs. I lather the lube on my hand all up and down Zevryn's crease before shoving three fingers inside him with no warning.

He yelps and bucks. I nip his shoulder. "Thought you liked the sting, baby?" I snark as I shove lube inside him. My hand cramps from the angle, but with the way Zevryn fucks down on my hand until my knuckles bump his ass, I couldn't care less about the pain.

Or anything but this. But him.

My boy.

Twenty-One

ZEVRYN

I hold my breath, and the pressure increases, sending me higher.

My heart hammers against my ribs, so hard it hurts, and the pain has never felt so good.

"Baby." My Daddy's voice echoes in my head, an anchor that keeps me exactly where I'm supposed to be.

I blink slowly at him, feeling a lazy smile tugging at the corners of my lips. "Fuck, you're beautiful." He tugs his fingers from me, eliciting a whine that gets cut off with a drawn-out moan when his cock enters me again.

He's gentle as he fucks me, every thrust like small waves lapping against the shore. Each one pulls me closer to the edge until I hover on the precipice where everything feels *more,* and then too much. But it's not enough.

I crave him the way I've never craved anything. Not cocaine, not booze.

Not even intimacy. *Or love.*

I just want Gavin however I get him. Whether he's married or not. Loves me or not.

I rock my hips, adding to the profusions blooming between the very spot our bodies are joined. Every sense homes in on all things Gavin.

The way the air smells of his deodorant, the salt on my tongue from his sweat, the gooseflesh singeing my hairs as they burn trails across my flesh.

When his pelvis smacks against my ass, I whimper, dropping my head to his chest. My rim is stretched impossibly wide. Daddy's arm is still wrapped around my waist, and he uses my new position to his advantage.

He presses against my stretched hole, tracing my rim with the tip of his index finger. The added sensation and pressure coupled with his cock dragging across my hypersensitive walls makes me clamp down tight to stave off the festering, blissful agony of my orgasm.

I lunge forward, knocking our heads together in a desperate attempt to claim his mouth. Daddy chuckles. "So desperate." The words themselves are demeaning, but he says them with a fondness that makes me feel proud.

He gives me what I need and drags our mouths together in a slow perusal of one another. His beard burns my face with each pass. My tongue slides against his teeth before he opens up wide.

When our tongues finally tangle, everything fades to gray.

Every messy, muddled shade twines between like gnarled branches in a flood. Vertiginous and exhilarating.

Just a Daddy and his boy.

This connection between us may not be normal or even

accepted by society's standards, but it's *us.* We both want it, and we can have it.

For now.

I don't know what's going to happen when I leave in just over a week. The clock ticking on our relationship chimes louder every day, the crisp wail of a sound like nails to a chalkboard. A reminder this has only ever been temporary.

The knowledge kills me. How this isn't it for us.

It'll never be this simple again—this effortless and all-consuming.

I'm a jumbled mess of a recovering addict, and Gavin, my temporary bodyguard slash lover, is married to a man that probably doesn't deserve a second of infidelity.

Daddy told me they've been in turbulence for a long time, and I believe him—because why wouldn't I? But the band wrapped around his finger makes me question every word to ever leave his mouth.

I know he cares for me. Not only has he said so, but he's more than proved it to be true. I feel it with every touch, especially the ones with no intent behind them. Like when we sit on the sofa together after we eat and his hand finds my wrist, his fingers stroking my pulse point absentmindedly.

Or when I have a nightmare and he rouses me from sleep before I wake on my own by pressing my face to his chest so I can latch onto him and suck in needy pulls. The motion alone lulls my mind into a state where it all fades away into a blissful numbness.

He *knows* these things without me ever having to say a word.

I was ashamed of my desires for him—the specifics of it

all. How I crave to let Daddy slip from my lips or the way it fills me with peace to be carried in his arms like I don't weigh a thing.

I'm more than grateful that Daddy brought up the research again. Having some answers to my lingering questions is exactly what I needed to feel *okay* with how I feel.

To know it's okay to want what I want and to need what I need.

There's nothing wrong with the undercurrent of desire and necessity that has long since bloomed between me and my bodyguard.

Daddy needs to be needed, to care for someone—wholly and completely—and I need to be taken care of. To have someone take the reins and guide me when all is lost and confusing. And how we do that is right for us.

He's my Daddy, and I'm his boy. The rest doesn't matter. Not to him and certainly not to me.

"Where'd you go, baby?" Daddy's breath is hot against my neck. Sweat drips and slides between us, slicking our skin as we writhe against one another. I shake my head, sending my curls bouncing.

"Just thinking." I squeeze my eyes shut at the unexpected sting and bury my face into his neck. I mouth at his salty flesh, nuzzling and humming contentedly as a dousing warmth buzzes through my groin. My dick pulses, and a dribble of precum smears between our stomachs.

"*Hmm.*" Daddy grunts, his hands tightening on my waist as he increases his tempo—only slightly. The drag of his cock inside my body makes me cry out, my back arching at the onslaught of pleasure as he nails my prostate with wicked accuracy.

"Love it when you're thinking about us, but I want you with me right now, so let's fix that, shall we?" With a hand knotted in my hair and fingers bruising my flesh, Daddy pins me against his thighs as he grinds his hips up. His cock shifts around inside me, but his cockhead stays pressed against my gland.

Sparks fly across my vision as it blurs. White morphs into blue. The pull in my groin is drugging. I scream, unable to contain the overwhelming sensations burning through me. In me. All around me.

Daddy growls and flips us. I lose my breath as air whips around me. He hikes my hips back and slams a hand to the base of my spine, pushing down until my stomach hits the bed but my ass stays in the air. I fist the sheets as he slams back inside me, stealing the breath from my lungs.

He's not gentle anymore. The hands holding me fucking *hurt.* I can feel the bruising all the way in my muscles, but the ache only sends me higher.

Slaps reverberate in the air, intermingling with Daddy's grunting moans and my mewling screams. He slides his hand up my spine until his fingers wrap around my nape. He squeezes the sides, making my eyes roll back.

Daddy shoves my face into the mattress as he pounds into me. I can feel my ass jiggling with every slap of our skin, the sting sharp and delicious. My neck throbs in time with my pulse, rapid yet chugging heavily.

As his balls slap against my taint with a particularly sharp sting, I clamp down as a scream rips through my throat. My balls throb, and my dick jerks below me. "Fuck!"

Daddy yanks me against his chest, sending me reeling as he wraps his hand around my length and jerks me through my orgasm, sending me higher.

I slump against my Daddy as he continues to slide his hand over my softening length, each drag of his calloused palm making me twitch and groan a sting of unintelligible words.

"Such a good boy." He kisses my shoulder and presses his palm to my lower abdomen, smearing my cum around as he works himself inside of me lazily, like he wants to drag this on forever.

I don't even mind the sharp pain twinged with pleasure because I know this is what he wants, and it feels good.

"I'll never get enough of this." He wraps his other arm around me, bracketing me in. I let my head fall back against his right shoulder. The angle is a bit awkward with my ass pressed back against his groin, but keeping myself upright is becoming harder by the second.

But I know I don't have to try. Daddy will take care of me.

"Daddy." Tears drip down my face. A few curve toward my mouth, and when I dart my tongue out to wet my lips, I taste them.

With a muffled moan, Gavin's hips stutter as he releases inside of me. His cum is warm as he paints my walls, staining me and filling me with him.

"This is good, isn't it?" he whispers in my ear after a few moments, his dick still flexing inside me. "Feels freeing. To be who we are—together. You're my boy, Zevryn." Daddy's voice cracks, making my heart clench in my chest. I try to turn to look at him, but he tightens his arms. I feel the bob of his throat as he swallows. "You're my boy, and I'm your Daddy. It doesn't have to be anything more than that.

"We are who we are, and we find that within each other. You don't have to overthink it, baby. We can just *be.*" His words snap the last tether keeping me here.

They're freeing—and I ascend.

Twenty-Two

ZEVRYN

"I'm ready," I say with confidence. Daddy beams at me, his smile transcendent. He hands me his phone, and I type in the password. Once the screen is unlocked, my finger hovers over the phone icon, the bright green, rounded square taunting me.

"Do you need help?" I smile shyly at his words before glancing up. His eyebrows are high on his forehead as he eyes me. His hair is pulled back into a tight bun, the messy knot placed at the crown of his head.

"Would you?" I hold it out to him. With a twitch to his lips, he opens the app before glancing at me again. "Gotta give me a number, boy."

I flush. "Right. Sorry, it's—" He grasps my chin.

"Don't apologize to me. Not when you have nothing you need to apologize for. Do you need another round of swats?" I reach back and brush my fingers down my clothed ass. The swim trunks do nothing to hold back the heat radiating from my bare skin just beneath.

My eyes flutter closed as I press deep, eliciting a groan I can't hold back. I shake my head, not bothering to open my eyes. "Maybe."

Daddy tweaks my nose. "Don't be a brat."

"Okay, Daddy." His bright smile returns with the utterance of his name. Ever since I spent hours reading articles and forums, I haven't been able to hold back the urge to say it.

He is my Daddy. It's not wrong. Or gross. It's not because I have daddy issues—or well, maybe not entirely—but Gavin's a Daddy in every way. He's a caretaker, a protector. My confidant. He respects me, cherishes me. Loves...

I suck in a breath, immediately shoving the thought away, deep down where I can no longer fucking feel it.

Except I can. It's right there, hovering in the small space between us like an oppressing weight.

I shake my head and plaster on a fake smile. Daddy doesn't buy it. His brows furrow before one forms an impressive arc. "What just happened?"

"I'm nervous." It's not a lie. I haven't spoken to anyone off the island since I arrived, but I'm leaving in a week, and it's time. I pull in a deep breath through my nose, hold it for ten seconds, and then blow it out.

"Good job, my boy." Gavin dips down and kisses me. As he pulls back, he grabs my hand and places his phone in my palm. The numbers sit on the screen, ready for me to type in the number and hit call. "Here. Give me the number."

I repeat Dillon's number by heart, watching almost in a daze as Gavin types each one in. "Are you ready?" His eyes dart between mine, searching.

"No, but I have to." I press the call button and shove the

phone against my ear. When the dial tone rings down my ear canal, I almost throw up. I have to swallow the burning rush of bile. Daddy's face tightens with unease, but he doesn't say anything. He just rubs his palm up and down my bare back, soothing me with his touch alone.

The tone cuts off, followed by a whisper of static, and then a voice fills the line. "Hello?"

My legs buckle, and if it wasn't for Daddy, I would've collapsed. He catches me easily and helps me down onto the sand. I stare out at the crystalline water, not really seeing it through the tears blurring my vision.

"Hey," I rasp, hating I can't say anything more. I don't even know *what* to say. Because there's nothing that would make any of what I did forgivable.

"Z...?" Dillon gasps.

"Yep." *Wow, Zev. Real fucking great.*

"Holy shit!" he shouts, making me yank the phone away from my ear. Gavin growls and sets me down in his lap. He wraps his arms around me. His hold feels solid, like there's no possibility I could ever go anywhere.

He's my anchor.

"Zev! Shit, I've missed you so much. How are you doing? Where are you? Do you like where you are? Are you sober now? Shit, sorry. That's probably insensitive. Am I allowed to ask? Is that bodyguard still with you? Your fucking dad won't tell us anything—go figure—and my dad's lips are sealed. Carmen! Z's on the phone; get the fuck in here!"

Dillon's rambling a million miles a minute, not letting me get a word in edge wise as he goes on and on. The sound of his voice makes me smile and fills a vacant spot in my chest I didn't realize was so hollow until now.

"Zev!" Carmen shrieks. There's a grunt, followed by a, "Hey!"

"I've missed you. Please tell me you're okay."

"Hey." I rub the back of my neck, suddenly feeling sheepish. I catch Gavin's eyes. "I'm okay."

"Put it on speaker phone, bitch! I want to talk to him, too! It's my fucking phone." Dillon and Carmen argue over the line, and I smile like I haven't in a long time.

"I miss you guys," I breathe. The tears fall, just like I knew they would, but they don't hurt—at least, not in a bad way.

It's rejuvenating.

"We miss you, too!" They both shout in unison, making me laugh. Daddy kisses the faded teeth marks on my bare shoulder before he lifts me from his lap. I whirl around in alarm, but he shakes his head and presses a finger to his lips.

"You're doing great, baby. You've got this. I'll be right here if you need me. Always." With a kiss to the top of my head, Gavin strides toward the water, leaving me alone on the beach. I watch the muscles in his back as he strides through the waves, blue shorts billowing around him from the trapped air.

"I love you." I let the words carry my whispered truth across the beach where it gets lost amongst the waves, exactly where it belongs.

"Zev? Ugh, we didn't lose you, did we?" With a shaky breath, I put the phone back to my ear.

"No. I dropped the phone."

"Okay, good. So! How are you? Tell us everything. We miss you so much." The repeated words of how they've missed me hit different each time. There's guilt, of course, but it's intermixed with relief and a sadness for my old life.

Not that I miss *who* I was, but... in a more nostalgic sense knowing that nothing will be the same.

"Who are you, and what have you done with my friends? We don't do feelings." We all laugh, and it feels *good*. "Nah, I'm kidding. I kind of do feelings now anyway. And I'm good. Sober, obviously." I crack the joke, holding my breath. They both laugh lightly, and I release it with a smile.

"This place has actually been really fu—really good for me." I catch the cuss word without really thinking, and the thought of my Daddy swatting my ass for it makes me shift on the sand. A few granules have made their way inside my shorts, only adding to the sting against my skin.

"I'm coming home in a week," I blurt.

"Oh, my God! That's so good, Zev."

"Yeah, dude. We're really proud of you."

I cough as unease creeps across my skin like darkness. "Look, I'm calling because making amends is part of the process. And I know I should've called weeks ago, but I just couldn't.

"I know that's just an excuse, but I've been working through a lot of shit and—" I swallow the lump choking me as I swipe at my eyes. Gavin dips beneath the water, and when he emerges, his soft, muscled body is dripping and glistening in the setting sun.

Solid, beautiful, and all mine.

For now.

"We understand, honey," Carmen says softly, her voice a gentle whisper. "We love you, and we *know*."

"But you don't," I correct her. "I'm an addict." I say the

words with confidence, the truth as strong as the resolve I try to obtain. "I hurt you because of what I've done, and I can't tell you how sorry I am for that. You two are my family, and I never wanted to hurt you—especially you, Dill. The way I abused you... I was blinded by my addiction, but that's no excuse.

"I see a lot of things differently now, and I don't ever want to go back to being that person."

Carmen's cries filter through the line, followed by Dillon's voice as he tries to soothe her, but I can hear the way his voice cracks. The sound of my two best friends losing it makes me sob. I nearly drop the phone again as it wracks through me, forceful and cleansing.

Neither of us speak for long minutes as we wallow in the sorrows of our pasts.

I'm not sure how much time has passed before Dillon speaks. "We've always loved you, Z. Even when you weren't yourself. I want you to know I'm so sorry for talking to Zion. I was just so scared, and I didn't know what to do. I just didn't want to watch my best friend kill himself anymore." The sob that rips out of his throat breaks me.

My heart splits wide open, and I suck in a gasping breath. My hand slams against my chest over and over, nails digging into my bare flesh as I try to breathe, but nothing comes.

I'm empty—clutching at nothing.

The phone thumps against the sand that suddenly feels like it's burning me alive. I watch with a blank stare as drops fall from my face, darkening the granules before it disappears in a blink. A high-pitched ringing is all I hear, like lost-lost screams of the past.

"Baby." Arms wrap around my waist, just below my ribs. A mangled sound I've never heard before rips from my throat, and I lash out. The hold tightens, constricting me to the point *I can't fucking breathe.*

The pressure in my chest amplifies, shooting to my head. My brain inflates, pressing against my skull. I bring my hands down, slapping and screaming. I dig my nails in, feeling coarse hair against my fingertips.

"Breathe for me." I hear words, but I *don't.* They echo, distorted and elongated. "Come on, my boy. You can do it. In. *In.*" I don't know what's happening, but my body obeys the command.

The rush of air that fills me is like a shock to my system. I splutter and cough, choking on nothing as life fills me. "That's it, baby. Take another breath for me." It's shaky and hesitant, but I do it. The arms around me tighten again, heightening my focus.

It's the kind of hold that centers me, keeps me grounded to the earth.

"Good. Again." Each one comes easier, brings back another sliver of clarity. Gavin's arms are strong. He's slick with water, soaking me as he pins me to his front. I slump against him when I realize, choking out breathless sobs.

"I'm right here, baby. Right here." He brings me back from the precipice of a dismal darkness, and I've never loved him more.

"You back with me?" I nod shakily. My body trembles uncontrollably, adrenaline from the panic attack coursing through my veins at hypersonic speeds. I swallow against the grit in my throat.

Gavin leans around me and clicks a button on the phone.

The sound of it cutting off makes me wince. "They heard all of that," I grumble pathetically into the comfort of his arm. I press my face in the crook of his elbow, breathing in the light scent of salt and *him.*

"Yes." He doesn't even try to lie, which is nice. I whimper, squeezing my eyes shut. Gavin seems to hesitate. "Are you embarrassed?"

"Yeah."

A slow beat. "Of me?" His voice is a soft rumble as it carries in the light breeze. I blink a few times.

"Of you?" I repeat, not having expected the question. I see Gavin nod in his shadow cast over the textured sand. I flip in his arms so I can see his face. His lips are downturned, beard still dripping water onto his bare chest. I play with the hairs there, finding comfort in the coarse texture.

When his eyes finally drop to mine, the look in his dark irises steals my breath. He looks open, vulnerable in the way I've mostly been the last two months. "No, Gavin." I use his first name instead of the name I crave to call him so he knows I'm fully clear-headed, even with the haze of my panic lingering.

"I'm not embarrassed of you. Ever. I'm ashamed of myself, for being easily triggered. For them hearing me lose it all because Dillon said he didn't want to watch me kill myself anymore. It's—" I swallow, then purse my lips. "It's strange hearing their point of views now that I'm able to recognize them as the truth. Their truth and also mine."

His unease never shifts, and my heart aches in a way that makes me want to cry forever. "Don't be ashamed of your recovery. You have triggers, and there's nothing wrong with that. You recognize it and try your damndest to work through it. You should be proud of yourself, Zevryn. I know I am.

"Seeing who you've blossomed into has been one of the greatest privileges of my life. You're so incredibly beautiful, baby. I've never seen someone work so hard to better themselves, and it's awe-inspiring."

I'm crying in earnest now, the tears wet and hot as they streak across my face. I try to hide in Gavin's chest, but he pulls my head back with a gentle grip on my curls. His eyes are tender and warm as he stares down at me with a love I never thought I'd see—or deserve.

"It's more than okay to break down, to feel with your whole soul when it all becomes too much. You know why?" He brushes a lock of hair off my cheek and tucks it behind my ear. His thumb drags down and traces the silver earring in my lobe. I shake my head, eyebrows pinching. It doesn't make sense. I mean, I know it's good to feel these things, to *want* to even feel them at all after I spent so long trying to be numb... but that's just the thing.

I didn't want to *always* be numb. My ultimate goal was to just feel *good.* But I didn't want the bad, which is where the numb came in.

But now I know there is no good without the bad—because the bad is what makes the good so *good.* Makes it worth it.

"Because there's nothing wrong with being in pain... o-or being vulnerable." My voice comes out far too small, but I don't have to be ashamed. Not with my Daddy.

"Well, yes. You're absolutely right." He caresses my cheek, and my eyes flutter closed as my heart clenches. "But also because I will be there to help you through it. I will always take care of you, boy."

His kiss is as soft and gentle as his words. Each second we're connected drags slowly and endlessly. There is no intent behind it other than to feel each other, to drift to a place where the sand is no longer beneath us and the waves of the ocean envelop us as we plunge into the deep trenches of a space we created just for us.

By the time we separate, I'm breathless and panting, but oxygen is the last thing on my mind. I lurch up, but Daddy pulls away with a tender smile. "As much as I'd love to keep doing this, I'm not as young as you are, boy. This position kills my back, and you're starting to burn." I glance down at my arm, noticing a faint pink blooming. My skin's hot to the touch, too.

"I wanted to swim after..."

"After the call, I know."

"I'm gonna call them back," I say with a confidence I don't feel.

"Do you want me with you this time? It's up to you, boy."

I nod shakily. "Please," I whisper. Daddy grins.

"Of course, my boy. Always, remember?" My nose wrinkles at the burn of tears. They fill my eyes, even as I try to blink them away. Daddy grabs my chin and tilts my head back. I can feel his ring as his hand slides across my skin. I squeeze my eyes shut, hating the place the touch of his ring takes me. One of pure, undiluted selfishness.

Kiss me. Please, just kiss me.

I part my lips with invitation, and my Daddy gives me what I need. Another slow perusal of one another. A kiss of passion, of love. His tongue drags against mine, rough and wet and drugging. I suck on it, making him grunt, which sends a spark of heat right to my balls. I flex my hips, veering toward my Daddy's arm stretched across my overheated body.

He pulls back, resting our foreheads together as he pants. I whine at the loss, but when he slides the phone into my hand, I sober quickly. I scramble to sit up. He keeps me in his lap, wrapping his arms around my waist and pressing his face into my neck.

His breath is hot against my sweaty skin but no less comforting. I lean into the touch as I redial, knowing with unwavering confidence that I have my Daddy to help me—at least until we descend from the jet and set foot back in the real world.

Twenty-Three

GAVIN

My boy's been in his head more than ever. We leave tomorrow, and I know that has everything to do with it. The weight of leaving our secluded world has got to be taking its toll on him, same as me.

I can't stop thinking about what's going to happen once we're back. When he's got his money and his friends again, he won't need me anymore, and the thought has nearly made me cry a few times.

I resist the urge to slam my hand against my sternum to add to the ache that's festering. It's deep, unwavering, and fucking suffocating. But my boy doesn't need my baggage along with his own trepidations.

I have to be strong for him. I *will* be. I just wish I could wallow in the sadness *with* him for a little while.

My boy's in his last session of therapy right now, so while he's occupied, I'm planning a surprise for him. It's hard since we haven't been separated practically at all since we both arrived, but I manage just fine through an endless stream of phone calls.

As a matter of fact, I love the forced proximity between us. It's the perfect excuse to keep him close, which is all I want anyway. I'm not looking forward to the separation that's coming.

I know it will leave a gaping hole in the shape of my boy —a space he carved for himself bit by bit with every needy touch and breathless sigh. Every whimper and cry, desperate and strong.

My head rolls between my shoulders. The muscles are stiff from sleeping upright against the headboard all night, but my boy needed me, and I'll be damned if I ever turn him away.

As distant as he's been during waking hours, at night, he's never been closer. I wake at all hours with his long limbs entangled with mine, every inch of him pressed against every inch of me.

I've never felt more consumed by another human being.

I think it's going to kill me to let him go. But I can't be selfish with him. Not yet, anyway. Not until I know I can take care of him the way he deserves.

I just need time.

"Would that work for you, Mr. Holt?" I shake my head, dispersing my thoughts.

"Yes, perfect. Thank you." I hang up and take a deep breath. I'm determined to give my boy a fantastic last day together.

"JET SKIS!" Zevryn shouts in my ear, rocking his pelvis against my back. I grunt at the feel of his softened cock rubbing against me. I tighten my hold on the backs of his thighs, digging my fingertips into the solid muscle.

"Yes, baby. Are you excited?" His laugh is melodic, a beautiful chime straight to my soul.

"Hell yes! This is fucking cool!" He's so excited, he doesn't even realize the words he let slip. I drop my hold, and he tightens his arms around my neck and his thighs around my waist to keep himself against me. I reach around and half-heartedly swat his ass. I mostly miss with the odd angle, making him laugh.

"Sorry, Daddy. I didn't mean to."

I roll my eyes, but my lips twitch. Two jet skis bob in the turquoise water in front of us. "Off ya get, boy." Zevryn slides down my back, every inch of his delicious skin rubbing against mine. He snickers from behind me, making me crane my neck.

"What's so funny?"

"Your back." His face is flushed from the heat, hair brushed back so it's clear from his face.

"What the hell's wrong with my back?" I try to peer over my shoulder, but I'm not that goddamn flexible. Zevryn giggles, and my eyes narrow.

"Tell me right now, or I'll beat your ass right here." He crosses his arms over his chest. The light dusting of hair on his chest leads down his abdomen in a perfect trail. My dick twitches.

"Let's just say anyone could take one look at you and know you got fucked." His choice of words make my brows fly high on my forehead. Even my lips part in surprise. I don't even care that he just let an F-bomb slip.

"Oh, yeah?" I take a step toward my boy. Zevryn retreats, arms falling to his sides. His black trunks are slung too low on his hips, showcasing the V of his pelvis. I want to drag my tongue through the grooves more than I want to breathe.

I drag my gaze heavily up and down my boy in a hot, heavy perusal. He knows what I'm doing too because he squirms, digging his toes into the sand. He lets me descend on him until we're flush and I'm towering over him. I may only be a handful of inches taller, but I use them to my advantage.

"I'm pretty sure they'd know it was *you* who got fucked and tore my back up." I swipe my tongue across his upper lip, moaning as his salt explodes on my tongue. "That's what they'd see, huh, baby? The evidence of your nails digging deep into my skin when you couldn't take how good my cock felt inside you?"

His sharp Adam's apple bobs, so I dip down to nip at it. Zevryn shudders but leans into the sting. I pull away with a chuckle, but not before soothing the fresh, red blemish with a kiss. "I do wonder what they'd think if they could see your ass though." I reach down and grab both cheeks. He fills my large hands easily, the muscle beneath firm but so fucking supple.

I dig in deep until my boy is panting and mewling, his hard, little cock bulging in the front of his trunks. "Now that

that's settled, let's go." I bring my hand down on a slap. He gasps and lurches just as I pull away.

"That's not fair!" he shouts at my back, and I'd bet a thousand dollars he's stomping his foot in the sand, in full brat mode.

"Keep it up, and I'll be forced to shut you up, brat!" Our little exchange gathers a few sets of wandering eyes. I don't make eye contact, but I do keep them in my peripheral. Zevryn catches up to me hastily.

"Everyone's staring," he squirms as we wade into the water. I yank him against me, mouth already reaching for his. He moans the moment our lips touch, and it only takes a sliver of time to get lost in the waves of our hunger.

"Let them. Then they'll know you're mine." I capture his full, bottom lip and suck it into my mouth before releasing him with a pop. "C'mon, boy. Let's race."

SEEING Zevryn in every version of freedom has become my goal in life, an effortless switch in a split second.

Watching the blinding smile light up his face, water spraying up around him, dark curls flapping and knotting in the wind was an elation like nothing I've ever felt.

I've never understood *his happiness defines my own* more than I do in this moment.

By the time we finally set foot on the beach, Zevryn's dragging his feet in exhaustion, but his smile never wavers. We both collapse, falling to our backs. Sand sticks to every inch of us, even creeping into places sand really just shouldn't be, but I couldn't care less.

My boy pulls himself onto my chest, resting his head against my heart. His hair flops in front of my face, making my nose tickle. I push it back, grunting when more sand trickles on top of us.

"So tired," he pants. I grunt in agreement.

The sun is hot but soothing as it hammers down on top of us. Like a warm blanket of comfort. It leaches the energy out of me, and it drains into the sand.

When a soft snore rumbles my chest, I twitch, not having realized I was in that disorienting place between sleep and consciousness. My eyelids fly open, and I scan the beach on instinct. There are a lot of people in the water today, even more relaxing on the beach, but Zev and I are in our own little spot near the green foliage of the jungle.

"C'mon, boy. Up you get." I swat his ass lightly, and he jolts awake with a groan far too sexy for someone so sleepy.

"Can't. Tired."

"I know. Let's go take a nap together." I push back with my elbow until we're sitting. With a grumpy huff, Zev pulls himself up.

The walk back to the villa is even more draining, and by the time I'm waving my band in front of the door to unlock it, I'm about ready to collapse—but my boy's already there, and I need to get him taken care of first.

I lead him to the bathroom and strip him of his soppy, sandy clothes, letting them fall to the floor with a *thwap.* Zevryn's boneless against me as I guide him to the toilet. I reach around and lift the lid before grasping his soft cock as gently as I can.

"Go for me, baby. Then we can get you cleaned up and in bed." He breathes out, and his whole body relaxes against me. I take the brunt of his weight, bracing him effortlessly—even through my exhaustion—as he relieves himself.

My heart thumps in my chest, but it's not a crazed action. It's one of peace, of pure satisfaction and gratification. The sound of his stream hitting the water fills the bathroom. My boy groans as he releases his full bladder, so I rub against his abdomen, hoping to ease the ache some.

"You should've told me you had to pee, baby."

"Was having too much fun," he replies sleepily. I hum, shaking the last few drops from his cockhead before patting him gently. "So good." Gently, I languidly stroke him as I shuffle us toward the shower.

My boy's all melty and dazed as I turn on the water and clean the salt and sand from our skin. The waterfall shower covers us both, so I don't have to worry about him getting cold as I shift him around to make sure I reach every crease and crevice.

When I drag the cloth between his cheeks, he moans and arches. I smile to myself, but I don't give in to his half-hearted attempt. I do clean his hole *very thoroughly,* and by the time I'm done, his cock is standing out from his body, hard and hot, ready and waiting for my mouth.

After dragging a fluffy white towel over him, I guide him into bed and wrap the duvet around him before crawling in on the other side.

By the time I've got him in my arms again, he's out like a light, snoring softly with the prettiest flush to his pale skin.

I drag him a little bit closer and hold him a little bit

tighter as the edge of fear and worry slip through the cracks of the façade I've fabricated to keep myself sane.

This is the beginning of the end.

My boy's going home and starting his life anew. He's so strong and so beautiful, I've never been more proud to hold someone in my arms. I know, without a doubt, that he's going to be okay.

His will and desire to remain sober and free from his demons is unlike anything I have ever seen.

He's worked harder these last two months than I have in the entire ten years of my marriage. Granted, the situation is vastly different, but my boy has only shed light on how frightened and weak I have been to tell Milo what I really want.

Zevryn has also made me see the undeniable value within the truth and how important it is to everyone involved. Skirting away from it only brings more pain, and it drags everyone down.

I've learned so much from him. He's irrevocably changed me into a better man. A man I hope can someday earn him back after I've gotten my shit together.

If he would even want me...

I twirl the gold band around my finger again and again until my skin stings with the fresh rawness of friction.

In order to have the man I love, I'm going to have to lose the other.

How can I hurt them both to save them? What does that make me?

Twenty-Four

ZEVRYN

I hardly recognize the person staring back at me. I can't help but to compare him to the shell I was two months ago.

Physically, I've changed a lot. I no longer look hollow. I've filled out, gained weight and muscle. I'm healthy, happy. I'm fucking smiling.

But beneath the massive changes I've sustained, there's a tiny flicker of the same Zevryn that witnessed too many evils. His presence is a scar on my soul. No amount of therapy or rehab could ever heal that part of me.

It's absolutely fucking terrifying, but I have to learn to live with it—to fight against the baser instincts I've done nothing but submit to since I was just fourteen.

I had my last session with Dr. Weaver today, which was intimidating but enlightening. She gave me a list of therapists she recommends in the city. Each name I scoured over was a relief, knowing that once I'm home, I still don't have to do this alone.

It was bittersweet, saying goodbye to someone that has quite literally changed my life, but she made sure it was exactly what I needed it to be.

At first, I wasn't sure why she asked me to bring the journal I'd been writing in since my first week at Black Diamond Recovery, but once I was sitting in her office, the weight of leaving sitting heavily on my shoulders, I *knew*.

Her smile was warm and accepting. We even joked as I tore those pages out and dropped them into the shredder, each loud grind of the machine solidifying my desire to never be that lost, angry, broken person again.

Haunted memories of my mother—gone.

Cruel, tortured realities with my father… not gone but eased.

The broken, warped essence of the addict at my core —*relieved.*

I'm not ignorant to the fact that I am going to struggle, especially when I'm no longer bound by the restrictions of rehab with a twenty-four-seven support system, but I'm confident I'll be able to push through it—because I'm not alone.

I have people that love me, that will do anything to help me, and it's time I swallow my shame and let them—except for my father. Where Zion is concerned, I could never see his face again and be completely fine.

I'll have to work through my anger and resentment with him eventually, but I'm just not ready yet.

"What's got that scowl on your pretty, little face?" Gavin comes up behind me from where I stand, naked in front of the mirror. I lean against him with a hiss, meeting his gaze through the reflective glass.

It lights me up inside seeing the way his eyes rake over my body, greedily and hungrily. He drags his hands down my bare skin, his callouses rough and scratchy against my tender flesh. His wavy hair hangs loose around his shoulders, a few locks brushing my collarbone as he leans down to kiss my shoulder.

His mouth travels along my back, each kiss a sting against my abused flesh. "I'm sorry, baby. I didn't mean to hurt you this badly." His words make me smile with contentment, the warm buzz of desire easing my disquiet.

I rub my back against him, giggling as he pins me in place with two strong arms. "You didn't hurt me." My Daddy scoffs and pulls away to spin me around. My face slams into his chest, and I nuzzle right in until the hairs tickle my nose and all I can smell is *him.*

"No. I did." He jerks my head back so I can stare at myself over my shoulder. The mirror gives me the perfect view of each scrape, small cut, and red lines of irritated skin. But that's not what really garners my attention.

It's my Daddy and the way he looks at my mutilated back with equal parts wonder and guilt.

I really wish he loved me enough.

I spin around until I'm facing the mirror again. Gavin's half-hard cock drags across my lower back. My lips twitch at the corners, and I know he sees it when his eyes narrow on me, dark orbs filled with *so many promises.*

"It doesn't hurt, Daddy. Not in the way you think. Yeah, it stings, but every time I feel it, it reminds me of the way you fucked me. Like you couldn't get enough and never wanted to let me go." I stare up through my lashes, hating the blush that skitters across my pale complexion.

I trace the imprint of his finger on my hip, dizzy as I'm brought back to the moment I felt him press the bruise into my skin.

"GODDAMNIT," *he growls as he shoves me up against the rocks. I cry out in surprise, my mind already flickering with the first bouts of haziness brought on by his complete and utter desperation to have me.*

Even now, in the water with the loud rush of the waterfall masking our intimate noises. Water sprays across our faces as Daddy slams our mouths together. It's not slow and sensual. It's not intimate.

It's pure, primal hunger and crazed desire.

Daddy rips my swim trunks off my legs, his fingers already delving into my crease. At the first probe of his digits, I clench up in anticipation. He sucks my lower lip into his mouth and sinks his teeth in deep enough to rip a gasp from me. "Open up for me, boy." His words make me shiver, even with his body heat leeching into me and the warm caress of the water lapping at our skin.

I clutch his shoulders, using his strength to let myself go. I relax into him, and he sinks two fingers inside with a soft, breathy grunt against the side of my neck. I'm still slick from this morning, his cum and the lube he used still lining my walls.

When Daddy spreads his fingers to stretch me out, I hold my breath at the feel of water entering me. It makes my gut coil with nervousness. Daddy's mouth turns gentle on mine for a moment before stopping all together.

He presses our foreheads together. "Let me take care of you." It's all I needed to hear. I nod against him, our hair dangling in front of our faces. I brush mine back carelessly before delving my fingers into Daddy's brown locks. I twine my fingers in the strands, gripping tight so I can pull his mouth back to mine.

He grunts but allows me to take control of the kiss—for a moment. I fall into subservience as Daddy commands me without a single word uttered. When he presses in too harshly, I ease my eagerness so he can have me any way he wants me.

The sensation of all my control washing away has never felt better. It sinks to the bottom of the reservoir, knowing I'll never need it as long as I have this.

Our teeth clash as we attempt to devour each other's mouths. Our lips are stretched wide, heads turned at an angle to get as deep as possible. I'm panting, breathless and needy. I've never felt so... consumed. So wholly owned by another person.

I've never felt like I've had luck on my side. But this... my Daddy and how badly he craves me... that feels like a strike of luck I'll only have once in my life.

I want to cherish him forever.

The stretch in my ass increases when Daddy adds another finger. I whine and wrap my legs around his waist. His feet are firmly planted on the sandy bottom, his upper half leaned forward as he keeps me pinned against the rock bed. The rocks scrape against my back, each granule making its own mark.

Using my heels, I dig them into Daddy's waist in an attempt to drag his shorts off his body, but the water works against me. With a cry of desperation, I release my hold on his shoulders and push through the resistance of the water to try to pull his shorts down just enough to free his cock.

It's so hard and hot, I can feel it radiating through the fabric. It makes me crazy. I need it. I need him inside me.

This fucking water!

"Shh, my boy. It's okay." I didn't even realize I was crying until Daddy swipes his thumb over my cheek to collect a tear. He sucks it into his mouth, and I gasp, watching his cheeks hollow from the suction.

It only makes me harder. My balls tingle, so full and tight, it's painful. Daddy pulls his fingers from inside me, making me wriggle at the emptiness in his place. "You have no idea how crazy you make me. I want to hurt you but not too much. Just enough to give you a reminder of who you belong to for days to come."

My eyes roll back as I nod, my chin dropping to my chest. Yes, that's what I want. So bad.

"Please, Daddy. I need it." Daddy shoves his arm between us, and I almost start crying again as I feel him finally free his cock. It slides between us, right up against mine. The heat and gentle waves of the water lapping over us sends me into a tailspin.

"Tell me what you need." He grasps our cocks in one of his hands. With half-lidded eyes, I stare through the water at us pressed together. My dick is lengthy but skinny. Daddy's is much bigger. Thicker and longer and so fucking perfect. I clench my asshole, thinking about him being inside me.

How full I feel. How his cockhead nudges all the right spots that make me go utterly insane.

The words tumble from my mouth with no thought, just feeling. Too much of it. "I need your big cock to fill my hole, Daddy. It feels so good stretching me. Like it's too much and you're going to split me wide open." I'm panting against his chest, clawing and whining as I try to reach his nipple.

Releasing our lengths with a grunt, Daddy lets me slide down just enough so I can lap at the peaked bud. Water and salt cling to my tongue. "For a second, I always think that's what's gonna happen. You're going to keep pushing in until I rip and then keep going. The thought makes me so much hotter because I know you would, but you'd make it so good."

I suck his nipple into my mouth, lapping at it and sinking my teeth in just to hear his grunt vibrate into my mouth. I smile around his bud as I soothe the sting away before pulling off to eat at his mouth again.

His tongue slides into my mouth, hot and eager. I suck on that, too. Anything he gives me is exactly what I need.

"Nothing has ever felt as good as your cock inside me. Not even cocaine. Fuck, I think I'm addicted to you." I slide my tongue across his lips, over every inch of his beard, loving the coarseness as it scrapes across my tongue.

Daddy's arm slides between us, and he clasps my throat tight enough to make me gasp out my last breath of oxygen. When I try to breathe in and realize I can't, he smirks at me, eyes heavy and so dark, they're almost black.

He slams my head back against the rocks—but not hard enough to actually hurt me. He never goes too far, and I'll never forget that.

My eyes roll back as he squeezes the sides of my throat a little harder. The pressure in my skull increases the longer my body screams for air. Daddy spreads my legs around his waist, nudging his cock through my crease. The slide of him along my tender flesh through the friction of water makes me tense up, only because I know it's going to sting so fucking good.

"You're addicted to me, huh, boy?" His voice is so low and gravelly, I shiver from the underlying threat. I nod as much as I can from how tightly he's keeping me pinned.

"I don't know if I love that or hate it. I don't want you to be addicted to anything, but if you had to be, then it's good that it's me." His angles his length until his cockhead nudges against my hole. I moan deep in my throat and bear down. He presses inside, so slowly it's agonizing.

It stings so bad, my eyes well up, but it's perfect.

I can barely keep my eyelids cracked, but nothing—not even the swimming in my head—could keep me from watching my Daddy as he sinks inside me. Each inch of his cock dragging along my walls is painfully delicious.

When black licks at the edges of my vision, Daddy releases his hold on my throat, and I suck in air with gasping breaths.

It all goes white.

Awareness creeps in, in drugging waves. Daddy's cock rocks inside me, slowly—just a tease. When my head rolls and my eyes find his, the first thing I notice is his smile. It makes his usually rugged appearance seem so much... lighter. Like he's happy and content.

I love you...

Words find me before I even realize I'm talking. "You're not cocaine, Daddy. You're just you—and you're perfect for me. It's a good thing."

You saved my life in every way.

Please, just love me... choose me.

Be with me, consequences be damned.

"You're goddamn perfect." Daddy's fingers dig into my hip with a precision that makes me scream. Gone are his slow, tantalizing thrusts. My back meets the wall so hard, my breath is gone in an instant.

Rocks dig in deeper than before. I can feel them shredding my flesh, but it's all background to the drag of Daddy's cock inside me.

Water rocks in unsteady waves, splashing up around us in a chaotic rhythm. Water from the fall still sprays as it thunders into the water, louder than ever.

All of my senses heighten each little detail until it's all too much to comprehend. My length bobs in the water, so I reach down to hold it, letting Daddy's thrust send it sliding through the confines of my fist so it's only him getting me off.

He dips down to slam our mouths together. It's not a kiss so much as a need to feel. Our mouths slide together with absolutely no rhythm, just the desperate need to be connected in every way.

Tingles burn at the base of my spine down to the tips of my toes. I flex them, then arch my feet as it shoots straight to my groin.

"Tell me when you're going to come, boy." Daddy's voice comes out strained, like he's as close as I am.

"Oh, gods, I am, I am. Right n—" I throw my head back with a scream that gets drowned out by the fall. My orgasm rocks through me, blinding me. All I feel is dousing, tingling heat.

"Fuck, you come so good for me." Daddy's cockhead bumps against my prostate as he buries himself as deep as he can, his head dropping between us. His dick pulses inside me, right against my gland, dragging out the euphoria of my release. My own length keeps jerking in my hand. I can't stop stroking myself, even though it's too much.

Tears fall from my eyes as sobs wrack through me.

"My beautiful boy."

"You like to hurt just a little, huh?" Daddy nips my shoulder, bringing me back from my reverie. I shudder as I melt against him.

"Yeah. You know exactly what I need."

"Speaking of, it's getting late, and you haven't finished your dinner. Then I need to get you cleaned up before bed. It's going to be a long day tomorrow."

I squeeze my eyes shut at the mention of what tomorrow is. The reminder makes me sick to my stomach.

And that's when it hits me—why Gavin's been doing all of these things. The jet skiing and swimming followed by a shower and a nap together. The walk to the waterfall, where he fucked me senseless...

It was all a goodbye, and it's like a slap in the face.

My eyes drop to the gold band still wrapped proudly around his finger. I sneer at it, hating the sight of it more than ever.

It's always been a reminder of what we could never be, but I've never hated him for it like I do now. The feeling sits like a lead weight in my gut, filling me with a resentment that nearly steals my sanity.

But I don't want to feel that way. Not toward him.

We've always known this thing between us had a clock on it. In fact, I told him four weeks were all we had, and now that time has come, so I'm determined to spend our last few hours together living in the bliss of a lie. A bittersweet, tender lie.

I eat the rest of the food Gavin puts in front of me. Each bite tastes like chalk, but I know it makes him happy to see me eat, and making him happy makes *me* happy.

After I set it on the table with a loud clank, Gavin wastes

no time bending down and carrying me to the bathroom. I know what's going to happen the second he sets me in front of the toilet, and I can't hold back my moan of elation knowing he's going to help me.

It's the most intimate thing I have ever done, like baring my soul in an inexplicable way. I shiver as he slowly undresses me; each drag of his hands over my body makes me shiver.

By the time I'm fully naked, my cock is half hard. I know what's coming before he even wraps his fingers around my balls. I lean back against him and nod, scrunching my eyes shut. "Do it."

With a hearty chuckle, Daddy squeezes my balls in his fist. I scream, then release my bladder immediately. Daddy grabs my now soft cock and aims my stream toward the center of the toilet. "Look at you, baby." He kisses my cheek, urging me to look down.

When I do, I nearly collapse. His hand looks so big wrapped around my flaccid dick. The thin, light yellow stream flowing between his fingers. When I'm done, he shakes me gently, expelling the last drops.

He releases me, letting my length hang between my legs. He pats me like he always does, then swirls his fingers through the coarse tangle of hair at my groin. The soft tugging makes my legs twitch, the sensation unlike anything I've ever felt.

"Take a bath with me?" I nod before he finishes his sentence. He steps back and swats my butt.

Watching him strip is unlike any aphrodisiac I've ever felt. Gavin's body is in-fucking-sane, and every inch of it drives me to madness.

He's all hard muscle covered with a soft, squishy outer-layer I love nothing more than to use as a pillow. His hair is dark, from his beard down to his legs. Dark patches stretch across his arms, his chest, down a thick trail that leads to the hair surrounding his cock.

My eyes are glued on him, my mouth watering to taste him, but he tugs me into the bath he'd started to fill while I was lost in my blatant perusal of him.

He pulls me back against his chest and grabs a sponge to pool water over my front as water spills from the tap, filling it up slowly. The water is warm and smells of lavender. I smile contentedly, closing my eyes as my Daddy holds me.

"I love being with you, boy. These last two months have been a light in my very dismal life." His words are unexpected, and I tense up. He brackets an arm across my chest, keeping me in place. "Don't move, baby. Just close your eyes and listen to me, okay?"

After a moment's hesitation, I nod, trying to ignore the trepidation in my gut. "Good boy." I shiver. I'll never get tired of hearing that.

"I know there are many unanswered things between us right now. And tomorrow, we'll both be back in the real world, which seems surreal and confusing." I sniffle, silently agreeing with him. "I don't know what's going to happen when we step off that jet, but what I *do* know is I am going to take you back to your apartment and let you go."

I cry out at his words, lurching away from him like they burned every exposed inch of me. Gavin only holds me tighter, burying his face into my neck. "I will not keep you when I don't have the right to, baby. I've got my marriage to deal with, and you have your recovery to focus on, and I *refuse* to get in the way of that."

Gavin mentioning Milo cracks something inside of me, a deep fissure that gushes blood. A gaping wound that I know, from this moment, will never stop bleeding.

"You've got your husband to go back to, and I've got my addiction and daddy issues to work through; I get it." Every truth is a bitter release on my tongue, but at least we're finally fucking getting it all put out there.

"No, baby, that's not—" I shake my head, dragging my curls over his skin.

"Please don't. I don't want to talk about it. Can we just enjoy our last—" I choke on the word. My nose burns, and it travels upward to my eyes. I'm grateful for the water below us because it hides how quickly they fall from my face.

"Can we just *be*? For one last night?" Gavin's beard scratches my skin as he kisses along my shoulder and up my neck until he's brushing my pierced earlobe with his lips.

With a sigh, he whispers his compromise. "Anything for you, my boy."

If only that were true...

Twenty-Five

ZEVRYN

The sun is but a blip on the horizon, emitting a hue of bright red throughout the sky. My eyes follow the endless trail stretching as far as the eye can see. Its ascension feels slow coming, but then I blink, and it's halfway up, then all the way, bleeding red the whole time.

I dig my fingers into the warming sand, thinking back on that fucking proverb that only ever comes to mind at times like this.

"Red sky at night, sailor's delight. Red sky in morning, sailor's warning."

A goddamn red sky and superstitious omens.

I've never hated a color more.

Especially since, this time, I feel that omen like I feel the breath in my lungs and my heart beating in my chest.

With every moment passing, I'm breathing life into it—solidifying a verity I've spent months denying in endless waves, only for it to fracture my core when its burden settles.

It seems I've found peace amongst the water I once saw

myself drowning in. Maybe it's because the water here is so clear, I can see straight through it, whereas the depth of the ocean in my dreams reached a place so abysmal, only the tentacles waiting for me existed.

"How long have you been out here?" The sound of Gavin's voice makes me flinch as it shatters the stillness to the early morning air.

I shrug, unsure of what to tell him. That I didn't sleep, that I couldn't. Or that I've been sitting in this very spot for hours, hating every minute of the inevitable sunrise.

"You know you're not supposed to be alone." He plops down next to me, grabbing my hand still buried in the sand. He feels warm with sleep, and when I flick a glance toward him, I can make out the sleep lines on his face, coupled with the bags under his eyes.

Looks like he didn't sleep well, either.

Guess we're both fucked over what today means.

I scoff, lifting a brow as I peer at him over my bicep. "Baby, you and I both know your *protection* was never necessary. Only an excuse for Zion to control me."

He rolls his eyes while he plays with my fingers. There's a sadness in his face I've never seen before.

It makes me ache all over. A heart squeezing, muscle spasming, veins screaming type of ache.

"Well, a hell of a lot of good that did him. I haven't spoken to him in weeks."

My eyes widen. "That surprises me."

"Why?"

"Because even though you dislike my father, you're still professional."

He laughs, a loud, hearty sound that makes the blood in my veins hum with satisfaction because *I did that.*

"Professional. Yeah, okay." *Daddy's crackin' jokes. How cute.*

"You know what I mean." I wrinkle my nose just to see him smile. *I'd do anything for it. For him. Even be a side piece in his marriage.*

But he wouldn't ask, and I'll never offer.

I won't make him choose.

"I do. And you're right, I am. But Zion does not deserve my respect or my professionalism. Not after the way he's treated you." His fingers tighten on mine.

"That's not your baggage or even your concern." My voice is dry.

"That's where you're wrong, boy. *Everything* about you is my concern."

"It won't be after today." *And I hate it so fucking much, it makes me sick.*

"Zevryn—"

"Wanna go on one last swim?" I cut him off, fearful of what his next words would've been. His mouth gapes, like he's vying between what to say. After a few moments, he nods, and his eyes soften.

"Of course, baby. Wanna skinny dip?" He waggles his brows, and I bellow out a laugh, throwing my head back. My curls brush between my shoulder blades.

"Like you'd let anyone see me naked."

He looks around the empty beach, head turning in all directions before he focuses on me again, one thick, dark brow raised playfully. "I don't see anyone. Do you?"

That fucking smirk...

I start ripping my clothes off as I run toward the water. "Last one in the water—" I don't even get to finish my sentence before my Daddy swings me into his arms and charges us into the ocean, sending water spraying into the air.

Laughter bellows out around us, a harmonized melody I know I'll never forget because it's the very sound that will get me through every dark moment that's sure to come once I'm alone again.

A bitter end to such a wonderful blip in time.

But I wouldn't trade it for the world.

My bodyguard, my lover. *My Daddy.*

There will never be another.

I ROLL my eyes at the ostentatious name sprawled across the side of the sleek, white jet. *Carver Breck.* My father will flaunt his name every chance he gets—even on something no one will ever see.

"Mr. Carver. Welcome." A stewardess I've never seen before welcomes me as I board. Gavin's right behind me, every step mirroring my own. We both stiffen at the sound of the voice, then continue forward in confusion.

"Uh, hi." I turn around to stare at Gavin. He's staring at her with a frown, eyebrows squished together. I move past the awkwardness and plop down in an overstuffed, leather chair.

"Guess your husband's not on the flight." My words come out bitter, but fuck if I can help it. I knew he was expecting to see him, and now he's probably disappointed he didn't.

"I suppose not."

"Sorry to disappoint you." I don't even know where that comes from. I'm just so bitter.

Gavin drops the bags near my feet and drops down into a crouch in front of me. I try to ignore him—I really do—but he fills every molecule of space so entirely, it's impossible. And when he grips my chin the way he always does—thumb resting against the dimple in the center—all my fight disappears in an instant.

"Don't be like this. *Please,*" he pleads with me. His brown eyes are soft and so gentle. It brings on another bout of tears and heartache that just *won't go away.*

I swipe at my eyes harshly, reveling in the sting of friction. "I'm sorry, I…"

Gavin's lips twitch, forming a sad excuse of a smile. "Don't be sorry, baby. Just be with me."

I've never heard better words in my life.

I let Gavin drag me to the sofa, pulling me on top of him. I yearn to suckle him one last time, but it's not the place for that. I'll just have to rely on my already fading memory to get me through until it all starts to ache a little less.

Hopefully, that happens soon… because I already feel like I'm drowning in despair.

My Daddy's strong arms wrap around me, fingers digging into my sides. It doesn't take long for the throbbing ache of pressure to develop, but it actually makes breathing easier. Knowing I'll be left with a few more bruises that will last for near days to come.

Anything to keep the memory of him alive.

My legs are sprawled out behind me, hanging over the edge, but I've never been more comfortable. Time passes all too quickly, and before I know it, we're flying through the air, leaving the mainland behind, with Black Diamond a blip in the distance.

The island that changed my fucking life—if only I could bring that kind of ascendency back with me.

NEW YORK'S skyline is bigger than I remember it being. I'm almost consumed by the sheer size of the buildings as we make our way through the city's stuffy traffic.

Gavin's hand hasn't left mine since we stepped off my father's jet. His gun is back on his hip, secured in the holster. My eyes keep catching on it every time I look him over. He wore it constantly in the beginning, but it mostly hasn't been a part of his attire for some time.

Now, it sticks out like a sore thumb—just like everything else.

I flex my fingers, hating the thin sheen of sweat coating my palms. When Gavin's eyes flicker over to me, I jerk my head back to the window to stare outside. I can't look at him. Because if I do, I'll break down.

I need to be strong, at least until I'm alone, and then I can feel... all of this.

The thought makes me scoff. *I actually want to feel things. Even the heart-wrenching tragedy of being left behind.* Because I know, without a shadow of a doubt, I don't want to numb Gavin away with drugs or booze.

I want to feel this. Every fucking moment of agony. The pain will be a reminder of how good we were, even if it was never meant to last.

"What's going on in that pretty, little head of yours?"

"You keep calling me little, and I'm going to get a complex," I muse as I chew on my bottom lip. Gavin reaches over and tugs it from my mouth to pinch it between his thumb and index finger.

"You're my boy, and even all filled out with delicious muscle, you're still smaller than me." My eyes drop down to his lap, greedily eyeing his thick thighs before dragging them back up over every thick, soft inch of him. Inches I'll never get to touch or taste again.

"Yeah," I breathe out, dropping my head against the hot glass. The sun glares down with a vengeance, even with it being so early, but this heat doesn't feel the same as it did on the island. It's suffocating. To the point I itch to strip myself down to my briefs just to get some relief. But that would mean taking off Gavin's T-shirt, and I'm sure as fuck not doing that.

I bend down, pulling the collar to my nose to catch a whiff of his scent. It makes Gavin chuckle. "I'm right here, you know. Get your *little* ass over here and smell me." He tugs my hand, pulling me into his lap.

His fingers find their place in my hair. He shoves me into his chest until my nose is completely squished. My eyes close with contentment. I wrap my arms around him, along the expanse of his ribs, and just hold on, leeching onto his impossible strength as we draw closer to my apartment building with every minute that passes.

"Come on, baby..." Gavin lulls gently long minutes after the car has lurched to a stop.

My heart is pounding erratically in my chest, fear coursing through my veins. My stomach is roiling, on the verge of spilling the food Gavin made me eat on the flight.

He's always taking care of me.

I wish I didn't need him to.

"Please," the plea slips from my lips the moment a sob breaks through my weak barriers.

"Fuck." Gavin squishes me so tight, I can't breathe, and I love it. Feeling so anchored when everything around me is spinning and sinking. "I promise it's going to be okay. *You'll* be okay." His words don't make sense. They *can't.*

"I don't—this—"

He tugs my chin, forcing me to meet his gaze. His eyes track over every streaky tear and line of snot leaking out of my orifices. Shame and helplessness churn through me, but he's seen me worse than this, and he still wanted me after, so I think it's okay.

"Do you trust me?" His eyes dart back and forth between mine. It's dizzying, the earnest warmth in his expression, even with the frown lines and crow's feet deepening by the second. I nod, knowing without a doubt I do and forever will. His eyelids flutter closed for just a moment before he bends down to kiss me, a soft, gentle press of his lips.

I can't stop my moan as his beard scrapes against my wet skin with a reverence that makes me feel alive.

"Let me take you home."

The lobby is cold and pristine, just how I remember, but

somehow, still different—like everything I'm seeing is with new eyes. My vision is clearer and more observant. Which I guess makes sense since I can't ever remember being sober longer than a couple of days at a time.

The heavy dip of the elevator's ascent settles in my gut. Sweat burns along my spine. My eyes are locked on the numbers as they slowly climb, each second another tick bringing me closer to my penthouse, to my life—without Gavin.

I tangle my fingers in front of me, twisting them and tugging at them until they ache. My neck screams from being angled upward, and the bright, digital numbers on the display just above the doors taunt me with every glitchy turn.

I've never wished for a nightmare more in my life. For all of this to not be real—I need that to be true.

I'm suffocating, and I can't take another second of it. With a cry, I whirl around and jump up, clutching Gavin's shoulders. He stumbles backward with a grunt, and his back slams into the wall. My bag drops to the floor as his hands find my thighs to hoist me higher.

One of his arms supports me under my ass while the other rubs up and down over my back, each pass of his hand drawing more tears from me. My face finds solace in the warmth of his neck. My tears dampen his neck and soak into his shirt, but he doesn't seem to care as he works to soothe me.

No words are spoken, but there's nothing left to say.

Gavin reaches over and slams his fist against the emergency stop button. A loud screech sounds around us, making me flinch. Gavin pulls me away from his neck. "Talk to me." He's pleading, eyes wide and glassy with worry. I sniffle and attempt to clear the snot from my nose, but it just smears, making me feel even more pathetic.

Gavin grunts as he shifts my weight against him, walking forward until my back thuds against the ice-cold, metal wall. I hiss, my back arching as the cold seeps through the thin material of his shirt hanging off me. "Don't hide from me, boy. Tell me."

"I'm scared," I rasp, tears still clogging my throat. I shudder.

"Of?"

"Being alone." I squeeze my eyes shut, whimpering when more sobs wrack through me. They shake me with their force, and I hunch over.

"Oh, baby." Gavin presses our foreheads together. His hair dangles in front of our faces so I can't see him properly, but I love the chestnut-colored waves. He shakes his head back and forth, a gentle friction across mine. It eases some of the agony.

When my Daddy kisses me, a slow, tantalizing, all-consuming kiss, I know it's the last one.

He steals everything from me. My control, my love, my life. It all belongs to him because the moment he walks away from me, I won't want it anymore.

None of it means anything without my Daddy.

"Daddy," I whimper against his mouth, "I don't want you to—" I cut myself off before I say too much. I shove my tongue into his mouth, licking every inch I can reach. My jaw aches from being slit open so wide, but I like it.

Daddy keeps his mouth open, tongue massaging mine,

letting me take whatever I want—but what he doesn't understand is I just want *him.*

Even if we couldn't kiss anymore, or even touch, I'd still want him.

I'd take just his friendship if I could. It would be enough. Just to see him. Talk to him. Breathe the same air.

But I don't have the right to ask.

It's too late.

"Please kiss me." A resounding growl vibrates my lips, where it travels down my throat and into my lungs. Daddy devours my mouth. Our teeth clank harshly, we're so deep in each other. It draws a long mewl from me.

Overwhelming warmth festers in my gut, a tight coil rapidly expanding. I rock my hips, rubbing my hard dick against my Daddy's stomach. He grunts and pulls back to nip my lip, sinking his teeth in deep enough to split the tender skin.

When he pulls back with a shuddering breath, I whimper and lean back in, trying to reclaim his mouth. He shakes his head and drops it down onto my shoulder.

I think I hate him a little for it. For being stronger than me.

Strong enough to walk away.

"Trust me, okay?" He's placating me, but what the hell, I'm desperate enough to take it.

What the hell does that even mean?! I want to scream, but I can't. I can't talk, can't breathe, can't do anything but kiss my Daddy goodbye.

He must've released the emergency stop because the screaming alarm breaks off, and the silence is jarring. My ears ring slightly, but the rush of blood in my ears blocks out most of it.

The dip of the elevator starting back up makes my stomach flip inside-out.

"I've got to put you down now, okay?" Every word Gavin speaks is so soft, so gentle, like I'm a fragile piece of porcelain teetering on the edge of a cliff.

I nod, panting against the side of his face as my legs slowly slide down. When my feet hit the floor, I wobble under my own weight, forced to grip the metal bar when Gavin steps away from me, leaving me cold and empty and so achingly desperate.

I try to meet his eyes, but he keeps his trained forward with a strength I admire. My throat bobs when the lift levels out. When it dings, my heart rises into my throat along with my stomach. Gavin's fingers are wrapped tightly around the handles of my bag, his knuckles white from the pressure. They clench and unclench many times in the few seconds it takes for the doors to slide open.

With a deep breath I don't even feel, my feet move of their own accord, dragging me into my apartment. Gavin steps with me. He dips down and places my bag on the floor at my feet before he straightens and clasps his hands behind his back.

The stance radiates professionalism. My heart tugs at the separation rapidly expanding between us.

I fucking hate it.

I blink a few times, my eyes flickering from my bag to the man who is now nothing but my ex-bodyguard. If it weren't for the sadness I've grown to recognize in his brown irises, I'd think that none of this meant a thing to him.

But it did. It had to... right?

He dips his head, sending a few locks of hair in front of

his face as he readjusts his stance again, backing into the steel box. When he peers through his lashes, fingers toying with that goddamn gold band wrapped like an endless promise on his thick fingers, I suddenly can't breathe. I clutch at my chest, nails already digging in through the cotton.

I can't survive this.

...But for him, I will.

"You're so strong, my boy. Please don't forget that." His voice catches just as the silver doors thud closed.

My legs buckle, and I collapse. A loud crack echoes through the widely empty space. So hollow and vacant—just like me.

My boy... Why did he have to say that? Something so irrevocable and so *loving...*

With a gasp and a silent scream, I choke on the words of his goodbye.

Twenty-Six

GAVIN

The drive to Ayers Security is an endless blur of cars and dull music. A constant start and stop that's enough to make me want to scream.

Zion's driver didn't even question my change in destination, just nodded his head and pulled into traffic. But now that I'm here, I'm not sure if I should be. I feel I don't belong anywhere but with my boy.

"Gavin," Deacon greets me as I stroll into his office, feigning a confidence I don't feel. He pushes back from his desk and rounds it to shake my hand. I drop down into a chair and get right to the point.

"Am I fired?" Deacon lifts a brow, his eyes raking over me, probably taking in my disheveled appearance. I drag my fingers through my hair to tie it into a knot at my nape. A pathetic attempt at straightening myself out.

"You look worn out. Maybe you should go home." I stiffen at the word home, knowing it's not that for me anymore.

"No, I'm good. I just want to work—if I still have a job." I shift in the chair, resisting the urge to tug at the hem of my shirt.

"The rest of your money was transferred this morning." Deacon changes the subject, *again.*

I grit my teeth, and my fingers clamp down on the armrest. "I don't want his fucking money." Deacon has the decency to look appalled. Hell, even I'm a bit surprised with myself.

"Well, you both signed a contract; don't have much say in it now." I huff but ignore him.

"I really just want to work, Deacon."

"You're not going to talk about this with me?"

"No. Why would I? I've said all I had to say over the phone, and it's none of your business anymore. The job is done—contract null and void."

"Jesus Christ, Gavin!" His palms slam down on his desk, making a few things rattle around from the jarring force.

I don't show my surprise, my face locked in the blank mask it always used to be, but I do glance up, eyeing him warily. "What?"

"You fucking idiot." He's shaking his head now. My brows furrow as I look him over. He's dressed immaculately in slacks and a dark button-down with the sleeves rolled up, showcasing the intricate tattoos etched in his dark skin.

"All right, thank you for insulting me. As if I don't already feel shitty enough."

"You deserve so much more than a few measly insults, Gavin. You *know* how bad this could turn out to be when his father finds out."

I roll my eyes and lean back in the chair, throwing my

arms on the armrests. "I understand your worries when it comes to the business, Deac. I know that has to be your primary concern, and I respect that. I would never ask you to jeopardize your company for me. But Zion Carver isn't going to do a thing."

"How can you know that?"

"Because I'll make sure of it."

"Again," he deadpans, eyes dark and narrowed. If I didn't know the guy so well, I might actually feel intimidated. "How?"

"My answer depends on whether I still have a job or not." Deacon bellows out a laugh, so loud and boisterous, he throws his head back.

"You're a son of a bitch, you know that?"

I dip my head. "I've been told a time or two."

He rubs his palm back and forth over his shaved head, eyes darting over every inch of me. I press my molars together and grind them, relishing in the minute pop from the pressure. "You look different. Sound different, too." His odd perusal makes my skin crawl.

"Do I?"

He hums. "You do. Lighter, in a way. More yourself, too. You've always been very laid back and aloof. But now I see who you've been hiding behind the smoke screen."

I visibly recoil at his accusation. His words bounce around my skull like the clatter of pins at the end of a bowling lane. My fingers brush over my beard as I mull it over.

Have I really been hiding my entire fucking life? Was I hiding from Milo, too?

"I feel different," I say mostly to myself. The statement is a weight off my chest, but I don't feel the ease of pressure. The loss of my boy is nearing the point of suffocation.

Is it possible to asphyxiate while I'm still breathing?

I feel Zev's absence like nails in a coffin. Each minute that passes hammers another in place, shutting me into a place where it's endlessly cold and void.

Every breath feels borrowed as it blows back in my face. Each inhale stings, like the deadly flash of a jellyfish's tentacles. It's a reminder I'm on borrowed time—my boy's time.

And I can't fucking hurt him anymore than I already have.

I need him to trust me.

"What are you going to do, Gavin?" His question makes me laugh. It's dry. A bit hysterical.

"I'm about to turn my life upside down and hurt someone I love." My hand finds its way to my chest. I dig the heel of my palm into my sternum, unsure if I'm adding to the ache or lessening it.

He seems to sit on that for a while. The clock ticks audibly, and I find myself timing each inhale and exhale to every fifteenth tick.

The watch on my wrist buzzes incessantly, and I stop breathing, already knowing what name lights the screen, but that doesn't stop my heart from yearning for it to be my boy.

He doesn't even have my fucking number.

I'm such a piece of shit, but I don't know of any other way to do this. I can't drag him into my life when it's about to be capsized. He deserves more than my baggage.

He deserves to own every inch of me.

"I'm not going to fire you."

"Really?" I blurt, making Deacon raise a dark brow. His face is rugged and harsh.

"Would you like me to change my mind?" His lip twitches at the corner, giving him away.

"No. I'm just surprised."

"Look, Gavin. Clearly, you're going through some shit. You know I've never been married, or hell, even been in a serious relationship. This company is my life. But it's not hard to tell you're turned inside out. And after working together for ten years and having a friendship nearly that long, I'd like to think I know you well enough to say with certainty that something like this will never happen again."

I shake my head, disgusted with the thought of ever being with someone the way I am with my boy.

For a decade, I thought Milo was it for me. My life partner, the love of my life.

It wasn't until Zevryn Carver stumbled into my countercurrent that everything fell into place.

"To be honest, just being away from Zevryn is killing me. I can't even think of entertaining a hypothetical scenario where anyone but him is it for me." *Not even my husband waiting for me at a home we've always shared.*

My thumb finds the band on my finger at the thought of Milo.

"You sound terribly in love; it's repulsive." I chuckle and shake my head, unable to hold back my grin.

"Fuck, I really am."

"Honestly, Gavin, if you keep cursing, you might just turn me on."

My eyeballs bulge from my skull. Deacon cracks a smile, and I blow out a breath, slamming my hand to my chest as I bust out laughing. Deacon starts up too, but mine dies off quickly.

"Thank you for not firing me, Deac. You know what this job means to me."

"I do. And I also expect you to never break my trust again. I don't forgive easily."

I nod my acceptance. "I know."

"Good. Why don't you go home and..." he waves his hand flippantly, "figure out your shit. I'm sure there's a lot for you to do. You can take the week off."

I open my mouth to protest the leave, but then I think better of it. It's probably best if I stay focused on what I need to do and not get distracted by work.

"All right. Thanks. I just need to check some things before I leave." I jerk my head in the direction of my office.

"I'll contact Mr. Carver to let him know everything is settled." The mention of Zion has me tensing mid-extraction of the chair.

"There's still a system in place of Zevryn's apartment, right?" My heart rate picks up speed thinking about him completely alone and unprotected.

"Of course. It was only put in two weeks ago."

"And you can access it from a cell phone, right?" Deacon's eyes narrow on me as he peers around his computer.

"If you have homeowners access, yes... which you already know."

"Yeah, you're right. Thanks, Deac," I rush out the words and slip out the door.

If anyone were to look at the cameras angled in the hall leading to my office, they'd see me move with a speed that is comical for an old man like me, but I couldn't care less—not when my boy is all I can think about.

I whip the chair out of the way as I lean down on the desktop and hammer in passwords and codes, my heart hammering in time with my fingers as they drill into the keys. My foot taps anxiously as I wait for the system to boot up.

The only light in the room comes from my screen as it illuminates my face, casting more shadows that disappear into the darkness.

My breath catches when the screen loads. I rush to click on Zevryn's file, scribbling passcodes on a sticky note when the screen loads, but once I'm done, my finger hovers just over the mouse, the pad skimming the sleek, white exterior. Sweat prickles at the nape of my neck, a thumbnail of just inside his penthouse staring back at me, mocking me.

I dig my fingers in just on either side of my neck and squeeze as I roll my head between my shoulders. Trepidation swirls in my solar plexus, adding a weight that makes me unsteady on my feet.

This is wrong... right? An invasion of his privacy. The security in place is for exactly that—to protect him.

But it's my job to do that, too.

It was never for the money but because of my compulsive need to care for him. To love him.

To be his Daddy.

"Fuck it," I growl and click on the large, daunting square. The feed rolls in, the time stamp showing it's live. I let out a shaky breath and force myself into the chair when my legs threaten to buckle.

It's only been a couple of hours since I dropped him off, and it already feels as if days have passed.

Being by his side every moment has distorted my perception of time. And I knew once we were apart, it was going to feel impossible, but I never once could have imagined this soul-sucking, live wire of separation.

I feel his loss in every vein and nerve ending. They scream out in yearning to feel my boy fill every part of me just by breathing the same air.

My gaze scans the screen, searching for any movement. There is no sound on the feed, so I'm hunkered over in the dark, staring at a brightly lit screen, craning my neck for just a peek at my boy.

Hours pass, I think, but again, time has no meaning anymore.

Just as I start to give up hope, my lungs deflating with the kind of sadness that surely kills, movement catches my attention. I shoot up in my chair and yank my monitor across the wood. It screeches loudly, enough to make my eardrums throb, but at the smallest glimpse of my boy, it all fades into white noise.

He has a thick blanket huddled around him and over his head so I can't see his face, but I know it's him. Even covered by inches of cotton, I'd recognize that body anywhere.

My eyes prick watching him move around so lethargically. His feet never even leave the ground as he shuffles into the kitchen. He grabs a bottle of water and then, before I can blink, he's gone—and I'm left despising my heart for pumping the blood through my veins, circulating oxygen, and keeping me alive.

SHOVING my own key into my own door feels awkward. The thought that this isn't my home has only gotten louder since I left Ayers. "Hello?" I call out as I step over the threshold. The door falls closed behind me with a soft snick.

"I tried calling you," Milo says. I startle and drop my bag to the floor. He's leaning against the wall, a dish towel hanging from his hands, which are covered in soap suds. My gaze rakes over him, seeing him anew after two months apart—but I suppose it's been longer than that.

I'm usually much more alert than this, but the weight of my decisions are settling upon me like an elephant to the chest.

"I know," I admit, rubbing the back of my neck. I tug at the hair tie in my hair, pulling it loose so my hair hangs across my shoulders.

"Are you going to look at me?"

"I'm afraid if I look at you, it'll break my heart. I don't want to hurt you, Milo."

He lets out a heavy breath. It chills me to the bone. "Jesus, Gavin, you're just diving right in." I wince and shuffle on my feet.

"You knew this was coming when we talked weeks ago. I mean, you had to, Milo..." I say as gently as I can.

"Not *this!* And sure as fuck not the second you walked in the door."

"Shit," I grate, tugging on my beard. "You're right. I'm

sorry." He shoves off the wall and disappears into the kitchen. I follow behind him, the weight of my footsteps imprinting them into the floor.

I stare helplessly at his back as he dredges his hands back into the soapy water and starts aggressively scrubbing a plate. "Milo—"

"Please don't, Gavin."

"We need to talk." *I need to do this, but I don't want to hurt you.*

His shoulders shake, and his head drops between them. His hair dangles in front of his face in straight, golden tendrils. Tendrils I used to love to wrap around my fingers, but now I prefer the messy, unruly curls covering Zevryn's head.

Jesus, I'm a prick.

He turns back around to look me in the eyes. *I wonder if he can see how far my mind is from this conversation, from him.*

"I know. But I need some time to think first. I... I think I knew this was coming from the way you were talking on the phone, but thinking and knowing are two vastly different things."

I shove my hands in my pockets and hunch my shoulders. "Okay. I understand." I glance behind me. "I'm gonna sleep on the couch." The surprised hurt that flashes over Milo's face is another blow to my solar plexus. I don't bother trying to rub the throb away, not when I deserve it.

His eyes crinkle at the corners as he squints. He crosses his arms over his chest, a purely defensive move. "Yeah, sure, Gavin. Whatever you need."

That fucking hurts, hearing his gentleness through his undisguised anger.

Unable to stand the sight of his cloudy eyes and shaking hands any longer, I round back to grab my bag before disappearing into our room for a long shower, feeling like the coward I am.

When I finally emerge, the house is empty. I search every room, quietly calling Milo's name, but I know it's fruitless.

He left me like I'm going to leave him. His is only temporary, but mine is a life-altering decision that will ultimately change the course of our lives.

My only hope is that he finds happiness once the culmination of devastation has settled.

The couch feels like a comfort I don't deserve as I stretch out on my back. My hands are clasped, resting gently on my stomach. They rise and fall with every bated breath I force through my lungs.

I pull my phone out, and with only trace amounts of shame, I pull up the feed for my boy's penthouse after logging in with his information. I don't see anything other than dark stillness, but the video alone—whether he's in it or not—is enough to quell my own despair to a more bearable level.

Resting my phone on my chest, keeping the screen illuminated, I let my eyes fall closed. The moment they do, my mind fills with every moment I can remember with my boy.

My nipples tingle as I think of his mouth on me, gentle and eager as he suckled me, uncaring if he could breathe. My fingers twitch with fantom caresses of his dark, tangled curls wrapped around them.

My heart capsizes, replaying the view I had of him playing in the water not even twenty-four hours ago.

Dunking under only to fly back up a moment later, water flying in all directions and rushing down his face in salty rivulets.

Rivulets I dived in to lick right off him, relishing in the sting of salt and *Zevryn.*

His laugh in that moment, bright and genuine, and his smile, beautiful and breathtaking, are the two things that assure me I am doing the right thing.

That taking the time to fix things before I go crawling back—on my hands and knees if I have to—is exactly what I should do.

Zevryn deserves to own me wholly, and he can't do that if I'm tied to a marriage, to vows that no longer mean what they should.

Death do us part isn't always forever.

But Zevryn and my love for him is.

An always kind of forever.

Twenty-Seven

MILO

Whenever I imagined my marriage ending—which had been occurring a lot more these last few months—I never once pictured Gavin, the man I fell so deeply for all those years ago, falling for someone else.

There ever *being* a someone else never crossed my mind.

Until now.

His face breaks my fucking heart. Guilt is written all over him, so tangible and thick, I choke on it.

I push away from the table to pace the kitchen, needing an immeasurable amount of space but unwilling to let this go.

It's clearly time. The moment I've been dreading for years.

The end of my marriage.

"Milo, I—" I hold my hand up, effectively cutting him off. Even the sound of his voice makes me want to scream—and not in anger.

"Please don't, Gavin."

"No, I have to explain. I *need* to. I didn't want to hurt you, I swear." His words, choked and raspy, make me smile. It's a sad smile. Bittersweet and agonizing.

With a deep breath and a resolve I'm mostly faking, I walk up to my husband and take his hands in mine. I drag the pad of my thumb over the gold band that matches my own. He's still wearing it, and I think that hurts even worse than knowing he's in love with someone else.

What the hell does that say about me?

"You're still wearing your ring."

This is all so confusing.

How *does* one end a fucking marriage anyway?

"Of course, I am, Milo. You're my husband, and even—" He clears his throat and shakes his head. His hair has grown out after our two months of separation—his beard, too. Even the sleep still etched heavily on his face after hours of being awake is different from before.

He's a different man. Inside and out.

Maybe I never really knew him through to his very core.

"Even though I cheated on you." I suck in a breath at the finality of his words. They *hurt,* like a vice around my heart. "Even though I disrespected you, I wasn't going to make it even worse. We made promises and took vows."

"That you broke." Gavin's head hangs between his shoulders in shame—or at least, I hope it is.

"Yes." Since the moment he walked through the door, he hasn't done a single thing to hide. No lies, no half-truths.

Full disclosure.

He wanted to speak the moment he got home yesterday, but I took one look at his face and *knew.* Like a lead weight in my gut, I knew he'd be ending it. So, selfishly, I told him to wait. And then I left, running from the truth I'd never be able to leave behind.

Now I wish I never would've postponed it. Because I have to look at him, knowing he slept on the couch thinking of another man in the home we share together.

"It would be insulting to say I didn't mean to hurt you. I knew what I was doing, even with the guilt it brought. But my intention was never to be deliberately harmful. I just..." He digs his fingers into his hair and tugs on the strands so harshly, I know it has to sting. "I couldn't fucking resist him." He says the words on a cough, eyes darting down.

I rear back. "I don't want to fucking hear that." He flinches but nods his acceptance.

"I'm sorry, I just want to be honest with you."

God, I want to be bitter. So rude and resentful and downright hateful, but when I open my mouth to hurt him in every way I know how, the words don't come.

I stand, gaping like a fish for long minutes before I finally snap my mouth closed. "We were so young, huh," I say with a dry laugh. I drag the kitchen chair out and plop down into it, feeling the weight of the end. I want to wear it like a shield, to protect myself from the inevitable blow that will surely knock me out. "But we're not those people anymore, are we?" Gavin shakes his head, dark locks still hanging, framing the frowning face I fell in love with so many years ago.

"Look at me. Please," I plead. He slowly lifts his head. Every inch of his shuttered expression he reveals solidifies my startling new reality.

Sharing a life with my best friend has come to an end.

Ten years of ups and downs, love and pain. Joy and peace and loneliness—gone. For reasons I'll never fully be able to understand.

I don't even realize I'm crying until Gavin's brushing my tears away with his thumb. His touch stings like it never has, knowing he's touched someone else the same way, but I'm selfish enough to not push him away.

One last time.

"It's been a hell of a ride, huh?" I peer up at him, eyes glassy and burning. His small, tired grin makes my heart soar, knowing he'll never smile like that for me again.

"The best." I nod through the pain, letting the tears fall unbidden, needing the release I know they'll bring.

"You were the best thing that ever happened to me, you know that?" He sounds sincere, too.

What I would give to do it all over.

"Were," I choke out, that single word sticking out amongst the rest. His face tightens. I shake my head. "I know; it's okay. You've changed. So much. And hell, I have, too. It makes sense in a way. For us to grow apart. To need different things, different people. Just sucks that it happened this way." *That I'm no longer who you need.*

"I'm so fucking sorry, Milo."

Not as sorry as me, baby.

Not as sorry as me.

Twenty-Eight

ZEVRYN

My room feels cold, bleached of the comfort I once found in it. But as I stare at the dark blur of my blanket wrapped around me, I know the solace was only ever in the drugs—my room had nothing to do with it. It's just a big, empty space filled with longing echoes and past regrets.

I pull the blanket tighter, willing for sleep to come back to me.

I think it's been a couple of days since I got home, but time eludes me. I'm either passed out, or when I finally wake, groggy and aching from the forceful sobs of the previous blip of consciousness, I lie and wait for sleep to take me again.

It's the only thing I have to look forward to.

I've never ached the way I do right now. It feels like Gavin punched a hole in my chest and left me gaping, and with every minute that passes, another whisper of my soul slips through, disappearing into the pungent air of despair that lingers around me like the plague.

My eyes close at the rush of another round of sobs. These ones are silent as they wrack through me with enough force to make my bedframe creak. I burrow beneath the mound of blankets surrounding me as I bring Gavin's t-shirt to my face and hold it against me, breathing in his rapidly fading scent with every gasping breath.

Living without him feels unthinkable. Every nerve ending in my body is screaming for him, for his touch, his words. His gentle comfort.

I need him to take care of me again. To make this all okay.

Why did he have to leave?

Why didn't he choose me?

Is it because I'm broken, and the harsh light of reality shined on parts of me that were masked by the shade of the island, and what he saw was too much? Too dark, too heavy.

Too burdensome.

"Come back to me, Daddy," I wail pathetically into his shirt, smearing snot and tears all over the fabric. "Please. *Please.*" Each word gets raspier, quieter, as my voice cuts out, too overworked from screaming and sobbing for endless hours.

My fingers dig into everything within reach, but nothing feels as tangible as my anguish. Each breath feels forced and labored. Each beat of my heart feels fraudulent, the blood pumping in my veins a stolen essence.

I sink into the mattress with relief when the first teases of exhaustion begin to seep into my bones. Sniffling loudly, I bring my hands to rest just beneath my chin, hating the scratch of my stubble because it doesn't feel like my Daddy's.

I'm curled into a fetal position, arms tucked tight against me, my heels digging into my ass. My hips scream for relief, but the ache kind of reminds me of Daddy's bruises still lingering. I itch to peek at them, to see the reminder I wanted so fucking badly, but I haven't been able to.

I'm scared if I look, they'll be gone. I know they aren't because I *feel* them. The same way I feel the scrapes and cuts on my back that still sting every time I roll over. But remembering brings a sense of security that actuality can fracture in a split second.

"Zev?"

Fuck. I hold my breath in an attempt to hold in a sob, but it breaks through like I didn't even try—and I'm trying *so hard* to be a good boy for Daddy. He said I'm strong, the strongest person he knows, but I think it was a lie...

Shame burns my face.

"Can we come in?" Dillon asks.

"You're already in," I rasp, wincing at how indecipherable my words probably are, but the tell-tale sound of Carmen and Dillon's footsteps tells me they heard just fine. The bed dips as they sit on the edge, pulling my blanket tight over my shoulders.

"Please talk to us," Carmen whispers into the darkness. I don't even know what time it is, but I don't care.

I just want to lie here for a little while.

"You haven't eaten since you got home, Zev. Pretty sure we haven't even seen you get up to pee. We're worried about you. You seemed..."

Haven't even seen you get up to pee...

I clutch at my chest with a silent scream. The ache in my belly is impossible to ignore, the pressure of my full bladder set to explode.

But I *can't. I need his help to do it. I need his hands wrapped around me, holding me steady as I release into the toilet, my weight pressed fully against his back. The relief would be transcendent.*

Tears flow. I don't care to stop them.

I can't do any of this without him.

I need my Daddy.

"Happy on the phone," Dillon finishes for Carmen. The sound of his voice startles me, but the reminder of what was makes me want to scream in agony, but all that comes out is a meek whimper.

"I was." I sound pitifully weak and hollow. My voice dissipates like mist in the rain.

"What happened, man?" Dillon crawls across the bed and presses against me. His touch makes me flinch away in shock. Then guilt. My heart slams against my sternum.

I don't want anyone but Daddy to hold me.

"Z, let me. Please." He doesn't wait for me to answer before he's wrapping his arms around me, knowing me undoubtedly. The weight of his touch burns me alive with shame, but I need it.

Need to be held, be loved.

Carmen comes around to the other side and rubs her hand back and forth over my arm, just beneath the blanket. Their touch feels foreign after only feeling one for so long, but I promised myself I'd let them help me—and I need it more than they know.

"SON." His voice is a blade to my neck and my bed beneath me the guillotine locking me in place. "It's good to see you home." I nearly laugh. Who the hell does he think he's kidding?

"I don't want you here, Zion." I don't recognize the sound of my own voice.

"Is it really going to be like that, Zevryn?" I can hear the muted shift of his feet. The sound of his quiet breaths.

I don't feel anything.

"There is no 'like that'. I just need space from you. For a while. Kick me out, disown me. I don't care anymore."

"I am not going to do that, son, but it's been two months—"

"Yeah," I rasp and force myself to sit up so my father isn't staring down at me while I look as pathetic as I feel. I lean back against the headrest to stare at him head-on. "It has been two months. Two months of me working on *me.* I'm sober now, Dad." The name still feels like poison on my tongue. "Things are different now, and I really don't need you in my life. Not when you're so bad for me. I'll take being homeless and broke over your toxicity."

Zion actually has the audacity to look hurt. His dark brows pinch as his lips curve into a grimace. "I..." His mouth purses. He's probably thinking of what lie to tell me next.

I don't even care. I just want him to leave so I can go back to sleep. None of this feels real anyway.

"I didn't realize my presence was harmful for you. I will go, but I would like to speak with you again once you're feeling better." His eyes drop before they angle back up toward my face, eyes tight and mouth pinched like he tasted something sour, matching the rest of his surprisingly disheveled appearance. Before I can even open my mouth—to say what, I don't even know—Zion's walking out of my room, latching the door shut behind him.

I sink back into the bed, burrowing under the covers until they form a thick wall around me. My breath blows back in my face in fast pants, burning to the point my skin crawls with the need to peel.

Tears spring to my eyes as I hyperventilate. Darkness swirls in at the edges of my vision, a dark, ominous cloud of dread ready to drag me down.

I'm strong. Daddy said I'm strong...

I repeat my mantra over and over, forcing my fingers through my hair the same way Daddy would to help draw me back from the precipice.

I yank on the strands until it burns, and I scream. The sound that comes out of me is different than the one in my head. Hollower and more distorted, but it relieves something.

A dam breaks.

I throw my head back and wail. The vibrations carry in the air and bounce off the high ceilings. My arms shoot into the air before they slam back down into the bed. The impact is blunt and dull, but it feels good to hit something. I hammer into the soft material, screams still ripping out of me.

My body's trapped in the space between crushing reality

and the first flashes of a fever dream. Can one have a fever dream while they're still conscious? It is all in my head: my flesh peeling from my muscle and shriveling into nothing, my brain pulsating from the pressure of my skull keeping it from expanding and bursting free from the confines.

I'm dying while I'm alive. Burning, drowning, sinking deep into the trenches, the impossible weight of the water forcing me deeper—and for the first time in my life, I feel myself wishing for the tentacles from my dreams to come and wrap around my throat just so I can feel something I recognize.

I vaguely recall the sound of my bedroom door opening, the drowned-out sound of footsteps. Arms encircle me, pinning my own. I kick out while I lean into Dillon—I'd recognize his touch anywhere, even through the haze of surreality.

"I got ya, buddy. Let it all out." His lips skim my sweaty temple with a slight tremble, the last thing I feel before I sink into my abysmal, black hole.

Twenty-Nine

ZEVRYN

I*t's only been three days.* A blip in time as forever stares me in the face—the same way my best friends are right now.

I slowly lift my head. It takes more strength than I have, but their continuous, worried glances and hushed whispers are blatant displays of how concerned they are, and they deserve to know.

"I'm not going to relapse," I say, getting it out in the open. They exchange glances, both of their eyes wide. I'd roll my own if I had the energy. "I'm not," I reiterate.

"Okay." Carmen nods with a smile. Her brown eyes are soft and gentle, open and expressive. "Thank you for reassuring us; that's actually really nice to hear you say."

I wince at the fierce stab of guilt. I brush my hair back from my face, tucking a few wayward curls behind my ears. "Sorry, I wasn't thinking."

"Don't be sorry, Zev. We're just worried. Especially because you seemed so good on the phone but ever since you got back, you've been..." Carmen trails off, chewing on her bottom lip. Her gaze drops to the table separating us, but it might as well be an ocean.

I'm in too fucking deep to see my way out.

"You're so strong, my boy. Please don't forget that." The sound of Gavin's rapidly fading voice repeating those words to me plays like a movie in my mind, giving me a sliver of the strength he always thought I had.

It's not enough, but it's something.

"Depressed," Dillon finishes without much class.

I snort. My finger traces the rim of the glass a few inches away. Condensation trickles down, settling into a ring around the base. "You guys have every right to be worried. I haven't been myself lately." *Well, I've been myself—just the most hollow, lost version.* "But you're right, Dill. I'm depressed. But I'm not going to relapse, okay?" I glance up at them through my lashes, hating that they're blurry. I blink rapidly, trying to clear the sheen.

"I need to feel this shit, but I don't know how. So, I'm kind of just treading the waters." My fingers curl around the glass and slide down. When I pick it up and bring it to my lips with a shaky hand, I nearly drop it.

After choking down a swallow, and nearly spluttering as I force it down my swollen throat, I drop it back onto the table, causing it to slosh over. I eye the tiny pool of liquid staining the dark-grained wood.

"Why, though?" Dillon asks. I avoid his gaze pointedly.

"Is it because of that guy?" Carmen's cavalier mention of Gavin has my stomach coiling into knots.

"What guy?" Talking about him feels weird, almost like

acknowledging his existence makes it all the more real. The elation—and the loss.

"The one we heard on the phone when you first called. He helped you."

My throat bobs with an obstructed swallow. The swirls within the wood blur and melt the longer I stare unblinking. I can feel the sobs building into a crescendo. It starts off small and soft. A few tears fall. My shoulders shake. The cavernous void in my chest expands beyond my body's capability.

My head drops into my hands as my body trembles.

A chair scrapes across the floor, and then Dillon's arm is stretched across my shoulders. He tugs me against him, knocking our heads together. "You love him, don't you?"

"Wasn't the plan," I rasp.

"Never is, man." Even through my bone-breaking sobs, I still manage to huff a laugh—which is a miracle in and of itself. "So, why isn't he here with you?"

The question is reasonable, but it brings a bout of jealous hatred I've been trying not to feel. Because I don't want to be that person, and Gavin truly doesn't deserve it. "Because he had a husband to go home to." My words are dry, even through my clogged-up tears. Carmen gasps, and Dillon stiffens.

I guess that does sound as bad as it is.

"Married?" Carmen exclaims. "Zev..."

"Yeah, man, what the hell?"

My molars grind as I try to think of a way to explain, but when it comes down to it, none of the little things matter. "I know. I'm a piece of shit."

"You're not," Carmen tries to placate me, but I shake my head.

"Nah, it's fine. I am. It's not like I planned it, but fuck. I fell way too deep way too fast. He's..." *My Daddy.* I swallow that down because there is no way I'm getting into that with them—now or ever, probably. "He's the most important person to me. He saved my life, gave me hope. Took care of me when I thought I was going to die and has every day since."

"Wow..." Carmen breathes out breathily. Dillon's still silent beside me, probably processing. At least, that's what I hope it is.

"Hey, this doesn't... I'm not, like, hurting you, am I?" I force my head to turn to meet Dillon's eyes. They're soft at the corners. A bit shimmery, too.

"Nah, Z. What we have—*had*—was out of need. Never loved you like that. Sorry to disappoint ya, buddy." He smiles through the straight blonde locks covering half his face. I laugh—loudly and warmly—a smidge of happiness peeking in through the murk.

"I fucking missed you." I knock our heads together, pushing against him just to feel him push back. His fingers clamp down on my shoulder. His thumb digs into a healing scrape, making my eyes flutter closed at the instant reminder.

The longer I reminisce on what I no longer have, the heavier I start to feel. I pull away slowly, my head hanging in shame.

Fuck, I really thought I was starting to feel better, but I should've known.

I can't do this alone.

I... need help.

"I'm gonna take a nap." I rush out of the kitchen, feeling their gazes burning into me as I disappear. After slamming my bedroom door closed, I hesitantly pick my phone up. Having it again feels weird. As I scroll through my contacts, elbows digging into my thighs, my thumb freezes at the sight of Darien's name.

It's a harbinger of agony as it stares back at me with a life force of its own. *I'm strong... I'm strong...*

I dig out the paper Dr. Weaver gave me from my bag and type in the first number on the list for a Dr. Justin Cray. The ringtone is loud in my ear as I wait for it to connect.

Hopefully, he can fucking help me because I don't know what I'm doing.

Daddy said to trust him. I don't know how or why, but I have to try.

For him.

I'd do anything for him—even if that means forcing myself out of bed and starting my life without him.

I can't be the shell of a man I was.

I KEEP my eyes pinched shut on the way down the elevator, refusing to face the last memory I have in it, but the moment the doors slide open and I step out with the few others on board with me, my legs twitch with the urge to turn right back around.

Yesterday, it seemed like a good idea to talk to someone

again. Having Dr. Weaver helped me tremendously, but now that I'm faced with the task of leaving the sanctuary of my apartment, I'm beginning to regret the purpose of it all.

And when my head rears back at the sight of Micah Richardson waiting for me just outside my building's doors with two beefy dudes at his side, the one place my mind goes is *Zion was right.*

What a fucking slap in the face.

My eyes dart between the three of them for a few, long seconds before I sigh and drop my shoulders. "Micah," I drawl tiredly.

"Get in." He jerks his head at the black SUV at his back. One of the dudes pulls the rear passenger door open, waiting. I hesitate as I stare into the dark interior.

"Are you going to kill me?" *Jesus, it's fucking hot out here.* I tug at the collar of my shirt. The cotton sticks to my damp skin, clinging to me in a way that makes me itch. Even locked away in my penthouse, it's been easy to forget the kind of power men like Micah Richardson and my father have.

Micah raises a dark brow, but that's the only shift in his stoic expression that I get. "Interesting. Who told you that—your father?" he sneers. My throat bobs, and I feel every centimeter of the lump I try to force down.

Gavin should be here. To protect me. Keep me safe from all of this.

I nod hesitantly, words lost on me. Micah laughs, but it's dry and a bit sinister, a foreign sound coming from someone so unflappable.

I don't know what role I should play. The scared boy or the defensive one. But when one of the guys grunts and swings his arm toward the open door, I realize with startling clarity that it doesn't matter.

My fate doesn't belong to me.

With one last flickering glance, I sigh and climb inside, pushing against the furthest door in a pathetic attempt to put as much distance between me and Micah as I can. He slides in effortlessly, the movement almost liquid. I shudder as apprehension licks along my spine, ice-cold and paralyzing.

"Give me your phone." I eye his stretched hand warily.

"I'd like to keep it, thanks."

Micah chuckles darkly. "You don't have a choice, Zevryn, and I think you know that." The goons in the front spin to face me at the same time. Their thick, meaty faces are domineering all on their own, which I'm sure isn't their only purpose judging by their steroid-influenced muscles.

This is what I get for trying to do the right thing.

With a silent groan for my own stupidity, I pull it out of my pocket and smack it into Micah's palm. Without looking at it, he tucks it inside his suit jacket.

"I want you to tell me what happened to my son."

I knew it was coming, but nothing could've prepared me for the way it would steal the breath from my lungs or leech the feigned strength from the marrow of my bones.

"We, uh..." I rub my hands together, hating the clammy sheen of sweat clinging between them. Staring at the backs of my brightened eyelids, I take a deep breath. "We went to the bathroom to do some coke, a-and that's when everything happened. After he did his lines."

"Whose cocaine was it?" My mind whirls, flashbacks hammering into me left and right. So much of that night is a blur, but I know the answer to that; I just don't know if I should tell him.

"Um..."

"Tell me, Zevryn. The truth." His cold, dark eyes cut to mine, making me twitch with nerves.

My throat bobs, giving away my apprehension. "His."

"I want the details." He doesn't raise his voice, but I hear the threat all the same. The lilt to his tone, the sinister gentleness.

My eyes dart across the bench. Micah is sitting straight up in the seat, his ramrod spine barely grazing the leather backing. A fucking statue.

The buildings outside begin to blur together as I tell Micah how his son died, eyes locked on a world that feels unobtainable. "He pulled the baggie out of his pocket and cut some lines on the back of the toilet. He did his first because it was his shit. I saw the way he began to sway, how he was sweating and breathing weirdly, but it didn't matter to me—not then. Not when the coke was right there..." I trail off with a swallow, vividly remembering the burn in my nose followed by the thick drip in the back of my throat. The addictive fire.

"You chose to snort some powder over helping my son when he was visibly in distress?" I wince. The dip of my eyelids causes the thick layer of tears that have built to drip down my face. They splash against the leather with near-silent *plinks.*

"When you say it like that..." Jesus. He makes it sound like I wanted him to die. But it's the truth—that I did choose to get high over saving him. I just didn't realize it then. The very moment a split-second decision changed *everything.*

"It's the biggest regret of my life—" I almost say sir, but I catch it right on the tip of my tongue. I may be a sad, scared sack of shit but there is no way I'm calling this prick sir. "I can't change what I did, but if it means anything, at all, I am sober now, and I feel every regret with startling clarity.

"Darien was my friend. We might not have been friends for the right reasons, but he was, regardless. And I'm sorry he died. Sometimes, I wish it would've been me."

The car is excruciatingly silent for a long time. My eyes keep darting to Micah's general vicinity, but he hasn't moved an inch or said another word. The car is still driving through the city. The buildings have slowly morphed from high, sleek opulence, to shuttered, dilapidated ones.

The car gradually slows as we near the mouth of an alley. The brakes are silent, but in my mind, they grate with a high-pitched squeal. Micah gives the slightest nod, drawing my attention for a split second before the two dudes in the front jump out. The door I'm leaned against flies open, and I lose my balance.

One of them catches me with a tight, unyielding grip on my arm. My chest heaves as I stare at the broken, uneven concrete a foot away. It's stained with oils and gods knows what else. The laugh that bursts from me is shaky and weak at best, a clear indication I'm losing my shit.

Oh, gods. What the fuck did I do?

Gavin never would've let me be so stupid. He would've pushed himself in front of me, probably with a hand already on his holster, ready to defend me at the first glimpse of Micah.

But he's not fucking here. I'm all alone in this shit, which is probably what I deserve.

My arm is practically ripped from my socket as I'm

yanked from the car and down the narrow alleyway. I don't bother putting up a fight, feet sliding over the loose gravel. The beefy dude slams me up against a dumpster, and my head bounces off the steel with a resounding *thunk.*

Gravel scrapes beneath my palms, splitting my skin. "Fuck," I groan. My eyes are bleary as Micah drops down in front of me in a squat. "Guess this is where you kill me," I huff before my breath is sucked back into my lungs on a sob.

"I'm not going to kill you, Zevryn. But I do want you to hurt—for what you did to my son. Choosing your addiction over his life." He leans in so close, I can taste the truth on his breath. "When this is all done and over with, just know your sobriety saved your life." He pushes himself up and redoes the button on his jacket as he takes a step back.

When his head dips with another nod, I let out a feeble groan, already knowing what's coming before the first meaty fist lands against my cheek. My ear pops as my head jerks to the side. A warped sound emits from the opened dumpster from the clash of my body against it.

But that's the only hit they land to my face. The rest are given in short, but heavy kicks to my abdomen. A few miss the mark and catch on my thighs, but I'm only grateful for the fleeting relief.

Each excruciating hit makes me scream out. I know it's fruitless, that no one is coming to the rescue, that I deserve each strike for every breath I've taken since Darien died, but the place between consciousness and survival instinct has long separated into shredded fragments.

My mind has closed off, a dull void without a single thought. All that's inside me is the impact of pain. The roll in my gut as a thick, leather boot nails me in what I think is a kidney. The whistle of each labored breath I have no choice but to force through a tight constriction because I have to live.

Death is far from me as I bask in the kinship of his near and dear friend—anguish.

I splutter and gag as the tip of a boot digs just beneath my ribs. My face scrapes across the rough concrete as I roll around, panting through my opened mouth. Copper is thick and pungent on my tongue.

My nailbeds throb, split open and broken off as I dig them into the concrete, for no other reason than creating a line between here and the place I'm drifting off to.

A place much darker and still.

A reprieve. As terrifying as it is welcoming.

Black licks at the edges of my vision, pulsating and wavering. Shoes scrape in front of me, but it's the fingers brushing against my cheek that drag my swollen, wet eyelids open.

Micah Richardson stares down at me with a hollow sorrow I recognize like I'm staring in a mirror. His cold eyes are pinched, dark skin shimmering with sweat from the sun glaring down with a vengeance that mirrors his own. He places my phone on the ground beneath my chin. "Forgive me." I flinch and whimper as he pushes up and walks away. He's sideways as I stare at his retreating figure, a dull wash of blurriness distorting the gray-washed world.

Forgive me...

Maybe I could if I could forgive myself.

Thirty

ZEVRYN

The piercing vibration of my phone against the gravel is what lulls me from the trance-like state between awareness and somewhere just behind. Somewhere better and so much fucking scarier.

"Fuckin' shit," I moan loudly as I finally rouse. I hiss when my palms hit the ground. The fresh scrapes sting like a motherfucker. It takes an effort I never knew I possessed to push myself upward.

Vertigo slams into me like a freight train, and I'm spewing the empty contents of my stomach onto the concrete beside me before I can take my next breath.

Vomit spews out of my nose and mouth as I gag and retch, the pain blinding and suffocating all at the same time.

"Hey! Are you okay?!" someone shouts from a distance, but the sound is still jarring. I wince at the throb at the base of my skull, gritting my teeth at the sound of footsteps drawing closer.

I hold up a hand, and with a strength only my Daddy knew I possessed, I force myself onto two feet, remembering at the last moment to grab my phone. "Fine," I rasp. My throat is clogged with blood, snot, and tears.

"You don't look okay. Do you want me to call someone?"

Using the dumpster for leverage, I reach and shuffle my feet, moving haggardly but purposefully. "No. I'm fine."

Each step makes me flinch, my breath coming out heavily as I pant through each new wave of agony. I swear to the gods my guts were rearranged—and not in the good way.

The thought makes me huff out a hysterical laugh—and I just can't stop. Even once I hail a cab and slump against the window, my manic chuckles never cease. The cab driver has the decency to look properly concerned, his eyes constantly darting to the rearview mirror, but it's not his job to ask questions.

He drops me at the front of my building where I stagger in, running on fumes. The front desk clerk bellows out in surprise—probably at the state of me—but I wave them off without a word as I shove my way inside the elevator.

I barely manage to type in the code for my penthouse through one very blurry eye—the other too swollen to see through. Once the silver doors slam shut behind me, I collapse to the floor, only to be startled awake by the dipping weight of the lift stopping, followed by a resounding ding.

I stare at the entrance to my apartment. Ten feet of distance has never looked so daunting in my life.

Refusing to let go of the phone clutched in my hand, I crawl out of the elevator, all traces of humility long lost the moment Micah's men started hammering the piss out of me

—literally. I think I smell urine wafting into my nose as I drag myself over the threshold.

It's silent—the echoing, hollow kind. Each haggard breath I force in and out of my lungs bounces off the high ceilings, coming right back toward me.

It's odd, hearing myself sound this way—as broken on the outside as I am on the inside.

My phone buzzes in my hand, startling me. My heart soars. It takes my eyes a long time to focus on the small words on the screen, but when I do, I nearly choke on the disappointment.

A fucking text reminder that I missed my appointment with Dr. Cray. I drop my phone, not even flinching at the resounding crack as the screen connects with the floor.

I curl in on myself right there in the foyer, the sleek floor cool against my feverish, split-open flesh. At the sound of the doors shutting with a dull thud, a sob rips through me.

But not because of the pain I'm wallowing in; because that elevator is the last place I saw Gavin, touched him and tasted him, and I wish for nothing more than for him to be here.

To get me through this in the way he always does. With his fingers in my hair, his chest against my face, and his legs curled like a lifeline around mine.

An anchor.

I deserved the blow to my face and every one to my abdomen after. Each hit was Micah's way of telling me what his son's death did to him.

It crushed him. Bruised and brutalized.

Killed a part of him.

I'm glad I know now. That I have his affliction atop of my own.

It only ensures I will never be that person again—someone so blind and selfish. Someone lost in the abyss.

If only Daddy could see how strong I'm being.

It's all because of him.

Thirty-One

GAVIN

My fingers thrum restlessly on my thigh, my left leg shaking uncontrollably.

"If you bump this table any harder, you're going to knock it over, Gavin." Milo's teasing drawl drags me back to the moment. I lift my head, finding two sets of eyes pinned on me. Milo appears amused, the lawyer annoyed.

Oh, what the hell.

"Nervous, baby? Cold feet?" Milo wags his brows, making me huff and shake my head. His tease is a throwback in time.

"No, I'm fine." My thumb rubs across the top of my now bare ring finger. Not having something there to fiddle with is a strange sensation, but the metaphorical weight of its disappearance brings a relief I didn't know I needed so badly.

"Good. Me, too." Our eyes catch, locking in the kind of moment you know you'll remember for the rest of your life. I memorize every sparkle and swirl in his blue irises. The way his golden lashes nearly touch his blonde brows. His hair—

long, golden, and sleek as it brushes his ears. The tattoos that were the very first things I ever noticed about him.

I'm saying goodbye to my husband. The man I've spent a decade with. My best friend and an epic love of my life.

It fucking obliterates me.

His smile is sad when I finally let my eyes land on his mouth. A mouth I've kissed, sucked, and fucked more times than I can count. Lips that have formed words that have scarred into the deepest point of my soul.

I love you, I mouth the words, unable to speak them aloud, but I want him to know, to see it, one last time. His mouth quirks, even as a stray tear slips from the corner of his eye and slides over his lips.

Love you, baby, he flips back, adding to the despondent sadness of this pivotal moment.

"If you both could sign right here," the lawyer rudely interrupts our moment. I roll my eyes, and Milo sniffles, shaking his head.

"Sure thing." He snatches a pen out of a small, cylindrical holder and scribbles his signature on the paper without a moment's hesitation. When he leans back, holding it out to me, I take it with a steady hand, pushing my chair back slightly as I lean forward to write my name on the solid, black line, the scratch of black ink on crisp white paper the final etchings of our goodbye.

My watch buzzes, snapping me out of my reverie. My eyes squint at the notification, my hand dipping into my jeans pocket to retrieve my phone before I even finish reading.

I click on the motion alert for my boy's apartment, heart in my throat as I wait for it to load. I watched him walk into the elevator almost two hours ago, dressed casually, looking harrowed and ragged. The sight alone almost made me collapse in defeat and rush to his side, but I *needed* to get this done first—to be wholly his when I showed up and begged for him to let me love him.

Deacon would have my ass if he knew I was accessing Zevryn's feed the way I am—with homeowner's access—but I *needed* to keep an eye on my boy the only way I could. And I know, when I can finally tell him, he won't care.

He'd probably love knowing I was watching, the little brat.

Fuck, I need him.

"What's that?" Milo asks, leaning over my shoulder, but I barely hear his words. They echo and bounce around my skull, sounding hollow and protracted.

My eyes are locked on my boy, lying helplessly on the foyer floor, blood smeared across his swollen face and body shaking uncontrollably.

"Who's that?"

"My boy," I gasp as Zevryn rolls. There's a pool of liquid beneath his face. It could be drool—or blood. "Fuck!" I shout, shoving to my feet. I race out of the room, heart hammering away in my throat. My feet slide across the carpet as I round the corner, my eyes locked on my boy splayed on the screen, so small and so weak.

God, what the hell happened to you, baby?

Why wasn't I there?

Each breath is uncontrolled and feeble, coming in too fast, not fast enough. I can't—I smack into the wall. "Goddamnit!"

"Gavin!" Milo's hands grip my shoulders and yank me back. I stumble, my head whipping around. "Gavin."

"What?" I pant. "I've gotta go." I try to pull away from him, but he slams me back into the wall. I grunt, already pushing back.

"Tell me what's going on!"

"I've gotta go help him. He needs me. I need to go!" I shout, pushing Milo off me, but even with our slight size difference, he doesn't budge—always so goddamn stubborn.

He presses his front against mine, and it feels wrong—so fucking wrong—but his breath, warm and minty, smelling faintly of his favorite mocha creamer, brings a sliver of clarity to the panic consuming me.

"Listen to me, Gavin. Focus on my words. Tell me what's going on; you're not making any sense." Our chests are heaving against one another. More like mine is heaving and his is steady and sure.

"Zevryn. He's hurt. I-I don't know what happened, but he needs me." I suck my bottom lip into my mouth, trying to bite back a moan of weakness. *He's all alone, in fucking pain, without me.*

"Zevryn... that's the guy you were hired to protect, right? On the island?"

"Yes." I struggle against him, the sight of him sprawled on the floor flashing through my mind again.

My little boy...

"Oh..." Milo stumbles back, his mouth as wide as his eyes. They lift from the floor to my own. "That's him." It's a whisper of acknowledgment, of realization.

Goddamnit, this is not how any of this was supposed to happen.

I yank on my hair, pulling it loose from the tie. "Yes. I'm sorry, Milo. I didn't want to—but I have—to go." I swipe my phone off the floor and rush through the building, my footsteps hammering and echoing in the stairway. I can hear Milo's behind me, but they're background noise.

It's all white noise to my boy and his need for me.

"Let me drive," Milo shoves his way into the driver's seat before I can slide inside. I growl as I stumble back but straighten myself in the next moment, rushing to the passenger side and jumping in. I slam the door behind me with a trembling hand.

"Where am I going?"

"East," I grunt as I type Zevryn's address into the GPS. My eyes automatically drop to my phone screen as Milo peels out of the parking garage. My boy's still in the same spot, but the shaking has subsided.

I don't know if that's good or bad.

I don't know a goddamn thing because I wasn't there like I promised I would be. To protect him, care for him. I left him vulnerable and susceptible to abuse.

I fucked up, did this all wrong when all I wanted was to do right by him and by Milo.

Traffic is light enough that Milo's able to speed most of the way there, but I can't tell for sure because my eyes never leave my phone screen. Milo doesn't try for small talk, which I'm grateful for because I'm not sure I can form a coherent thought.

Nothing that's not Zevryn.

My stomach gurgles and lurches, hot bile shooting up my esophagus and sitting just behind my uvula, making it impossible to breathe. I swallow constantly against the pressure, gritting my teeth at the raw burn blistering my throat.

Sweat licks across my palms, causing my phone to slip against my fingers. I tighten my grip, but all that does is make my phone creak and groan under too much pressure.

"You're going to break it."

I startle, whipping my head around toward the noise. "Huh?" Milo's head nods toward my hand. I glance down, not realizing how close my face is to my phone screen. My elbows are dug deep into my thighs, and I'm hunched over, phone inches away.

"Your phone. Might wanna loosen that death grip." I blink. It takes great effort to get my fingers to respond to the command of releasing.

The molars on the right side of my mouth grind together as I work my jaw, gaze flickering between the GPS and my boy, watching the time slowly tick. An endless taunt of my stupidity.

"Is this it?" Milo asks as he pulls up the circle drive, but I'm already swinging the door open and running up to the front doors, leaving him behind as the car inches up. The front doors swing open as I shove against them. I nearly trip over my feet as my gaze zeros in on the elevator. I hammer my finger into the button, eyes darting between the arrow and the digital numbers displayed above the doors.

Sweat drips down my forehead and into my eyes. I hiss and grit my teeth at the sting. My palms grip both sides of the sleek metal as the doors slide open. The two people on board jerk back in surprise at my close proximity.

"Move!" I growl as I shove my way on. Someone gasps, the other huffs, but they shift out of the way to let me on before they exit. I shake my head, scrunching my eyes closed to try and clear the static burning and bouncing around.

I'm dizzy and sick to my stomach. Every inch of me is on fire.

A tattooed arm slips through the slowly closing crack, blocking the doors from closing. It dings as they slide open. "Come on!" I shout, slamming my hand against the wall. Milo slips through, sweaty and panting.

I balk at him, not really sure I'm seeing things correctly. It's all distorted, blurred and consumed by my need to get up to my boy's penthouse.

Penthouse... A goddamn penthouse.

"Fuck!" My head hangs between my shoulders. A few tears of anger slip from my eyes. I'm so goddamn helpless. Milo's hand rubs between my shoulder blades. All it does is smear the sweat beneath my shirt around, but I get the point of the gesture.

I just don't need it from him.

I need it from my boy, who I cannot fucking get to without the goddamn code.

"What's wrong?" Milo asks like he can actually fucking help me.

"I don't have the code." I jerk my head in the direction of the keypad.

"Code?"

"He's in the penthouse."

"Jesus—a penthouse." Milo huffs. My teeth ache from the brutal pressure I'm putting them under. The doors slide shut when I hit a random number, and the ascent starts. My eyes drill into the floor as my phone rings loudly against my ear.

I may not have the code, but I know who does, and so help me if he doesn't give it to me...

"Mr. Holt, didn't expect to hear from you again."

"What's the code to the penthouse?" I get right to the point. My foot hammers restlessly on the ground as I watch the digital numbers tick higher.

"Excuse me?"

"You fucking heard me, Zion. The code. To Zevryn's apartment. I need it."

"And what on Earth would you need it for?"

I growl and yank on my hair. "Because I do! He's hurt, and he needs help, so fucking give it to me now!"

"Fuck. It's twelve, twenty-seven, thirteen." When the lift stops, I hammer in the numbers, and my eyes flutter in relief as it clears and we ascend to my boy's apartment.

"Did it go through?"

"Yes." I'm seconds away from hanging up when his question stops me.

"How do you know he's hurt?" He sounds like he genuinely cares, but I couldn't care less if he does or not. Not after all the shit he's put my boy through. Zion Carver is a selfish, pathetic excuse of a father, and he doesn't deserve my boy or his love.

With my eyes locked on the glowing numbers, I dip my head until my eyes strain under the pressure. "Let me ask you a question. How many times have you checked the security feed since Zevryn has been home? Did you just glance at each motion alert or did you not even bother to turn them on? Do you even have it downloaded to your fucking phone?" My voice is low and menacing, each word filling my blood with vibrant hatred.

How can someone be so fucking careless?

The blaring sound of his silence says it all. I click off the line and shove my phone back into my pocket just as the lift dips and shudders to a stop. I wait with bated breath for the thick, silver doors to slide open.

And when they do, my every reason for living flashes right in front of my eyes as my boy, so small and vulnerable, consumes every sense I possess.

I sprint out and drop to my knees at his side with a resounding crack. "Oh, fuck," I pant as my eyes rove over his scraped face. The left side is swollen, with a split in his lip and a bruise on his cheek—similar to the very one he had months ago. There's a trail of dried blood leading from his nose, down over his beautiful lips, his chin, where it disappears behind the collar of his shirt.

I cradle his head in my lap, hesitantly brushing his knotted curls away from his face, fingertips grazing the grown-out length of his once-shaved head. The scent of copper and sweat and urine wafts into my nose as I move him, and the air is disturbed. I suck in a breath, choking on the scent of his pain.

"Baby..." I rasp, then clear my throat. Brushing my fingers along the side of his face that isn't abused, I tap his skin lightly, not wanting to hurt him but needing to rouse him. "Zevryn, wake up for me." I alternate between patting and rubbing, drawing a flush of color to his unusually pale skin. The dark stain of blood makes him appear even more washed out with the added shadows of his darkened apartment.

"Is he okay?" Milo asks from somewhere behind me.

"I don't know. Zevryn, baby, come on. Wake up for me." I

grip his shoulder and shake gently. His lashes flutter against his cheeks. I hold my breath. "Get the light," I tell Milo.

"That's it, boy. Show me those pretty, hazel eyes." I choke on my own words as he does what he's told—always so beautifully obedient. Stark, red veins stain the whites of his eyes. His pupils are large in the darkness, the rest wholly unfocused as he gazes up at me without really seeing me.

"Zevryn." A light flickers on, illuminating the space with harsh fluorescents. Zevryn winces, eyes crinkling at the corners. The light shines on his injuries with shocking clarity. My breath stills in my lungs as I rake over what I can see. He's clothed from the neck down to his knees, so I can't be sure of his midsection, but the damage to his pretty face isn't as gruesome as the dark made it appear to be. It's still swollen and scraped, with the freshness of bruises starting, but it could've been so much worse.

"Tell me what happened," I whisper, shifting on my haunches to draw him closer. I want every inch of him on me, but it's not the time for that yet.

Just seeing his face after days away breathes life and purpose back into me.

"Daddy," he croaks, eyelids fluttering open. His bleary gaze focuses on me with intent. My heart clenches, making me gasp. I bend down at an awkward angle just so I can brush my lips against the tip of his nose, now wet from the tears that leak out of his eyes.

"My boy." I nuzzle against him, my heart throbbing.

"*Daddy.*" His voice breaks with a sob, and I die a thousand times over hearing it.

"Fuck." I ease my arm under his neck, and with another beneath his knees, I shift onto my feet and haul him into my arms. He groans at the movement, and I wince. Pressing my lips to his sweaty forehead, I murmur, "I'm sorry, baby."

I ease him onto the large, dark, sectional sofa, ignoring the way my quads burn as I squat. He lands on the soft cushion with another groan and curls into himself, his hands clasped beneath his chin in a gesture so childlike, I nearly lose all reason and climb in beside him.

He's shivering again, so I reach over to grab a throw that's lying across the back of the couch. I tuck it in around him, careful of my touch against his skin. Zevryn looks to have fallen back asleep, so I gently nudge him awake again.

"What happened to you?" I nearly ask why he didn't call me, but that would be utterly insensitive seeing as I didn't give him a way to contact me. I'm such a fucking prick.

When his dark lashes flutter, revealing hazel, the glassy sheen has dissipated, leaving some newfound clarity in its place. He speaks with a whisper so light, I'm forced to lean into him, ear to his mouth. I shudder at the brush of his skin against mine, no matter how innocent.

"What my father hired you to protect me from." My blood, which ran so hot, now freezes like ice in my veins. Every muscle atrophies as if years have passed, and I've remained stoically immobile for every one of them.

His exhale against the side of my face makes me pull back so I can stare into his eyes. They're so fucking sad—glassy, wide, and perfectly innocent.

My boy may have gone through hell, but his soul has remained beautifully untarnished, vibrant with the innocence of the lost little boy inside.

"What did he do to you?" I jerk back, hands already reaching for the blanket and ripping it off. Zevryn tries to protest, but his attempts are weak at best. “Sorry, baby, but I need to see.” With a grimace, I grip the hem of his damp t-shirt and drag it up his body. Each inch of bare flesh revealed to me kills a little more of my soul, each piece shriveling up and flaking away.

“Oh, shit,” Milo blurts. I flinch, but I don’t stop—not until I’m tugging it off Zevryn’s head and dropping it to my lap. His skin is mottled in bright red blotches, some already turning a deep, vibrant purple. My hand lifts, fingers hovering a hair’s breadth away.

“You can touch me,” my boy rasps with a hint of desperation that kills me. My eyes pinch, and I drop my hand back into my lap. His skin is swollen from the abuse it took, and, apparently, his abdomen took the brunt of it.

“I don’t deserve to touch you, baby.” I choke on the words of my despair. I’ve never hated myself more. I should’ve been here. I was supposed to fucking protect him—and I failed. My marriage, my boy. My one fucking job.

“Not your fault.” Zev tries to placate me, and it’s so endearing, my heart splits wide open. I lean down, pressing my mouth to the top of his curls in a touch so light, I’m sure he can’t even feel it.

“No lies, remember?” I remind him, even as they taste like acid on the way out. How dare I say that to him when he’s lying here, bruised and beaten, like *I’m* the one who needs to be mollified. I hover over his ribs. “Do you think any are broken?” Him having a punctured lung flickers into my mind, and once I think the possibility into existence, I can’t stop the turbulence.

He could be bleeding internally. Something could’ve ruptured or broken. He needs a doctor. Now.

"Time to go." Before I can take my next breath, I'm hauling my boy to my chest and striding toward the elevator with intent.

"Milo, grab that blanket, and let's go. I need you to drive."

"Milo?" my boy squeaks, face buried into my chest. My eyes flick down to the mass of curls blocking most of his face. *He's my home.*

"Yes, baby. He brought me here. It's okay; there's nothing to be worried about. You're my boy, yeah?" He stares up at me with eyes so wide and full of devotion I don't deserve. His nod is jerky, but seeing the slight movement is all I need.

"Then let me take care of you." Milo lays the blanket across my boy, carefully tucking it in between the places we're connected. Zevryn's eyes dart between us, wary and apprehensive, but he nods.

"Okay." *That's all I need.*

As the doors close and we descend at a pace far too slow for my liking, I repeat four things over and over, using the strength of their meaning to keep me sane.

He's talking. He's breathing. He's alive. And he trusts me.

I don't deserve his confidence, but I'll be damned if I make him question it ever again.

"Where are we taking him?" Milo asks from beside me as I carry my boy through the lobby and out into the mid-day sun. He sinks deeper into my chest as the light glares down on him. I hunch over, trying to block as much light as I can.

Our car is still idling by the doors. "I told them to leave it alone if they didn't want to lose their jobs. I threw out Carver, too, just so they knew." I snort at Milo's comment.

"Good thinking. And the closest place—it doesn't matter." I slide across the back seat, keeping Zevryn tight against my chest. My eyes flicker to Milo as he shuts the door behind me. Sadness lingers in the creases at the corners of his eyes, but when they dip down to my boy in my arms, I think I see raw, honest acceptance. The corner of my mouth lifts into a sad smile, which he returns a split second before the door latches, and he's jumping into the driver's seat.

His finger taps on the GPS, pulling up the closest hospital, and then he's peeling out of the circle drive. My eyes never stray from my boy as he breathes against me, into me, filling me with a love so selfless, I can't stand the ache of it.

Thirty-Two

ZEVRYN

Daddy's fingers card through my hair, and if it weren't for the tangible proof of his body against mine, I'd think it was all a part of a feverish dream, scraped up from my deepest, most desperate fantasies. His smell is so strong, it nearly burns my nose with every inhale.

My fingers dig as deep as they can into the soft flesh of my Daddy's tummy. Coarse hair scratches across my palms, easing the torturous throb of pain into a radiating ache.

Something vibrates beneath me. Daddy's arm drops from my legs, and I whimper. "I'm not going anywhere, my boy." He digs into what must be his pocket and pulls out his phone. I feel his entire body tense up. I mouth at his chest, uncaring of the chemical taste of cologne on my tongue. Daddy deflates and delves back into my hair. Color bursts behind my closed lids.

"What?" he snaps, making me flinch. His nails scrape across my scalp in reassurance. "No, he's not fine. We're on our way to the hospital." The car veers as we turn, making my stomach flip alarmingly.

"I'm not having this conversation right now." Our eyes connect for a brief moment, and his mask of steel fractures into a smile for me. A voice on the other end rattles something off, and Daddy's steely expression flips right back.

"You should've been there, Zion."

Zion.

I start shaking my head frantically, the mere mention of my father's name upending my lure into tranquility. Gavin shushes me by pressing a cool finger to my lips. "I'll tell you what hospital, but if you cause a scene, I'll have you escorted off the property. Don't push me." Daddy hammers his thumb down on the screen before typing one-handed, then he drops his phone onto the empty space on the seat just above my head.

"I don't want him there." I don't know how I manage the words, but the strength comes from somewhere.

"I know, baby. Just relax, okay? We're nearly there, and then you won't be in so much pain. You've been so fucking strong, my boy. I'm so proud of you." His lips against my forehead are the best feeling in the world. I want to protest my strength, to tell Daddy how strong I'm *not*—not without him—but the scrape of his blunt nails against my head and the rhythmic drag of his roughed palm over the back of my thigh lulls me back into a restless state of unconsciousness.

HOURS OF TESTING and imaging later, and I'm finally back in my hospital bed, sleep already tugging at the edges of my vision. But I don't want to sleep—it's all I've done since Daddy carried me in and I was hauled into a room.

They tried to give me IV pain killers, but I refused. Even Daddy protested my decision. *"Baby, you're in pain. It's okay to have some help with that."* And I knew he was right, but I still didn't want any.

I'm too scared. Of liking it. Of *needing* it again. So, I vehemently refused. They gave me ibuprofen, which doesn't do shit, but it's better than nothing, I guess.

"How are you feeling, boy?" Daddy's at my side, my hand trapped between his two much bigger ones. The callouses there are rough and textured against my sensitive skin, making me shiver.

"I'm okay." His eyes narrow pointedly. I swallow. "Um..." I curl my lips between my teeth. "My ribs ache, and my stomach feels wonky, but I'm better."

The truth seems to appease him. His smile is small but warm, and his fingers never stop rubbing over the back of my hand. The movement draws my attention. I still at the sight of Daddy's finger, bare aside from a thin tan line striped across it. I lift my hand, bringing his closer to my face.

"It's gone." *Wow, Zev. How fucking astute.*

Daddy chuckles. "Yeah, boy. It is."

"Why?" My heart shoots into my throat. Hell, I think my intestines do, too. Daddy's right brow arches, causing a few wrinkles to form across his forehead.

"We can talk about all this stuff later, boy. I want you to get some rest. It's late." His eyes flicker toward the black and white analog clock centered above the door to my room.

"I want to talk now. There's nothing wrong with—" A low rumble emits from deep in Daddy's chest. I give an involuntary shiver. "There isn't *much* wrong with me. Nothing serious, anyway."

"I'd say getting beaten is serious, baby." The term of endearment is said with enough gravel to turn my guts to mush. I sigh, melting into the plastic-y pillow wedged behind my head.

"I missed being your baby," I tell him.

"You never stopped being my baby. Or my boy." He kisses the back of my hand, rubbing his mouth back and forth over my hand free from an IV. His beard is the same length it was the last time I saw him, only less neat like he hasn't bothered to trim it.

In all actuality, Daddy looks run ragged. "Are you okay?" I ask timidly, unsure if I have the right to ask. We haven't talked about anything other than me and my injuries.

"Yeah, boy. I am now." *Ugh, I don't think my heart can take this.*

"Sleep with me?" I ask, puffing out my bottom lip and lowering my eyes so I have no choice but to peer at him through my lashes. Daddy knows exactly what I'm doing, though. He laughs, throwing his head back, causing his hair to flutter across his shoulder. I beam with elation at the sound.

"You're a little minx, even lying in a hospital bed." My smile never falters. It feels good, even while the rest still hurts.

After a few moments, Daddy stops chuckling and gets

serious. He even does that thing where he pinches his brows, so they form a little divot between the two. Even his crow's feet deepen. "I'm not fucking you, boy."

I pout and huff even though that's not what I meant, and he knows it. "Cuddles?"

Shaking his head, he stands in front of the bed. My eyes drop, taking in every thick, clothed inch. I press my palms into the thin mattress when Daddy stops me. "Don't do that, I don't want you to tug on your IV." He tucks his arms beneath me and drags me across the bed, my ass skimming over the sheet in a light graze. He even pulls up the extra guard rail along the bottom of the bed.

I stare at it. "You know that's ridiculous right?"

"Ridiculous or not, it's staying." Then, he shucks his shirt and drapes it over the back of his chair, and I lose all thought. "Tell me the second it hurts if I do something wrong." His face is so stern and serious, I can't fight back a giggle.

"Yeah, Daddy. Okay."

That seems to appease him because he gingerly climbs on, keeping his bare back pressed against the plastic rail. It's gotta be cold and uncomfortable, but he doesn't complain—because *of course,* he doesn't.

"Come here, boy." Daddy wraps his arms around me and gently tugs me against his chest. The second I land against his soft, squishy skin, every trace of the outside world falls away. The heart monitor, the near-silent drip of my IV, the crackle of a TV from across the hall.

Daddy's the center of my world again, holding me against him and taking care of me—exactly how it always should be.

Thirty-Three

ZEVRYN

"I don't need—" Daddy swings me into his arms, effectively cutting off my protest—not that I'm complaining.

The hospital discharged me a couple of hours ago after my night of observation. All that's wrong with me is a lot of external bruising and a split lip, believe it or not, which Daddy certainly didn't after he proceeded to question the very doctors he sent me to. It was unbelievably hot, watching him fire off rounds of questions with his lips pinched in a tight line, fingers clamped around mine.

Apparently, Micah's goons didn't kick me as hard as it felt like they did, which I'm grateful for now that I've sobered from the despondency I was drowning in.

Those few days without Gavin feel like a fever dream now, dark and nearly untouchable, like it was only ever in my head.

Daddy's footsteps echo in the lobby as he takes us toward

the elevators, ignoring the clerk's welcome. "You don't have to be rude," I whisper.

"I'm not. Zion is literally two steps behind us, and it's grating on my nerves." At the mention of my father, I jerk my head back, peering around my Daddy's thick bicep. Zion's standing a few feet away, hands clasped in front of him, his gray suit crisp and pristine, and his dark hair is nearly perfectly styled.

I wince the moment our eyes connect and burrow back into Gavin's chest. "What's he doing?" I murmur. He somehow still hears me.

"He's been at the hospital all night, baby. Even when you refused to see him, he wouldn't leave."

"Why?" I groan. "Why won't he just go away?" I mumble mostly to myself.

Gavin chuckles as he steps onto the lift. "I asked him the same. He said he wanted to speak to you." Before I can respond, Zion is stepping on and typing in the code, all three of us staring at the doors as they glide shut.

The wait to my penthouse is tense, like electricity snapping between live wires.

It doesn't occur to me until right then that I'm being carried in Gavin's arms, right in front of my father, and he hasn't said a word.

The Zion I know would be all over reprimanding me for my disrespect or some shit like that.

"Zev!" both Carmen and Dillon shout the second the doors open. Gavin steps into the foyer, giving my two best friends his back as they try to hound me.

"Give him some damn space, for fucks sake."

"Daddy, you're swearing an awful lot," I giggle, wrinkling my nose up at him.

He rolls his eyes as he trudges across the open floor to set me on the couch. "You make me crazy, baby." My stomach flips, warmth pooling and spreading through my extremities.

Once I'm settled and tucked in with a blanket, he plops down next to me and wraps his thick arm around my shoulder to pull me into him. With my face practically in his armpit, inhale deeply, relishing in his musk.

After a few minutes, I realize how silent it is. I peek around Daddy's arm, finding four sets of eyes drilling into me. Carmen, Dillon, Dillon's fucking dad, and Zion.

What the hell is this—a party?

"Why are you all staring at me? The doctors said I'm fine," I huff. The amount of attention makes me feel like this is another fucking intervention or something. *News flash, guys, I'm unquestionably sober.*

Carmen clears her throat, a light, meek sound as Dillon coughs, shaking his head as he stares at me. "Daddy?..."

I refuse to meet Zion's gaze—and Hugh's.

Oh...

Oh.

"Uh..." A rush of heat blooms across my face and down my neck, making my skin crawl. It's not that I'm ashamed of Gavin or our... whatever we have, but I'm not exactly chomping at the bit to reveal intimacies in front of my father.

"It's none of your business what Zevryn calls me. Don't pressure him on it. He'll talk about it with you *privately* later on if that's something he chooses to do." Gavin squeezes me, rubbing his palm over my bare arm. The rough glide eases my trepidation.

"Uh, yeah. Sure," Dillon mumbles. When our eyes meet, his face flames—probably close to matching my own. I shoot him a toothy grin, which he returns a moment later.

"Are you hungry, Zev?" Carmen asks.

"Yeah, actually. But nothing too heavy?"

She smiles. "I gotcha. Dill, come help me." She grabs his arm and tugs him into the kitchen with her. Gavin swipes up the remote and clicks the large, flatscreen TV on. I stare at it for a moment.

"Is this new?" I ask. Gavin's lips purse.

"Yes. I replaced your old one after you left, since it was broken," Zion answers my question. I roll my eyes, unable to help it.

"I didn't ask you to do that," I say, hating that I sound slightly bitter about it.

"I know, but I wanted to." He takes a step forward, coming into my line of sight. Gavin's just flipping through channels, the movement almost absentminded.

"Why?"

The question goes unanswered. I don't even bother looking at my father as my eyes drill into the screen, not really seeing anything on it. Gavin sets the remote down and leans in to press his lips to my forehead. I careen into the touch, increasing the light pressure. I feel his smile as it shifts, making my own pop up.

"I'm going to get you some medicine and water to go with your food, okay? I'll be right in the kitchen if you need me." He pulls back. His eyes flicker between mine, soft and warm and everything I need. But as he pulls away, I tighten my grip on his thick forearm.

"You're not leaving, right?" I hate the panic laced in my tone, but I need to know.

His eyes smile. "No, my boy. I'm here as long as you'll have me. You and I will talk later." The promise of later is enough for me to release my hold.

"Okay. But you have to kiss me first."

His eyes close with a chuckle. "Whatever you want, *brat.*" His lips are cool, but his mouth is an inferno as he slips his tongue between our lips for a quick swipe into my mouth. I gasp as he pulls away, leaving me cold and wanting.

"Talk to him. For *you.* Not for him." I swallow at the reminder from rehab. Something I've tried not to forget, but it's so hard now that I've been thrown back into the throes of real life.

This is the time to figure out what's best for you. The words of wisdom from a stranger in group.

I never did get their name because they never returned to group after that. It makes me regret not paying attention before then, but I'll always be grateful for their selfless wisdom.

It helped saved me from more years of unnecessary torment when I'd already been on that train for too fucking long.

"Zion," I finally acknowledge him. I hear his exhale—controlled but loud.

"Zevryn."

"What are you doing here?" I finally look at him, noticing Hugh ventured into the kitchen as well, leaving us alone.

"Can I sit?" He gestures to the couch. I shrug, which he takes as an invitation—because of course, he does.

"I'm here because I feel guilty—"

I bark out a laugh, cutting him off. "Oh, that's nice."

"You didn't let me finish," he grates. I huff out a breath.

"Whatever. Continue, I guess." I feel Gavin's eyes on me from all the way across the room.

"I feel guilty about the way things happened between us."

"Which time?" I mean, is he fucking kidding me?

"All of them. I know I haven't been a good father to you, Zevryn. I regret a lot, but I realize I fucked up."

I rear back at his use of a swear word. Something he almost never lets slip through his masked exterior. "What made you realize that?"

"You leaving."

"You mean when you sent me away. Forced me to go to some fucking remote island rehab center where you wouldn't have to deal with me and send a bodyguard with to keep an eye on me."

His dark eyebrows tug together as he rubs his index finger over his top lip. I never noticed the shadow of stubble smattered across his face. Something I haven't seen on my father since my mother's funeral.

"Hiring Gavin was for a legitimate reason. Micah Richardson—" the sound of his name makes me wince with flashbacks of feet and fists and his cold, forgiving face, "really did speak on a threat. I was worried about you because I know the power men like me hold."

"Yeah," I huff in agreement. Gavin's eyes narrow at me, and I shake my head, giving him a small flip of a smile, hoping I'm reassuring him and not sending a smoke signal. My whole face feels contorted.

"And after you were away, the... drama, for lack of better

word, settled. Micah seemed to have grieved—as much as he could—and I truly didn't think I had anything to worry about by the time you got home. But I was wrong." His eyes land on my face, not nearly as swollen as it was, but I know that fucker's fist will leave a bruise for a while.

"I don't want to talk about that. It has nothing to do with you, and it's over with."

"How can you be sure of that?" he asks, sounding like he genuinely cares, but I won't fall for that.

"Because I know."

"All right," Zion concedes. "As for the rehab... Dillon and Carmen came to me with their concerns before everything happened with Darien. It's why I confronted you at the launch party. I will admit I did not handle that the way I should have, and I take full responsibility for the impact of my threats and the pain they caused you."

"You're not responsible for my actions, Zion." I don't know why I'm telling him this, if for no other reason than me taking responsibility for myself.

"You may be right, but I still played a hand in it all. By being a shitty father. Not just then, but always. I've made mistakes, Zevryn. More than I can ever atone for, but I do want you to know I regret every single one that caused you harm."

I rear back, eyes wide, jaw hanging slack. *Is this even happening right now?* "Did some alien come and abduct the real Zion Carver and replace him with—" I wave my hand up and down in his general vicinity, "this thing."

My father, ever the cold, manipulative bastard, laughs. He fucking *laughs.*

I'm going to lose my mind. There's no way this is real.

"I guess I deserve your apprehension. I suppose all I'm asking for is the chance to try and make it right with you." He grips his knees with both hands, palms sliding back and forth over the expensive material.

I scratch my upper lip. Shit. I never expected this. I've been telling myself since rehab that I'd never made amends with Zion because he wasn't worth it—that it was better for my recovery and my sanity to cut him out.

And now here he is, asking for a chance to be... *my dad.*

Yeah... definitely an alien.

"Can I think about it?"

He nods resolutely. "Of course."

"Uh, cool." My fingers twist in the blanket wrapped around my legs. Zion lifts his head, glancing around the room before meeting my unsure gaze.

"Gavin?"

I immediately stiffen. "What about him." It's not a question.

"Are you together?" He's being blunt, which I appreciate.

"Think so." I want to say yes, to scream it without a doubt, but we haven't talked since he saved me... again, and I don't want to jump the gun on the possibility of him—or us.

"He's a great deal older than you."

"And?"

"Just be careful, son." He pats my leg twice, the touch sturdy yet cautious, before he pushes off the couch and walks into the kitchen. He and Hugh share a few words before they both head toward the elevator. Gavin leaves his place at the counter. He places a hand on Zion's shoulder, halting him.

Zion turns around, listening to whatever Gavin says

before he nods and then leaves. My mind whirls with confusion. *What the hell is going on?*

Now that my father has left, Carmen and Dillon venture back into the living room. Carmen sets a plate of toast, scrambled eggs, and fruit in front of me. Dillon's carrying two more, and in comes Gavin with a plate of his own and two bottles of water clutched in his left arm.

My first bite is hesitant. I haven't eaten in hours, but the rumbling growl of hunger has been present for almost just as long, to the point I only feel nauseous. With the first swallow, I feel immediate relief and dive in for more, practically scarfing it down.

"Slow down, boy. Your stomach is still uneasy."

"Just hungry."

"I know. Here—take these." He holds my plate so I can wash down a few tablets. "Good boy," he praises after I've swallowed. My face heats, eyes darting toward Carmen and Dillon, who are sitting on the other end of the large, sectional sofa, seemingly engrossed in the silent movie playing, but I know better.

Gavin pinches my chin the way he always does. "Don't look at them. Look at me. Better," he says once our gazes are locked. I see so much in his eyes, it's unbearable. Love, devotion. Respect and adoration.

Or maybe it's my own feelings mirrored back.

"We'll talk later, remember?" he reminds me gently, probably sensing my anxiety.

"I know."

"Good. Eat some food. We're just gonna relax for a little while. But don't forget," he lowers his voice, ensuring he has every modicum of my attention, "you will tell me everything." I nod, words stuck in my throat. Convincing my Daddy to leave what happened to me alone will be a challenge like no other, but I'm up for the task, and I'm not above using sexual favors to my advantage.

I mean, he doesn't call me a brat for no reason.

I lose track of how many movies we watch. Sleep dips in and out, voices nothing but hushed murmurs.

I vaguely recall the shift of movement and the sensation of being weightless as Daddy carries me. "*Mmm,*" I groan, smelling and feeling him all around me.

"Shh, go back to sleep, baby."

"Don't wanna," I whine, clutching tighter as Daddy lowers me onto the bed. My head lulls to the side, leaving a string of drool connected between us. Daddy swipes it up with his finger and wipes some off my jaw with a caress so tender, it makes my sleepy eyes burn.

"Do you have to pee?" he asks tenderly. I smile and shake my head.

"I'm not leaving you, boy. You can sleep, and when you wake up, I will be here."

"Promise?"

His kiss is reverent, a gentle brush I feel as deep as a wave crashing over the shore on a dark, summer's night. Drowning, all-consuming, and scarily beautiful, even basked in the shadows of darkness.

That's who my Daddy is to me.

He clutches my pinky, wrapping his around mine. "Pinky promise."

I giggle sleepily as he rubs our foreheads together, our hair tangling in our embrace. Daddy slips into bed, still clothed from the waist down, but when he pulls me on top of him—the only place in the world I wanna be—it doesn't matter that every inch of our skin isn't bare.

With a gentle tug, he guides my head toward his chest. My mouth is already open, the same way his nipple is already peaked in anticipation. I sleepily drag my tongue over the hardened flesh, groaning loudly at the scratch of the surrounding hair on my tongue.

I lap and lick, soaking his skin, tasting every inch, caught in a daze. When Daddy's hand tightens in my hair, forcing my head back, I whine, trying to get closer again.

"Quit being a tease and go to sleep, boy." His voice is husky with arousal. It makes my own groin pool with heat.

"Please," I cry. "*Please, Daddy.*"

"God, I never could fucking resist you." With a gentleness I'm surprised he's capable of this deep in his lust, Daddy presses my mouth back to his nipple. I'm careful of my split lip as I suck the peak into my mouth, eyes falling shut as my head drops, supported by his arm.

"Just suck and sleep, my boy."

And just like with every command from my Daddy, I obey with eagerness because I know, even if I mess up, he'll be right there to pick me back up again and help me make it better.

Thirty-Four

GAVIN

The curtains are pulled tight, only a few minuscule beams of light sneaking in through the gaps.

My boy's wrapped around me, every limb cinched tight, even in the depths of sleep. It soothes some of my tension of what today is for us. Like maybe yesterday wasn't a mistake. That maybe, after everything I've done, he'll still want me.

I brush my fingers through his hair, holding tight onto his slim nape. *He holds me like he does.* That has to mean something.

I'm unsure of what time it is, but it's bright enough for the black curtains to glow with the rays of the sun. My bladder is full, but I'm not risking waking him. Not when his body has been through trauma and needs to start healing.

I still hate that he didn't accept any pain meds. I know that when the body is in pain, healing can take much longer without any reprieve, but I also hold a deep respect for my boy for saying no.

Not many could've done that—especially someone with a past like his. It only proves the depth of his strength. I only wish he could see that.

My eyelids droop with contentment as I hold my boy in my arms, feeling nothing but peace and serenity at my core. It wavers outward, similar to the rays of the sun peeking through the gaps.

There's still so much to be said between us—first and foremost what happened to him. I've got to give the boy credit, though. Despite all the attention on him and what happened, he kept his pretty, thick lips sealed up tight.

He gave the doctors every bit of information they needed to treat him, but as far as *what* happened...

With a swallow, my fingers flex against his bicep, kneading into the flesh for the reminder that he's warm. Breathing. Alive.

He's okay.

But I'll be damned if he ever gets this close to being hurt ever again—not if I can help it.

"Hey," he croaks out in a sleepy voice. My heart cinches as tight as his grip on me at the low, kid-like tone.

"Hi, my boy." I let the thoughts of him being worse than just bruised settle into the back of my mind as I focus on him, here and now. His head is nestled into the crook of my arm, dark curls fanned outward. The entire front of his face is pressed into my armpit. His warm breath tickles with every exhale, but it's a sensation that only brings me satisfaction.

"You're still here," he whispers against me. I tighten my grip on his nape, drawing him out of hiding. He blinks warily up at me, hazel eyes so soft and cloudy with sleep.

The scratches coupled with the tender bruise marred on his cheekbone chokes me, and I nearly splutter on my next attempt to breathe.

"Of course, I'm here." I will him to believe me, but I know it is something I'll have to prove to him every day—and I'll do so gratefully if he gives me the chance. He ducks his head, seeking comfort in my body.

"I wasn't sure after..." Hearing his insecurities laid bare shifts my last slivers of doubt into perspective for me.

"Milo," I finish the thought for him. He nods but doesn't look up. But that's okay. I don't need him to see me for this, as badly as I crave his eyes on me. I brush my hand back and forth over the exposed skin of his pale arm. I trace the pattern of a few scattered freckles.

"We're getting a divorce, baby. Or, I guess we did. Signed the papers yesterday. We just have to wait for them to go through." His head jerks up, nearly nailing my nose. I jerk back with a chuckle, heart hammering in my throat. Zevryn stares at me, wide-eyed and confused.

"That was... but it's only been..."

"Yeah, just a few days."

"Feels longer," he whispers. The tip of his index finger traces around my nipple over and over in a tantalizing pattern that has the bud peaking almost instantly and my dick hardening in my boxers, despite the pure innocence of it.

"How?" It's a whisper nearly lost in the gentle stillness, a raspy whisper blown almost as if he didn't want to utter it.

"I already had the papers drawn up, baby. I left most of our stuff to him and the rest was an even split down the middle, which Milo agreed to easily. All we had to do was sign—which we did the other day, right before everything happened." I need him to look at me, to give me those hypnotizing, hazel eyes, so impossibly full of the kind of love and devotion I never imagined I'd be lucky enough to experience. The kind of love only read about or seen in movies.

His body is still stiff, no longer lax with the lingering traces of sleep. I'm not sure if it's because he's in pain or due to the conversation. "Are you in pain, boy?" I change my tone so he knows I need an answer.

"Nah. I mean, it hurts, but it's bearable." He buries his nose into my armpit.

"Are you sure?" I knead the tendons in his neck, smirking as I watch his body physically melt into the mattress—and into me. He nods, sending his nose running through the hairs in my pit. Most people would find it disgusting, to breathe in someone in such an intimate spot, but fuck, is it arousing. Seeing the proof of how deeply he needs to be buried in every part of me.

My dick stirs to the point of pain the longer he rubs his nose against me, a gentle, nearly soothing back and forth motion. Like waves lapping against a buoy. "Boy," I rasp. My voice cracks, giving me away. "As much as I love what you're doing, you're going to have to stop. I only have so much self-control where you're concerned, and we need to talk."

A hot, wet stripe swipes across my skin, lighting me on fire. I inhale sharply, every muscle tensing. My fingers tighten around my boy's arm in warning. He pulls back only enough to meet my eyes. "But, Daddy, I don't wanna stop." Keeping his gaze locked on my half-lidded one, he teases his tongue through the hair. My eyes glaze over, and his face blurs.

I throw my head back against the pillows as my boy has his wicked way with me. I drop my hand to the bed and curl my fingers into the sheet, needing something of purchase before I lose my mind. "Baby, I can't. You're hurt," I groan.

"My dick isn't hurt. Neither is my hole, and it's *throbbing* for you, Daddy." I shoot up with a growl. Zevryn flops back against the bed with a breathless giggle. I roll on top of him, shoving my way between his spread legs.

My heart is throbbing in my chest. "Watch your mouth, brat." Zevryn's eyebrows furrow before his lips kick up in a grin.

"So, I can't say dick now?" I lean down, careful not to bring our abdomens together. Our mouths hover millimeters apart, our breath washing over each other's faces.

"No." I'm being an ass, but I don't care.

"What do you want me to say, then? Penis?" he asks, appalled. I can't hold back my scoff, but I nod, feigning seriousness.

"Yeah."

"Oh, whatever." He slaps my bare chest. His laugh is a breath in my lungs. "I'm so not telling you *my penis isn't hurt.* That just sounds fu—juvenile."

My brow arcs at his near slip. He grins at me. "I don't know... you *are* my boy. Perhaps it fits." I brush our noses together. He lifts his chin, nuzzling into it.

"It's not sexy."

"It is," I counter. "Everything about you is. Especially when you're being all small and cute."

His eyes widen, mouth falling open. *There's that innocence.* "Yeah?" he asks, hope in his words.

"Yeah, my boy." Our mouths finally brush together in the barest hint of touch. Zev gasps, arching into me, and who am I to deny him? I drop down, only until our fronts are just grazing. My arms shake with the effort of keeping myself up, but as I lose myself in my boy's mouth, it all fades.

Our tongues lap against one another's, a slow massage of taste and discovery. I explore every inch of my boy like it's the first time—and in a way, it is. The first time we can be us, wholly and completely.

"Please, Daddy." My eyes roll back at his breathless plea. Such a perfect, little boy.

"What do you need, baby?" I draw back to trace his lips, reveling in the scratch of his stubble as I dip down his neck. I ignore the bruise like my life depends on it because I refuse to ruin this for him, not when it's more than I ever could've hoped for after what I did.

"Need *you,* Daddy." His hips thrust against mine, grinding against my pelvis with fervor. With a gentle hand, I guide him back down against the bed and pin him.

"Where do you need me?" My teeth catch on his nipple ring, and I tug, drawing out a strangled moan.

"Everywhere," he cries, back arching as he follows my mouth.

"I won't hurt you, boy. So, this will have to be gentle." He whines but nods, water leaking from the corners of his eyes. I swipe my tongue through his belly button, following the dark trail of hair leading to his pretty cock, straining beneath the silky fabric of his small briefs.

They're cute little things, hugging just beneath his ass

cheeks and wrapping around the tops of his thighs. The desire to avert my gaze from his bruises is strong, but I will myself to look. To see the outcome of my choices. No matter how good my intentions were, the result was the same.

I'd left my boy when he needed me most.

I'll never be able to forgive myself.

"Hey, hey. Come back to me, baby." Zevryn's hands are clawing the sides of my face, fingers tangling in my hair and yanking hard enough to make me hiss. I shake my head, blinking at him dazedly.

"I'm okay, Daddy. Really."

"There's just—" He nods before I can continue.

"I know. Just give me this first, *please,*" he whines. More tears fall from his eyes, and I don't think I've ever seen him look more beautiful. His cheeks are flushed from pleasure, eyes glassy and half-lidded. Lips slick with spit and parted to allow his panting breaths. "Please give me this. I missed you so much, and I'm scared this is the last time, and I just want it so bad—" I slam my mouth down on his, stopping his ramble before I hear anymore.

I don't want to hear about last times. Never fucking again.

I try to be careful of the split in his lip, but with the way my boy is fucking devouring my mouth like it's his last meal, I don't have much choice but to swallow him whole, willingly drowning together because there is no other option.

We'll sink together before we ever ascend apart from one another.

And that's when it hits me—this is the always kind of forever. When I know, without a shadow of a doubt, death would be better than living without him. That anything other than *this* is impossible—practically unfathomable.

I shove my hand beneath the sleek, black waistband of my boy's briefs and fist his cock. He's hard, and his cockhead is slick as I drag my thumb over his slit. "You're already wet for me, boy." He nods frantically, unable to form any words, which is just fine by me.

I drag my hand down his length, curling my fingers around his slim girth and squeezing at the base. He mewls, and his hips jerk, still carefully pinned by my left hand. I work him over slowly, relishing in the slow torture I'm putting him through.

The noises ripping from his throat singe my nerves, and I'm pretty sure I'm seconds away from coming in my pants. I pull back, chest heaving as I stare down at my boy, sprawled so wantonly, flushed and glistening with the thinnest sheen of sweat.

I shove my hand in my boxers to grab my balls, bypassing my cock completely, and squeeze until I grunt and nearly double over. My boy's eyes blink open. "What are you doing?" he asks timidly.

"Trying not to come, but it's fucking hard when you're so goddamn sexy." I grit my teeth, hissing as my fingers tighten further. My balls throb, and my eyes roll back.

"Oh," he squeaks. *So fucking cute.*

"Yeah, boy. This is what you do to me." I roll my balls around, panting through the throb. My cock has deflated some, but I know the second I get my mouth on my boy, it'll be like I never tried to stave off my orgasm.

"I like that," he whispers cheekily. I smirk.

"Yeah, I'm sure you do, *brat.*" I rip my hand out to yank down his underwear. I'm careful as I pull them off.

"I'm not fragile," he huffs at my caution.

"That's where you're wrong, baby," I say as I dip down to lick a long stripe up the length of his cock, smirking as it jerks. "You're the most fragile thing in my world. And I'll protect you any way I see fit. Even if that means not fucking that tight little ass until I no longer see a single bruise." I spread my lips around his cockhead and slide my mouth down in one fell swoop until he's nudging the back of my throat. My stomach convulses on a gag, but it only makes my head swim deliciously.

"Oh, gods," he moans as he curls his legs around my head. The rough scratch of his leg hair against the sides of my face is heavenly. I bob on his length, slurping and sucking every long inch. I'm just grateful he's not any girthier because my jaw would be aching tenfold right now.

I pop off to catch my breath, dragging my mouth down to his balls and sucking one into my mouth. I roll it around, curling my tongue around the curve before slipping to the other one. Spit drips down my beard and onto the bed.

My boy grinds against my face, shameless and so *hot.* My tongue follows the tight line in the center of his sac, all the way down to his taint. I slurp and spit against his skin, getting him as wet as I can as I work my way between his cheeks.

I don't want to push his thighs up and risk adding pressure to his abdomen, so I push his thighs apart and dig the tips of my fingers into his cheeks, spreading him as wide as I can. The dark shadows of his center are revealed to me. His asshole is light pink and furled and so pretty. I drag the pad of my thumb over him, smirking as it tightens at my touch.

"Fuck, I missed this hole." My nose drags over his taint as I push between his thighs. The angle is difficult, and I know my neck will be throbbing later, but none of that is enough to deter me from eating my little boy's ass.

He's mumbling and groaning incoherently, shaking the bed as he twitches.

"Baby. *Baby,*" I try again when he doesn't answer.

"*Hmm,*" he moans.

"Grab your cock and jerk off. Make it feel even better. My hands are gonna be busy keeping you spread for me." Zevryn fists his dick and starts jacking slowly. "Good boy." I lower my head back between his legs, spread him wide again, and bury my face into him, nuzzling back and forth to get as deep as I can.

"Oh, fuck!" Zevryn screams, his upper-half launching off the bed. The urge to reprimand him sits on the tip of my tongue, but I'm a little preoccupied, so I take it out on his ass. I flex my tongue and probe his hole, grinding my hips into the bed at the texture of his wrinkled pucker against my tongue.

His hand delves into my hair, yanking painfully on the strands. I grunt, then groan when he shoves my face even deeper. *Fuck yeah, that's my dirty boy.*

I ravish every inch of him, slurping and growling. I switch between fucking him with my tongue and sucking his furl with fervor. The sounds coming out of my mouth echo, bouncing off the high ceilings, but it's my boy's wonderfully loud mouth that fills the air.

He's mindless, switching between screams and moans.

Each decibel he reaches shoots straight to my cock. His hand speeds up, the raunchy *shlick* of spit and precum tunneling into my ears, even over the sounds he's making.

I pull back from his ass just long enough to watch his hole wink at me, not quite stretched but loose enough to feel my missing tongue. He wriggles against the bed, ass dragging through the obscene wet spot just below. I catch the edges of his cheeks, hating and loving the red blemishes from my fingertips with equal measure.

"You ready to come on my tongue, boy?" I growl the words into his chafed skin. The scratch of my beard has to burn by now, but it only seems to make him hotter.

"*Nngh,*" he moans. I chuckle and lick a stripe across his asshole. His legs jerk and try to close around my head. I tease the slick rim with my thumb, circling his pucker a few times before pushing inside. His muscle is relaxed, making it easy to slip inside. His walls are hot as they clamp down, locking me in.

"Fuck," I grunt as my boy halts any movement. His walls quiver around me, and I watch with reverence as his balls, so tight and drawn up close to his body, pulse with his release. Shoving my thumb as deep as it will go with him clamping down on me, I lurch upward, catching the head of his cock between my lips just after his cum starts spurting.

Some of it flies across my face and into my beard before I latch on and swallow the rest down in greedy pulls. His cum is hot and bitter and so fucking good. I keep up on the suction, even after he's all drained. He whimpers and tries to pull away. With a resounding groan, I give his cockhead one last gentle suck and pop off.

Zevryn's legs fall flat onto the king-sized mattress, feet

angled inward, pressed against my calves, while his knees are pointed out. I sit back on my haunches between his spread legs to stare down at my thumb still inside him.

I push it in a little more just to draw another moan out of him before I gently pull out. I flop down beside my boy and tug him into my arms. His head rolls onto my chest, mouth already seeking my nipple. I grunt at his gentle suction as it shoots straight to my balls, but I'm more than content to let my boy float where all is blissful and rapturous for as long as he can.

Hopefully forever.

Thirty-Five

GAVIN

"How're you feelin', boy?" I ask once Zevryn rouses some time later. He groans and stretches out, wincing as the injured skin of his torso is pulled taut. I try not to look at the deep, purple bruises, but I can't exactly look away either.

When he catches me staring, he flushes and tries to cover himself with the comforter, but I tug it away. "Don't hide from me," I tell him.

"I don't want to," he repeats the same words that seem from another lifetime. I swallow my shame with bitter resistance. I brush my thumb along his cheek.

"How are you feeling?" I repeat the question, needing an answer.

"Good. Really," he adds like he knows I need the reassurance. When I hike a brow, not fully believing him, he says, "Coming actually helped. Released a lot of tension." I huff.

"Yeah, I'm sure it did." He smirks, scrunching his nose in that way he always does. It makes my heart flip.

"I was thinking." I take a breath, suddenly needing to steel myself in case this goes in a different direction than I'm hoping it will. My boy stares up at me like I have all the answers, and it's fucking terrifying. *Doesn't he know he has all the power here? I'm at his mercy—now and always.*

"Let's curl up on the couch and put on a movie? I want to get some food in you, too. And... we need to talk." The air stills, crackling with the tension of unanswered questions.

"Yeah, okay. But I think you'll have to carry me. My legs are still jelly." Zevryn glances down, making me follow. "I have to pee, Daddy..." he adds after a moment. My breath catches.

I find his eyes. "You want help?" He nods, face blooming such a pretty shade of pink, an elegant caress down his jaw. My head nearly rolls back in relief. I kiss his forehead, already clambering off the bed to haul him into my arms. "Thank you, baby." I bring our mouths together in breathless devotion.

"Feels good when you take care of me. When you..."

"Help you pee?" I help him out as I take us into the bathroom across the room. The opulence of my boy's penthouse isn't lost on me. The shower is huge, big enough to fit probably ten or more people. The tub, pretty much the same.

I ease his feet to the floor directly in front of the toilet. "Yeah." He nods shakily, but the moment I wrap my index finger and thumb around the edge of his flared head, his body drains of any tension, and he slumps back against me, releasing his bladder with ease.

I'm rapt as I watch his pale yellow stream hit the water in the bowl. The sound echoes around us, filling me with pride. He's come such a long way—I couldn't be more pleased. I flatten my palm against his lower abdomen, keeping my touch feather-light.

When his slit drips with the last few drops of his urine, I shake him then pat his flaccid length a few times. "Such a good boy." I nuzzle into the side of his neck, dragging my nose over his skin.

"Thank you, Daddy." He sighs, pressing his head against mine.

"No, thank you, boy. Do you want to get cleaned up?"

He shakes his head. "No."

"All right, baby." I help him to the sink to wash his hands and face, then repeat the same for me, needing to wash his cum out of my beard. After drying my face, I take Zev's toothbrush and gently scrub his teeth before treating my own, then I'm back to carrying my boy.

Once we're in the living area, I get him situated onto the couch before throwing something quick together—which just so happens to be a peanut butter and jelly sandwich and a banana. Quick and easy, but it gets the job done.

I take that and a glass of water to my boy, along with a few tablets of ibuprofen. He purses his lips at the medicine, but when he catches my stare, he swallows them down without protest.

He picks up his sandwich and eyes it for a minute. "What if I don't want the crust?"

"You want me to cut it off for you, baby?" I ask softly. His eyes twinkle, shining with that sliver of brat that's always present, even when he's being such a good boy.

"Yeah."

"Too fuckin' bad. Eat it." I lean back, stretching my arms across the back of the sofa. Zevryn's mouth hangs open for a moment before he snaps it closed with a small giggle. He takes a bite, moaning provocatively, just to push back.

I flip through channels while he eats, not feeling hungry myself with the nerves swarming around my gut like moths chewing through cloth. I finally settle on some racing movie filled with loud noises and fast cars.

After a while, Zevryn finishes all of his food—only after making me feed him his banana, which was certainly a test of my control with the way he wrapped those goddamn lips of his around the fucking fruit.

I force myself to sit up, hands clasped and hanging between my spread legs. My hair is hanging down as well, a curtain between my face and my boy's seeking gaze. "We need to talk."

"Ominous words."

I snort. "I hope not."

"What do we need to talk about, Daddy?" I let my eyes fall closed, hearing that name fall from his lips with breathless ease. *Nothing* has ever felt as right as this—what we share together. It may be unconventional, outside the realm of what most deem is normal, but nothing about Zevryn is *wrong.* It's all fucking right.

"Everything, baby. What happened. Why I left. The *way* I did it."

I feel him shift on the sofa. "I don't want to talk about that stuff." I force myself to look at him. He deserves my undivided attention.

"I know, but we need to. And you're the one that said you

need honesty. I want to give that to you." He takes some time to think over what I said, eventually nodding his agreement.

"Okay."

"Okay," I repeat, freezing for a moment. Where the hell do I even begin?

"Tell me about the divorce. You said you already had the papers drawn up, but I don't understand."

"Yeah, I can do that. So, not long after we got to the island, Milo called me. It was when we were at the beach. You were in the water, swimming and splashing. Looking so fucking breathtaking—even after you ran from me..." I smile at the memory, then shake my head. I need to stay on track.

"Anyway, Milo called, and it wasn't a good conversation. We didn't argue, but I think we could both feel the loss between us. And honestly, I was jumping the gun when I called the lawyer a couple of weeks later, but I couldn't stand the thought of being with you while I was connected to someone in that way.

"As much as it killed me to betray him and our vows, you were always at the forefront of my mind. I couldn't do that to you—make you think you were *ever* a second choice. But I also couldn't disrespect Milo. I don't know if that even makes sense, but he's been my best friend for a decade."

Zevryn's face is taut, and my anxiety grows, but I force myself to continue. "We've known each other since we weren't much older than you. He's always been there through everything. And we built a life together. But it wasn't a life that was sustainable for either of us. And I'm not going to go into detail because it's not really necessary—unless you really want to know?" I search out his gaze, relieved when he shakes his head.

"But our split has been amicable—and mutual. Milo's a good person, and I'll always care about him, but we both knew we didn't have that forever kind of love—at least, not in the way it matters most." I reach out for my boy's hand, needing to feel his touch. He slides his palm against mine and interlocks our fingers. The weight of his touch eases the one in my chest.

He's so quiet, it scares me. I'm not used to him being this reserved since he let some of his barriers down with me, but I respect that he might need some space. It is a lot to process.

"Do you think we could have a forever kind of love?" he asks so softly, I nearly miss it.

"Oh, baby." I haul him against my chest, tired of the separation. The moment he's curled in my lap, everything clicks into place. No more questions. No apprehension. "We are that forever love. The always kind."

"Always?" he whispers into my bare chest as he swirls his index finger through my chest hair.

"Yeah. No doubt in my mind."

A breath shudders out of him. It squeezes my heart—knowing what he's been carrying. Doubt. About me. About us.

"I get why you had to do it the way you did. I wish you would've told me, though. I thought you left me."

It kills me hearing what I did to him, but I deserve the lancing pain to my chest. "I know, boy. And that's the last thing I wanted, but I couldn't risk breaking your heart in case things didn't go so seamlessly with Milo. It all happened the way I hoped it would in the end, but I refused to have you wait around for me on the off chance it didn't. I'd much rather you move on and live your life without me. I never wanna drag you down, baby. Not when you've fought so hard to claw your way out of the trenches."

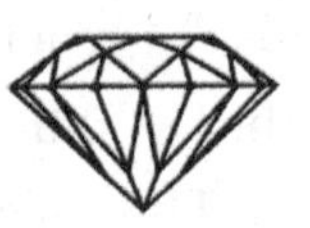

Zevryn

DOESN'T HE SEE? He is *my strength. The only reason I was able to drag myself out to begin with.* I tell him as much, too.

"No, that's where you're wrong. I was there. I watched you fight the endless torture and agony that your body put you through for days—and you fucking pushed right through. Sure, I was there to help you drink water and bathe, but, baby, you're the one who did it.

"You fought to survive—not only physically but mentally and emotionally every day since. I see it, even now, the fight churning within you. The endless battle of your addiction. Because I know it'll never fully go away—the urges and tendencies. You know it, too. But you resist every day. All day. *That's* the fucking strength in you, my boy.

"You are so incredible, and you have no idea how deeply I admire you. Watching you become this lively, bright, wholesome person who emerged from some dark, abysmal place has been the greatest pleasure that I will cherish forever—even if this doesn't work between us."

My mind is reeling with Daddy's confessions, and I don't

even know where to begin, but his last few words are what snags something in my brain, sending everything reeling to a halt. "What do you mean if this doesn't work?" Gods, I hate how small and insecure my voice sounds, but I can't hold it back, either.

Daddy's thumb drags back and forth over my knuckles. "I'm not going to assume that you want this—or me—after we get through what needs to be said."

"Why would you say that?" *Why wouldn't I want you?*

"Baby," he sighs, like I'm just not getting it. "I hurt you. I left you, and you got *hurt*."

"Yeah, and? You're here now." I don't understand. Does he not want me anymore? Is this all just to relieve his conscience?

My breathing picks up as panic swarms.

"I am. And I'll be here as long as you want me, but I don't want to pressure you into any decisions that you might not feel ready for. You're pretty vulnerable right now, and I don't want to take advantage, Zevryn."

"I'm not some weak little thing that can't make decisions for himself, Gavin." Saying his first name feels odd on my tongue, but damnit, I'm pissed. "Yeah, I got the shit kicked out of me, but I'm pretty sure Micah would've managed it, even if you were by my side or not." When he opens his mouth—probably to ask about that very situation—I hold my hand up to stop him, which he at least respects.

"And no, I'm not going to talk about it. There's nothing to say. And no, you will not do anything to Micah Richardson. Is that clear?" Fuck, trying to sound stern with my Daddy is a head trip, but I need him to know how serious I am.

His dark brows are tunneled together, and his slight frown lines deepen considerably. "Zevryn... that's not fair of you to ask."

"It is. Because it was *my* baggage. And it's taken care of now."

"How can you be sure?"

"Because I know. I need you to trust me on that." I search his gaze for a long moment. When he nods his acceptance, albeit stubbornly, I exhale a breath of relief. "Thank you. It wasn't your fault. It was mine, and I've accepted that. I had to. Now, I'd like to try and move on, if that's okay with you."

"Yeah, baby. If that's what you need, I'll... work on it." My smile is beaming.

"Good." Fuck, he may be right about my strength... I feel inclined to believe his truths to be my own, but I can't deny that his presence alone makes it feel so much more tangible.

"I love you, Daddy. I've loved you for a long time. I don't know if it first happened when you got me through my withdrawal. If it was when you beat my ass in the jungle or when you first held my cock to help me pee. I couldn't tell you the exact moment I realized I felt something, but it's been lingering inside me a long time, building under the touch of your worship.

"Because that's how I feel when you touch me. Worshipped. Cared for and loved in a way people only dream of. Hell, it doesn't even feel real for *me* sometimes, but when you look at me the way you do..." I glance up from our clasped hands, finding his eyes on my face, just like I knew they would be. His dark irises shimmer with the reflection of the movie in the background. His crow's feet are soft and etched with his relaxed expression, his lips kicked up in a gentle smile that makes his mustache curve up, too.

"Like that," I breathe, feeling my own smile break across my face. It's freeing, like the bounds of elation have shattered, and I'm drowning in bliss, locked in a state of consciousness that *can't* be real because nothing real feels this good.

But Daddy's hand in mine, his other clasping my neck, thumb pressing just beneath my jaw, is tangible proof it is real.

"Like what, baby?" He leans in, close enough I can taste the hint of mint still lingering in his mouth.

"Like you love me." His mouth slams into mine with a force that startles me. I gasp as our teeth clank together, tongues sliding into each other's mouths with careless desperation. My fingers tangle in Daddy's chest hair, loving the rough scratch as I dig into his soft skin.

He growls as he pulls back, just enough for our lips, slick with our combined spit, to brush with every word he shoves down my throat, like he's forcing me to accept them—knowing I need him to.

"I do love you, Zevryn. The forever kind." I chase his confession down with his tongue as I nearly swallow it; that's how deep he gets inside me. But I *love it.* Love how wholly he consumes me.

I get lost in the drag of our skin for so long, I don't realize I'm not breathing properly until Daddy forces himself away, uttering the reminder—probably for the both of us. I obey—because of course, I do—but I remain lost in the illusory clouds, floating higher than I've ever been.

But it's the safe kind of high. The high I get to experience with and because of my Daddy for the rest of my life.

"Be my boy." It's not a question because it was never refutable. At least not in my mind.

"I've always been your, boy, Daddy." It's cheeky to remind him when he's being so sweet, but I can't resist.

"You're goddamn right." He pulls back just to show me how big he's smiling. Every inch of him is alight with happiness, and I know I'm radiating the same.

We settle back on the sofa, the weight of the pasts buried deep in the depths we were once buried in.

"What now?" I ask hesitantly. The future is staring at us in the face, but I have no idea what it means. I've never thought this far ahead. Hell, I never thought I'd *be* here. Let alone experience the complexities of just living life.

"Well, let's just cuddle and finish this movie, and we'll figure out the rest as we go." I frown, not expecting such a vague answer. Daddy chuckles and draws my chin up. "Don't like that answer?" I shake my head, knowing I'm pouting, but I can't help it. "Why not?"

"I wanted you to tell me."

"Baby, I can't tell you because I don't know." He smiles tenderly like he gets it—my fear of the unknown. "But I do promise to take care of you while we navigate life together." My heart squeezes, eyes burning in relief. He knew exactly what I needed, even when I didn't.

"Yeah. That sounds good." I sniffle, nose wrinkling as I fight the burn. Daddy's finger swipes under my eye, catching a tear that he sucks into his mouth. I feign a gasp, and he laughs, the rumble working through his chest and vibrating into me.

"It better, little boy." He swats my ass, but it's just a tease of a touch. A hint of the pleasure I know he'll give me when the bruises are long gone and that blip in time forgotten.

"Daddy," I sigh, just because I can.

Thirty-Six

ZEVRYN

"So you're..."

"Together," I finish Dillon's question. He and Carmen are sitting beside me out on the terrace. The cool, summer evening air is a nice wash against my fevered skin. I'm fucking nervous.

"Wow."

"What?" My tone holds a bit of bite, and I know I sound defensive, but fuck if I can help it.

"Nothing. It's cool."

"As long as you're happy," Carmen butts in, and Dillon nods, his blonde hair falling in front of his eye.

"I am." I smile as my eyes flicker toward the glass, finding Gavin seated on the sofa, staring right back at me. His mouth curves up in encouragement. "And I really hope you guys don't have a problem with it. I know he's older than me, but he's not taking advantage of me, so don't even think that."

"We don't, Zev." I look to Dillon.

"Nah, dude. We can see how much you adore him."

"Yeah, it's actually really cute, seeing how you act around him."

"I'm not acting," I say defensively. "It's who I am. Without—without the drugs." Their lips form perfect O's at the realization. I hate the way my face heats with embarrassment.

"Oh."

"Yeah, so. If we could move past that—"

"Is that what the Daddy thing is all about?" Of course, Dillon doesn't let it go. My chest raises with a deep breath.

"Not that it's any of your business, but sort of. It's just who we are. He's my Daddy, and I'm his boy. Again, I hope that isn't a problem for you guys, but I'm not going to change what's right for me."

Carmen's hand grabs mine. Her fingers are long and cool, nails perfectly manicured and painted a pale pink. Dillon grabs my other hand, probably so he doesn't feel left out. I chuckle.

"We love seeing you happy and *in love,* Zev. Be who you are. We love you." She nudges Dillon's shoulder with her own. "Don't we, Dill?"

Dillon shakes his head, eyes focusing back on us. "Yes. Absolutely. It's cool to see."

"What's got you so distracted?" I ask curiously.

"Your..."

"Boyfriend, Daddy, partner, lover. Take your pick." I relish in the blush that blooms across his cheeks. It's too easy.

"Uh, yeah. Him. He's glaring at me, so I'm going to let go of your hand now." His hand slips away and slinks back into his lap. I bark out a laugh, tossing my head back. Dill looks like he's about to piss his pants.

"Oh, Jesus Christ. It's fine, Dillon."

He shakes his head so fast, his blonde locks whip around his face. "Nuh-uh. Not gonna risk anything. No, thanks. Does he know… about… us?" He nearly chokes on the words.

I lift a brow, glancing over at Gavin in thought. "I don't know. We haven't really talked about it, but I'm sure he can tell with our sexual tension." I wag my brows, and I swear Dillon's face drops three shades to straight-up translucent.

"Absolutely not, Z. You better fucking set that shit straight. I am not getting on that bear's bad side."

"Bear," I muse thoughtfully. "That's cute. I love it. He kinda is a bear, isn't he?"

"Yeah, looks all soft and cute till you fuck with it." Dillon shudders.

I've never felt better.

"Oh, Zev, quit fucking with him," Carmen blurts with a laugh. In the moonlight, I notice the ease on her face. She looks different, too.

"How have you guys been?" I ask, then take a sip of my water.

"Good," Dillon says. "Working at CB now. Full time. Legit job." The mention of my father's business makes me tense up.

"Yeah? How do you like it?"

"It's good. I really like the work, Z." His eyes search mine.

"Well then, I'm really happy for you."

"Really?" he balks.

"Dillon," Carmen hisses. I snort.

"Yeah, dude. It's all fine. Things with Zion aren't great,

but they're... fine? I guess. I don't really know, but it's all good."

"Wow, it's like we're in the fucking Twilight Zone."

"Dillon, I swear to God—"

"Carmen, chill. It's cool. You guys don't have to walk around eggshells with me. If something's up, I'll tell you. Otherwise, let's just get back into shit." *Wow, Daddy would beat my ass black and blue if he heard the things coming out of my mouth.*

The thought makes me giddy. Maybe I should tell him...

Carmen sighs and fiddles with the tail end of her braid. "You're right; I'm sorry. I'm probably being too much, I just... I'm scared and don't want to trigger you or anything."

"I know, and if anything ever does, I'll tell you. Honesty is all part of this... whatever the fuck this is." I wave my hand around. "So, let's just agree to try and move on?"

"Fuck yeah."

Gavin pulls me aside as we all walk back in from the terrace. "Did you have a good talk with your friends, baby?" he whispers in my ear.

"Yeah. It was exactly what I needed. Thank you for telling them to come over."

"Good. I'm glad. Anything for you." He kisses me, which turns deep and frantic in a split second. My arms wrap around his neck, and I lean on my tip toes to press our groins together. Daddy grunts against me, hands cupping my ass and squeezing.

"Um..."

Daddy pulls back, barely holding in a growl—and just because I like to fuck with him, I blurt out, "You know,

Dillon and I used to sleep together. It was never anything but mind-numbing fun and something we both needed—"

"You *what?*" Daddy whips around, facing Dillon, who's just a few feet away. His eyes dart from Gavin to me, mouth open in shock.

"Z, what the fuck!" He takes a step back, and I laugh. Every inch of Gavin is rolling with tension. I knead his soft, thick muscles.

"Daddy, I'm just fucking with you." He spins back around and shoves me against the glass.

"Oh, really?"

"Well, what I said was all truth, but it was only to rile you up. Don't hurt Dillon. It's not his fault. And I was serious when I said it never meant anything." I wrinkle my nose. "I also slept with Carmen a couple times, too," I blurt out.

"Hey! That's insulting!" Dillon shouts but shuts up real quick at Daddy's glare, which then gets turned onto me, but instead of withering under it, I shine, bright and rejuvenated. He doesn't even glance at Carmen.

"So, you're being a fucking brat again."

I nod, not even trying to pretend. "Uh-huh."

"You know what brats get, don't you?"

"Spanked." I wiggle my ass, sending our hard cocks bumping together. Daddy reaches down and squeezes said ass until I groan, knowing there will be bruises. I can't wait to stare at them in the mirror.

"Spanked and no orgasms."

I gasp, jaw falling slack. "Daddy! What the—"

"You heard me. Don't *fucking* argue." With a bruising, chaste kiss, he pushes off the glass and saunters into the kitchen. He starts pulling takeout containers out of paper bags, lining each one on the counter. "Dinner's ready."

Still dazed against the glass, I slowly make my way into the kitchen, plopping down on a barstool next to Carmen. Dillon, ironically, chooses the one on the far end.

"Thanks, Daddy," I say easily as I dive into my Lo Mein. I groan the second the rich, salty flavor of the sauce explodes on my tongue. Daddy's hand grips my nape as he rounds the counter to take the barstool to my right. He dips down, brushing his lips over the shell of my ear.

"Watch it, brat." He tugs on my lobe, and I groan at that and the added sensation of his beard scratching me.

"So, Dillon," Gavin says as he picks up his chopsticks. Dillon splutters, sending a chunk of beef flying across the counter. Daddy just lifts a brow in question, making Dillon's face burn crimson.

"Uh, sorry, Da—uh, Gavin."

"Were you about to call him Daddy?!" I squeal, nearly jumping off my stool.

"What?" Dillon scoffs. "No, absolutely not. It just—I just —oh, what the fuck. I hear you say it all the time! I'm sorry!" He throws his hands up.

We all bust out into a fit of laughter that lasts for minutes on end. Poor Dillon hunkers down on the stool, hiding his face in the crook of his arm. "Fuck all of you," he mumbles.

"Oh, Dill," Carmen splutters all over again, nearly spewing her water.

"It's okay, Dillon." Awe, Daddy tries to ease Dillon's embarrassment.

"Yeah, Dillon, it's okay if you call Daddy, *Daddy*."

"It sure the fuck isn't," Gavin thunders, making me and Dillon jump. Carmen just snickers.

"Oh, well. Yeah, you're right. I wouldn't like that, but it's okay that you almost did."

"Can we *please* just drop this?"

"*Hmm.* I suppose."

"Great." He lifts his head and grabs his fork.

I wait until he's got a mouthful of food before I say, "For now."

"Goddamnit, Zev!" He mumbles through the food, making us all start cackling again.

Daddy leans into my side. "You look happy, boy." I turn my head, resting my chin on my shoulder as I stare at my Daddy.

"I am." His eyes smile, and it shoots straight into my heart—and my balls, if I'm being honest.

I really fucking am.

I'm no longer walking the line between reality and a dream-like fantasy.

This is real. This is life in all its painful, messy, wonderful waves.

Epilogue

ZEVRYN

One month later

I finger the thin material of my new shirt absentmindedly. The hem sits just below my ribs, showing off my entire stomach and the defined ridges of the abs I've worked my ass off to get. My trunks are untied and hanging off my hips, the patch of hair on my pelvis out and on display.

The sun burns my skin as it hammers down over my exposed flesh. For September, the sun is awfully hot today, but it happens to work in my favor, even as I bend myself into a downward-facing dog pose.

I've kept up with yoga since I left Black Diamond. The burning stretch and exhilaration help keep my mind free from the static life brings sometimes, but things have been good between me and Daddy. More than good. It's almost surreal, but Daddy works hard to ensure I never forget that I deserve this.

To be happy. To live my life.

It's why I not only work for my father—of my own free will—but why we're also moving out of the penthouse and into a much more respectable apartment in just a few days. I need the freedom of living in a place not tainted with haunted memories or under the nearly indistinguishable control of my father's money.

Working at Carver Breck Technologies was a decision I made after talking about it with Gavin for days on end, going over every possible pro and con. When it came down to it, I decided I'd like to give Zion a chance.

We're merely coworkers at the moment—a distinction I made more than clear to him—which he accepted assuredly. He seems to be making an effort, and I think I owe it to myself to try. The same way we both should have with Mom, but we know it's too late for that, and all we have is *now*.

And if it doesn't work... well, then Daddy will be there to pick up the pieces and fit me back together again. Of that, I have no doubt.

Now all that's left before Daddy and I move out is to create one last raunchy memory to take with us to our new home—the place we'll have together.

Just us.

"Boy?" Daddy shouts as he wanders out of the bathroom from his shower. I hadn't had much time to work with, but I didn't exactly need much to show myself off to him. I stay silent, waiting for him to find me, which doesn't take long.

"What are you—fuck." I peel my eyelids open, peeking out from under my arm from where I'm bent over.

"What, Daddy?" I ask as I push myself up and turn

around to flop on top of the lounger, panting through the dousing sweat coating every inch of my heated flesh.

"You little fuckin' tease." He strides across the terrace, each step thunderous and dominant. My insides quiver with anticipation. Daddy leans down over me on the reclined chair. He tugs on the hem of my shirt.

"*Daddy's boy,* huh?" He reads the print on the front. I peek down at the shirt like I don't know exactly what it says. It's dark blue with light blue lettering that reads the very words he spoke. I blink up at him, feigning innocence.

"Is that what it says?" I jut my bottom lip out.

"You drive me crazy, baby." He dips down and captures my mouth, stealing my oxygen. But that's okay, I don't need it when he kisses me like this.

Like he owns me—because he does.

His finger traces the V lines leading to my groin, a tantalizing back-and-forth pattern. I squirm and buck up, but he pins me down. Then, he scratches a nail over my pubic bone. "You look good enough to eat."

"You wanna eat me, Daddy?" I lick my lips. His head blocks out most of the sun. The light radiating outward gives him a warped halo.

"Oh, I'm gonna eat you, baby. But first, I'm going to fuck you and fill you up. Then I'm gonna eat you and make you eat me."

Oh, my gods.

I think my brain just short-circuited.

I stare up at him, mouth agape. "You like the sound of that, boy?" I nod because I can't fucking form any words. My blood rushes with agonizing heat, making my balls throb from how fast they fill with a big load just for Daddy.

"As fuck-hot as you look, you're gonna have to ditch the trunks. Leave the shirt," he barks when I reach for the hem, shorts already down to my ankles.

"Yes, Sir." I shimmy my trunks the rest of the way off and lay on the lounger bare from the waist down, one eye scrunched shut to block out the sun. Daddy drops his shirt to the ground and follows with his jeans, leaving him naked and so fucking yummy.

"Up." He hikes his thumb, and I jump at the command, chest heaving, cock bobbing between my legs, harder than it's ever been.

Daddy takes my place on the lounger. He sprawls out, spreading his legs and jerking his cock so leisurely behind a half-lidded gaze that makes me feel drunk. I sway, and Daddy reaches out to grip my thigh, keeping me steady.

He drops his cock to pat his thigh. "Climb on, boy." I scramble on top of him, spreading my legs around his thick, hairy ones, sweat slicking the way. I dig my fingers into his flesh. Daddy doesn't waste any time. He reaches around and swipes a finger down my crease. His chest rumbles. "Knew you'd be ready for me."

"Lubed and stretched, Daddy. I just want you inside me."

"Fuck, you're so needy, it makes me crazy." He says that so often, and it never fails to give me butterflies—large, hammering ones that make so fucking horny. I reach around to the small table and grab the nearly empty bottle of lube. I douse Daddy's cock without having to be told.

He grunts his approval, eyes shining with devotion as I drop it to the ground and lift onto my heels. Daddy's cock is too long for him to push inside me while I'm on my knees, but that's okay with me. I work out almost daily just so we can fuck any way we want.

The first slip of his head against my stretched rim has my eyes rolling back. "Damn, boy." Daddy grunts as he slips inside, lube paving a *very* smooth entry. My thighs shake under the strain as I slowly lower myself. Daddy's palms slide back and forth over me, soothing and gentle, even when his eyes blaze with uncontrolled lust and hunger.

When I finally settle in a deep squat, I move to my knees, groaning at the shift of his cock against my walls. "You're so deep, Daddy." I nearly whimper.

"Yeah, wanna be in your guts, baby, so get to it." His hand cracks across my ass cheek, making me scream at the rip of fire.

"Fuck," I breathe, head rolling between my shoulders as I slam my ass down on Daddy's lap. Our skin sticks together from the sweat.

He slaps my ass again. "Watch that fucking mouth."

"Uh-huh." I roll my hips, relishing in our combined moans. Daddy presses his hand against my stomach, raking his blunt nails over the ridges of my abs. He teases and tugs against my pubic hair, adding a sharp sting to the endless bliss of rapture.

My cock bobs in the air between us, growing hotter from the sun's heat blazing down. I feel a flush all over my skin. Perspiration drips from me and onto Daddy's glistening skin.

My hips roll in one continuous, drugging motion. When Daddy wraps his hand around me, I arch back, planting my hands just above his knees. He grabs onto my hips and takes over as the heat bleaches my energy.

I don't know how he manages it when he must be as hot

as I am, but damn, he knows how to fuck me so good. I moan uncontrollably, head rolling around between my shoulders as Daddy thrusts up, slamming his cock into me. The slick sound of lube and animalistic grunts is the melodic tune that carries me toward my release faster than I anticipated.

With my balls squished against Daddy's soft tummy, getting their own bout of rough friction, I press my fingers to the head of my cock, teasing and tugging and adding dull pressure. My eyes crack open so I can stare at my Daddy as I come.

I fall forward from the force of my release. Sparks shoot off at the base of my spine in a delicious tingle that spreads throughout my limbs and into the head of my dick. My hand slides over my length as it rushes through me. "Oh, gods, oh, fuuuck." My cum spurts from my slit in thick globs. They streak across my shirt, a thick, white shimmer over the letters.

I slump against Daddy's chest, hand trapped between our stomachs as Daddy lifts my ass with his strong arms and continues to work for his release.

I clench my ass to make it easier for him, and sure enough... he grunts and rotates my hips through my contracted channel, spilling his load inside me. I groan as he lazily humps against me, working his cum in deeper.

My ass squelches from the various liquids, warming my tummy. I find Daddy's nipple and suckle on it, humming contentedly.

Eventually, his movement slows, and we both melt into the chair, slick with sweat and cum. Flushed and burning up but sated. Daddy's fingers dig into the muscle of my ass cheek, spreading me apart while his other hand traces my rim, following the girth of his cock.

Before I have time to think, Daddy's pulling out and pushing me face-first into the sweaty fabric of the chair. I inhale deeply, reveling in my Daddy's fresh sweat against my face. He's behind me now, hiking my ass into the air.

He doesn't tease me, just shoves his tongue inside where his cock just was, slurping and sucking his cum out my hole, and fuck, I've never been more glad I decided to clean up before sex. Normally it doesn't matter too much, but this is the kinda scenario a guy wants to plan for.

I moan unabashedly into the chair, my screams echoing out into the autumn New York City air. The sounds coming from Daddy's mouth on my ass sound illegal in at least forty different states, and fuck does it make me feral.

I press my ass harder against him, urging him to eat me deeper, harder. Forever. Daddy slurps and sucks loudly—and then it stops. It takes a moment for my brain to catch up to the loss of sensation.

My head turns, searching for Daddy. "Wha—" His tongue is thrusting into my mouth, hot and wet with so many different fluids. I moan pathetically.

"Swallow me, baby." He seals my lips with his tongue and the scratch of his beard. I've never guzzled cum so fast in my life.

"My dirty little boy." Daddy praises me once I show him my empty mouth. And with a finger in my ass and his tongue against mine, *I fucking ascend.*

The End.

Afterword

I was equal parts relieved and despondent when I typed the end on this story. Gavin and Zevryn took me on quite the journey and this book is actually the fastest I have ever written one. I just couldn't get it out fast enough.

I fell irrevocably in love with them, and their beautiful bond, and I never wanted it to end—not that it ever does in my mind, but I am wholly content with their story and where I left them.

Happy, healthy, and healing in a life together. A Daddy and his boy—exactly how it should be with their always kind of love.

Thank you for taking the time to read their story and I really hope you enjoyed it, and maybe even fell a little bit in love with them too.

Make sure you check out the other twelve fantastic stories in this unique shared world! Each one is absolutely incredible, and I am so lucky to be a part of the Unlucky 13!

Acknowledgments

As always, I have to thank my family. For bearing with me every day while I poured my soul into this book for hours on end. Your grace is the reason I am able to do what I love, and I am eternally grateful.

My best friend for always talking me off of every self-deprecating ledge.

Rae, my alpha and soulmate, for being there since literally day one. I couldn't write a single book without you.

My betas; Kayla, Taylor, Liz, and Sam. Thank you for reading my work when it's still so raw and loving it anyway. And also a massive shoutout for catching all my typos—y'all are amazing.

My street team for being the best support system. I got pretty lucky in who I have in my corner, which is pretty fucking cool.

To the other authors in this shared world. Thank you for inviting me along on this awesome endeavor. I love that we were all able to create something so uniquely cohesive.

And last but not least, my readers. To my OG's, THANK YOU. Never could've done this without y'all. I really can't thank you enough. And to every reader that has recently delved into my work—or if this is your first read of mine—

thank you so much for giving me a chance and I truly hope you loved this story!

Books by Marie Ann

Standalones

Inevitable Destruction

Quiet Is the Night Now

Strangled

Fragmented Illusions

Abysmal: A Black Diamond Novel

Monsters In Us Series

Creep

Monster

Fiend (A Monsters In Us Sequel Novella)

Poetry

Skin&Bone

Coming Soon

Visceral Series: Make Me Pretty: Vol One

A limited release Phobia Anthology

About the Author

Marie Ann is a writer of dark and depraved romance. Her characters are always toxic and damaged to some degree—which is just how she likes it.

You can find her on almost all forms of social media where her awkwardness is blatantly obvious, but we pretend it isn't.

Stalk her @authormarieann

Made in the USA
Las Vegas, NV
22 April 2024

89033780R00262